DANIEL LIGHT

AND THE CHILDREN OF THE ORB
SERIES

BOOK TWO

THE BLOOD ROSE
OF PANADOR

BY
C. MICHAEL PERRY

Leicester Bay
BOOKS

Salt Lake City

Paperbound Edition(CS) 2013 by Leicester Bay Books –
ISBN-13: 978-0615694702
ISBN-10: 0615694705

Kindle Edition available

BISAC: Fiction / Fantasy / Epic --
Adventure – Coming of Age

Leicester Bay Books
3877 Leicester Bay South Jordan, UT
www.leicesterbaybooks.com

Cover art and layout by Brook Bowen
of Bowen Design Works, Salt Lake City, Utah

Visit us at: **www.childrenoftheorb.com**

Contents

NOTE: Ꙣ after each chapter, are the initials "M. L." standing for **Miraden Light**, the historian of the Realms.

NOTE: If you want to see maps of the world and the structures of The Realms of the Crystal Orb please visit:
www.childrenoftheorb.com

Books by C. Michael Perry

DANIEL LIGHT AND THE CHILDREN OF THE ORB

Book One: **The Miracle Of Mirador (2012)**

Book Two: **The Blood Rose of Panador (2014)**

Book Three: **The Prophecy and the Circle of Light (2014)**

Book Four: **The Prophecy and the Child Of Promise (2015)**

See the layout of the entire series at:

www.childrenoftheorb.com

COMING SOON!

WEMBLEY TEWKES AND THE EDGES OF TIME

Book One: **Imperfections On The Edge (middle 2014)**

Book Two: **Living From Edge To Edge (early 2015)**

Check out other publications by this author,

and by other authors at:

www.leicesterbaybooks.com

DEDICATION
*To Robert G. Peck Jr., Charles W. Whitman
and Max Chatterton Golightly,
the men who first placed deep inside of me a love for
writing and where it comes from.*

ACKNOWLEDGEMENTS

*To Brian Whipple, Geoff McCalla and Stephen Carter
for their advice and encouragement;
To my wife and family for their support.*

The First Prophecy

The magic will grow strong in the
Realms of the Crystal Orb.
There will come a time
when those who have sought to destroy
The bonds that were created by Orb and Talismans,
For their own selfish and greedy purposes,
Will find that there is a Champion of Light
that their Darkness will not overcome.
He will rise, white and strong in youth, power and
innocence
After Darkness' long reign.
Many others will also rise to aid him in his eternal quest –
both mortal and Immortal.
He will unite all of the Realms and bring new voices
To the influence of the Orb. He will be the son of Gregory,
born of humble yet noble circumstances.
He will sink below all experience.
He will approach death,
Only to rise above all mortality in love and greatness.
He and his companions will protect
and expand the Realms forever.
They will return all Light to the Realms.

The Creators speak and it is written

CHAPTER ONE
NEWS
(End Month: 2701)

DANIEL GREGORYSON HAD BEEN CALLED to the Cottage of the Dwarves of Hope. Alder, the eldest of the clan, was on the floor dying. It happened; a natural part of the five-hundred-year life-cycle of a Dwarf. Daniel wondered why he had been called to the bedside of his friend. Hadn't he seen enough of death? He was not certain at all if he could bear to lose another friend. He also wondered why they had not moved Alder to the comfort of his bed.

Then he felt the strong hands of Miraden on his shoulders as he watched the Dwarf gasp his last breath. Daniel's hand rose up to brush a tear away from his eye. He heard a whisper in his ear – and it wasn't the Creators this time, it was Miraden.

"Watch closely."

Daniel tried to see through his blurry vision. He felt a huge ripple in his chest. He hoped it wasn't another of those personal 'growing pain' things. They came at the worst of times. But he felt the reassuring hands on his shoulders and remembered the advice of his grandfather as he focused on the now still face of Alder Hope.

Suddenly, there were two faces of Alder Hope: one peaceful and calm in death, and the other coming very much alive – smiling and screaming – as it rose out of first the face, and then the remainder of the body – spectrally, then corporeally – it just stepped out of the lifeless corpse leaving it behind on the floor.

Daniel turned to Miraden, his face awash with questions and confusion. Then he felt a small but strong hand on his forearm. He turned around and stared down into the eyes of his friend, Alder the Elder. The face was smiling and the room was beginning to fill with the loud and raucous laughter of Dwarves.

Daniel didn't know whether to take offense, or not. His own mother had always cautioned him not to take offense, especially where none was meant. He felt the arms of his grandfather wrap lovingly around him, and that voice whispered again.

"You have witnessed what no other Human has ever seen. The renewal cycle of a Dwarf."

Daniel turned again with that one word question on his lips. Miraden had anticipated it.

"Every five-hundred years each Dwarf is renewed. His old self dies but is immediately reborn in his new self; an exact copy, a replica, with all memories and experience retained in a newly invigorated body."

Daniel turned back to Alder Hope and threw his arms around him. Daniel thought, *Young again every five-hundred years?* Then the thought came to him, *I'll be young forever.* The silent embrace spoke volumes about Daniel's love and respect for the men who had helped him save his new mother, Liliana, and her daughter, Bianca.

"All of you will go through this?"

The Dwarves were nodding.

"All in the next week. It will be our fourth regeneration."

"But you've only been alive for seventeen-hundred years."

"The War of the Realms sapped us of our strength and the Creators are granting all living Dwarves a regeneration."

"Every Dwarf?" Daniel was flabbergasted.

More nodding.

"How many are there?"

"Not so many as there were."

Nothing more came from the smiling lips of Alder, The

Elder – The oldest Dwarf alive.

"So, wait – when a Dwarf dies, his replacement is just there?"

"Yes, Daniel."

"So – why… why are there only seven of you where there once were twelve?"

There was silence again. Elderberry, the youngest and the magician of the group of brothers, stepped forward. "Our brothers were killed in battle."

"I don't understand."

Miraden interceded. "When a Dwarf reaches the end of his cycle, he is prepared to die. His replacement is ready. But when he is killed in battle, his body has not had the time to regenerate."

Daniel hung his head and wiped his eyes again. Each Dwarf stepped in to The Miracle, The Prophecy, and embraced him. It was all Daniel could do to control himself. He felt … honored. Humbled.

He thought right then, he knew that he was a part of some greater whole. How could he ever hope to fulfill whatever task was his to fulfill? He had no greatness in him. He barked out a sudden sob, or was it a laugh? He felt the arms of his grandfather wrap around him warmly again. Even in that warmth, he felt so inadequate, so young and inexperienced. Awkward. He heard the whisper again.

"Never doubt!" and Miraden hugged him fiercely.

Daniel remembered what had happened with the Dwarves just days ago as he again stood in the hall of the great Crystal Dome. This is where it began – his journey to Immortalling, and responsibility, and growth beyond his imagining. He had hoped to find some answers by coming here – to this place of origin. Lily, his adopted mother, had taught him much since their co-Immortalization. But she had no experience at all in raising a son or providing him with useful information about the process of growing up. Miraden had few answers because he had as many questions about it all as Daniel had. The Creators had been silent on the matter, as they usually were; letting Daniel find his own way through the maze of his life with nothing but an inspired lead here, or a pertinent thought there. Daniel was supposed to connect the dots; but there weren't enough dots yet to connect. In spite of his present location – the spiritual and geographical center of The Realms – the youth did not feel anywhere near confident that any solutions to his problems would be forthcoming from anyone inside or outside of his life.

He gazed up at the United Orb and Sceptre, and at the Frosted Flask – that power-imbued Talisman of the kingdom of Mirador; the representatives of the power of the Creators. They both connected in the brightness they shared, which radiated up and out of the apex of the dome, sending protection across the Realms of the Crystal Orb, but especially Mirador.

Daniel felt so small, even though he had grown at least a foot in height over the last 18 months. He was unequal to the tasks set him by Miraden and the Creators. At least he felt that he was. Isn't it true that people outside of us seem to sense, even to know, that what we are capable of goes way beyond what we know at the moment, but will only come to learn over time? Daniel didn't know, but he wanted to – desperately.

He closed his eyes and concentrated on the beam of light shooting upwards. He also did not want to see the Dwarves of Hope watching him, as he knew they would. The Guardians and Protectors of the Orb and Sceptre were resolute in their duties. There was no outward appearance that they even knew that Daniel was there. If Daniel had been someone who was not supposed to be there – he would have been dead! So he closed his eyes to blot out the presence of his friends. He knew they would wish him well, but still, he felt that he could not perform in front of a crowd.

His arms slowly rose from his sides. He had the thought, *What? Am I crazy? I'm seeking a vision?* Those thoughts faded as his elbows bent and his fingertips touched in front of his face and he concentrated on whiteness harder than he had ever focused on anything before. He did not begin to feel that funny, stomach-swirling sensation of all his other visions. He opened one eye and looked down to see that he was still wearing all his clothes. He sighed in relief – and frustration. Then he felt almost nauseous and his chest heaved. He took his hands from the triangle they made in front of him to press against the pain in his upper chest. He found a great discrepancy there, as one side of his chest, his left pectoral, was suddenly much larger and seemed stronger than the right. He was twelve and suddenly had a left pectoral the size of many very fit adult men. The longer he kept his hands there, the more it did not go away. He sure hoped it wasn't noticeable. Then the queaze hit him again and his body rippled and shook.

When he regained his balance, he opened both eyes, for the smell was different; the echoes of the room were not the same. He found he was standing in the cavern that served as his bedroom at the White Dragon Mount, Miraden's home. His home now, also. He felt his chest. He was still misshapen. Oh, well. It would all catch up – he hoped. It had happened the same way with his feet just last month. One of them grew suddenly one day and then on another day a few weeks later the other caught up in size. It was unsettling, for a while, but as everything on his body was going wild, and usually through the same manner of drastic and radical sudden change, he was growing accustomed to it, but not really. It always set him off, set him apart, set him up for a round of questions he had no answers for.

Every thought in his life was interrupted by another happening, or a disturbing thought, or a vision. This time was no different.

Then, he heard a large 'boom'. Greenish-black smoke from the explosion sped down the central hallway of the White DragonMount. Daniel heard coughing and cursing coming from the laboratory. As the smoke invaded his own room, he began to cough. It was thick – oppressive. As the cloud overwhelmed him, he passed out.

Daniel was naked. Again. A robe of exquisite whiteness was once more being wrapped lovingly around his white body. He was seeing things – people – that he could not fully perceive. He was hearing things that he didn't entirely understand. He was feeling things that completely overwhelmed him.

He had been here before, but that had been a dream! Hadn't it? Or had it? He was no longer too sure about the 'honor' of being 'The Prophecy.' This Miracle-of-Mirador thing was still just too much for him sometimes. Here he was, wrapped in brightness, surrounded by the glow of a light that transcended even his own body's whiteness.

He felt safe. Confused, but secure – somehow.

This was not a vision – or a dream. It was a visit. He had been summoned somewhere – for some purpose.

He endured it. He could do nothing more. He tried to remember – to retain and take with him what was said and done during this visit. A voice repeated the same words over and over again, but he couldn't remember them. He didn't understand that his mind would recall them when he needed them. It did not require a conscious effort on his part – this time. A hand caressed his cheek. Another one patted his back. Then, all too suddenly, the robe was removed and he was naked again before he felt the pull of something from some other where. Or was it a push from this present, but temporary where? Wherever this place was! Then there was no nakedness, no sight, no feeling – no where.

In the center of the smoky cavern, Miraden wrapped the palm and fingers of his right hand around his old friend, Wand, as the sunstones of its handle connected with something deep inside him. He then extended his index finger out and along the Alderwood shaft. The connection between heart and hand was completed, as it had been thousands of times over the last twenty-seven-hundred years, when he had called upon it. His fingers and palm drew power from his wrist, which flexed as it turned the wand, urging the power through his forearm, elbow and upper arm, drawing it along the blood lines that led directly from his heart.

All wands are of Alderwood – even Tophet's. The very heart

of the tree was used to craft the slender instruments of magical amplification. Then came the handle, the receptor from the palm of the magic of the heart of the Enchanter, which was then focused and amplified through the heart of a tree. The handles of each wand are what differed from others, varying in their composition; but only three types of stone were used. Most dark Sorcerors preferred Obsidian, because it was of volcanic origin; a tie to PanAlta. The other wands of the Enchanters had handles of either Moonstone, or, in Miraden's case, Sunstones; beautiful, speckled brown and creme stones, that had been fused through a magical spell to expand their own magic. The wand almost hummed, resonating with power as it awaited the command of its Master and friend – Miraden. The last of the smoke in the room disappeared into the tip of the wand and Miraden bent over his grandson, fully dressed and prostrated on the floor.

Daniel's eyes finally opened and he found himself staring at the ceiling of his bedchamber. He felt his stomach. Too queasy to move, he let his hand drop back to his side as the images solidified in front of him. He saw two blue eyes appear through the blur; then a head of white hair appeared around the two eyes.

"Ah! Awake again, I see."

"Grandpa, what happened?"

"Nothing. Just a stubborn potion."

"Are all of your potions stubborn?" It was an innocent question posed by an almost innocent, twelve-year-old. Daniel put the dream – vision – visit – he had just experienced aside. It was not solid enough in his memory for him to talk about yet.

Miraden reacted with a huff. "What are you implying?"

"Nothing, Grandfather. Just that there are an awful lot of explosions around here."

Miraden looked shocked. He had never really considered it before. He had lived alone for most of his life. Well, alone since Liliana left to live at The Crystal Castle; alone, before Liliana was born; alone, after the deaths of his first wife and children. He smiled down into the trusting and loving face of the child-now-youth that had been linked so inseparably to him. His smile turned into a laugh, which rang out along with that of his Grandson.

"Where'd all the smoke go?"

Miraden waggled his wand between his fingers. "I ... took care of it."

"Why do you live here, Grandfather?" Daniel felt weak but struggled to a seated position, eyes never leaving his grandfather's face.

"I ... I ... like it here."

After long and careful deliberation, even while looking around at the strangely smokeless and dustless room, regretting his earlier confusion, Daniel added, "So do I!"

Daniel's arm flopped up and his knuckles hit him in the face. He had not intended for that to happen. It was every once in a while, as he was trying to work some simple magic or accomplish the easiest of tasks, that his body rebelled. It didn't just malfunction. He had been stirring together the ingredients for Miraden's potion in the lab. Just a flick of his wrist had initiated the face-punch. He rubbed his jaw with the non-offending hand and placed the other one between his knees, to hold it steady, hopefully free from other twitchy surprises.

He began stirring with the other hand. He saw his fingers rippling and enlarging; enough to allow him to drop the glass rod he was stirring with. It shattered on the floor and the cauldron of green, slimy potion belched a response as if saying, 'Klutz!'

As Daniel's hand continued to vacillate between how it had always been and its newer, larger cousin, Daniel hopped about the room, not forgetting about the potion but unable to manage it with this latest of twitches. He decided to stand still and wait out what was happening. His feet came to a halt but his arm did not. He was soon on his back on the floor trying to control the spastic actions of his once trustworthy arm.

He heard a sound to his left and looked over to see Miraden enter the room; face fully alarmed at the position that Daniel was in on the floor. As Daniel's arm spasmed and jerked, Miraden knelt beside his grandson not really knowing what to do. He waved his wand slowly down the length of Daniel's body. The arm, thankfully, was quieted, but Daniel was now asleep. Miraden 'popped' Daniel to his bedchamber and let him rest on the bed. He knew there would be questions, but he would deal with it later.

If the White Dragons, Willamere and Imadar, had used fire and claw to carve a dwelling place out of solid rock 2000 years ago leaving twelve Dragon-sized rooms; if it was a cave in the tallest mountain around; if you were twelve years old and had recently acquired the powers of an Enchanter; if your Grandfather was the oldest living Enchanter in the world and had invited you to live there with him, would you?

Don't lie! You would.

Daniel had started out by spending only weekends with his adopted grandfather. The weekdays were spent with his adoptive mother and father, King Marble and Queen Lily White, rulers of Mirador. But now, after a year and a half, that had kind of switched, due to the fact that magic took up more and more of his educational time, since the requirements of history, science, math and literature had been met. He had become a great archer (born to it as his real father had been: Gregory, the Huntsman of the Blue Mountains). He was also a pretty good swordsman. As for his scholarship? Well, he dutifully learned everything that his mother, Lily, had taught him – even how to dance. (Which he had, at first, only secretly enjoyed.) He had loved dancing with Bianca as Prince Valerius just got to sit and watch them. He knew, that as she was now his adopted sister, and five years older than he was, he could never have her love and devotion in anything but a sisterly way. So, he had resigned himself to that sad fact and suppressed his boyish crush on her. Was it boyish? Was he a boy?

After the war in which his entire family was killed he also had some very tough times. He had spent many nights crying himself to sleep – despite what his mother and father had said to him in

9

his first vision in the Crystal Dome; the vision he had received just before his Immortalization; just after the murder of his father. He loved his adopted family – truly – but he missed the people who had given him birth and life and direction.

They had been the ones who had, since his birth, inculcated in him the qualities that made it possible for him to become The Miracle of Mirador. Hadn't they? He was so 'not sure' of all of it. Except for sometimes. There were times he knew for sure that he was where he was supposed to be.

He was still having those nightmares – dreams of war and death and the massacre of innocent youth – something he had witnessed during the War of the Realms. He would awaken in a cold sweat, sometimes yelling out, while the images of 150 boys of the supply train, dead on a Zanadonan battleground, flashed through his mind for the hundredth time.

Someone had always been there, so far, to hold his hand and help him back to sleep: Lily, Bianca, Marble or Miraden, his adopted family; Valerius, Bianca's husband; Elias and his parents, Sarai or Matthew; one, or more of them had been there to calm him – reassure him. Elias was Daniel's closest friend. There were many times when they stayed over at each other's houses, playing, eating, fishing, hunting, eating and talking until dawn, that his younger and best friend had had to help Daniel through something that he, himself, didn't even remotely understand. But he did it. Even though the dreams were ever present morning rituals, almost – loved ones were there to shield, protect and comfort The Miracle Of Mirador.

The laboratory was filled with smoke the next day as well. But this time it was Daniel who had wielded his grandfather's wand in the combining of powders and oils and animal parts. The experiment had almost instantaneously evaporated along with the workbench, and everything else on it.

At the same time as the explosion, Daniel felt suddenly taller on one side. He looked down and his left leg was noticeably shorter, by about a knuckle, than his right leg. He waited and watched. His right leg popped and he was standing even again. Miraden rushed into the room to find his grandson tottering, dusty and blackened from the ash, but alive.

"What's wrong?" was the only question that a frustrated and confused Daniel could ask.

"This potion came from the Creators. There cannot be anything wrong with it."

"No, Grandpa, I meant, what is wrong with me!"

It was difficult to be twelve years old and realize you were not perfect yet.

"There is nothing wrong with you either." Miraden suddenly left the room.

Daniel's life had changed. So many shifts that it was a real wonder how he could process them all. His life was still changing; would continue to be modified in many ways completely unimagined by the people living on the continent of Colabos.

That additional, necessary, inevitable change that comes upon all Humans, the one that takes us from childhood to adulthood, had been hastened along for Miraden's grandson, by the application and ingestion of Miraden's potion in the form of the chocolate he provided to his adopted grandson, Daniel Gregoryson. Some time after the changes began, or even if they had already finished with Daniel, Immortality would soon take over and start to draw out and lengthen the years and the life span of the Human youth to that of the Immortal Youth. Thereby, a child who was changed at fourteen or fifteen would not appear to be a year older for at least a decade of Human years, because of the physical maturity already gained; and, more likely, not for a period of decades would he or she appear to age even one Human year. Daniel was the first to go through it. A living experiment, so to speak. That is how Miraden had planned the potion, which served this dual purpose: to speed up that change and to lengthen the over-all lifespan, aiding the Immortalling.

In those seventeen months that had passed since the War of the Realms, Daniel had turned twelve in Human years. Still very young. Because of his Immortalled status at the age of eleven, his changes were more rapid and fully perplexing. No one had ever been through what he was going through; not even Miraden. The Miracle of Mirador was growing rapidly through adolescence and was as big as most fifteen-year-olds because maturity must be reached quickly so that magic can take its place in its full power in an adult-like body. Yet the person must still have the teachable mind of the child – or youth. So, you could see what could have been happening in Daniel's mind when he told Miraden that another type of dream had entered his life.

"Things are happening."

"Things, Daniel?"

"You know, things! My body's gone crazy. And the dreams are not very ... comfortable. It's been happening since I was Immortalled."

"Oh! Yes, – well, you see I never went through those changes."

"You didn't?"

"No. I was created in an adult body. I never had a childhood like yours. But I had the mind of a child, open and empty but keen – and ready for all the thoughts and feelings I was about to experience. The power that was there was amazing. I could do anything I was asked or told to do.

"So, you never had these dreams?"

"No. But many others who have, have described them to me." It was not really a statement, but a hopeful question. Miraden was wishing that Daniel would tell him about it.

Daniel took the cue and tried to launch into an explanation, even though it made him feel terribly – exposed. With guarded looks, he began; "It's always the same. I see green eyes – beautiful green eyes – that are surrounded by red hair ... and freckles. We're having fun and playing games and then we're not playing games...and I feel all strange and funny inside – and then whoosh, I'm feeling ... well, really good ... and tired and then I wake up, sometimes suddenly, like I've been catapulted out of my bed, or up off my pillow, and then..."

"Yes, I see."

Daniel waited, expectantly but the old man's face was a masque of confusion, elation and ... "Grampa?"

Miraden nodded. "It is just like all of the other times I have been told this. You are growing up and these ... dreams will continue for a while."

"How long?"

Miraden shrugged. "Week ... months – years." He turned and rummaged through his shelf. He handed a slim, brown volume to Daniel. *Magical Changes: The New Enchanter.*

"Grandfather – a book? I don't need to know what and how. I need to know why! Father taught me all that other stuff a long time ago – before he ..."

"Oh, he did! Oh! I see. Well, good. Good for him! Good ... for you."

It was an awkward moment. Daniel was feeling things that he did not want to feel. He couldn't let it overwhelm him; not in front of Miraden, who noticed anyway. He waited for Daniel to suppress the turmoil of the moment.

"Grampa, I thought immortality slowed everything down!?"

"It slows down the aging process, almost ends the process of a body's deterioration, but ..."

"But not the growing up process?"

"Correct. That, actually, is sped up."

"Oh, great!" Daniel was not happy so far with Grandpa Miraden's explanation, or with the fact that the disturbing dreams that weren't nightmares woke him even more than occasionally. But at least it was an answer. He looked up into Miraden's face. There was something more and Daniel knew it; but the old Enchanter was hesitating.

"Especially when you are given the gift so young."

Yes, at eleven, Daniel thought. "Is it a gift?"

Miraden peered at the youth, thoughtfully, through his round spectacles. "You need the body of an adult and the open mind of a child to learn and store magic effectively. That is why I and the race of Enchanters were originally created with adult bodies. We were all new, like children; no experience, no knowledge. But our bodies were large enough and had the capacity to store the power necessary."

"I'm sorry, Grandpa."

Daniel still did not think that Immortality or magical powers were a terribly wonderful gift. Not if it made him feel like this. His body had already undergone most of those changes that turn boys into young men, and in a very short time, too; all accelerated by the potion in the chocolate. It had also been very painful; still was painful much of the time. That pectoral thing had made his chest sore. His legs ached and his fingers crackled sometimes as he gripped things. Daniel felt that his body was out of control – every day some new something. He feared for his mind as well. In the year and a half since 'it' happened, Daniel's body, voice and emotions had changed daily and drastically. His bones ached. His muscles twinged. His skin stayed perfect: that glowing white that had overcome him in the Crystal Dome had remained; had made his skin as pure as snow. 'Things' were ready for Daniel, but Daniel was not sure that he even wanted to be ready for 'things.'

His crush on Bianca hadn't helped either. Since she had dark hair, these dreams were not about her. That was a great relief to Daniel. We have all felt that pang of confusion, the infatuation we call puppy love, or a crush. Inevitably, for each of us, it usually has been on someone totally out of our reach; as it was with Daniel. Bianca was his newly adopted sister. She was already married to Daniel's second best friend, Prince Valerius Red of Panador. It was all just happening too fast. He felt terribly uncomfortable – and as we know, confused! Daniel had finished paging through the book that Miraden had given him.

"Grandpa, there's nothing in this book. The pages are blank."

Miraden retrieved the book and looked at it.

"Oh, yes, well – I guess I never got around to writing it. But at least, now, I have someone to write it about?"

"Grandpa!"

"It must be written! Will you write it?" and he shoved the book at Daniel.

"Grandpa!"

From the laboratory came the sound of gongs being struck.

Miraden rushed to his sleeping quarters, "Oh, we're late!"

Even Miraden isn't helping! Daniel thought, as he dropped the book in the dust of the table.

The Village of Panadar was twenty leagues west of Panador City and it's Castle. The High Road slowly rose across the Plateau of Peace as it climbed to the eastern city from the little village nestled against the mountains of the West. Even from the edge of the plateau you could see the distant City of Panador and it's brilliantly colored castle, Castle Panador, home to Queen Mother Alidah and King Father Comera. The castle stood out in pastel colors of blue, lavender, green, yellow and pink against the darker, plainer greys, blacks, greens and browns of the mountains of the Eastern Barrier Ridge; the mountains that marked the border with the wastelands, farther to the East. Multiple minarets and towers spiraled or shot straight to the skies, all topped with roofs of bright red slate. The castle was on a small hill just southeast of the city and was built with an outer and inner wall completely separate from the walls that surrounded the city. It could stand on its own in the case of the town walls being breached.

The road wound around the hill on it's way to the main gate, on the South. The walls of the battlements rose to a height of ten spans (some sixty feet) with a barbican or double-gated entry. Once inside the second gate there was an inner yard or bailey, thirty spans wide where it ran into the inner wall with it's own ten-span height and solid portcullis.

Between the inner and outer walls, in and around the bailey, were the stables, both Royal and military, servants' quarters, outhouses, blacksmiths, troop garrisons, armories and other military offices, along with the military kitchens, dining halls and training yards for the soldiers. Also, on the West side, a small theatre, seating many thousand, took advantage of the afternoon sun to help light its stage.

The beautiful grounds and gardens of the castle opened to view once inside the inner wall. A large set of steps climbed to meet a five span high red door set in the central lavender keep. This opened to the Grand Entry. Off this expansive room was the main Court and the Throne Room, a large banquet hall and the stairs to other levels of the castle. It was splendid. Of course it was, it was Dragon built – just like all the other castles in the Realms of the Crystal Orb. Castle Panador – as Panadorians believed it to be the best of all the Castles – was built by the Red Dragons, Rindamere and Andradar, under Miraden's direction during the Age of Magic.

Rose, the lovely red-headed younger sister of Prince Valerius, and daughter of Comera and Alidah, was rushing to the gardens, on this warm, winter morning, to visit her newest sister – Bianca. The Kingdom of Panador was a happy one – it had been so for generations, but the King and Queen, Rose's parents, had decided to let Valerius and Bianca assume those duties that pertained to the running of the Kingdom. Rose was incessantly happy for she and Bianca were the same age – just seventeen – and had become like twin sisters.

They shared everything; especially that there was to be news today at Court.

"Court! Oh, no! I'm late!" thought Rose. She turned around and ran back to the Castle. She had forgotten. Her visit would have to wait.

No one knew exactly what the news was, but something was to be proclaimed. As Rose arrived, she was announced (which she hated because she could never just sneak in, for she was often late). She proceeded to her chair, which was located to the right of the throne now occupied by Bianca and Valerius. The former King and Queen (Rose's Dad and Mom) also sat to one side – observing. They smiled indulgently but lovingly at their tardy daughter.

The Chamberlain banged for order with a rap of his staff and silence reigned in the large hall that was the Throne Room of Castle Panador. The banner with a large, Blood Red Rose crossed with a silver sword, surmounting a white crown centered between sword hilt and rosebud, was emblazoned on a Chevron field of blue with white dots in the field. It hung behind the thrones with an occasional billow from the warm winds.

Just as Rose sat, Miraden popped in with Daniel. Miraden did the popping though. Daniel still just followed along.

"Sorry, I'm late – or am I late? Well, I'm sorry anyway." But Miraden was always late, lately.

He joined the growing throng around the throne. Valerius led Bianca to the front of the dais. The trumpets heralded the announcement:

"The Queen is with child!"

There was an audible gasp and then shouts and yells and general excitement burst forth. Valerius' parents surrounded him, while Bianca was swarmed by Daniel, Rose and Miraden. Miraden held his hands up for quiet. He took Bianca's face in his hands and planted a very nice, grandfatherly kiss on her forehead. He then shook the hand of Valerius warmly. He held his hands up in the air again. His face went slack as the crowd grew silent, expectant. Then his eyes clouded over as those in the room leaned in toward him.

"He's having a vision," Daniel whispered.

"Yes, little brother – I know," and Bianca smiled back.

Daniel wilted a little at her smile but realized that his crush on her was officially over. It had to be.

"I'm gonna be an uncle!" Daniel beamed.

All present waited patiently and then life came back to the Enchanter's face and the crowd reanimated.

"It's a boy!" Miraden exclaimed.

"Long live the King!" and other similar shouts proceeded from the mouths of those in the throne room. Miraden held his hands up yet again and the room quieted quickly. "He is to be – a

Child of Promise!" The words of another Prophecy spilled out of the oldest man alive, as he looked to be in the midst of another of his catatonic states:

A youth will arise like unto the Miracle.

All eyes in the assemblage turned to focus on Daniel, as he blushed – crimson. Miraden, clearing his throat, again required their attention:

He will grow fast and strong

Daniel nodded to himself. His 'growth' still hurt him.

He will inspire love and loyalty, hatred and fear;
Fear of the Light; hatred of the right.

There were gasps; the least surprising of which was Daniel's.

He will grow close to all who know him.

Miraden paused, for effect. There was silence on that one. Maybe he was not as catatonic during these utterances as most thought him to be.

He will give the most ultimate of ultimate sacrifices in the salvation of others.

Daniel heard it; but he didn't believe it. It sounded like he, himself, was going to be born all over again;

He will live forever.

There was a final silence – a collective sigh. It was the kind of silence that occurs after you have heard some specific news, different from the sigh that accompanied the act of merely wanting to hear it. They were appreciative. *It is about time,* many of them thought, *that something new and exciting and of real import happened in Panador.* Not that Valerius and Bianca were not new; or that winning the War of the Realms wasn't thrilling! But this was prophecy! Prophecies had a way of writing themselves into the history books. Those peoples and kingdoms associated with the prophecies were chronicled also. Panadorians were no different from anyone else – they wanted their little piece of immortality – one that didn't necessarily include magic.

ML

CHAPTER TWO
THREE ROSES
(1st Month: 2702)

THE CASTLE WAS SURROUNDED BY 'them', the inner walls holding 'them' hostage to the rays of the sun. The Castle walls reflected that sunlight. The flowers, especially the Blood Roses, thrived and bloomed in the hothouses, patches, designs, mazes, planter boxes and pots of Castle Panador. The ground inside the inner wall was covered in nothing but flowers as they encompassed the Castle completely. Roses, daffodils, chrysanthemums, tulips, marigolds, pansies, Sweet William, begonias, rhododendron, camellias, magnolias of every size and color of the rainbow existed in a flood of blooms; a cascade of color. There were even some blooms that you or I would never recognize, for they were unique in origin to Colabos.

The Kingdom of Panador was located at the perfect elevation for sunshine, it's breezes and water conducive to floral growth. It also had a favorable latitude – thirty degrees north of the equator of its world. That is where Castle Panador sat – the ideal place to grow flowers. The climate was similar to central Florida on our planet – and maybe also the Gulf Coast from Texas right through Alabama, but a little drier here than there, as it was between two very high mountain ranges and not near an ocean. The Creators had chosen well for the location of the Realms of the Crystal Orb.

The gardens of Panador were an exploding artist's palette of hues, shades and tints because of its fortuitous location. And the smells wafting from place to place along the paths and byways made you forget that the stables and the sweat of the training yards were just on the other side of the walls. (Maybe that's why the gardens were planted in the first place?)

That one thing could not be forgotten – the profit to this treasury, the thing that helped the Kingdom keep taxes low for all citizens, was that the flowers from this garden were shipped as bush and bloom, tonic and treatment, all over the kingdoms of the Realms of the Crystal Orb. There was even a rumor that some of the roses had gone beyond the borders of the known Realms. Mirador had its timber and freshwater fish to trade. Aradon provided salt-water fish and grains. Caladon furnished some fish, timber and rice. Balador had timber, and lots of it. Zanadon used to harvest timber, rice and rock products. Panador had its flowers, fruit products and wheat.

The Blood Rose of Panador, the live bloom not the Talisman, measured at least ten knuckles across (about eleven inches) and was a very hardy flower for a rose. As the petals would slough off they were gathered up to make a delicious tea or were crushed into powder for a curing and healing salve to be placed on wounds. So, not only decorative, this flower was practical and useful.

The second rose, the Talisman called the Blood Rose, is an enchantment of the first bloom ever formed by The Creators, and loaned to the Humans who inhabited Panador, for their protection. Its unbreakable glasslike petals pulsed with the magic and power with which the Creators had endowed it. It gave energy to and fed on energy from the Crystal Orb – as all Talismans do. The Twelve Dwarves of the Clan of Hand have been its guardians since their creation. Six Dwarves guard from sunup to noon; the six others from noon to sundown. All twelve of the Dwarves guard it through the night.

The third and remaining Rose in the Castle was, of course, Princess Rose. She was an enlightened seventeen – and if she had been living with your family, you would hear nothing but solid evidence about the abilities of women being equal to those of men; which is not a falsehood, just a bother when it is the only thing one hears someone talk about. She was an independent thinker, with a strong will, but she was one of the most beautiful young women in all the Realms. Zantha's magic mirror would most certainly have homed in on her beauty if asked who was the fairest in this land. Young men had lined up several years ago for the chance at her hand but she dismissed them all as silly little boys. Maybe they were. So, there was no promise of marriage for her, no betrothal, as of yet. A heart-break for her royal parents.

Rose ran down the long corridor of the central maze. She turned right at the end, then, took a left in the middle of the next run. Then an immediate right and another left.

"Rose! I don't know these mazes like you do. Where are you?"

Rose laughed and continued on. A right and two lefts and she was on a sprint to the center of the bloom-shaped maze. With a final right she turned into the maze's flower-laden heart, with its swings and benches. She hid behind a topiary tree and waited for Bianca's arrival. Bianca came carefully – knowing Rose's caprices – but before Bianca could discover exactly where Rose was hiding, hands were over Bianca's eyes.

"Got you again!"

"Yes. You always do." Bianca collapsed into the double glider swing and Rose gave it a push and joined her in the seat opposite. They leaned back and relaxed.

"So, did you know that Daniel had a crush on you?"

"I knew. And I discouraged him. It was not serious anyway. Besides, I have Valerius."

"Yes, my noble brother. I keep looking for someone like him. But no one can measure up – not even me."

"I thought you were the equal of any man."

Rose shrugged.

Bianca suggested, "There's Daniel!"

"Yes, there is Daniel. He's only a boy – I must say that he is much more of a man than any of the silly things who have come to court me. If only he were older, there might be a possibility – but he's just too young."

"Who's too young?"

The girls jumped and screamed – even the stately Rose – for there was Daniel standing by the topiary, laughing at them.

"Daniel!!"

Both girls got up and chased him around the circular enclosure. They finally dragged him to the ground (or he let himself be caught) and they tickled him mercilessly; all three laughing and giggling.

Then Daniel gasped. "I'll wet myself – stop!"

Again, laughter of all three filled the air. They did stop just short of embarrassment for Daniel.

"How did you find us?"

"Miraden has a new orb and he spied on you two to try it out and then popped me in. So, Rose, dear cousin, if I was older ... ?"

"If you were older you'd be even more of a nuisance than you are now!"

She playfully kissed him, full on the mouth, and got up and went over to the glider again. Daniel sat there – stunned. Bianca laughed, just a little bit.

Daniel looked at Bianca. "What?"

"Was that your first kiss?" was asked in a very sisterly way.

Silence a moment, a downcast look – "Yes," came the mumble.

"I think it's terrific! I won't tell. I promise," and Bianca kissed him on the nose and spit on two of her fingers and held them out. Daniel spit on two of his fingers and matched them up to hers and they shook. It was a custom of theirs developed over the previous year and a half of companionship. Another pact to keep between brother and sister. They had grown close in that time. He comprehended then and there that he would rather have this relationship with Bianca than any other. His crush days were definitely over; at least on Bianca.

Rose intruded. "You really shouldn't have a crush on your sister."

"I know – and I'm over it. Sorry, Bianca."

Bianca smiled. Daniel turned his adoring gaze to Rose. She had kissed him!

"And I certainly can't encourage you – you are one of my favorite people, Daniel – but not as a suitor."

Daniel was a little startled at that revelation, but he managed a rejoinder. "But you don't seem to be able to find any suitor!" Daniel was hopeful; optimistic that he still could be the one.

Bianca laughed. "My little brother is quite right, cousin!"

Rose looked at Daniel. He certainly did not look like a child. There had been other twelve to thirteen-year-olds within the Realms who had been married, but not to seventeen year olds! At least, not older girls to younger boys. As she really took a careful look at him, as a possible suitor, not as her step-cousin, she had to admit that Daniel was no longer just cute. He was tall ... handsome. His voice was deep and full. She stopped the inventory right there. She couldn't think those thoughts! She couldn't do that with Daniel. Her weak thoughts led her to weaker words.

"Daniel, you must realize that you are only twelve."

"I know." He sounded a little dejected – almost defeated.

"Daniel there will be hundreds of girls lining up at your feet – girls nearer your age – and soon by the looks of you. Even though I'd like to be, I can't be one of them." It hurt her to say it – pained her to admit it. It was placation not admission, really. He still looked incredibly stunning to her. But she had to maintain control of herself.

"I'd rather have just one right one than hundreds of them."

The girls smiled. He was so incredibly wise beyond his years.

"When you choose – choose one like Bianca and you will never go wrong. Choose one like me and you'll always regret it."

"I don't see what's so bad about you! Except that you're too old!!!" Daniel smiled that incredible, beaming grin.

Well, if that wasn't an invitation, I've never heard one. Daniel laughed and Rose was after him again. Maybe that was Daniel's intention. Maybe the 'child' in him did not realize that his crush had shifted from Bianca to Rose; it had not just ended. The adult that was forming there, inside him, already knew something that the child didn't. Daniel took off. Rose pursued, playfully. Just when she thought she had him, he disappeared.

Rose shouted to the skies. "Miraden – that's not fair!"

A voice came, as if out of the sky, "Neither is toying with the affections and emotions of my grandson."

"Touché, sister dear, touché," Bianca intoned.

Rose, sobered momentarily, laughed again as Bianca joined her. Rose's laugh was to cover her embarrassment. She really did like Daniel – but deep down she knew it would never work. Still, the attraction was there; and she had to deal with it. She and Bianca walked hand in hand to the exit as if they were still eight-year-old best friends forever. Bianca was singing and Rose was ... whistling.

ᴍ

CHAPTER THREE
DRAGONSIGN
(1st Month)

WHEN DANIEL FOUND HIMSELF BACK at the Cave of the White Dragons — due to Miraden's transportation spell – his room had changed slightly. There were dozens of books with pages open, and sheaves upon sheaves of drawings of Dragons. Small ones, tall ones, colors! Six to be precise: white, blue, red, orange, green and gold. Each color portrayed, not a single beast, but a pair of Dragons.

"Grandpa, this is the best stuff you've ever shown me!"

"I'm glad you feel that way. We are going to recreate them ..."

Daniel was thunderstruck for a moment. "Really? When?"

" ... Soon – not too long – but not tomorrow."

"Will I help?"

"Yes – you will do more than help."

Miraden began to outline the plan as Daniel stood there in stupefaction.

"You will need to research each of the original twelve Dragons, their colors, their habits, their names, the locations of their DragonMounts. Then, you must visit each DragonMount and bring back DragonSign."

"What's DragonSign?"

"Anything that comes from a Dragon – scales, claws, teeth, eggshells, bones – anything of their bodies that remained

25

behind."

"Even dung?"

Miraden thought, *Twelve-year-olds!* "Well, yes – even that."

"What do I do when I have it?"

"You bring it back here."

"Here? Maybe I'll leave the dung alone. What happens after we have it all?"

"We recreate the Dragons – well, maybe resurrect is a better term."

"You're serious? We are going to create Dragons?"

"Yes – that is what I said."

A shout that could have been heard in the farthest corner of Balador left Daniel's exultant throat. In reality, the shout did not leave the vicinity of the cave due to the silencing charm Miraden had placed so wisely on the mountain. Miraden covered his ears and the cave shook a little. "All six Kingdoms will be visited, so the sooner <u>you</u> get reading, the sooner <u>we</u> get started."

Daniel ran to the shelves in the laboratory, reached into the back of the topmost shelf and grabbed a small casket and ran back to Miraden and threw it open.

"Ready for the White Dragons?"

Miraden was dumbfounded.

"How did you ...?"

"Grandpa – I've been here almost two years – I know every ingredient on every shelf. I know what most of them are used for, too. I do watch you. So when do we resurrect Wallamere and Imadar?"

"Two years? That long? It seems like two months to me."

"Funny, Grandpa!"

"Like all things worth doing, it takes time to do it right. You can't have everything now. That is too easy. Ease is usually the first step toward disinterest and boredom – and error. Just ask Tophet! We start preparing now. What's in the casket?"

"You don't know? I know something that you don't?"

"Regrettably, yes. In 2700 years one can forget a lot of things ..." he peered over his glasses, imperiously, "...even that you liked someone."

"Sorry, Grandpa. I just thought that there was nothing that you didn't know."

"Thank you, boy, for that vote of confidence. But I was serious about my memory."

Daniel smiled. "These are the teeth of Wallamere."

Miraden looked at Daniel.

"It says so on the casket."

Miraden inspected the scrawl on the outside of the casket and nodded. "Go look in the white book on your bed and tell me what we do with the teeth."

Daniel rushed to his chambers and brought back the book, leafing through the pages. He was scanning intently, fingers racing across the words. When he found what he was looking for he plopped the book on the table and pointed.

"We need to soak them in a paste of eel meal for at least forty years. That's too long to wait."

"You'll only be nearing fourteen, Immortally."

"Where do we get the eel meal?"

No sooner said than Miraden had taken Daniel's hand, then all four of their feet were covered by the waters of the River of Fear in Zanadon. *Sometimes things are immediate!* Daniel thought. Miraden reached into the murky stream and pulled up an eel with each hand. Daniel did the same and soon they had 'popped' back to the cave.

"I am most glad to have developed this potion," as he nibbled on a piece of chocolate.

Daniel was still not too sure about it, but he nodded in a half-hearted agreement.

The potion is the one that enhances magical powers; helps grow them in young initiates like Daniel. And restore them in already seasoned ones, like Miraden.

"Saves a lot of time." Then he muttered, "Something I've had too much of in my life, anyway."

They enchanted a cleaver and chopped the eel into tiny bits after removing the bones and the head. Miraden got one of the larger beakers and put the eel into it and then placed the sixteen teeth of Wallamere into the paste and covered them over with more meal. He gave Daniel a vial of potion.

"One drop only! Right, Grandpa?"

Miraden nodded. The sweat began to bead up on Daniel's forehead, determined to let only one drop escape that vial. He tilted it gently, the liquid moved to the lip of the flask and then one drop dripped off the edge of the vial.

"I did it!"

"Yes, you did."

Usually, but not always, Daniel's attempt at only a drop turned into two or three – or a plop of a drop. Daniel passed the vial back to Miraden who stoppered it and placed it in the pocket of his robe again. Daniel looked at Miraden. Miraden looked at Daniel.

"Don't you have something to read?"

"Oh…yes."

"I suggest that if you don't find something about Imadar, Wallamere will be very lonely. And believe me there is nothing worse than a lonely Dragon" – *unless it is a lonely boy*. The bit about the boy was said to himself. "Once you are done then move on to the blue book."

A quizzical look from Daniel.

"Aradon. Best to start close to home."

Daniel went to his chambers and dove into the reading of the book of the White Dragons; especially the female, Imadar. He found some information and noted it in an empty book Miraden had given him in which to record his findings. Then he attacked the book of the Blue Dragons of Aradon – Kallowmere and Ekladar.

ML

CHAPTER FOUR
LO*SS* OF BLOOD
(1st Month)

DANIEL WAS STAYING THE NIGHT in his room at the
Crystal Castle. It was not a good night, as he had hoped it would
be. Tossing and turning, he flopped around on the bed like a rag
doll being flung into the corners of the room by a careless owner.
He was aware of eyes – dark eyes, this time – and Daniel felt that
his entire being was full of one thing – fear, but he could not
wake up. He could not get away from it, or put it out of himself.
Pain seared through his insides and he was suddenly in the
position to see his heart and lungs – inside of him – shrink and
constrict and stop.

He was abruptly outside his body again, where he saw himself
– all gloriously white, naked – and still on the bed. He heard
laughter coming from somewhere else. It was not in the room
with him. His body appeared strangely white and lifeless. As if
there were no blood left in his strong and maturing body.

Then, in a flash he was drawn back into himself. His eyes
popped open and he saw a dark, cowled face, hovering over him
and smiling broadly. He saw dark, gnarled hands reaching for him.
He felt the cold, spectral fingers ice their way across his white
flesh. He recoiled but he could not move; could not wriggle away;
could not push the hands away. He was bound without cords. He
screamed. As he scuttled, but only in his mind, away from the

29

rushing and roaming and uncomfortably invading and probing fingers – over every inch of his body – he began to sense a peace, a warmth washing over him. He also felt his heart begin to beat again. There was a scream from that someone, somewhere else.

Then his own blue eyes were reflected back to him as his eyes changed slightly, his reflection-hair shifted to that of grey, not white, and a glow enveloped him as Miraden's face now hovered, protectively, in the place of Tophet's face, now vanished. Yes! It had, somehow, been him.

As Daniel came out of whatever it was that he had just experienced, Miraden's wand was glowing with the brightest light Daniel had ever seen from it. The eyes, still hovering over him, were full of concern. A familiar voice came to his ears.

"Not green eyes again, I hope? Not this time?"

Daniel shook his head as he pulled his covers to him, seeking to gain warmth and comfort from their folds. A welcome hand brushed aside the errant strands of hair off Daniel's sweaty forehead.

"Dark eyes. And a horrible voice. I only remember seeing him close up once. In the Crystal Dome."

"Tophet?"

Daniel nodded and cried and remembered the flash of light that had killed his father, there in the dome; and Tophet's smile then, just as now.

Miraden scanned the body of his grandson, looking for marks or burns or something. All he could sense was that he looked more pale than usual; a dull white, not a bright one. – as if the blood had left him for a time and only now was renewing itself.

The thoughts that then coursed through the mind of the Enchanter were, *Is it Tophet? How can it be? We took his powers from him! How could he have regained them? Already!*

There was a shadow across the moon. Brief, sudden – but noticeable – barely. The reflected light of the fully rounded orb permeated the rose gardens of Castle Panador. It fell through the window of the Room of the Talisman in the castle tower, just above the gardens. The light crept its way across the floor as the moon rose in the East. It climbed up the boots of one of the Dwarves of the Clan of Hand, Guardians of the Talisman of the Blood Rose.

Another shadow, this time on the floor of the room. Silent. Deathly. Potent. The Dwarves stared ahead, axes held in front of them as they had done for three lifetimes – 1500 years. Wary, but not alarmed. Just a bird or a bat. Probably just the Great Royal Snowy Owl, Martinian, let out at night by the gamekeeper to feed on the mice and rats around the Castle. For even though, as you have seen, castles are pretty wondrous things, there are still some things in them that are not so nice.

The peaceful silence of this perfect late-winter evening was interrupted by the flap of leathery wings, the snarls from a monstrous throat, the slashing, ripping and tearing of Dwarven flesh and the clatter of axes as they fell from lifeless fingers onto the cool stone floor now smeared with the blood of the entire Clan. The attack was sudden and terrible. Not one of the dozen of the Dwarven Guard had seen or heard anything until the sounds of their own and their brother's deaths was no longer able to reach their ears.

Then a shadow filled the room almost blocking the light from the window. Claws clacked against the hard floor, wings folded back and red eyes gleamed in the darkness as Rosenblad, a creature of the night, approached the glass case that contained the Blood Rose of Panador – the Talisman from the dawn of time which aided the Crystal Orb in its protection of the Kingdom of Panador.

Rosenblad was almost as ancient and Dark as the Rose was old and full of Light. Turned during the Age of Magic, as Tophet sought to spread his powers and solidify his position, Rosenblad was once a proud member of Zanadon's Dwarven Clan of Blad, protectors of the Burning Branch, the Talisman of Zanadon. Withera had kept him from dying and had changed him, over a period of time, from a creature of Light to a Dark Vampire, living only on the blood and occasional flesh of his victims.

Guildenblad, then entered the room through the window. He was also a creature of death: a Necromancer, A Dark Dwarven Wizard created over the span of a thousand years through the patience and dedication of Withera. He was also Rosenblad's brother. He was given the power to reanimate life – not resurrect it, but to make the dead bodies walk to kill the living, not caring if they, themselves, died again; but maybe even hoping for the chance of a real death. Once fully turned, he had learned his Dark arts well from Tophet – and also much other magic.

The brothers Blad had been defeated in the War of the Realms and were driven away from the battlefield injured and hungering for more than blood. It was the time for Valerius and Bianca, Son of Panador and daughter of Mirador, Guildenblad's greatest enemies, to receive the revenge he and his brother had plotted for nearly two long years. Panador and Mirador would pay for the defeat of the two Dark brothers!

But together they had just committed the ultimate of horrors: there is no worse crime for a Dwarf than to kill another Dwarf. Now, the Dwarven Brothers, in un-Dwarf like shapes, had killed twelve Dwarven brethren; but were they really still Dwarves? Or had their blood, or lack of it, taken them away from any knowledge of Clanship other than their own shared Dark brotherhood of kinship?

Rosenblad's tall winged shape, partially blocking out the moonlight, transformed into his Dwarven self again. Wings disappeared, claws became feet and hands, fangs changed to uneven teeth, but the skin was still a deathly grey. His Dwarven features, now stretched and leaner, revealed themselves as he stood much taller than his former Dwarven-self ever had. He was taller than his brother who had retained his Dwarven size but had taken on the Dark, almost rotten skin of the Necromancer – not brown, but black, or at least, blackish-grey.

Guildenblad reached for the protective glass encasing the Rose. His hands trembled. He was so close! A Talisman again! He touched the glass. He felt it, the vibration, the hum of the power of the Talisman. He lifted the glass and a light shot out from under the bottom edges that momentarily blinded him. He held still for a moment until the light subsided, or at least equalized. He carefully lifted the glass casing off the Rose and put it on the floor. He took a wooden chest out of his rucksack, set it on the floor, opened it and reached for the Rose. His touch on the Rose caused shockwaves of electricity to be sent deep into his dead tissues. He paused, waiting, unaffected. He lifted the Rose from its vase and the electrical current ended. He then placed the Rose in the chest, closed the lid and replaced the chest in his sack.

"My brother, I am in your debt."

"Someday, Guilden, I will call in the favor." The voice was menacing in its depth of tone.

Rosenblad re-transfigured and leaped out of the window, taking flight with his huge wings spread just before hitting the ground of the gardens below and then streaking off in the moonlight to his lair. He had fed for this year on the flesh of other Dwarves.

Guildenblad pulled out his wand and created an enchantment that carried his nearly weightless dead body to the carpet of living grass in the gardens below. Wherever he stepped, and whatever he touched, it turned brown in decay. Many of the leaves and blooms wilted at his mere passing, hastened also by the passage of their protective Talisman. He made his way to the North garden wall, and with his wand, lifted himself over it and disappeared into the darkness, which is the place where he was the most comfortable.

Rose Red was leaning over the stone railing of the very window in the Room of the Talisman through which Death's creatures had gained entry just hours ago. She was emptying the contents of her stomach after having discovered the massacre of the Dwarven Guard when she had come back to check on The Rose. The Palace Guards she had summoned were now arriving and began to go through very similar motions to Rose's. They had managed to return a messenger to the King and his parents before joining Rose at the railing.

It was unthinkable! Who or what could have eliminated all twelve Guards? Miraden had also been summoned by Bianca, through her Orb of Communication.

"This is the work of a vampire," was Miraden's conclusion.

"But what vampire?" Daniel blanched, if someone with skin as white as his could do so.

"The same one that threatened you on the Plains of Youth, Daniel. He has fed now and will doubtless sleep for a month, a year – maybe ten. The bodies, of course, must be beheaded. Then they must be burned to stop the curse of the vampire from transferring and growing in them."

"But they are dead!"

"If left as they are, each will live again as an undead thing on the next full moon."

Miraden, of course, must be obeyed. So, a state funeral was set for two days hence. In the meantime, the grisly task of 'preparing' and wrapping bodies for cremation went forward.

A funeral for twelve Dwarves! Struck down before they had been renewed. Their renewal was to be held in a few weeks, but that was not necessary now. Who could have foreseen it? It had not come in a vision to anyone with an orb, or dreams or even a remote connection to the Creators.

Silence caused it. That's what Daniel thought.

Miraden sensed Daniel's fury at the oversight.

"Not all things are seen, Daniel."

"This should have been!"

"It is not for us to tell the Creators what should have been seen."

Daniel caught himself before he said something unwise. Which, of course, was a wisdom in and of itself. Miraden smiled, sadly. Daniel left the room.

There was more portent in this than just the death of the brave Guardsmen. The safety of all the Realms was in question. If this could happen here – it could happen elsewhere. There was also the loss of the Talisman and the power and protection that it brought to the Kingdom. All present felt the sense of confusion. Plus, they wondered why.

Miraden had recognized Rosenblad's handiwork; but what use could he have for any Talisman, let alone the Blood Rose? Someone was working with Rosenblad. Was it Nightbane? No! He had never been concerned with any Talisman! Could it be Tophet? Or Withera? Could they possibly be active already? Could Daniel's dream have been more than a dream – a premonition? A message that even Daniel had missed? Were they trying to regain their powers?

Was it Guildenblad? He had sworn revenge right there on the battlefield. It could be him. Or it could be some other Dark Sorceror that had been lost to Miraden's awareness since the Great War; or who had risen without his awareness. It could not be Tophet! Everything inside the Enchanter recoiled from that thought. He would have to trace the magic used. He would have to examine the room again. He searched for Daniel. He wanted the boy to be with him as he used this particular magic. But the boy was not to be found. Miraden could not wait or the most important traces might be lost.

He went to the Room of the Talisman. He soaked his wand in his potion first, and then ran the wand across every surface, touching every item in the room. The window and balcony railing revealed the effects of a hover charm. Anyone with a wand could use that enchantment. Something interesting came up when he examined the unbroken glass casing, found on the floor at the foot of the Rose's pedestal, as if it had been carefully set there instead of having been knocked off or having fallen. How was it possible for something to have absorbed the electrical charge that was built into that unit without leaving a mark of any kind? That protection was built into the workings of the glass itself and no living thing could handle it without severe burns. Plus, the glass was clear. No prints of any kind. Which only left one conclusion – dead, lifeless, printless Guildenblad! But how to find him?

Daniel was terrified. Angry. Even more confused than usual. The memories of the destruction caused by this particular Vampire raced across his mind and it was no dream. No nightmare. It was a living, breathing hell. Daniel was awake and his body shook as each image of wing and fang and claw, of young bodies decimated; – limbs and heads and other things unattached and bloody in the grass – assailed him. He saw Zantha's Castle as a pile of rubble. He recalled the Fortress of Fear as it had tumbled into the surrounding swamp.

He heard the cries of boys and men as they were ripped apart.

He saw a burned out hulk of what used to be his home; the bodies of his family; six graves; then, the murder of his father, and a seventh grave.

He had not been forced to remember these things for two years, at least not while he was awake.

His stomach churned at the thought of the noble Dwarves of Hand, massacred. He wretched. He ran. He stopped and heaved again. He bolted across the bailey of Castle Panador and threw himself against a wall. His fists became bloody and raw as they railed at the stones. Still, his body raged as the memories repeated themselves over and over again, mixing with the new images from the Room of The Talisman of Panador; mingling with the dreams of terror that had plagued him for months. He could not rid himself of the horror he had witnessed at age eleven. And now again at age twelve.

He sped up the steps from the bailey, winding and winding ever upward to the top of the outer wall. Once he achieved the parapet, he ran towards its crenellated walls as if there were truly no end to it. Like a madman followed by shadows, he fled. It was as if he were possessed; Darkness clouding his mind. Suddenly he was airborne and falling. He saw the ground hundreds of arms below him for he had jumped off the castle on the side where the cliff beetled down to the High Plains. He screamed. He folded his arms and shot toward the ground. He closed his eyes.

ML

CHAPTER FIVE
REVENGE IS NOT LIKE CHOCOLATE
(1st Month)

DANIEL FELT WET, SOAKED, SOPPED. His eyes were still closed. He expected not to feel anything. He had expected the bliss of peace, of nothing remembered. But all he was was wet. Had his bladder loosed itself? Was he lying at the bottom of the cliffs, bloodied and soaked in his own waste? Was he alive, but just barely?

He opened his eyes. He was underwater. He was unexpectedly confused because the river was on the other side of Castle Panador than the one he had jumped from. He scrambled toward the surface. He floated, sopping wet but completely undamaged; except for the slight sting in his bloody hands from where they had met with the wall of the bailey. He was alive. He knew that. He was glad of it. Why had he run off the parapet?

He looked around and found the shoreline quite close to him. This was not a river. It was a lake. But which one? He struck out, swimming to reach the shore. In less than a minute he crawled out onto the rocky bank and collapsed. He wasn't asleep or unconscious. He was just tired. He waited there for his energy to return. He looked out across the waters to where an island sat. He felt his pockets. There was something in one of them. It was a chunk of chocolate. It was wet, almost soft and runny, but he folded it into his mouth. He felt better almost immediately. How had he expended enough magic to require chocolate already? He looked around, trying to get his bearings. This was definitely not Panador.

The trees were blackened hulks with few leaves on them. Bare. Eerie. The area inland seemed to be darker the further you probed into it. He started to walk. He had to find out where he was. He didn't remember that he could transport himself yet. He couldn't! He knew that. But somehow, here he was, not even remotely where he had been a few minutes ago. He trudged across a low hill. The trees around him were stunted, misshapen, twisted versions of those in other places of the Realms. Then he saw a castle, stuck back into the woods, looking a lot like the trees around him. He flattened himself against one of those trees, hiding from the castle. Whose was it? Where was he? Who could have seen him? A terrible thought flashed through his mind: had his anger brought him directly to where Guildenblad lived? Stranger things had happened.

He gradually gained control of his heaving shoulders. He couldn't face Guildenblad! He was only a child. A strong child but ... he was alone. He started to shake, to cry. He calmed himself again by asking himself, *What would Miraden do?*

He would 'pop' home; that's what Miraden would do! But Daniel was not Miraden and he could not 'pop.' He gained control, once more, of his overactive chest. He opened his eyes. He saw the sun climbing in the sky. It was higher now than when he had beached himself. He was facing east, into the sun. So this castle was west of where he had been? He peeked around the tree and saw tall, dark mountains behind the forest, which was behind the castle. He looked back in the direction from which he had come, the lake was also east of him, and south. He saw no mountains beyond it. Only that island not too far away. Was he in Mirador? Zanadon? Somewhere no one knew about? He had had dreams about strange new places. He didn't know where this place was but he knew that he had not been here before and that this was not happening in a dream.

He set his hands gently against the bole of the tree and thought, *grow!* He waited. Nothing! Had he lost his powers? Was he alone and completely defenseless? He then thought, *break apart* as he lifted his hands toward another nearby tree, but not the friend that had hidden him from this strange castle. The other tree shattered. His powers were still there. But they were not operating as they should be. This place must be cursed!

His eyes widened at the realization that he could destroy things but not make them grow. He had never experienced this before. He had to be somewhere Dark; some place that dampened his natural ability to work the Magic of Light. The only place he knew about that could still do that was Zanadon; or at least parts of it. This wasn't the Swamps, or the Mire, nor was it the Plains of Youth. (Where he had lost his friends.) The Forest of Fear did not reach to the shores of the Crystal Lake. He could be in The Wicked Wood! The place where the murderer of his family had lived.

He jumped out from behind the tree while at the same time raising his hands and pushing a bolt of energy toward the castle that was not too far distant. The energy rebounded and shattered some trees off to the left and right of him, missing the castle entirely. This place was still protected. There was a residual magic here that was not Miraden's. It had to be Tophet's. Or Withera's!

He began to walk slowly and cautiously toward the strange, misshapen, yet seemingly intact structure in the hollow of the woods. Behind it, if he was in the Wicked Wood, there was that range of low mountains that would be the Fearful Mountains. Behind them, another range towered in the distance: The Black Mountains. That had to be it!

He scanned ahead, around and behind him as he progressed forward. He felt no other physical presence. But there was a magical one. He began to dart from tree to tree. Then he thought, *If this place is Dark then the trees as well as the castle are Dark.* He began to stay away from the trees; avoid their branches. Maybe it was from them that he was feeling the magical presence.

The closer he got to the castle the thicker the air became;

more oppressive, more dangerous. Was he letting fear get the better of him? He was only twelve. Thirteen would come next month. He could still be frightened of things and be considered totally justified in that fright. But he was Daniel – The Prophecy – the Miracle of Mirador. Not that he exulted in those positions. He was still just a boy from Valley Vale whom the Creators had deemed worthy to touch with Magic, and responsibility, and honor, and death. He could be dead and this was just ... No!

He sagged against a tree trunk. He prayed to the Creators to help him. Miraden had taught him that he could call upon them at any time; that they were gratified when their creations asked them for help. He spent some time in the hollow of that tree with his eyes closed. When he opened his eyes the branches that had been quietly wrapping themselves around him cinched tightly across his chest and arms and grasped his legs, holding him to its trunk. He felt his chest swell, pulsate, and his right pectoral now matched his left. *Timing,* he thought, *is not always inopportune!* The strain had brought about sudden equalization. He flexed the considerable muscles over his entire body while he thought, *'Light!'* He began to glow. The heat from his body expanded and sent fire into the tree that was holding him. He hated to destroy any tree. He had already been able to make so many trees live in his short lifetime. The tree 'screamed' as it was suddenly ablaze. The branches that held him released him. Well, they didn't actually release, they were just no longer there. They had been turned to ashes at his feet. The heat of his body subsided and he returned to his normal, warm-white glow. He pulled his father's red-handled long-knife from its sheath at his calf and it glowed. A bubble of red formed about him, as it had over a year ago and not too far away from this very place.

He knew now, for certain, what it was that he was facing: The Wicked Wood and Withera's magic castle there. They had never destroyed it. It had been on their 'to do' list – Miraden's and his – but they had never gotten around to it. He squared his shoulders and thought, *Now is the time.* Encased in his red warding, the same as the first warding that had magically protected him against the wolf, he marched toward the castle. He had led a charmed life. Not an easy one, but it had been one where he could have died a thousand deaths before he was eleven, and he was still alive at twelve.

Black lightning crackled from one of the towers of the Castle. It hit his warding and bounced off of it, angling into the trees where it was absorbed. Daniel noticed that the tree it hit did not disintegrate. He shot his own beam of Light at that same tree and it exploded. The Castle sent another bolt, which his warding deflected into another tree that shook like it had just tasted something it relished and had missed for a long time. Withera couldn't still be here! She had been banished, with her father Tophet, to the Unknown East, never to return. But this sure smacked of her magic. Her spells, any spells or enchantments, can last a good long time as long as the caster of the spell is alive, somewhere.

Daniel prepared himself. The next bolt launched itself at him and he responded with a bolt of Light. They met midway and their energies wrapped around each other, sizzling and scorching the earth beneath them. Then they winked out. It was like the bolt of Light just consumed the Dark one and they disappeared. Another shot was met by Daniel, so that the two bolts were deflected high into the sky where the swirling column of energy dissipated for lack of something to electrify.

Daniel continued to advance on the creepy castle. He was within fifty arms of it now. It loomed over him, much taller than it had appeared, earlier. It's battlements stood at about forty arms high with scraggly, pointed towers that rose up at odd angles another thirty to forty arms in height above the battlements, looking much like the trees surrounding them. As he took another step he heard screaming. He stopped. Shadows were vomited upwards, out of the center of the Dark mass that soon corrected their course and came right for him. He had met them before. They could be instant death to those who were unprotected by a warding. Their screams increased as they came in contact with the red edges of his protection. They sizzled, almost like they had real bodies. But they were Shadow, somewhat corporeal, but still ethereal. He repeated what he had seen Miraden do when they were attacked by the Shadows in the southern part of the Forest of Hope. He formed a small pulse that he sent out through his warding from his empty hand. His other hand still held the glowing long-knife, that seemed to act strangely like a wand; but only in the formation of a warding. It had never manifested itself as magic, elsewhere or otherwise. The energy obliterated all of the shadows in its path. Again and again he pushed the balls of energy through the walls of the warding as he rotated in all directions and Shadows turned to ash around him.

Then Daniel stumbled. He was tired already. He sent one more pulse at the Shadows and it took many of the remaining entities out. The others took to hiding behind the trees, waiting for the bubble of red to come by them. Daniel faltered. He fell, long-knife still in his hand, bubble remaining around him. The Shadows attacked, all six of those that could. They flung themselves at the bubble, certain in the fact that they could now get through. Daniel, even in his weakened state, could maintain the energy around him, and the Shadows – an ancient conjured evil – sizzled to an ignominious end on the warding of a boy Enchanter.

But Daniel was spent. He could not rise. The Castle sent bolt after bolt at him. He crawled or rolled away in his warding, for he could not stand. The warding was taking a beating and Daniel lost consciousness as he hid behind a very large tree with a thick bole. The lightning stopped as if unable to reach, or even detect its enemy.

Daniel awoke to darkness around him. He stretched out his hand and felt the warding still in place; protecting him. He patted his pockets. No food. No chocolate. He thought about the stack of rejuvenating ambrosia that supplied his room at the DragonMount with that heavenly smell of chocolate. All he wanted was one bar. And that's all he got. It appeared in his hand. He broke it into pieces and placed one on his tongue to melt. He savored the taste as he felt the reinvigoration of his body.

Miraden had invented some marvelous stuff. He placed another morsel on his tongue. Then a third. As his strength returned to him he stood, still behind the tree. Its great girth had protected him as surely as the red warding that was still around him. Why had it not tried to hold him? Then he took another look. All around the warding ashes were scattered across the grass. He looked up. The tree had no branches, no leaves. It had tried to capture him and had already paid for its folly. That served it right, since Daniel had thought that it was also his shield, his protector, and it wasn't.

All of a sudden Daniel ran, still inside the bubble, as it rolled beneath his feet. He headed straight for the portcullis of the peculiar Castle. He was determined to gain entrance. Bolts of lightning arced out at him. Explosions rent the air around him. He was using none of his magic, except to maintain the warding. It was doing all the work – that and his legs. But he was a good, strong runner. He ducked his head as the warding crashed into the castle gate excising a warding-sized hole from the crossbars of the gate; melting them away like a soldering iron through a piece of plastic.

He was inside. He stopped to catch his breath. The warding hummed around him. He watched as the pieces of the gate left barely attached to its bastion dropped to the cobbles below it. The lightning had stopped. He collapsed his warding, but he kept his knife in his hand.

He proceeded slowly to the other end of the gate-house, where he peered around the edges of the archway. It was silent, eerie, spooky – empty. The sunlight didn't necessarily stream into the courtyard, more like it dribbled around the towers and battlements as it reluctantly dripped onto the earth, afraid that it would be sullied or contaminated forever by the evil of the place. Daniel felt it. He was not comfortable here. He reengaged the warding. There was something about this place that ...

He heard a growl. Or was it a bleat? Or maybe a caw? Out of the shadows across the courtyard there was something emerging. He was not alone after all. As it stepped into the uneven sunlight

Daniel's nightmares of The War seemed to return to him, again. He stood still and spellbound. It was a Ballark. One of Tophet's created creatures. It was missing one of its four legs and half of one wing was torn away. It opened its fanged beak and screamed at him. Maybe it recognized him? Maybe Daniel had been the one who had crippled it! He almost felt sorry for it, in its mutilated state; a creature with no volition of its own, created to do the will of others.

It charged him. He was surprised how fast it could move on only three legs. But he stood firm; knife out in front of him and bubble of protection all around him. Suddenly it stopped and snapped at him. It seemed to know what a warding was and was not going to be tempted onto it. It hobbled around this new enemy. Daniel looked it right in the eyes. It roared again in defiance of that human stare that most animals only wither under. Daniel rolled forward. The Ballark screamed at him and jumped into the path of the warding, which sizzled against its foreleg causing it to jump away again. It extended its long, purple tongue and bathed the burn on its leg. It wasn't so bad, there were only a few feathers missing, and the skin was just a little red. Daniel wanted to reach out and heal it. He could do it. But the hiss as his hand began to extend beyond the warding made him retract it to the safety of the inside. Again the two beings looked at each other. Stalemate.

Daniel rolled forward again, trying to attain the archway opposite him in the courtyard. It looked like it led to the rest of the castle. The Ballark hissed again but made no move to intercept him. Daniel rolled in a circle, studying the creature. It looked back at him out of its red little eyes, following him. It reached down and preened the feathers on both forelegs as it settled onto the cobbles of the courtyard. Daniel continued to roll around it. It began to ignore Daniel. Daniel just proved to himself that something doesn't always have to be destroyed in order to be overcome. It was a deep wish inside him. He hated to kill and maim and hurt. 'No harm' was his hope. But he was up against the Dark. Its minions had no such ideals. The mantra of the Dark was: Power, control and influence; they are to be gained at any cost.

Daniel was saddened yet upbeat as he rolled to the archway that hid the grand doors into the castle proper. As he passed uneasily under the arch he turned and looked at the peaceful Ballark, head nestled between its forepaws, resting. He gained the doors, which were wide open. As he rolled inside he collapsed his warding, shutting and barring the doors against the attack of anything from outside, including the now peaceful Ballark.

Nooks and naves and crannies and a dais greeted him. This was the Throne Room, not the Great Hall he had expected. It was fascinating in its intricate simplicity. Arches and tree-like columns joined as in a cathedral on our Earth, forming wonderful 'wooded' designs. It was very pleasant for a place of Darkness. He looked up. He saw the underside and the inside of the monumental towers he had seen from the outside of the building. They rose a hundred arms above his head. He realized that there must not be any upper floors for this castle, for everything that he had seen from the outside was now visible to him inside. It was a carefully constructed ruse. A mirage. A shadow of itself.

There were two doors behind the throne. He carefully stepped up on the dais. He heard a click and engaged his warding immediately, which, as it enlarged, shot the throne against the back wall. The throne rebounded to lay on its side near the right door, smoking from the burn on its side. But a huge blade descended from the ceiling and would have sliced Daniel in half had his warding not been engaged when he jumped to the side. He watched it as it pendulumed back and forth in front of him. It finally came to rest and then was drawn back up into the shadows of the archway above, as if magically resetting itself.

Eyes still on the blade, he ran to the door on the left. He opened it and rushed through it. He was in a bedchamber with a lonely, dusty bed at its center. No other furniture decorated the room. Bare walls of stone surrounded him. As he stepped forward he heard another click and four Shadows rose out of the bedcovers and threw themselves at him. He had collapsed his

45

warding to get through the door, so he raised his long-knife, held, ready in his hand, and sliced the air as the Shadows darted around, weaving through the rising dust, trying to reach him. He rent three of them into cloth-like confetti on the floor. But the fourth got one of its spectral hands on his face and he started to burn. He slashed again, this time in desperation, and the Shadow screamed as it crumbled to bits. He felt his face. It was indeed burned. He placed his hands against his cheeks. After they were cool, he felt better.

He found an alcove to his right. It was curtained off. He walked over to it and after finding the cords, drew back the curtains, knife poised to repel attack.

There was a mirror placed, hidden, there. His brow knitted together. It was the mirror he had seen Lily storing away. The one she had known nothing about, except that it was there, in the Crystal Castle, and very pretty. How did it get here? He ran his hands over the surface, around the gilt-edged frame at the intricate designs and filigree he found there. It was dusty, but beautiful. He withdrew his hand and saw that his fingers were blackened – with the dust of years, probably.

He looked into the glass, which reflected his face while his fingers traced his reflection and the fading burn marks on his cheek. He saw a swirl, a smoky whirlpool, beginning in the center of the mirror itself. He backed up. Thinking that it could not reach him if he were further away from it. He was shocked and amazed as a face formed out of the whirlpool and looked right at him. He knew, then, that this could not be good. He reformed his warding.

The forehead on the face wrinkled in recognition. "You!"

Daniel just stared back.

"The Prophecy!" was spit at him. It was almost as if he could feel the moisture, with so much vituperation.

"So, I am. What of it?" Daniel stood strong and tall and defiant.

"My Masters were supposed to have killed you."

"I know. But it doesn't look like they succeeded, now, does

it?"

The blade of Daniel's knife flashed and the face in the mirror reacted, fearfully, to the gleaming metal. If it had had working legs and could have backed away, Daniel thought for sure that it would have.

Daniel realized, then and there, "You can't hurt me, can you? They created you, didn't they, but gave you no defenses!"

The mirror was silent. It knew that the type of thing that could destroy it was in the hand of 'The Prophecy' right now. Not just a knife, or a piece of metal, but an enchanted object. It was a strange thing to see this talkative mirror silent. Zantha had wished it to be mute many a time. Daniel had never seen it talk before, but he had heard it speaking as he listened through the door of Lily's chambers in the Crystal Castle. The boy contemplated the Dark object; the frown on its evil face. The fear reflected in its unreal eyes. He had to admire the craft with which it was created; a craft similar to his own – that had to be respected. The reflection was almost human. Almost. Miraden had taught him that no good could come from a Dark object. He believed his Mentor.

He stepped forward again, holding his knife around the back of its blade, and raised his arm, swinging it up, then down again, crashing the butt end of the knife into the glass itself. It shattered. The pieces fell to the floor amid a wail of sound that almost overcame Daniel with its piercing intensity. He wobbled and reeled back and forth as the shriek buffeted him. He placed his hands over his ears until he was certain that the sound had ceased. It was several minutes before he dared to take his hands away from his ears. The room was tranquil. He stepped back from the mirror and raised his hands. He hated to do it, but it must be destroyed completely. Pulse after pulse of flame shot from the palms of his hands. The mirror's frame caught fire, incinerating itself almost instantaneously. The enchantment had been within the glass only. All that was left was a small pile of ash on the stones of the bedchamber of Withera, the Witch of the Wicked Wood.

As he looked to where the mirror had stood there was another door beyond. Hoping that it led to the same place that the door on the right side of the dais would have led, he opened it. Or tried to. It was locked. He threw a burst of sound at the wooden door. It shattered away from him. He walked into a room lined with shelves. They were completely empty, except for the dust. So were the tables filling the center of the space. This must have been Withera's work-room; her laboratory. A giant fireplace opened up in the back wall. Empty. No irons, no grate. Not even ash from a fire, or a cauldron of any kind. Except for the wooden furniture, the room was a void.

He found the door to the dais and headed there. He stopped short, though, to pull out the drawers in the tables. Empty also. Not even mouse tracks. He returned to the door and opened it. It was not locked. He turned in the doorway and spewed flame back into the room. The old, dry wood crackled and spit and caught fire quickly. It burned hot and fiercely enough that Daniel had to back away from it while being bewitched by the flames themselves. Even flames of destruction, like the flames of a campfire, could be comforting; knowing that the things that were on fire were never going to bother anyone ever again. It brought a peace to the boy. He continued to watch and back up slowly, arm up and shielding his face from the intense heat. He bumped into the back of the throne. It skidded a few knuckles along the floor and Daniel heard what he thought was another click apart from the noise of the crackle of the flames. The sound of stone scraping against stone began to overwhelm both the room and the noise of the fire. Daniel's warding was up in an instant. A large stone landed near his feet. Another one hit the throne and toppled off onto his warding, exploding at the increased contact with a magical presence of the bubble. Then it started raining stones. Daniel ran. The flames came into the room after him, eating away anything that they could. Even the falling stones could not extinguish the flames crawling along the wooden inlays of the intricate flooring.

With each and every step Daniel's way was blocked by

another stone dropping from above. Then he stepped up on one of the stones, that then stone raised up and took him six arms higher into the air. He leaped from it immediately and found that another stone plummeted on top of the one that had raised him up, just missing him. He screamed and ran. It wasn't a little girly scream, for Daniel was no longer a child. As he neared the large double doors, already aflame, a gigantic stone landed directly on top of his warding. It pressed down threatening to crush him, smoking but refusing to disintegrate against the power of the warding.

Daniel concentrated, harder than he had ever done before. Rivers of sweat coursed down his face as he tried to reinforce his warding to repel or obliterate the stone. But he was tired and had expended a great deal of magical energy, even though he had tried to conserve it. His warding managed to hold, but just barely as the stone slid off to the floor with a major thud. As it did so it pinched part of the warding to the ground, as it rocked back on itself, it caught Daniel's heel in the process. This time he screamed in pain.

He managed to extricate his heel. It was just a glancing blow, but he had to limp now. The archway began to collapse around him. He ran through it and out into the courtyard to find that a tower had collapsed, its spire pinning the poor Ballark to the stones of the yard. It was dead. It was a merciful death for a creature that had no choice in its life.

The castle began to bulge outward as the stones exploded toward Daniel in his warding. He rushed to the gate, stones as big as he was crashed into him and propelled him along. Then the Barbican came crashing down. He jumped through it in time to be missed, but the outer walls of the battlements toppled over on top of him and he was surrounded, trapped and slowly losing consciousness and energy. He could hear the thunder of the rocks and stones disassembling themselves on top of and around him. Then he heard nothing.

The next thing that Daniel was aware of was the face of his grandfather, again peeping over the rims of his glasses at him. He was laying down in his own bed in the DragonMount. He felt his face. There was no pain from the burn. It was no longer even tender. There was a pain in his legs, they were still there, but he tried not to move them.

Miraden chuckled. "Yes, you are all together in one piece."

Daniel reached up and wrapped his arms around the old Enchanter. A pain shot through his lower body, but he didn't care.

"How did you find me?"

"When we noticed that you were no longer with the rescue party at Castle Panador we started searching the grounds. We did not find you anywhere. It was not until you began to use your magic that we were able to locate you – or that my Orb was able to find you. How did you get to Zanadon?"

There was a long silence as Daniel thought about it. "I don't know. I was running so hard that I fell off the parapets of Panador. I was about to hit the rocks when I found myself swimming in the Crystal Lake off the Isle of Fear. I got out and found Withera's Castle. I explored and it exploded."

"I noticed. Why?"

"Traps that were set by Withera herself demolished her castle."

"Why did you engage the castle in the first place? That is why we did not destroy it yet. Its magic is purely defensive. As long as we stayed away, there was no danger to us."

"I was angry."

"You wanted revenge?"

"I know it was stupid, but I didn't expect it to … do what it did."

"You are very lucky."

"Tell me about it."

Miraden looked at his grandson in a very quizzical manner.

"Sorry, Grandpa. It means that I know I'm lucky."

"Oh. Well, you are here for a day or two. I have placed an enchantment around your room. If you stir one foot or finger, magically or physically, out of this area, I shall know it and you will be bound!"

Daniel huffed. Miraden turned and laughed, silently of course. Then he left the room.

"But, Grandfather ..."

All that greeted Daniel was silence.

ML

CHAPTER SIX
NO ROSES
(2nd Month)

THE BLOOMS WERE PUNY, THE colors were lifeless, the stems were spindly and weak – and that didn't take into account the bareness of the rose bushes. The power from the Talisman had brought blessings to Panador that no one really fully appreciated or understood. Until now. Even the hothouses were troubled with failure to produce. And the Royal Gardens were not alone in their barrenness.

The overall harvest of fruits, vegetables, grains and other foodstuffs was down, along with the production of livestock. The farmers and ranchers would have a meager season. If the farmers were down, then the merchants in the cities and towns would have no supply (and thereby, no customers) and the citizens would have no income as well. The outlook was bleak. But the Royal Storehouses, kept full for just such an emergency, were opened up. It would be a scant, but survivable season.

And late winter was approaching. The kind of winter where the sun hides its face for weeks at a time – leaving behind it only a cold rain. Leaves were falling off many of the trees for the first time since the freeze of 2178. So, once 2nd Month had hit there was little joy in the everyday eking out of a living. Once they found the Talisman, all would be renewed. That was their hope.

The Court was fairly empty as Valerius had delegated the apportionment of the food to the Mayors and Townsmen. Re-supply would all be handled locally – it had been planned that way and it was working according to design. Valerius and Bianca sat in Court, conferring with Comera and Alidah, trying to decide the best way for Panador to maintain now that it had little to offer the rest of the Realms in trade for goods or services. There could be no exports of flower or bloom. The other Kingdoms tried to be helpful but there were reports coming in from all over – massive sheep and cattle deaths in Balador and northern Panador; empty fishing nets in Mirador; catastrophic crop failure in Aradon, presumably due to the theft of their Talisman, The Gentle Jewels. The Crown Prince, Emeron, was missing as well; feared dead. Zanadon seemed as impenetrably Dark as ever but nothing particularly useful had come from Zanadon for over a millennium. Only Caladon seemed to still be thriving. But no one had much to trade with them.; nothing but the promise to repay as soon as possible. This is the way that the Realms had operated under the guidance of Miraden for seventeen-hundred years; and with the Kings and Queens for seven-hundred of those years.

At the Court of Panador, there was a disturbance in the hall. The Guards were refusing to do something. Rose went to investigate. She found a dirty and indeed very old man asking for food and shelter and a job. Rose brought him into the throne room, against the protestations of the Guards, so he could make his appeal, himself, to the King and Queen. She placated the guards, reassuring them that they had only been doing their duties. She would now do hers. There was an unusually strong odor about the man. Most people present kept some distance betwen them as he passed by. It makes it very hard to help someone when you can't open your mouth for a breath of air, or to talk, simply because of the quality of the air around the person.

"Please, sir – tell my brother your story."

The man sighed, took a deep breath and launched into his tale.

"I am a traveler who has not seen lodging for the past six weeks. While I was away our home was burned out and I have been searching for my family. We used to live just east of the Springs of Peace."

"You live in the Unknown East, then?"

"Almost, Your Majesty, but still within the boundaries of Panador. I wandered the eastern edge northward into Balador for three weeks before I found my family dead – slaughtered by some animal. My wife and children must have been trying to get to my wife's family there. It took me three weeks to get back to you here, as I had nowhere else to turn. I have wandered hungry and alone. I throw myself on your mercies."

"Valerius, may I remind you that we need a gardener?"

"You would really give this ..."

"He can be cleaned up."

"I certainly can. Just haven't had the opportunity."

"Rose, you shall have your gardener."

"Thank you, thank you, Your Majesty. And thank you to the young lady, also. I can tell a tulip from a horse chestnut. I will do my best for you, Sire."

"Guards – take the Princess and ..."

"... Boncaster, Your Majesty.

"... Boncaster – show him what a tub of water looks like, burn his clothes and provide him with new ones and a room in the servant's quarters."

"How about the hut in the garden?"

"Very well, Rose – the hut."

"Thank you, thank you, Your Majesty."

Rose went to the kitchens to have the water heated and the servants carried the tub into the lean-to outside the kitchens. The Guards had to peel Boncaster out of his clothing, they then wrapped him in a blanket, which they also later burned, and sent him in to bathe. The Royal Barber arrived and cut his hair and removed his beard until he looked really quite human again. Several servants, after giving him a good long soaking, scrubbed his body from a distance, with long handled brushes, and poured scented oils and soaps into the water from bottles strapped to the ends of other poles.

"Ye'll have me smellin' like a blooming rose!"

"That's the point." (After all, there was nothing wrong with the aroma of a rose, or a Rose.)

The bath was done, and emptied. The clothes were brought and a new man appeared before them – but a fairly young one, younger than had at first been suspected, at not over forty years of age, they all reckoned. They took him in and fed him stew, and bread, and wine. He ate noisily but gratefully, thanking and praising with each bite.

Rose then showed Boncaster to his hut in the garden. He said goodnight and fell onto a soft, federdekked straw tick for the first time in six months. He was asleep before Rose reached the gate of the garden. Her hand paused on the latch.

Have you ever had the feeling you were being watched? The little hairs on your back and neck and arms start tingling. Your stomach feels like there is all of a sudden no bottom to it. Your eyes can't stop looking around, searching for the eyes of whoever, whatever ...

"Rose?"

Rose jumped a league out of her shoes as Bianca came up behind her. Bianca was terribly startled herself as Rose leaped passed her.

"I'm sorry, Rose, I didn't mean to startle you. Valerius wondered if you would be joining us for dinner."

"Yes, of course I was just feeling – odd – like I was being watched."

"It was me, silly."

"No, it was some ... thing else."

Daniel, at the Pinnacle of Perfection, dropped the Orb he

was peering into. As he had recovered from his battle at Withera's Castle he had had little to do, even with the warding on his room released, so Miraden had taught him how to use the Orb but he had forgotten to explain how to shield the Orb from being sensed. Daniel spoke the word 'end' and the Orb went clear. Miraden came into the room as Daniel fumbled the Orb back onto the table.

"Been spying again have you?"

"You've done it!" Daniel said with a twinge of guilt.

"Yes, I have, when I needed to know something or check on *someone's* safety. Not just to be a nuisance."

"Fine then!" and Daniel stomped out of the cave and down the path a short distance to his 'thinking spot;' his 'quiet place'. His legs were working well enough, now. It was his custom to go there when he was confused, angry or just wanted to think – sometimes he went there because he knew he was wrong but couldn't let anyone else know it. This was one of those times. More mad at himself than anyone else, he sat there on the rock ledge looking out over the Crystal Lake, angry, yes, but knowing what Miraden knew; that the old man didn't even need to chew him out because Daniel would be hard enough on himself.

He watched the glittering, blue-purple waters of Crystal Lake playing with the golden-orange light of the setting sun. He let it wash over him and felt his insides calm slowly; felt it all taken away. It always helped. Was he that predictable, then? No – he just knew what worked for him. He knew that Miraden realized these things also.

Suddenly Miraden was there; standing in front of him. But Daniel was no longer seated on his 'thinking spot' – he was back in the cave. Miraden had transported him!

"Come with me."

And without even time to take a breath Daniel found himself in a village square. There was music coming from somewhere nearby – and laughter. Miraden directed Daniel, with his hand, toward the sound and followed him at a short distance. Daniel peered over the fence. He startled. He'd never been tall enough to peer over fences before! (Almost thirteen was better!) He saw people of all ages dancing to the music of guitar and flute with a few small drums keeping the beat. There was a roaring fire and the whole enclosure was even warmer for a night in 2nd Month. Miraden settled into the background by the fence as Daniel strayed inside what turned out to be the side yard of an Inn – The Lakeside Lion. They were in Laketon, a little hamlet on the shores of Mirror Lake in southern Panador.

Daniel began smiling and clapping to the music and Miraden, now seated nearby, nodded along as well. The boy's feet also began to move in rhythm, and then he found himself dragged into the dancing. He took hold of the hands that were dragging him and looked up into the eyes of – a girl! She smiled – and her eyes seemed to flash – green!

He was petrified. The movements that had come naturally to him moments ago had suddenly vanished to the point that he could not remember which foot was his left. Lily had had much success in teaching the young Prince of Mirador how to dance. Why now? He tried to jump. He lifted one leg. He flapped one arm then the other. He felt like a goose about to be taken for someone's supper table. Or a three-legged Ballark! Where was everything he had learned? Somewhere – anywhere where the green eyes weren't, that's where!

"Can ye not move about, then? Do ye know ye're dancin' all in one place?"

Something finally broke inside him and Daniel started dancing. The very thought that this girl mocked him for his dancing! He had danced since he was a little child with his real mother; then with Lily and Bianca, even with Rose. He tilted and whirled this presumptuous girl – a very pretty girl; oh, yes, he noticed – around the yard and many others stopped to watch the boy who could somehow, finally dance! The girl laughed and threw herself into the joy of a boy who could dance! Daniel executed some very intricate steps as several people joined in the dance with him and his mystery girl; seemingly a mystery only to him.

Then the music changed to a reel and the couples formed two lines. Of course he held on tight to this – really nice girl! He'd never had fun before with a girl who wasn't his mother or sister -- she definitely was not his sister -- for which he was extremely glad. She continued to laugh and seemed to be really enjoying herself. But not half as much as Daniel was. He had never felt so – light – so free, not even when he was dancing with Bianca while Valerius was watching. Every once in a while, he even caught himself just looking at those green eyes. They peered at him, into him, over him and made him uncomfortably comfortable; that feeling of elation right behind the belly button.

The couple threaded the needle, do-si-doed, took a grand right and left and came home to their partners where the music stopped and the young Miss caught Daniel staring again at her shining face. He looked down quickly, ashamed.

"Sorry, didn't mean to stare."

Daniel always the reactionary!

"I dinna mind. Do ya mind 'fi stare at you?"

Now Daniel thought *who would want to stare at me?* But he didn't realize how handsome and strong his youthful features had become: a gentle but firm jaw line with high cheekbones; a supple mouth with full lips, really good for smiling (and maybe other things as well); a small nose and piercing blue eyes; not to mention the shock of long white hair that cascaded to his now broadening shoulders, the strands of which hung down over his deepening chest. Much more sixteen than almost thirteen.

"I don't mind at all," Daniel managed to squeak out. He hated it when his voice betrayed his real age.

So, they stared at each other for a few minutes. And this girl was something to stare at. Long, auburn hair to her waist, slender and tall, with those haunting green eyes as deep as the forest, and a narrow, sharper-featured face with small lips that made Daniel want to lean in and ...

"Ahem!"

Daniel and the girl were abruptly startled out of the reverie into which they had sunk themselves. Their mutual admiration society had been interrupted as they were jolted, not rudely but firmly, back into reality. They realized how close their lips had been to touching.

Daniel turned red and so did the girl. On Daniel, with his white skin and hair, it was certainly more noticeable than it was amid the freckles of the girl.

"Can I get you a drink? I'm sure thirsty."

"Love one. Thank ye."

He walked, no not really, he floated over to the table and took two mugs of some sort of cider. He brought them back and gave her one.

"Umm, I'm Daniel."

"I know."

He stood there. *That went well*, he thought. "Oh. And you are ..."

"Tilly."

Daniel sipped. "I like it."

Tilly sipped. "Yes, good cider."

"Oh, that too – I like your name."

Tilly suddenly sunk her eyes into her cup – smiling – and took a deep drink while trying NOT to look at Daniel. He took a large sip and ended up coughing and spluttering, and he didn't know why, but he thought it might have something to do with Tilly's 'not looking at him'.

The music started again. A quadrille. A little slower, a chance to watch each other as they danced. They played tag with their eyes as the complex steps of the dance were flawlessly executed by their feet, they tried to catch each other trying to sneak a look at each other without catching each other, while looking at each other. It was not a terribly successful endeavor. Not at all like the dancing!

After the quadrille finished, Daniel took Tilly's hand and led her to a bench nearer to the fence, out of the center of attention, into the recesses of the light. Miraden was keeping a watchful eye and Daniel knew it. The youth found out that Tilly was the Innkeeper's daughter and that she was Daniel's age exactly (as long as you didn't count his immortal status, which he was something he was determined to do for the rest of his Immortal life). They were both almost thirteen and only six days apart in human years, they would each have their birthdays in just a few days, it being Second Month. Tilly liked to sew and cook, dance and shoot a bow and arrow. She loved dogs and cats and horses. Daniel confessed that he liked dogs and horses, but cats he had no opinion on, or pretended not to at any rate. He loved archery and dancing, but admitted that he was a terrible cook, and that every time he picked up a needle he only ended up drawing blood – his own. Tilly laughed. Every time she did so Daniel felt something tighten in his chest. It was a good sort of discomfort, not one of the twinges of change, and Daniel welcomed it; almost invited it. They talked about this and that and other things.

"Tilly – time to clean up!"

They hadn't noticed that the music had stopped; that the gathering seemed to be over for the night.

"I ... have to go."

"I know. Will I be seein' you again?"

"If I have anything to say about it, yes!"

Tilly's father approached. "Now, Young Master Daniel, there'll be other days and you, a well-behaved young gentleman, will always be welcome 'ere."

Tilly smiled and so did Daniel. Tilly's father's comments had surprised them both.

"Thank you, Sir. Goodbye, Tilly. It was great ... I ... I had fun!"

Daniel got up and went to the gate in the fence. He thought that what he had just said would make him seem like a real dolt to Tilly and her Da. Really lame, as we would say today, here and now. But he turned to look once more at Tilly and found her right in front of his face where she stole a quick kiss from his lips and left him standing there, like usual, just staring. Why did every girl in his life just kiss him and run? (Because he's lucky, that's why! But really, it was only two girls so far: Tilly and Rose.)

"Goodbye, Daniel."

"Uh, yeah ..."

Tilly giggled and Daniel stumbled out the gate to where Miraden was waiting. The two Enchanters walked in silence through the moonlight for a short distance.

"Grandfather, is every girl like that?"

"Not all will be. But that is neither your fault nor theirs. There are people who fit and people who don't fit. You and Tilly fit – or so it would appear."

"Yeah," was a dreamy, somewhat stupid expression typical of the male teen when his emotions, especially those new and jumbled up ones, are overruling his brain. "How did you know?"

"I didn't. But I knew you, and I was familiar with Tilly because I come here a lot."

"For the lemonade?"

Miraden hemmed and hawed, and eventually said "Yes. Then there were the dreams you told me about."

"Yeah. I just thought about those. It was her?"

"I think so."

"How did you make the connection?"

"She was always happy, singing, responsible, when I came to eat here. I just had a hunch she was the one in your dreams. Sometimes that is all you can have."

"I think your hunch was a good one."

"Obviously," with a little laughter in his grandfatherly tone.

"Is she…'the one'?"

"There is never only 'the one'. I think that you will find that there can be many 'ones' in your life. I've been fortunate enough to have two 'ones'. Only time will tell, in your case."

Pop!

They were home. The cave was warm. Daniel was warm and lightheaded. He slipped out of his clothes and then fell back into his deep, soft bed covers. He pulled them up to his neck and sighed. He mouthed the words, *"Thank you, Miraden."*

"You're welcome, Daniel – now get some sleep," came audibly from the other room.

How does he do that?

"It is to Mirador tomorrow."

"All right. Good night, Grandfather. I love you."

Miraden was silent as a tear misted his left eye. His own children had died so long ago, except for Lily, who was still over eight-hundred years old. He had forgotten what it was like to have the unconditional love of a child.

The private gardens of Queen Lily and her son, the Prince of Mirador, were not so private on the seventh day of Second Month. It was Daniel's thirteenth birthday and Miraden, Lily, Marble, Valerius, Bianca, Rose, Matthew, Sarai, Elias, and their other children were frolicking about in a great game similar to Blind Man's Bluff. Even Miraden and Lily took their turns behind the blindfold. How can you blindfold an Enchanter? He, or she, has to promise not to cheat – just like a human must.

Six of the Dwarves of Hope were stationed about the enclosure, the seventh having remained in the secret room of the Talisman as a guard. Their countenances appeared cheerless, but they, too, were having fun. They were needed. They were useful. They would follow Daniel, or Miraden, anywhere. The Prophecy himself had grown much in the last two years since their first meeting. He used to be closer to their size. Now he was twice their height and as strong as an ox. Yet, he retained – or maybe he had gained – the bearing of a Prince of the Realm. What he had retained was his childlike heart. Lily and Miraden had both worked wonders in a simple, humble, teachable youth. Wonders that seemed to be already a part of him; not just added on. The youth had taken to their love and attention like he had been born to them.

Elias and his brothers and sisters, along with Daniel, crowded around Miraden as he levitated objects, and made things appear and disappear. They were thrilled, but Daniel knew the secrets, although he would never reveal them or his knowledge of them to the younger children, including Elias. Elias had only experienced magic through Daniel and Miraden, so far. It was still a world of mystery and fascination to him.

It was time for the birthday boy to make his speech. These were, traditionally, meant to express hopes and dreams. Daniel tried to stick to the typical agenda but he had some thoughts that would not leave him alone.

"I know that I can never be mortal again. I know that I will outlive most of my family and friends. I have a real difficult time adjusting to that thought, even though it is not a new one for me. So, this birthday, and the birthdays of those who are closest to me, are important. They remind us of our Human mortality. I have decided to count myself in Human terms. I love being young and Human, and at the same time, I know that I must grow up. I do not want to stay a child forever. Even though I may have to. I don't really know how it all works – yet. But I will cling to my Humanity and my childhood by counting my age in mortal years. In ten years I may not look twenty-three, may not feel it, either, but I will count myself as being twenty-three. But I may look a lot like I do now. I think in that way I will be able to celebrate my Human origins as well as my life as an Enchanter. I will get the best of both worlds. Besides, if I look like a child, I can get away with acting like one – sometimes!" There was laughter. "I will love my friends and family forever, even though some of them may not be with me that long." He couldn't help it, but he looked over at Elias. Tears formed in his eyes. He saw that Elias, too, was struggling. "My love, and I hope theirs, too, cannot be limited or even contained by a mortal time span. Life and love are eternal. So are memories. My birth-family is gone. I think of them every day. I miss them but still they are with me; somewhere inside me. I can call them up anytime I wish. My new family, and my friends, will also always be with me. I will not forget; like Dark wants us to do. Part of our fight against the Dark is to remember – then to love – then to live!"

He was silent, like those who had heard him. The Dwarves began to bang their axe-poles on the ground of the garden while the others applauded the thirteen-year-old Prince of Mirador. He was hugged and kissed by every member of the party, except the

Dwarves. Elias hugged him the longest, but they didn't kiss. Daniel thought about placing a kiss on the cheek of his 'brother', but decided against it. Lily and Bianca and Rose lavished their kisses on him. He did not mind it. He even enjoyed it; reveled in it. Then it was time to eat.

Miraden and Lily levitated a huge cake onto the table in the garden. Everyone surrounded it, ready to devour it. Daniel cut it and served the children first. Elias' youngest sister clung to the birthday boy as he tried to hand her a piece of cake.

"I love you, Daniel."

"I love you, too, Hester."

"I don't just love you because you can beat up Elias, or because you have fun parties. You're my big brother, too – just like Elias is. I have the best brothers." She looked at Daniel, Elias, and then at the younger Jeremiah.

Elias and Daniel looked at each other, a single simple thought transferred as if by magic between them. They lifted her into their arms and placed a kiss on each of her cheeks. As they put her down, Daniel handed her her piece of cake. She went over to her parents and solemnly ate what Daniel had given her. Jeremiah placed his arm around his slightly older sister. Even the Dwarves felt the tug of a heartstring on that one.

Food was consumed, the pond was swum in by all the children while idle talk (and not-so-idle-talk) of this-and-that was engaged in by the adults. Daniel chose to swim! But he longed to hear what was being talked about! Ah, the complexities of being a child-adult.

Before long, the sun had quickly dissolved into the mountains of the west. Night-time brought the fireworks. Magical explosions of color and light created by Miraden appeared in the skies over the garden. Even the Dwarves provided a reaction to the marvelous phenomenon. The children, this time fully including Daniel, were awestruck. The other adults were delighted. As an arc of white streamed up to explode into blues and reds and purples and oranges a cloud of Darkness moved in and hovered, quickly extinguishing the bright lights and obscuring the stars and moon behind them.

Dark lightning struck from the cloud and shattered a statue near the pool. Miraden and Lily went into action, along with Daniel and the Dwarven magician named Elderberry. Their wands and hands pointed to the sky sending a shield of Light arcing toward the cloud of Darkness; covering the entire gardens from wall to wall to wall to wall. The arc pressed up and the cloud pressed down. A battle of wills developed. Lightning flashed between the two very different manifestations of Light, providing another stunning but dangerous display, wholly unintended, for the little crowd inside the gardens of the Crystal Castle. But no-one was laughing or ooohing or ahhing, now. Miraden thrust his arms up. The shield moved upward. Wordlessly, he had communicated his intentions to the rest of his defense force on the ground. Miraden flexed his arms twice and on the third flex all the others joined him. They sent the arc higher into the sky, repelling the Dark cloud little by little with their repeated actions.

After the constant barrage Miraden sent as much power as he dared skyward while at the same time dissolving the shield. The energy hit the Dark cloud with such pinpointed accuracy that it began to burn. The sky was alight with flame as the dark cloud was eaten away, dissolving into nothingness. As the last shred of Dark was incinerated, like a Shadow, Miraden and Lily re-erected the shield while a scream was launched at them out of nowhere. The shield recoiled at the impact of the sound of the voice, but it held steady. The scream repeated itself, but got softer and softer as its power lessened and the stars and moon reappeared. The night that could have been an end was not. Miraden and Lily, connected on a telepathic level, alarmed over the suddenness and intensity of the attack, ushered the children into the castle where they would all spend the night. The Enchanters did not want to risk undue exposure for their guests to this sudden Darkness. The children were thrilled. Every child crowded into Daniel's room, where additional beds were summoned and the room was warded with an extra warding beyond the one on the castle, and on the gardens.

Daniel was a great host as he quieted their fears and told them humorous stories and stories of bravery – some of them including their two oldest brothers, Daniel and Elias, who was prominently featured, but he never used his own name.

ML

CHAPTER SEVEN
BLOOMING AND NOT
(3rd Month)

THE CLANK AND CLATTER OF two pieces of metal clashing together filled the air of the training grounds. A tall knight with a bold stroke was backing up from a shorter knight who had a vicious attack. This attack caused the tall one to parry madly. The tall one was dressed in a white tunic while the shorter one wore blue. Their arms and legs were covered with metal greaves and their helmets were closed, with visors down over their faces. There was a crowd watching, soldiers and villagers mixed, silent, breathless, as the two combatants fought around the obstacles of the yard. *Ching – ching – ching – clinch – break – clank – ching – crash.* The taller knight stumbled over the bracing for the trebuchet, a sort of sling-like catapult, that his smaller opponent had managed to maneuver him into. His helmet bounced up and askew as he landed hard on his backside and scrambled to his feet again, re-seating his helmet, his opponent giving no quarter. *Ching – ching – clash – ching – ching – ooof! – ching* again as the sabers rattled against one another, blade to blade. The smaller of the two knights seemed to be the more agile swordsman. Then the smaller knight was down. No – a feint and an upper cut by the downed man took the sword out of the hands of the white knight who was then knocked to the ground with the blow and pinned there by the sword point of the smaller, blue knight.

"Yield?"

"Yield.

The point came away and was sheathed. A hand was extended and the downed knight was helped to his feet. Their helmets came off with laughter and labored breathing. The tall one was exhausted but the shorter one – who had on the blue tunic – had a recognizable shock of white hair – there was no mistaking him now, it was Daniel. The tall knight was Miradorian Master at Arms, Jeremiah.

Daniel shook his mane of white hair. Bianca, Valerius, Miraden and the King and Queen crowded around him, congratulating him. Daniel stood calmly but winded, taking the compliments. Miraden stood behind him with his hands on the boy's shoulders and hugged him to him. The Master at Arms then kneeled in front of Daniel.

"Daniel, I have not seen a better. With the permission of the King and your Mother, I would like to present you with this sword …"

Marble and Lily nodded and an attendant brought over a sword, shining brightly in its red scabbard. The Master at Arms took it and handed it ceremoniously to Daniel whose face almost out-shined the brightness of the weapon itself as Jeremiah drew it's gleaming length from, and then returned it to, the sheath after swooshing it through the air.

"… a Sword of Light that marks you as a protector of Mirador and a full-fledged Man At Arms for the Armies of the Crystal Orb."

Daniel reverently took the sword and clipped the scabbard about his waist. He extended his hand and shook heartily with the Master at Arms.

"Thank you, Jeremiah. It will be an honor to be counted as one of you and to serve the Orb."

With a lot of backslapping the little group moved off to the armory to return the battle swords, talking animatedly about future contests. Then they proceeded to the castle. Daniel was left in his chambers where he took off his swords and ensconced them with great care in a place of honor in the brackets on the wall next to his bed. They were to hang right next to the bow and arrows that his father had given him two years ago in the High Forest of Hope. He unbuckled his leg and arm guards, his greaves, and wormed his way out of his tunic and chain mail shirt. His linen undershirt clung to him with the sweat of his battle labors. In linen shirt and breeches Daniel moved to a panel in the wall by the head of his bed. The panel slid aside from the pressure he placed on the trigger and revealed a set of stairs. Daniel descended them quickly and burst out into the private gardens that he shared with the Queen, his mother.

He dove into the pond and came up sweeping his long white hair out of his face. He wriggled out of his wet breeches underwater and wrung them out, throwing them onto the rock to dry. His linen shirt then followed. Then he got an idea. He stood in the waist deep water next to the rock where his clothes were. He clasped his hands together and rubbed his palms across each other. He thought, '*hot and dry – hot and dry*' and he ran his hands over his clothes. Steam swept off the garments and they dried out immediately as if the sun had been at them all day. He then swam about the pool for almost half an hour, splashing and diving. When he was ready he pulled himself out of the water and stood there dripping. He thought, '*hot and dry*' and ran his hands over his skin. It worked. He was dry and he jumped into his clothes. He hurried to his chambers clean, dry, refreshed and tired. He fell onto his bed.

After a few minutes, there was a knock at the door.

"Daniel? We must leave now for Panador if we are going to be able to eat and see the play tonight."

Daniel sighed. He was not looking forward to a sixty-league coach ride. Maybe he could catch up on his sleep! But he was excited about the play!

"And Daniel, I almost hesitate to mention it, but the next time you swim naked in the gardens put up an invisibility shield so that the servingmaids don't have so much to talk about. It is not good for them to know too much about the heir to the throne.

And from what I heard, son, there was a lot to talk about."

Daniel turned crimson!

"Sorry, Mother. It won't happen again!" *You can bet it won't,* Daniel thought! Something horrible then occurred to him. He wondered if his mother had really 'seen' for herself? Was she just posing as the reporter of the incident? Daniel's crimson level rose from toes to nose! Daniel had to know, however painful, "Mother, did you ...?"

"No, son, but as I said, I heard plenty. Now, hurry!"

On his way down to the front steps of the Castle he wondered why Miraden couldn't just 'pop' them all over to Panador! But no! They had to make a royal entrance in the royal coach. Giggles from the side corridors and nervous scuttling about in the shadows greeted his rapid passage down the hall. Daniel was crestfallenly crimson again! He must remember that he did not have the same freedoms, here at the castle, that were his at the cave. It was funny how he thought of the cave, now, as a home. It was a good thing. He had moved on in some ways. He realized that there was nothing he could do to bring his own family back; that there would always be a large chunk of his heart that would ache just for them.

But his consolation, at least about the ride today, was that he would have his new family around him. Marble, Lily, Miraden and Daniel. It felt pretty good to have people who cared how well you were, who you were, that you were, and whom you hoped to become.

They boarded the coach at 12:45 and at 1:00 they were at the Waves of Wonder where the horses plodded right across the twenty league span of water and made their way across the lake to the City of Mirador in less than fifteen minutes. It was almost like being on one of those moving sidewalks at an airport in our world. The water itself seemed to move you along, but yet your footing was sure and dry. (Slower traffic stay to the right!) It was incredible what Miraden had come up with when it concerned the enchantments of Mirador.

They traveled through the city to the cheers and huzzahs of

the people. He was certainly glad that the people were not the chambermaids back at the castle! Soon they found the Eastern High Road. In one hour they would be to the pass. Just north of them now were the Cascade Cliffs, where the waterfall of the River of Peace dropped 1000 feet to the bottom of the escarpment. The Cliffs were higher than anything Daniel had seen anywhere else. Flocks of birds patrolled the skies. Herds of deer and antelope gamboled on the grasslands. He had been west, seen the sea – but he had seen little to nothing of the eastern parts of the Realms, except for the Castle itself – and its parapet. As they neared the cliffs Daniel stuck his head out of the coach and craned his neck, awestruck at the height and the sight of the cliffs with the water shooting over them.

Then they were lost to his view as the carriage entered the chasm where the road would lead them up to Hart's Pass. The climb up to the pass was incredible. Secretly now, Daniel was so glad they had decided to ride instead of 'pop' over. Just because something was easy doesn't mean it was always better. He just couldn't tell anyone – yet.

The canyon was full of offshoots – arroyos, trees, more cliffs, deer (hence the name of the pass), and Daniel was enchanted. Then they topped the pass and he saw the glimmer of the distant city of Panador, their final destination, shimmering in the sun over twenty leagues away across the upswept plains. He had not seen it this way before. After a wild ride down the other side of the pass, breathtaking and scary in its switchbacks and hairpin curves, Daniel was really glad he came. All thoughts of sleep had faded from his being. The village of Panadar, at the eastern head of the pass would begin the last twenty leagues of their final leg of the journey.

The Plains of Peace were golden and magical also. He could see the gentle rise to the east as the plains swept up to meet the City of Panador with its Castle Panador, a multi-colored blot through the shimmer of distance, with the range of the eastern mountains flanking them. The vistas of the plateau swept by. Farms, horses, cattle in herds passed by beyond the window of the coach. It was really the coach that was passing by. Daniel saw hundreds of animals, maybe even a thousand. He was spellbound. Those traveling with him smiled an inner, secret, 'I-told-you-so' smile. They knew. Daniel didn't have to admit to anything. Nor would they force him to.

The proud white horses pulled the gleaming coach along the High Road. The adults were asleep. Daniel laughed to himself at the irony as he thought, *How can they sleep through all this good stuff?* Then he got another one of his ideas. He slipped Miraden's wand out of the old man's sleeve and pointed it at himself while thinking hard about the seat next to the driver, right above his head – and he was there! The driver startled and the coach lurched a bit. Daniel's view of Panador was even more spectacular from the top of the coach. You could see all the way around. And the city was getting closer. The castle looked like you could almost touch it.

Just before they rolled up to the gates of the city, Daniel returned to his place inside.

"My wand, please?" and Miraden smiled.

Daniel handed it over.

"Sorry, sir. I just tried to 'pop' and it worked! I got from here to the driver's seat and back just by thinking about it!"

How typical it is for a thirteen year old to want to 'pop' into the driver's seat!

"Very good."

"Thank you."

"But don't do it again without my permission."

"Yes, sir." Daniel wondered why, but knew that Miraden never asked for something unless he had a reason.

The red, silver and blue banners were flying from the turrets and towers of the Castle. The trumpets atop the battlements blared an official welcome to the Royal Coach of Mirador. The coach pulled up to the outer wall and drove through the raised portcullis into the bailey and then veered left to get to the theatre. A banquet had been prepared and the Royal houses of Panador and Mirador were feted with a fine, outdoor repast to celebrate the beginning of Spring: the planting of new hope as well as new crops. Musicians, dancers, jugglers and acrobats entertained them as they feasted.

Afterwards, the audience members made their way from all over the city, from their dinners and feasts and other entertainments. They filed into the large semicircular seating area for the play. The seating, as in our old Greek amphitheaters, rose away from the half-circle stage, which it also partially surrounded. The scenic wall at the back of the stage was made up of rotatable scenery, which we call periaktoi. They are three-sided towers with a different scene painted on each surface. When the five towers were rotated properly, the scene behind the actors changed so that, as an audience, you knew where the actors were supposed to be. It was a fun device because at least once in the performance a stagehand or an actor missed their cue to turn it so there would be say, four panels of forest scene with maybe a chandelier of a castle remaining erroneously unturned. The audience would chuckle, and an actor would stamp or cough and the unit would be turned and the play would proceed.

Tonight's play was a double bill: a comedy followed by a tragedy. The comedy was one of Lily and Marble's favorites. As Daniel had never seen a play at all before, he was excited for anything. Well, Money Madness was about a very miserly old man whose misuse of money brings riotous calamities to all around including himself, and makes him realize and reevaluate his selfishness. Daniel laughed and laughed and laughed. His favorite part was where all of the servants, armed with mops or brooms, came down the stairs to catch a would-be burglar in the parlor – only to find, later, that it was really their miserly master stealing his own money. In the ensuing melee and confusion of discovery all were solidly trounced, smacked and whacked – and bowled over with an artillery of cleaning implements until each was sore and the Master was properly chastised. At one point in the action, the Housekeeper swung at the Master who ducked, allowing the broom to hit the Butler who swung his mop and hit the cook in the face; the cook's pot then conked the Maid who fell over into the Master and, as he caught her in his outstretched arms, the money he was carrying flew into the air and the Maid landed in a very uncomfortably compromising position with the Master. Daniel screamed and shouted and applauded and whistled, he enjoyed it so much. Others also received great joy from the performance, and at the curtain call the audience was standing.

After the comedy there was a half-hour intermission for the actors to rest and reset. There was more food and drink for all – it seemed almost as if there were no national emergency – no famine – but remember what entertainment is meant to do: divert us from our troubles. Since most of Panador was there, witnessing the fun, with their invited guests, there was a lot of diverting that needed to be done. Many were able to successfully lose their worries and reassess their hopes in the several hours they spent being entertained.

The audience reassembled for the main event, and unknown to several in the audience, they would witness a tribute to their own individual efforts and patriotism. The title of the play was The Four Heroes and had been specially commissioned and rehearsed for just this occasion. It was not a bad title for a tragedy. I will not go into the details of the plot because you know the story; if you have read The Miracle of Mirador. It is the story of the heroes of the War of the Realms: Miraden, Valerius, Gregory and Daniel. All of whom were honored that night with awards and thanks but only three of whom were physically there to receive them. Daniel's father, Gregory, had been killed in that war. Daniel was profoundly moved by the play and the ceremony for the heroes. For you see, theatre does not only entertain – it stands to remind us of who we are, where we came from and what it is that we live and fight for.

As each of the living heroes was called to the stage, they were soundly applauded and cheered, then presented with a special shield: the four great Crests of the Four Fabled Kingdoms of the Realms – Panador, Mirador, Aradon and Caladon – were etched into each shield and over the tops of the crests the silhouettes of the Four Heroes were emblazoned across the shield. Daniel received two of the shields and he hugged them to him in great, yet tearful, humility. His eyes shone particularly blue that night.

Miraden and Valerius were speechless. How had this been kept a secret from them? Miraden had the Orb of Sight, after all! It was such an honorific surprise! Daniel received hugs from his family and loved ones. The audience then remained standing and motionless as the heroes and their families exited the theatre. Daniel wept the sweetly bitter tears of pride and loss. His growing frame shook noticeably as he made his way up the steps. Once outside the theatre, his mother – adopted mother, really – covered him in a cloak, kissed his forehead and bustled him into the coach for the short ride to the castle where they would stay the night. This was a night that would last forever in the memories of each of those who either participated in it, witnessed it or were honored by it, but particularly for the boy who had become, too soon, a man.

Boncaster was in the gardens the next morning, bright and early, well maybe not so bright, but still elated by the performance of the previous night. Soon, he was joined by Rose and Bianca. The garden seemed to be returning. All the plants, except the roses, were in bloom. The rose bushes remained dead and barren.

Daniel found his way into the garden by midmorning and helped to dig about and water. He placed his hands around the base of one of the rose bushes and tried to will it to live again. But they, like his father, were beyond his powers to cure which caused him to grow momentarily frustrated and sad.

Miraden came out also. His favorite place to be was surrounded by plants or animals or family. Here, he had all three. But he caught Daniel's attention and held out his hand. Daniel took it.

Pop!

They were back at their cave. Miraden instructed Daniel to fill his pockets with five or six vials of potion and he did.

Pop!

They were back at the garden where Boncaster and the women, who had barely recovered from their disappearance, were again startled when their reappearance sort of knocked Boncaster over onto his back.

"Sorry, my good man, but we figured that some of this potion, mixed and placed in your watering cans, would go a long way to returning your lovely garden to its former splendor."

"Thank ya, Miraden. They'll be put to good use, all right."

A brunch was called and the servants brought out tables and platters of food to the garden. Everyone sat down to eat, servants too, for in Panador each person may have had a different job or responsibility, but not one person was any better, different, or more important than anyone else. They suffered together and they celebrated likewise. Their Talisman of power and protection may be missing but there were some things that were not poor substitutes; friendship, companionship, and love were never out of place.

Daniel was on his bed leafing through the pages of a white book. "Imadar, Imadar, where are you, Imadar?"

He was just being dramatic. Last night's play had made a great impression on him. He figured that if he didn't make it as an Enchanter he would become a great actor. (Like being an Enchanter was a job, or vocation, or something!) But right now he was searching for the DragonSign of Imadar. He had found Wallamere's teeth but he had turned the cave upside down and still had no sign from Imadar, the mother of all White Dragons.

That's it! A mother! "Miraden!!!!"

Miraden hustled into Daniel's chamber.

"Grandfather, where was the hatchery?"

Miraden looked at him blankly. Daniel was rifling through the books and pointed at a page in the white book.

"Imadar's hatchery! I've been reading in the books and all DragonMounts had thirteen rooms. We only have twelve. Where's the hatchery?"

Miraden sputtered, his mustache flying away from his face; he chortled, he chuckled, he laughed out loud and clapped his grandson on the back.

"Congratulations, my boy, that's the answer!"

Miraden rushed to the bed and looked for a large purple book that did not seem to be there.

"Daniel, have you read 'The Designs of DragonMounts' by Araden Light?"

"No, Grandpa, I haven't even seen it."

"Acquire 'Designs of the DragonMounts'!"

A thick, purple book came flying through the air, just missing the back of Daniel's head by a knuckle, and arrived in Miraden's outstretched arm. Daniel wiggled close to Miraden and both peered at the opened pages of the book. The White DragonMount was depicted on the first few pages and there were thirteen rooms! Where was the entrance to number thirteen? Now, Miraden's laugh blasted out in one loud: "Hah!"

He rushed to his potion room. Daniel followed.

He stood in front of his desk and bookshelf. He moved them, with Daniel's help and the help of a small transportation charm, to the other side of the room. Then he inscribed a magic arch up and over and down and then across the bottom of the wall in front of him. When the red light of his wand stopped arcing through the stone wall, he said to Daniel, "Push!"

Daniel placed his hands outward and leaned against the incised portion of the wall and it slid, then fell away from him.

The astonished look on Daniel's face matched the smile in Miraden's eyes. They stepped through the arch and went down a winding, descending passageway that led to a cavern below all of the other rooms of the cave. It seemed as big as all of them put together. It had gotten dark fairly quickly.

"Light!"

Miraden's wand lit up the room, with white light this time.

"Grandpa when do I get one of those?"

"Soon."

"Grandpa, look – eggshells!"

Daniel picked up a sherd of one of the shells.

"That's good but we need a second thing. Remember that with the females we need an eggshell and something else."

"How about this?"

Daniel stood holding a claw – a white claw as big as his forearm. If you think that is big then you should see a Dragon egg before it hatches. It's about four times the size of an American football. The eggshells around him were all white, like a chicken's egg. But the eggs of other Dragons would have striations, or stripes, or lines of color, matching the color of the parents. A Dragon egg took fifty years to hatch as long as it was kept warm. Daniel now looked around.

"Grandpa there must be fifty or more shells here. Were there once that many White Dragons?"

"Sixty-six, Daniel. But Tophet and his side of the family inflamed the minds and opinions of the citizens of the Realms against the Dragons and they were systematically hunted down and slaughtered during the Dragon War which led into the Great War."

There was a great sadness in Miraden's voice, for you see it was from his wand and through the power of the Orb, that Dragons were born in the first place. Daniel placed his hand on his Grandpa's shoulder.

"They will live again, soon."

"Yes, my old friends, soon," he promised to the almost empty room.

"But if an egg takes fifty years to hatch hadn't we better get started?"

"We will create Dragons, not eggs. The Dragons will then create their own eggs. But before we can think of creating Dragons, all six of the Talismans must be in their homes in order to help the Orb supply the power to do the task. Before the Talismans are in their homes we must have DragonSign!

$\mathcal{ML}$

CHAPTER EIGHT
BLUE
(3rd Month)

RUCKSACK! SHOES, STOCKINGS, CLOTHES, FOOD, more food, plenty of Miraden's chocolate, knife, map and compass, bedroll, two vials of potion, matches, notebook, water skin, walking stick. Daniel stood by his bed, ready for travel.

"Haven't you forgotten something?" and Miraden pointed.

Daniel looked down towards his feet to see that he only had his nightshirt on – no traveling clothes. He grinned sheepishly.

"I guess."

He shrugged his shoulders and shucked his breeches over his legs and removed his nightshirt and pulled on his chemise.

"What will you do while I'm gone?"

"Find Guildenblad. I've almost got him. I must travel to the Fortress of Fear and see if there is anything left of Tophet's records. I know where he isn't, I just have to pinpoint where he is."

"But there is nothing left!"

"There is always something."

"There wasn't at Withera's Castle. It was ... more than empty."

"There will be something. I'm sure."

"Good luck, Grandfather."

"Thank you. This is for you."

He opened his hand, palm up and passed the wand over his

empty palm with a great flourish. A clear orb, about the size of a lemon, appeared in the center of the Enchanter's hand.

"It is to contact me – or for me to contact you. Speak my name, I'll appear." He held up a second Orb, matching the first.

"Thanks!"

Daniel's eyes were bright. His first and very own magical object. (Well, if you don't count the knife, which he wasn't quite sure about, yet. It had been in his family for centuries.) He hugged Miraden who seemed to take his time before releasing the boy.

"What's wrong, Grandpa?"

"It's nothing."

Now you know and I know that when your parents, or another grown-up, or sometimes even a child, says 'it's nothing', that it really is something. But they either don't want to bother you about it, don't want to burden you with it, or it was none of your business. This was something that Miraden did not want Daniel to be burdened with. He felt he was sending his grandson into danger. But Daniel was a capable and intelligent young man. He would do all right. Miraden kissed him on the forehead.

"Come home to me soon. And no monkey business."

Daniel nodded and threw his pack over his shoulders, picked up his sword and buckled it on, grabbed his bow and quiver, took hold of his staff, slung his water bag over his shoulder and walked out of the mouth of the cave and down to the shore of the lake where Matthew and Elias were ready and waiting to take him to Harborton.

As Daniel walked away Miraden realized that the boy was much taller than he used to be, or at least than he thought he had been. Childhood is a precious thing and as each moment shines it is then replaced by another moment. Some of those moments get lost in the living of them. Pity.

Before he stepped in the boat, Daniel turned and looked up at the cave. Miraden was still there and they exchanged waves and then Daniel sat in the boat and Miraden went back into the cave.

Daniel would spend the night with Elias and his family. He was welcomed in the house of the Master Fisherman with hugs from the entire family. If he didn't have Lily, Marble and Miraden, he would choose to be here.

They had a lunch of fish and bread. Daniel played all afternoon with Elias and his brother and sisters, and their dog, 'orace! He hadn't 'played' in weeks! They giggled and laughed and sang and shrieked. It was fun to be with Elias. It was good for Daniel. No one was near his age at the cave or the Castle, except for a few of the servingmaids! (Blush!) But there was something else; here he was able to remember that he was still a child and could act like a child. He was allowed to be a child, even encouraged to be one – especially by those who seemed to discourage childish things at the other places in his life. Miraden knew that Daniel had grown in many ways in a very short time; in ways that most children never have to suffer through. He also knew that Daniel would have to continue to grow up too fast, too early; so his childhood must be experienced while it was available to be experienced. Miraden may not remember everything. But he certainly knew many of the most important things.

Darkness. Miraden hated Darkness, literally and figuratively.

"Light!"

The room around him was a wreck. It was the room Tophet disappeared from when Lily was rescued: his underground laboratory. The bookshelves were mostly empty. The ceiling was partially gone and the room was open to the sky. Tophet must've taken very few things with him; just what he considered important. Miraden began to paw through the books, papers and scrolls scattered across the shelves and floor. He thought, *"Guildenblad."* Four papers and two scrolls came flying at him. He began to peruse them.

"... *Guildenblad created by Withera in over a thousand* ... "

"... *His powers to animate the dead are* ... "

"... *Guildenblad has learned a most prodigious amount of magical* ..."

"My Dear Master, Tophet--"

Jackpot! A Letter!

"I have indeed made a home for myself ... "

"Yes – yes, where?"

"... in the Forest of Anan. I am protected by your greatest magic and no one can ever get to me if I don't want them to. Your two creatures and two wardings make my home impregnable and undetectable."

Miraden stuffed the scroll in his robes. A letter from the Disciple to the Master. An incredible find. He raised his wand.

"Acquire Nightbane."

A scroll fluttered to him.

"Acquire Rosenblad!"

Nothing.

Well, it was worth a try. He stuffed the Nightbane scroll in his robe and then with his wand, swept all remaining scrolls, papers and books into a trunk. He sat on the trunk and 'popped' home with it. When he got an idea, it was a good one. So, why did it take so long for him to get the good ideas?

It was a happy and convenient coincidence – or maybe Miraden planned it that way – for the evening before the expedition to the Blue DragonMount to also be Elias' eleventh birthday. It was only a small family party, like all of the boy's other birthdays. But this time Daniel was there. In the morning, Matthew and Elias would help Daniel along to his destination, but for the evening, Daniel belonged to another family that loved him as one of their own. As Daniel had said before about Elias: "We fit!"

Ten-year-old Ruth was as clingy as seven-year-old Jeremiah. But Daniel didn't mind. Neither did Elias. And eight year old Hester, after her special cake at Daniel's own party, was infatuated with the boy she called her older brother. Two-year-old Jonah added his special laughter to the occasion which endeared him completely to Daniel as well as to his oldest brother, Elias.

After the meal and games were over, it took a long time to get the children settled down and into their own beds. They all wanted to sleep in the big bed with Daniel and Elias. The boys didn't mind, but Elias' parents put their foot down. They knew the importance of the Quest tomorrow; Miraden had impressed that on their minds. Daniel needed his rest. So did Elias, for that matter. Elias and Matthew had a very important part to play in this second quest. It was a recurrent happening that just as Daniel and Elias were alone and drifting off to sleep, one of the younger children would come in to say goodnight again, or give the older boys a hug, or offer yet another birthday wish for Elias. Jeremiah couldn't be shuffled off to his own room because he shared his room with Elias, and now Daniel, who was reawakened by a shivering Jeremiah poking at his chest.

"Daniel?"

"What is it, Jeremiah?"

"I'm scared."

Daniel didn't hesitate. He pulled back the covers and Jeremiah hopped in to the bed between Elias and Daniel. It stirred a memory of his own little brothers and sisters; and long, dark nights of comfort and companionship no longer to be enjoyed. Elias was awakened.

"What's wrong, Jeremiah?"

"I saw something outside my window." And he pointed toward the attic gable at the other end of the room.

Daniel was out of bed and to the window in a flash, Elias following. "Stay there, Jeremiah."

It was dark outside but it was not the usual dark of a 3rd Month night. It was truly Dark. Daniel looked at Elias in horror, "Shadows!"

Immediately Daniel erected a clear shield-warding and pushed it around the house to protect them all. He then began to cover that warding very carefully with a red one. If whatever was outside tried to get in, it would be eradicated. Fingers of black reached into the room through the window, grasping, clutching at what it couldn't yet reach, just knuckles from Daniel's face. Elias placed his hands on the shoulders of his best and closest friend, as if to lend him mortal support and power. He saw the fingers clutching at them. His eyes opened wide but he didn't step back.

Elias witnessed what this warding was costing his 'brother.' Sweat was pouring from Daniel's brow and off his chest and back. His breathing was rapid and labored. His shoulders heaved under the strain of the demand for power. Then Jeremiah, ever obedient, came and put his smaller hand on Daniel's back. He wanted to add comfort and peace to his friend, too.

The three boys stood there, near the window and watched as their house was covered in a red glow. They saw the swirling apparition of Darkness cut off as Daniel's red filled its place and severed the curling, smoky fingers from the entity outside. There was a scream that had to have been heard all through Harborton. Suddenly the boys' room was full of family. The girls and their parents had entered and quickly became very frightened at what they saw happening to Daniel. He was shaking. As the scream ended and the warding finished its wrapping of the house, Daniel collapsed. Elias and Jeremiah caught him and kept him from hitting the floor until Matthew came and picked Daniel up and carried him back to the bed.

The little family gathered around the stricken Daniel, unaware that some small part of the entity that was outside had evaded the warding and gotten inside and was hovering in the room, waiting, reaching for more victims than just a boy-Prophecy. Daniel revived suddenly and saw the Shadow over the shoulders of his friends. He moved quickly and effectively, grabbed his sword from its temporary hanging place on the wall, drew it and barged through the crowd of family, swinging. There was another scream, much like the first, that rang through the house and hurt the ears of the family gathered in that upper room to the point that they all had to press their hands to their heads tightly, and cringe.

Daniel slashed and swung and ripped and tore at the apparition that dared to attack him again. As each portion of the Shadow was sliced off it turned to ash and littered the floor. Daniel was so quick at it that he was almost a blur. The scream lasted until the last bit of dust fell to the boards of the attic floor. Daniel's sword drooped, point down into the wood, and held him up as he leaned on it.

Matthew again helped him to his bed. "Wot was it?"

"A Shadow."

Matthew's eyes opened wide. Miraden had told him about the spectral creatures. They were fearful, that was their main offense. They were terribly dangerous if not seen. If the victim were asleep or unaware, they could inhabit a human, or other creature, and rip them apart from the inside out, if they desired to do so. Once seen and recognized, they could be destroyed.

Daniel's shoulders started to heave again. He was crying. Tears flowed. He couldn't speak. Six pairs of hands held him, pressed their love against him and into him. He felt the infusion but it couldn't stop the outpouring of emotion. He had to let it out. He knew that. The family seemed to understand it also. As he gained control, quieted and calmed himself, he stood and hugged Elias' mother, Sarai.

"I'm sorry," was Daniel's despondent reply.

"Ye've got nuthin' ta be sorry for."

"But I do. I have allowed this house to be found by the Dark. I have marked it. I may have put you all in danger."

The water dripping off the oars fell back into its crystal-clear brothers and sisters still in the lake. Their cousin, wind, filled the sail. Their guardian, Sun, gave light and warmth. Daniel rowed, not out of need, but for want of purging, and maybe to show off his growing strength. Work helped him take his mind off the events of the previous night. Rowing was work as the honest sweat, not the sweat of horror, dripped down his body under his chemise. He took it as a penance. He was also thinking that maybe he had overreacted and said more than he should have last night. He had caused fear in a family that had had none until he showed up.

The boat, except for the sound of its slipping through the waters, was silent.

Elias steered the little craft and Matthew was in the bow on lookout. The sunlight almost bounced off the surface of the lake, blinding the three as it came from the South. Daniel tried to be happy about having an important task to do; trying to shake off the gloom; which was difficult, but not impossible.

Elias, who was worried about his friend, and a little scared still from the happenings of last night, tried to fight that feeling with the pleasure that he felt over the fact that his father thought him capable enough to steer the boat for the first time, that he quite forgot about the brightness of the sun even as it stared him in the face. (He had just turned eleven, after all. He could handle these things.) He managed to put his fears to rest for the moment as he watched Daniel row. Ceaselessly, not seeming to tire. It did help when the wind picked up a little and shot them across the lake.

Only Matthew shaded his eyes as the boat approached the mouth of the River of Hope. They steered west at the inlet, which put the sun on their left and in their eyes no longer. They pulled in the sail and somewhat rowed down the river. For it was downriver they were going as the River of Hope helped to drain the Crystal Lake into the distant sea.

As they passed into the Forest of Hope, Daniel remembered Valerius' story of Nightbane; he managed to spot the place, just up the bank, where his father had sheltered and protected him from his own little fears all through the night after the story had been told. Daniel was certainly glad he was on the water now for Nightbane could not touch him here. Other thoughts of a wolf – the one that attacked him two years ago – began to overreach his active mind. Was that Nightbane? No, that wolf was dead now. A relative? Another servant of the dark? Or merely a wolf? That was the time when his power was first manifested through his long-knife. The only type of 'wand' he had ever used, except for 'popping' once. He wished he still had that long-knife but it must have been lost at Withera's Castle, for he couldn't find it when he was packing for this trip. He had not seen it since he came home, even though it was in his hand as he was entombed by the falling wall of the castle. Then he remembered the battle and the pack of wolves on the Plains of Youth, ripping and tearing at the flesh of boy and man. He was grateful for the water around the boat. For the safety it offered him. Did it protect against Shadows? Were they only after him? Would they leave Elias' family alone, now that he was not with them? His thoughts were interrupted by Matthew.

"Ship yer oars there, son."

Daniel hurriedly pulled the oars back into the little craft as it passed from the entrance of the river into its strong current. The water began to get a little swifter as they slipped into the Pass of Hope, entering the canyons of the Blue Mountains.

"Father, maybe you had better take the tiller!"

"No need. You'll do fine!"

Elias gulped and looked at Daniel like a death sentence had just been passed on all of them.

"You're Da's right – just do it!" It sort of brought Daniel out of his self-recriminating reverie.

Elias gritted his teeth and gripped the handle of the rudder more tightly. They bolted through the canyon. The water was swift, but not too rapid. Daniel screamed in delight as they hit the small cataracts. He held tight to the gunwales and they shot out of the mouth of the canyon and into the slowest portion of the river that flowed through the Yellow Plains. (So named because of the leagues of wheat that had been grown there since man first lived on these plains.)

"That was incredible – and we're alive. Elias, you did it!"

Elias beamed and his father gripped his knee in silent agreement with Daniel. It was a lot of responsibility for an eleven-year-old boy to steer a small boat down a raging river. Elias maneuvered over to the bank and got out.

"Be right back."

He disappeared into the wheat field. Then returned a minute or so later with a relaxed and empty look on his face. Daniel looked at Matthew and they laughed. Elias ignored them and got into the boat and steered them back out into the lazy current.

There was a good breeze blowing so they put up the sail again and made good time down the river with the current and the wind working for once, in their favor. Elias easily avoided the few rocks and snags in the way. The effortlessness of the journey allowed them to eat a light meal for their lunch. Soon they saw the bridge of the Arafel Road, where a wagon would be waiting to carry the boat, Matthew and Elias back to Harborton. As they pulled the boat to the bank by the bridge, Daniel hopped out and Elias followed. Matthew pushed as the boys pulled and the boat came up on the rocky sand. The wagon master winched, while Matthew and the boys pushed the boat up the short rise and into the wagon. Goodbyes were said. Matthew laid a particularly heavy hand on Daniel's shoulder and squeezed. Elias hugged him.

"I'll be all right."

The Matthewsons, not entirely reassured by Daniel's statement, climbed into the wagon, which started north to the City of Aradon. Daniel stood and waved until the wagon disappeared from view over a small rill in the undulating rise and fall of the surrounding farmland.

Daniel actually felt alone for the first time in a long time, probably ever. He gamely shouldered his pack and water skin, buckled on his weapons and picked up his stick as he started along the road to the south.

Daniel walked and whistled – he even sang – something he would not do in front of others because, whenever he did, his voice would crack trying to reach the notes. Who could hear him out here? So he sang with gusto. It is a sure thing that many scarecrows in the fields did not have to do their jobs well that day with Daniel passing anywhere nearby. Not that his singing was bad. Just that it was loud and full of … heart! (And cracks!)

Eight leagues down the road he would find the turn off for the shortcut to Halla Tarn. Night would be coming soon and he would barely make the turnoff before sundown. He walked along steadily, after all he was young and strong and free! The eight leagues were eaten up, it seemed, in a matter of minutes, but it had really taken not quite two hours.

He was just in time to set up his camp in the field, get a fire going and roast some cheese and bread before the sun withdrew its light from southern Aradon. He was settling down for the night, when he realized that he had seen no one since the bridge. *This must be the loneliest part of all the Realms,* he figured.

There was no windbreak, aside from the tall stalks of wheat among which he rolled out his bedroll hoping to get at least some protection from the prevalent west winds of the southern plains. The fire was only embers now. He was fed and ready for bed. He laid his sword on one side of his kit and his bow and arrows on the other. He closed his eyes as the fire popped and sputtered a little. He took his orb out of his pack.

"Miraden?"

Soon the orb was no longer blank. "Yes, Daniel?" came a bleary reply.

"I'm safe at the Halla turnoff. Just wanted to say goodnight."

The figure in the glass seemed to smile. "Good night – and thank you for checking in."

The orb went clear again and Daniel put it back in his pack, then squirmed into his blankets. He realized that he had not informed Miraden of the incident of the previous night. He would tell him in the morning. Then a wolf howled and he sat up – rigid. He unsheathed his sword. Another howl – farther away. He sat there. He decided to erect a red warding to protect him as he slept, and felt better once the hum of energy was around him. It's funny how the first warding that he had ever erected, by accident, was becoming his first method of protection. After what was probably minutes, but seemed like hours to Daniel, his eyes drooped and he fell asleep.

When he awoke in the morning he was back between his blankets. He roused himself and rolled up. He ate a little cheese and sipped some water, then was packed up and back on the road, headed southwest towards the mountains by Halla Tarn, before the sun had peeked over the eastern Blues behind him.

Later, when the sun was well up, he was walking along a footpath that led through the wheat. He stopped. He had looked down. Across his path were the paw prints of a wolf. He'd know them anywhere. The hackles started to rise again on the back of his neck. He looked more carefully and found that the edges of the prints were not crisp. They were full of dew. He knew that they were at least from yesterday. Maybe from as recently as those howls last night, but they were not fresh. He took in a calming breath and walked on.

Did these fields ever end? He saw the mountains. He knew they were there! When would he arrive at the foot of the seemingly elusive peaks?

The path he was on finally attained the rocky foothills. Still he had seen no living person. He sat on a rock and ate a little bread and cheese and drank a little more water. Oh, and a bite of chocolate! It would be a little cooler in the canyon. This 3rd Month day was hot. Even though it was a typically, nice, sunny, warm Spring day, too much of any good thing can lead you to want a change.

The canyon took him almost directly south and the trail began to incline as he made his way up the path. He came out on a small ridge about a hundred arms above the canyon floor. He heard the snarl of some wildcat. His bow was in his hands and an arrow nocked before a few seconds had passed. He listened – he watched – he sniffed – everything his father had taught him was instinct to him now. He stood absolutely still. Some rocks scrabbled down the mountainside off to his left. He heard a 'snuff' and a 'grunt' as the cat came into the clearing. It wasn't huge but it could kill him! It stopped, arched its back and sprang – and fell dead, pierced to the heart by Daniel's arrow. Daniel finally took a breath after what had seemed to him like hours without breathing. He retrieved his arrow, wiped the blood and gore off on the grass and put it back in his quivver. He wished there was something he could do with the cat but they were not good eating for humans. He left it near the edge of the clearing for the wolves or something-elses to find. He hoped that the something-elses wouldn't be bothering him. After all, he was leaving them a cat!

He trudged upward and onward across the ridge trail. He had already covered two leagues, comparing the map with the local topography, so there were two more left. He would be there in an hour. Well, at least to Halla Tarn. It's waters sounded refreshing right now. He heard a crashing in the trees down below him and to his right. It sounded like a bear. Daniel kept moving by picking up his pace, and the crashing sounds got softer behind him.

He came to a rise in the ridge and the waters of Halla Tarn flashed at him from behind a turn in the trail; still far below him. The sight of the waters distracted him, fascinated him so fully, that he just stood there entranced. It was more than beautiful. He did not hear the beast until it growled and struck him. He was thrown to the ground several spans away, where he had rolled up against the bole of a tree. As he scrambled to his feet he saw nothing but a large bird-like beak snapping at him. He didn't notice the tear in his chemise and the gash that was dripping blood down his arm until he raised his hand in front of him to send a stunning spell at the beast and pain ripped through his shoulder. He clasped his other hand to his wounded shoulder to hold his arm in the air. As the wave of energy from his wounded arm hit the creature it stopped and shook its head, as if some fly had been buzzing around it and annoying it. That was enough of a distraction for Daniel to painfully scramble up the nearby tree, where he sat on a branch several spans above the creature. He could see it now, but he wasn't believing his eyes. The body of a bear was below him, but it had the feathered legs, talons and wings of an eagle. Then there was that beak! Bird-like, it replaced the muzzle of the bear – while it still had teeth – fangs. Daniel also noticed stubs of wings on its back. Was this another one of Tophet's creatures that had escaped from Zanadon during the War of the Realms? It had to be. Daniel had fought off many of them in that battle in the Mires of Mist. How many of them had survived? So far, there was the one in the Wicked Wood and this one – so far away at Halla Tarn! It was not a welcome feeling to think that any had escaped.

Daniel felt safe knowing that its wings could not lift it up to him. Then the bear rose up and leaned on the tree. The tree shook under the assault of the creature. Daniel wrapped his arms around the bole and hung on. The bark of the tree tore into the wound on his shoulder and Daniel winced. He covered himself in a red warding as he sat precariously on that branch trying to stay out of the reach of that beak and talons. He heard snaps and crackles as the beast continued to lean its considerable weight against the tree. Daniel had thought it was a sturdy tree when he climbed it, but now with the sounds coming, apparently from its roots, he was not so sure. The tree began to cant towards the ground.

Daniel tried to prepare for impact. Another shove by the bear and Daniel was tipping over with the tree. He jumped out of the tree as it crashed passed its neighbors, and he rolled to a stop as the bear headed straight for him. He doubled his warding. The bear began to rail on the outer shell of the warding and its talons sizzled and burned. Too bad the stench from the searing could not be kept out by the warding. Daniel sickened at the odor. With each hit the bear howled in pain but kept striking the warding. It then rose up on its hind legs and stood there staring at Daniel – looking directly into the boy's eyes. Daniel stared back. Somehow this bear knew him – remembered him. He could see it in the demeanor of the creature. Then it crashed down on the warding with such force that it shuddered. Daniel held his hands out toward the bear. Power streamed from them, reinforcing the red protection. The bear yowled as its talons disappeared from the ends of its forelegs and the feathers there burst into flames. Again the bear stood and fell against the red. More of its forelegs were sheared off by the protection as it screamed at this intruding human cub.

The bear curled to a fetal-type position and whimpered, bringing what was left of its forelegs close to its body. Daniel stood in his bubble of red and began to walk, rolling his bubble towards the stricken bear. He stood close, not knowing what to do. The bear, with a last flash of energy, stood, sudden and powerful. It fell onto the warding with such force that the warding shattered, while at the same time the bear's body was disintegrated and blood and skin and ooze dripped over Daniel, coating him with the remains of the bear.

Daniel sat there, covered in bear parts. He didn't believe what had just happened. Every time he encountered something Dark, it fought him to its death. He didn't understand it, but he did file that fact away for the future. He hated fighting and killing.

He ran his hand along his arm. The bear guts vanished. He ran his hands over his torso and the red masses disappeared along with his chemise. He blinked and laughed and ran his hands all over his body removing what was left of bear and clothes, because the blood and gore would not separate itself from the weave of the cloth. When he was satisfied that he had gotten it all he summoned a fresh chemise and breeches, and a pair of boots, from his cave. (That made him wonder why he had bothered to pack a pack.) He jumped into his breeches but then, before putting on his chemise, he had to heal his shoulder. He placed his hand against it, securing the flap of skin in place that the bear had almost torn away. The muscle re-knit itself and the skin closed up. He poured energy into his flesh. And the whiteness returned. It was tender as he tested it, shrugging it; but that, too, would heal, and soon.

Donning his chemise, he ate some chocolate and started downhill, where he had to really strain to keep himself from going too fast down the steep incline and rolling into the forest at the base of the hill or falling off the edge of the switchbacks of the trail. After making innumerable 'z's in the mountainside, he arrived once again on flat land: the basin that held this forest and its tarn.

It was cool and peaceful with only squirrels chittering and woodpeckers pecking. The howls of the creature still somewhat reverberated in his memory. Then he caught another view of the waters of the tarn through the trees and the echoes of fear were swept away, replaced by euphoria. The shadows in this little mountain valley filled the place with greens, browns, greys, purples and blues. Calm. Peaceful. He saw that down by the tarn there was a small cabin. No smoke. Nobody home?

He crept up to the cabin. He knocked. No answer. He

opened the door. No one had been here in a long time! Small animals had taken over the cabin but there was no sign that a larger animal had come inside. It would be safe for the night. He stowed his gear. And you'll never guess what happened next!

A boy, a lake and no one around for leagues? You guessed!

After a pleasant and relaxing swim, washing the dust of the trail off of his body, he dried himself off with his new 'hot hands' technique and got dressed. He started a fire and roasted some bread and cheese and sat at the edge of the tarn munching on his dinner. How he loved being outdoors! He was truly his father's son. He thought about days spent just like this with his father. It's funny, that he could think of it now without it tearing him apart. The slightest image of either of his parents in his mind used to trigger waterfalls of tears and earthquakes of sobbing. But he was older now. A little. Maybe a lot. He was perplexed, himself, that these thoughts hadn't stressed him. Did he no longer care? No! There it was – that tug of emotion that usually began it. This time only a single tear fell from his blue eyes. He sniffed once, ran the back of his hand across his nose and stretched.

He laid back on the rock with his hands behind his head. The sun was warm on his face; finishing the drying of his hair, eyebrows, chemise and breeches. He remembered his father and thought about someday having a son, himself, and spending days like this with him. Thoughts of a son brought on other thoughts – of how to get a son. He clamped down on them. He didn't need that kind of distraction.

But those unwanted thoughts led to thoughts about Tilly – he thought about Tilly a lot – could it be possible? How completely was he smitten? Was it just a fancy? Or a friendship? Was it only a momentary, never-to-be-repeated meeting? If it was not to be Tilly, would there be someone else who would strike him as she had? Could it be Rose? If it couldn't be Tilly, he came to the conclusion, that it could be Rose; maybe even should be; even though she was almost eighteen. These were confusing and impossible feelings for this thirteen year old. So, he got up from the rock and took a walk. He circled the tarn, every so often tossing or skipping a flat pebble across its surface. He just couldn't rid his mind of thoughts about a son – Rose – his father – Tilly. Everything he saw reminded him of her. Her laughter was in the trees. The wind was her voice. The water of the tarn was the comfort he felt when he was with her. The pebbles in his hand stirred thoughts of holding her hand. The leaves that brushed his shoulder as he walked passed were the whispered conversations of her lilting voice and soul. The sunlight was her smile. He realized that he did not feel bad when he thought about Tilly. Quite the contrary. Tingles lingered; were even recalled. But there were so many times in his past where he thought this way about people – and then they were no longer in his life. He had to stop. He was The Prophecy.

Eventually, he walked back to the cabin and picked up his orb.

"Miraden?"

"Daniel – safe?"

"Yes, at Halla Tarn. But I almost didn't make it."

Daniel had debated whether or not to tell Miraden about his bear encounter. A lone Ballark was not terribly significant – except that it almost killed him. So he told his grandfather the story. Miraden was alarmed but felt similarly, that one lone, now dead, escapee was of little significance. The only thing that really bothered Miraden was how the Ballark had seemed to 'recognize' Daniel. Much like the one at Withera's Castle had. Tophet had managed to build a malevolence into his creatures. They were more than just creations. It seemed that they had a mission. Very advanced magic, for the Dark. Daniel interrupted Miraden's thoughts.

"I also found a cabin. Do you think it's safe?"

"Show me?"

"What?"

"Hold the orb up and show me what is around you."

Daniel ran the orb slowly through the air.

"No alarms come to me. You have checked out the cabin?"

"Yes, sir."

"Then have a pleasant night."

"You too, Grandpa. And Grandpa?"

"Yes."

Daniel had neglected to inform Miraden of that other incident. "Something happened at Elias' house two nights ago."

"Matthew told me."

"Oh. What should I do?"

"Nothing you can do except what you already know how to do. Just be careful. Be prepared."

"Should I ward myself?"

"If you feel you must. But sometimes a warding can draw the unwanted attention of that which you are warding against."

Daniel had discovered that. He thought a lot over the past few days, about his drawing attention to the house of the Matthewsons with the wardings he created.

"But at least they can't get to me – like the Ballark."

"True. Until the warding is removed."

"I can't go around warded all the time!"

"My point exactly. Good night."

"Night, Grandpa."

The orb went clear again and the boy bedded down on an old slatted bed in the corner. The light of a full moon illuminated him through the window. His night-light. He slept well. No worries. No nightmares – then Tilly's face appeared. *They were dancing, talking, racing on horseback – flying through the air.* All the sharp jumps that our minds make when we dream. *Then Tilly was limp in his arms and Daniel was crying.* He awoke with a start. He was dripping with sweat again. He went down to the lake, took his shirt off and rinsed the sweat out of it. The moonlight reflecting off the water helped him to feel secure as he looked up to the light. He splashed himself with water and used his drying technique on his shirt and torso and when everything was dry but his eyes, he went back to bed.

He didn't sleep much the remainder of the night. He rested, but he didn't sleep. Maybe he didn't want to. There is that fear of what sleep sometimes brings with it that keeps us from it, sometimes.

The birds welcomed him as the dawn approached. At least that mangy rooster from the Crystal Castle wasn't there for him to try to ignore!

He went out to the tarn and found a rock to climb on and fish from. He rolled the legs of his breeches up tightly onto his thighs and slipped silently into the water. It only came to his knees. He could see fish everywhere. He hunched over, elbows on his thighs, and steadied himself. With his hands motionless in the water, down between his calves, he waited. Fish swam by and soon some swam through, between his calves, he closed his hands slowly, almost stroking the fish, and soon a fish was wriggling in his hands and he was headed for shore. It was a small fish about a hand long, perfect for his breakfast. He cooked it and ate it with some water and bread.

Ready for his adventure, he wiped his hands and mouth on his clothing and looked around. The DragonMount was supposed to be on the East side of the tarn and a little to the south – that's what the map told him. With his compass he plotted the direction and located what he thought would be the DragonMount. He headed for it. He had to skirt the edge of the tarn for a league before he saw the path halfway up the mountain. He scrambled up the scree to the path and followed it around to the south and east. He was right. He had found the tallest peak, sighting it from his position at the tarn, and it was indeed the DragonMount.

He could see the mouth of the cave but there was no path up to it. There was a series of ledges about three spans apart all the way up, which was about 30-40 spans higher than where he was standing. He got an idea. He thought of standing securely on the first ledge above his head, like the distance from the interior of the coach to the driver's seat. But he didn't have a wand! Oh, well.

Pop!

He was there! After looking around to make sure that he indeed was where his eyes told him he was, he ascended the mountain by 'popping' from ledge to ledge. After a few wobbly minutes he was standing at the mouth of the cave, looking down and eating chocolate. He got dizzy and almost fell. The ledge was narrower than the one at the White DragonMount. He staggered back against the wall outside the cave. He realized that no animals could be in there, unless there was a bird, but it was going to be dark.

He couldn't use a fire, as the smoke would choke him. A torch? Perhaps.

"Miraden?"

"Yes, Daniel."

"I'm at the cave."

"How did you ..."

"Sorry I didn't ask you but I 'popped' from ledge to ledge."

"No wand?"

"No, Grandpa, no wand."

"Very ingenious."

"Thanks, but there is no light. No torches on the walls like at our cave. I can't see a thing inside."

"Any white stones around?"

"Yes."

"Hold them in your hand – you know what to do."

"Goodnight and thanks. I might sleep in the cave tonight."

"Good idea – goodnight."

He found some small white rocks and held them in his hand and thought *"light – I need to see – Light!"* His hand started burning and he dropped the rocks on the floor. They were glowing. He grabbed a shirt out of his pack and picked up the stones and dropped them one by one along the cave floor. He found more rocks and heated each one up. His surroundings took on an eerie, frosted kind of glow.

The cave seemed to be laid out similarly to the white cave. So, Daniel went to the back room on the right and there it was, the tunnel to the hatchery, undisguised and open. But he'd run out of rocks. He went back and picked up half of the rocks he'd dropped and relit them. He spaced them out along the incline and soon found himself in the hatchery. He first picked up a piece of eggshell, wrapped it and labeled it and put it in his pack. Then he turned and looked behind him and the room went dark.

Guildenblad was talking to someone as they walked around the tumbled stones of his former home – Withera's Castle. He was glad that he had managed to get everything out before it had been destroyed. But who had been the destroyer? That question gnawed at him. It had been set with enough traps that anyone, human or otherwise, could have triggered them and caused this destruction. He hoped that whoever had destroyed it had been destroyed themselves. Maybe it was for the best; if there is a best where Darkness is concerned. He had been here only months ago salvaging the last of Withera's magical equipment. He had returned today to see if they dared to use it as a base. It seemed to have been forgotten about. Not any longer.

Something glinted in the sunlight filtering to the floor of the Wicked Wood – not as wicked as it used to be – there between the tumbled stones. Guildenblad reached in and plucked the object from the ruins. It was a long-knife with a red handle. Guildenblad tucked it into his sash. He would trace its origins. He could feel magic in it. It was not Dark magic.

"It is most unfortunate that we have lost yet another of the places of Dark Magic." He paused, saddened at the state of his surroundings, anger mounting. "I have hidden the two Talismans safely in the Forest of Anan. For our plan to succeed completely we must gain at least one more Talisman. The Frosted Flask is utterly unreachable. Zanadon's and Balador's are lost to the ages and I have yet to find a way to the Talisman of Caladon. I need you to scout it for me. The guard has doubled throughout the castle and they have moved it to a locked cell in the center of the dungeon. Wardings and charms guard it. I cannot find a way in."

"I will see what I can do." It was a deep voice. A hollow voice: Rosenblad's. He was no longer asleep.

Miraden had also redone the charms and changed the

location of the Frosted Flask of Mirador. The Orb and Scepter remained in the Crystal Dome, at the center of the Realms, where it was destined to stay. Its amplifier, the Flask, was in a new home, that no one but Miraden and the Dwarves knew about. He would 'pop' in occasionally with food and drink for them, for they were used to a lonely life, but not a long fast. In fact, they thrived on loneliness, unlike their cousins, The Dwarves of Hope, who seemed to get along famously with 'company'. Miraden enjoyed the companionship of the taciturn Dwarves. They were lively enough at times and that pleased him also, but he held a great amount of respect for Dwarves fulfilling their sworn duty. It wouldn't be too long and they would be out from under the present danger.

Did Daniel see what he thought he saw before the light vanished? Before he had dropped the rocks out of fright? Was he alive and in the cave or dead and who knows where? It was dark. That is all he knew. He heated up three rocks again that he had managed to find on the floor of the cave while he was fumbling in the darkness. He was alive. He opened his palms.

What the glow helped him to see startled him again but he did not drop the rocks this time. He placed them on a ledge that ran around the hatchery.

The dim light revealed a complete skeleton. Daniel held up both hands in front of his face, fingertips touching thumb, and let his hands puppet-talk to each other.

"Ekladar, Ekladar where are you, Ekladar?"

"Here in the cave for two thousand years – no longer prone to laughter and tears."

Daniel laughed at his little rhyme. Maybe he would be a playwright *and* an actor. His hands quickly dropped to his sides s the scene before him began to make sense. There laid Ekladar. The head of the skeleton was resting on a rock about ten arms high. And Daniel wasn't laughing anymore.

He enlivened the remaining stones and laid them along the

ground until the entire skeleton was illuminated. She was lying on a Dragon made bench, which had kept most of her skeleton intact. The skeleton was gigantic. It must have been forty arms long. So Daniel had his choice of DragonSign.

Pick a bone – any bone. He was a little intimidated. The skeleton looked like it could come alive and really chew him up. He figured that he could sit in that Dragon's mouth and have room left over for Elias also. He didn't mean any disrespect, but --

"Ekladar – I need one of your bones to help Miraden bring you back to life. Please, may I take one?"

The skeleton seemed to move and Daniel found a bone from the Dragon's foot flying into his hand. It had flown without an acquire charm. He had asked and it was there. He stared at it hard.

"Thanks ... I think?"

He took the rocks, the piece of the egg sherd, more of which littered the hatchery floor, and made his departure. At the portal to the hatchery he stopped and looked back, he didn't want to leave the Dragon while at the same time he had to get away from the skeleton. Daniel went back up the ramp-like corridor to the room that would have been Miraden's lab if they were in Mirador. He studied each room and then thought of something he had seen Miraden do once.

"Kallowmere, come to me."

Nothing.

He said it again. Again nothing.

He moved into each room and tried the incantation there. After twelve tries there was no response from anything Kallowmere-like. He took out his notebook, reenergized the stones as they were fading, and sat down to study the pages of his notebook on the Blue DragonMount. He then decided to go directly across the central corridor to the room he'd find there. He took stones with him. The notes said that this had been Kallowmere's chamber.

"Kallowmere – come to me."

This time some dirt rattled from the ceiling and fell to the floor.

"Kallowmere – come to me."

More dirt hit the floor from the ceiling of the cave. Daniel looked down and there was a long bluish tube-like thing with a sharp point at one end.

"Kallowmere – come to me."

The blue pointy thing leaped into his hand. He studied it carefully and decided, from the books he'd read on Dragon anatomy, that this was one of Kallowmere's horns that had gotten broken off and stuck in the roof of his sleeping cave. Maybe he threw a tantrum, or woke up suddenly from a nightmare. Or was he trying to defend himself from the attack of the Dark Ones? Daniel fumed as he wrapped it and labeled it, along with Ekladar's sign, and left the room. He ran to the mouth of the cave and dropped every rock. He then saw that the sun was still high in the sky. He decided not to sleep here. The presence of the skeleton had kind of unnerved him. He chose to return to the cabin since it was still early and he had all of his DragonSign. He held his breath, peered over the edge and thought *next ledge down*.

Pop!

Thus he continued all the way down the cliff. He was three ledges from the bottom and decided to try something daring. He imagined himself on the path below him and,

Pop!

He was there!

He reached into his bag and ate an entire bar of chocolate on the way back to the tarn and its cabin. Upon his arrival there was something different! Smoke was billowing from the chimney! He should have hidden his kit. How stupid had he been? Never leave a trace! Both Miraden and his father had taught him that. There was only one thing to do.

By keeping his cover in the woods he snuck up to the side of the cabin away from the lake. He heard movement and humming and smelled something delicious cooking – venison! He looked over the window ledge, slowly, carefully, like an ancient Kilroy, and found two blue eyes staring back at him.

Rosenblad had made his way across the skies toward the Palace of Caladon in the full moon of the previous night. He found it easy to travel during the full moon. His large wings carried him quickly along the many leagues so that when the moon had set and his powers vanished, he only had a few leagues to walk to reach his destination. He studied the castle from the top of one of the gates to the city. It came within half a league of the nearest castle tower. He was looking for Dwarves and found none. Pity, they were so easy to ambush! Their blood was thicker and richer than many of the other creatures of the Realms, including Humans. Transforming to his Human self, he drifted to the ground, landing at the base of the gate, clothing himself, and was immediately noticed.

"Move along there," and the patrol passed around the corner.

In his human form, Rosenblad obeyed. No need to draw attention. He had been waiting for the next moon. This small planet revolved relatively quickly and the moon, at its own high velocity, passed through the skies twice in a night. He could still get some more time in his vampiric form but not for six hours yet. So, he moved along, closer to the inner walls, and settled down in a dark alley near the back door of the Castle, called the Queen's Gate.

The moon rose again and he snapped awake; his eyes already seeing shadows of red. He felt the change affecting him. He quickly disrobed to save his clothes for he had brought no others with him. He hid in the shadows. His skin tore loose, splitting open, revealing the monster inside, and his wings sprouted and unfolded, his talons grew where his fingernails and toenails had been, his teeth elongated and his red eyes shone in the light of the moon. His muscles rippled, lean and strong as any three or four men.

He left the ground, on the wing, and soared on the updrafts to the tallest castle tower. This is where the Talisman was supposed to be, but it was nowhere to be found. His brother was right. They had moved it. He took off out the window and floated to the ground underneath the westernmost tower of the triple-towered keep. The portcullis, with its Murder's Gate – what an appropriate name – was locked. He grabbed the edges of the door and tore it away from its position in the frame, then crept through and repositioned it.

Dungeons! That is what he smelled, mingled with the scent of Dwarf. He hated dungeons. They had no ready access to the sky. He found stairs and heard a clank of armor coming up them. He waited. He tore the guards apart silently. He left them in pieces and proceeded down, continuing into the depths of the castle as the blood of the slain slowly dripped down the stairs after him.

He could hear a Dwarven song. He may have chosen correctly. He forged ahead. The song was a somber one and it almost touched something deep within him – something lost – almost forgotten. He hesitated, then shook his body to rid himself of the memories that were too painful. They were Dwarven – unwanted, now.

He stopped when he was just outside the door that the song was coming through. He peered into a small opening and saw the Dwarves. He caught a tiny shaft of moonlight with his night vision. The room seemed to be at least three or four levels high. There was a small, barred window that let moonlight in from way above, somewhere. He retraced his steps and on the way up ripped apart two more guards who had thought, unwisely, to challenge him. He was then outside and crept along the wall of the castle and found the very same little barred window leading to the new Room of the Talisman.

He flew up and over and retrieved his clothing. He waited as the moon ebbed. His body was wracked as all of his vampire trappings withdrew with the light of the moon and his human form took its shrunken, normal shape. He dressed and found his way out of the castle grounds.

Blue eyes?

"Miraden?"

"Daniel – come in – come in – I wasn't expecting you 'til tomorrow morning. I had wanted to surprise you – for a job well done. But here you are! Surprise?"

Daniel ran around to the door and went in. The place was spotless, decorated – even homey.

"How did you get here? I thought you had to have been to a place before you could 'pop' there."

"I have been here. When you told me about the cabin, and showed me around, I remembered." What it was that he remembered he did not elaborate on. That was just Miraden's way. His life was full of non-sequiturs. "What have you got for me?"

Daniel's hand moved and then halted in his retrieval of the items. "How did you know I'd succeed?"

"My dear, boy, I knew. I am a Seer, after all."

"What else have you seen?"

"Nothing that needs concern you at the moment." Miraden had said too much.

Daniel looked his adoptive grandfather right in those blue, twinkling, eyes. "Everything concerns me, doesn't it, Grandpa?" He was making it plain that he was no longer a child and would not accept any dismissive attitudes; no condescension.

"True enough. But if I tell you of my visions, then maybe they will not come true. If you know where it is that you succeed, you could choose to be lazy or unprepared, thinking that you will succeed no matter what."

"Well, won't I?"

"Not necessarily. Each vision is provided on the basis of present attitudes and circumstances. If we alter those circumstances, or change our attitudes – even the slightest shade from where we are when the vision is given – many things could not end up as I have seen them."

Daniel was disconcerted at this revelation. His entire life changed in this moment. He found his voice. "So I do have a choice?" It was something that had been vexing Daniel over the last year or so. He had begun to feel that he was just a puppet of the Creators; to be summoned like an obedient lap-dog. Now, in a flash, he saw the possibility that he was just being prepared, being given the information with which to make the best possible choices.

"I, too, felt that way for a century or so after I was created. But it could not be further from the truth. Every action, every thought, every thing that we feel is a choice. The Creators cannot force those upon us. They can provide some circumstances where our abilities to make choices will be tested. No one else forces a specific choice except those of the Dark. They try to ensure that what they want to happen will happen. Their Quest is an impossible one."

"Then why do we have to worry about them?"

"Because they can affect each of us, or all of us, and provide opportunities for us to make negative choices – decisions we would not have made without their influence. Our journey becomes longer and more arduous if we choose their way. What if there had never been a War of the Realms?" Miraden had hated to say it, but it needed to be said.

"Well – then – many people would still be alive – including my family."

"So you realize how the Dark can affect us – even when we are fighting it?" Daniel could only nod. "It was that interference, caused by Withera, that led us to such sorrow."

Daniel chose, at this moment, to repress the emotions swelling within him. His shoulders slumped but he did not let a tear fall. He could not. He had spent too much time putting it behind him, accepting it, dealing with it. "So, the Dark is at the root of our problems, not the Creators?"

"Precisely."

"Then why don't the Creators just do away with the Dark."

"Because that would erase our opportunity to make choices. They cannot act in such a way. It is contrary to the nature of all things to do so. They will sometimes show us things through visions ..." Daniel startled at that one because his visions had already begun. Something he had not told his grandfather, but Miraden saw the truth of it in the boy's reaction, and paused. "I see that you have had some experience with that already."

Daniel nodded again, somewhat reluctantly. His visions so far had been both terrifying and glorious.

"So what I have seen does not have to happen?"

"No, Daniel – not necessarily – our ability to choose is everything!"

"I can make choices that might change the bad visions?"

"You could, yes. But through a choice based on wanting to alter a vision, you could also cause something even more disastrous to happen. You must live in the moment and make choices based on the present from information you have gained in the past. If you decide everything, completely, right now, it may even remove some of your own opportunities for choices in the future. Prepare. Remember. Use the information that you collect."

Daniel chewed silently on that one for more than a moment.

"What is it that you have seen that troubles you?"

"I had a dream – but it wasn't a dream. I can already tell a vision from a nightmare. It was about carrying Tilly in my arms and she was dead."

"Oh, dear. Thank you for telling me. I can say that I have not had such a vision, if that is any comfort. But if you spend all your time making decisions to counteract that one single happening, you may cause many more discomforts to Tilly, or to others – even to yourself. Best to think through each situation you are presented when you are conscious, remembering the visions, but making sense of them while you are awake, and move forward from there."

The expression on Daniel's face was one of uncertainty. He felt that what Miraden had said was true. His heart knew it. He just had to convince his brain about it all.

"Is that what you do?"

"It is what I attempt to do – always."

Daniel smiled, gamely.

"It has mostly given me success."

Daniel startled and looked his grandfather in those sparkly blue eyes. Miraden smiled. Daniel brought out what he had found at the Blue DragonMount. He told Miraden about Ekladar and Kallowmere. There was wonder in his eyes, fear and doubt forgotten for the moment, as he recounted the story, both from his experience at the cave and from what he'd read in books. But there was also a little bit of fear, mixed with sadness, encapsulated in the tale as he described the skeleton he had found.

Another tear escaped from Miraden's left eye. Two more friends and creations accounted for. Miraden almost had to turn away from his grandson. He really had to get that leak fixed.

Daniel also told him of his new 'popping' skill. Miraden's tears dried up quickly as he laughed and exclaimed at each joy that was Daniel's. He loved the boy so. The oldest man in the world had a companion again. He was no longer one lone Enchanter facing the Darkness. He stroked Daniel's long white hair. It was a gesture that comforted both men.

Miraden had prepared dinner and they sat down to venison, potatoes and vegetables. Afterwards, Daniel climbed into bed in his linens and Miraden slung up a hammock, his preferred method of sleeping, even at home in the cave. They settled in and slept well for the night as Miraden put up the warding around the cabin, if only to ease the fears of his growing and changing grandson.

ⱮL

CHAPTER NINE
YELLOW
(3rd Month)

THE FOREST WAS ALIVE WITH birdsong and Daniel was again taking a morning swim. Miraden was puttering in the cabin. Eggs and bacon were on the table and potatoes were finishing up in the pan when Daniel, dry and clean, walked through the door.

"It's to Caladon today!"

"But it will take me three days to get there!" and he stuffed his mouth with potatoes. He still ate like a child, thank goodness!

"No, you will be there tonight. We will 'pop' over to the city of Caladon together and secretly engage a cart to take you up the Blue River trail. You will leave the cart at the mouth of the canyon and walk half a day into the mountains to the Golden DragonMount. There is something I can do in Caladon; something I must do. I will wait for you in the city and then we will 'pop' home."

"But Grandpa, why?"

"We must travel together to accomplish separate missions. Time is growing short. Guildenblad is close to getting at what he wants."

"And what is that?"

"All four of the remaining Talismans! He has two, unless you had forgotten. He'll never get Mirador's but Caladon's is a possibility. If he destroys even the Talismans he has ..."

"We'd better go."

Miraden and Daniel went out the door of the cabin after finishing breakfast and tidying up. Daniel put on a hooded robe that Miraden had supplied so as not to draw attention to his white hair and skin. Caladon was more populous than Aradon, and he would be recognized there. Miraden threw up a warding to protect the cabin in their absence. He would return, someday. He raised his wand and thought *Caladon City*.

Pop!

They walked through the streets of the merchant section looking for a stable from which to hire a horse and cart. When they found one Miraden plunked down some Caledonan coins, waved his wand, and no questions were asked. Miraden checked into the Dragon's Gate Inn and told Daniel to return to him there.

Daniel mounted the cart and directed it to the western gate where he passed through and onward to the bridge over the Blue River. It was not a long drive. He took the cart track off to the right on the east of the river and moved along at an easy pace as the trail into the mountains of Caladon rose in front of him. The wide path ended where the trail began. He tied his horse up to a tree, where it could get to the grass, and left a tub of river water for his equine friend. He placed his robe on the seat of the cart and buckled on his sword – again, the one he had been awarded in Mirador – and slung his bow and arrows over his shoulder. He marched off into the mountain canyon towards the DragonMount of the Golden Dragons.

It was a pleasant, forested canyon, birch, aspen, pine, hemlock and fir – and the trail stuck right by the side of the river, so it was cool; the walk was calming with the sounds of the water. The further up the canyon he traveled he found that the river was narrow but deep. Its waters seemed to slog by, now. But really, they were fast with a good undertow. The slow speed was a deception. A non-swimmer would quickly lose a battle with this river. Daniel was tempted, because he was a great swimmer, but he continued on. He followed against the current for two leagues before he saw the object of his quest, off to his right – the DragonMount. He studied the mountain. There appeared to be a trail or pathway most of the way up. He traced it to its base and headed for where he supposed the start of the path would be.

There he ran into five playful Gnomes who demanded the solution of a riddle before he could pass. They were obnoxious and giggly little creatures and had sharp sticks which they were poking in Daniel's direction. Daniel decided to humor them even though he had a sword at his side and could encase either them or himself within a warding.

"Ask your riddle."

More giggling.

What is lesser than a Dragon King?
What strives to add up everything?
What lives upon a DragonMount?
None other than ..."

There was silence and an expectant but smug look on the faces of the Gnomes as they crossed their arms awaiting a reply that they knew would not come.

"That's it?"

There was more of that infernal giggling.

"Let's see, now ... lesser than a Dragon King, added up everything, lives DragonMount ... King ... thing ... mount ...?"

Daniel turned away apparently disheartened and beaten by the Gnomes. He even let his shoulders slump, playing his game. They giggled louder. Then he suddenly reared and faced them down and yelled out: "A Dragon Count!"

The Gnomes got so angry that this little Human (really a young Enchanter) answered correctly that they ran at him brandishing their little pointed sticks. Evidently they had not noticed the sword hanging at Daniel's side for he drew it and slashed their sticks out of their little hands and spanked their little bare bottoms with the flat of his sword, sending them off howling into the woods. Daniel almost doubled over in laughter. Then he heard the sound of a 'raspberry' sent in his general direction. If it was a 'raspberry.' Gnomes could be disgusting little creatures if provoked enough.

He proceeded up the path. It was an easy, gradual climb but as he drew closer to the cave's entrance he found that the trail just ended in a shear drop-off, leaving ten untrailed spans to the ledge by the opening of the cave. He thought hard. *Cave entrance!* He found himself in midair about an arm's length out from the ledge. As he fell he grabbed the edge of the ledge and hauled himself up, gradually, and painfully, and soon was standing in front of the cave on solid ground.

He remembered reading that this particular cave was marked by unusual magic and special enchantments.

"I seek Tandamere and Ostradar, the wise and ancient Dragons of Caladon."

The cave answered him with silence and darkness. He leaned forward onto the wall, placing his hands there, palms flat against the stone, and called 'Light!'

Torches sprang to life along the walls of the main corridor, lighting the entire way to the back chambers. The heat they emitted felt good after being in the cooler shadowy places of the mountain canyon. He strode down the corridor and a huge gust of wind blew him backwards off his feet and extinguished the torches. He heard a sound like wheezing laughter. He placed his hands against the wall again and called 'Light!' This time the gale was immediate and he was nearly blown to the mouth of the cave and over the edge. Again, the torches were extinguished and the laughter returned.

"Gentle Tandamere and Ostradar, I have been sent by Miraden Light to bring him DragonSign so that you may live again."

"Speak you truly?" aspirated eerily through the tunnel.

"On my honor as Miraden's grandson."

"Prove yourself!"

The torches flamed to life again with a wave of Daniel's hand. Wow! He didn't know he could do that! Look ma, no words! A need for magic must bring new powers to fruition. That's how the first magic he ever worked had been accomplished – out of a need to do it. He never ceased to be surprised, even a little awed, at the powers that were at his command.

"What more can I do?" he mocked. "How did I get in here without magic? How do I light the torches without spoken charms?"

The breath again. "Ahhhhhh."

"I am Daniel Gregoryson."

"The Prophecy? We have heard the name."

There was a flash of light and a piece of eggshell and a golden scale appeared in his left hand followed by a curved, horned yellow tail-spike in his right hand. Daniel was mesmerized and a little more than spooked.

"Th-th-thank you, noble Golden Dragons. I ... I ... live for the day to see you in the flesh again."

Daniel backed out to the entrance. The torches went out and he felt himself blown out of the cave. For a moment he was terrified until he realized that he was not falling, he was floating; down – down – down – like a feather.

"Goodbye, Daniel Gregoryson" wafted to his ears as the wind supported him. After a full minute of gentle descent, a minute he filled with gazing upon the highest sights of western Caladon, with a quick glimpse of its forbidden border with Colabos, he alit on the ground and looked back up at the cave, fifty spans above his head.

"Goodbye, Tandamere and Ostradar." He even bowed, so awed had he been by the experience.

He turned and headed to the river after wrapping and labeling the DragonSign and placing each in his pack. He tried 'popping' to the river path and ended up only going about fifty spans and landing flat on his face. *A little too far too soon, I guess.* He picked himself up and walked to the river. He took his boots off and pulled the legs of his breeches up and thrust his feet and legs into the cold, clear water. He felt it first. then he heard laughter, then he saw a beautiful water Nymph standing across the river, staring at him. She was naked, but a Nymph is somewhat androgynous, so Daniel made reluctant eye contact after a moment or so and found that there was really nothing to see. She had probably sensed some sort of magic within him. She just wanted to see who this human was. The word *'handsome'* kept repeating in Daniel's ear. It was not a word he was used to using when applying it to himself. It was as if the many-voiced whispers were all around him.

"Hello?" came from the Nymph.

She laughed again and the water of the river rushed up and over Daniel getting him soaking wet. And it was cold! More laughter. *Do these mountain creatures do nothing but laugh?* he thought. He maintained his temper and blew on his hands and whispered 'hot and dry', and ran them over his body effectively drying himself off. The Nymph must have been impressed as she sat down and studied him from the opposite bank.

"Hello?" Daniel cooed at her.

"Hello."

"I'm Daniel."

"I'm Nyara."

"I am completing a DragonQuest."

"I am a water Nymph and your feet are in my home."

Daniel quickly pulled his feet out of the water. "I'm sorry. Excuse me for my rudeness? I didn't know there were any of you left. I'm glad though."

She cocked her head to one side and her eyes sparkled in appreciation. "We live in out-of-the-way places, where no one is likely to notice us."

"Unless they stick their feet into your home."

She giggled.

"I am sorry for the intrusion. I will keep your secret, Nyara."

"How do you know for sure, young one?" came a deep voice. A Dryad stepped out of the woods.

"Because I am Daniel Gregoryson, grandson of Miraden Light – one of your creators."

"I sense truth from him, cousin."

"He has weapons. He could have killed you."

"But he didn't."

Daniel was tired of being left out of the conversation. "Those Gnomes could have killed me. But I didn't kill them. Besides, I would not hurt anyone so magical as you, if I had any choice about it."

"You must go."

"I'll be gone." He stood up and rolled down the legs of his breeches. "Thank you for the use of your water, Nyara."

The Dryad disappeared as Daniel put on his boots. The Nymph giggled and vanished, like a fountain, into the water.

Daniel trotted down the path to his horse and cart. He found the horse tethered where he had left him. He donned his robe and mounted to the seat of the cart, then headed down the river trail. Once on the road he passed walkers, horsemen and women, other carts – but no one seemed to pay him any mind at all. It felt very nice to be inconspicuous; something he rarely felt in Mirador.

He came up behind a very shapely woman on a chestnut charger. She wore a brilliant green dress and was riding side-saddle with her golden hair flowing down her back. Her noticeable attributes had naturally caught his adolescent attention. Then he caught up with her. He sneaked a peek out from under his hood at – the ugliest face he had ever seen. He swallowed and choked and hitched his horse to go a little faster. Once he was ahead he did not look back. Life was strangely funny. *Appearances can be deceiving*, he thought; especially to the point of misleading him.

He was not challenged at the gates of the city of Caladon and walked quickly to the Dragon's Gate Inn. He boarded his horse and cart at the stable down the street. He went inside and found Miraden seated in the great room of the Inn. Miraden motioned for him to be quiet. Daniel went to remove his hood and Miraden slowly shook his head from side to side. Daniel kept his hood up. Daniel sat. Daniel was quiet. Miraden pointed his index finger up toward the ceiling, flashed three fingers at Daniel and touched his left shoulder.

Daniel figured – *the third room on the left upstairs*. He got up slowly, walked to the stairs and went up. Miraden watched the room. No one's eyes seemed to follow Daniel. Miraden stood and went out the front door. He walked around to the alleyway. It was deserted – fortunately. He 'popped' to Daniel's room. Daniel was waiting for him and startled a little at Miraden's appearance right in front of his face. Daniel's questioning look at his grandfather was enough to get Miraden started.

"Guildenblad is in the city. Rosenblad slaughtered four of the Palace Guards the day before we arrived and it is thought that Guildenblad has two human spies working for him; mercenaries from the fringes. They wear black cloaks, black boots and have this red mark on their left cheek below their eye."

Miraden made a motion with his wand and in the air Daniel saw, inscribed, the mark in fire hanging in front of him:

"It comes from outside the Realms and, from what we know, is the sign of a secret society of assassins: The Taradalnock Brethren. They serve the god Dal, a Dark and evil presence. They have never come into the Realms before, to my knowledge. The original Taradalnock were outcasts of the Realms; malcontents who left during the Age of Men and Dwarves. They are thought to live in the Unknown East on the fringes of the Eastern Desert, past Balador. If they have re-entered the Realms, it must be because of the loss of so many Talismans and a weakened warding around ... Quick! Take my hand."

Daniel did. Miraden looked out the window.

Pop!

They were gone from the room. The door opened and two black-cloaked men entered with swords drawn. They waited.

From his perch across the alley, Daniel noticed a little red "T" under the left eye on each of their faces. He gulped. A black shimmer started in the center of the room. (If black can shimmer.) Guildenblad appeared in front of them. Unknown to the three now in the room, there were four eyes watching everything from behind the chimney on the rooftop across the way.

Miraden was startled. The first time Daniel had ever seen it happen. Daniel looked at him. Miraden kept watching the room with wide-eyed wonder.

"So, Guildenblad has learned the art of magical transportation through the Talismans he possesses."

Daniel wondered what else Guildenblad could do.

"My thoughts precisely," Miraden sensed Daniel's unease. Luckily, Miraden traveled with only his wand and everything that Daniel needed was on his back already, so nothing had been left in the room. Miraden pointed his wand at the room and placed his ear near his wand hand. Daniel leaned in also.

Guildenblad snarled. The mercenaries backed up.

"We were careful, Lord Blad, nobody saw us."

"You don't need to be seen by Miraden – he knows."

"That was Miraden, Lord? He was very young for an Enchanter."

"No – that was his grandson, the brat!"

Daniel tensed and then laughed – a little.

"And I too, am an Enchanter!" The men stepped back, cowering. "Miraden is here, all right."

"How do you know?"

"No trace – he never leaves a trace. Return to the castle. We must prepare for tonight."

"Tonight?"

"I cannot wait another month."

And the three left the room. Guildenblad did not '*pop*' out as he had '*popped*' in. Maybe his powers were limited! Or he needed rest.

"We must 'pop' to the cave, then to Harborton. Then I will 'pop,' back here to the castle and see what I can do."

"Why can't I come with you?"

"You and Elias and Matthew must travel to Zanadon. The DragonSign must be gathered from there as well."

"I understand." There was a regret in his voice but he knew

Miraden was right. Too much was happening and neither he nor Miraden could be everywhere together. But they each could be somewhere different.

"How are the Golden Dragons?"

Daniel whispered, with the greatest amount of respect he could muster, "Are they still alive, Grandfather?"

"No, but their spirits are. Somehow only their bodies were destroyed."

"It was weird, Grandpa, but I think that they are well. They made the DragonSign appear in my hands. I didn't even have to search for it."

"Yes – they are old friends."

"I met some Gnomes and a Water Nymph and a Dryad."

"Good."

"I liked the Nymph."

"Spoken like the son of your father!"

"Grandpa, not that way! She was ... nice."

"And pretty?"

"Well, yes."

"Thought so."

"Grandpa!"

Pop!

"She sure beat the lady I saw on the road back to town."

They were at the cave. Daniel handed the trophies to Miraden and cleaned out and re-supplied his pack.

Pop!

They were just outside Harborton and found Matthew's cottage there. Matthew and Elias were waiting.

"There will be three horses held for you at the Glen of Goodness. That was as close as I could get them for you. I did not want to set off any alarms that there might be, alerting anyone too soon of your presence. If there is anyone there to be alerted, but better not chance that, had we? You will travel to the Green DragonMount from there."

"Grandpa, I can't go across those plains again."

"You must."

"I can't!"

There was real panic in his voice, in his eyes, in his breathing. Otherwise Daniel was silent. He seemed to be kind of shutting down. He bit on his lip. His fists clenched, fingernails digging into the palms of his hands. Miraden, Matthew and Elias stood, watching, none of them really knowing what to do. Daniel's teeth released his lips as his mouth moved without sound, as if repeating a mantra of some sort. His eyes were glazed over. His hands jerked in tiny spasms. His breath rasped in staccato blasts. Elias stood in front of his friend. He took both of Daniel's hands in his smaller ones. He squeezed them lightly. Miraden and Matthew each put a hand on one of Daniel's shoulders. Miraden was quite alarmed. He had never seen this kind of reaction from his grandson. Daniel's breathing slowed. He came out of his trance and hugged Elias tightly to him. Elias didn't know what to do so he placed his arms around his friend. He felt a great intake of breath as Daniel began to relax out of his fit. He released Elias. Elias, reluctantly, let go. Daniel took Elias' hands again.

"Thanks."

"No worries." Elias smiled. But he really was worried.

Daniel smiled back. The men patted him on the shoulder blades. With a shrug he hitched them into place as a Prince of the Realm.

"We'll get him through, Miraden."

"Thank you, Matthew."

Daniel smiled, a half-smile. Miraden's eyes twinkled, but there was the hint of a tear at the outer corner. Daniel noticed. He was pretty good at noticing things; especially if they came from Miraden.

Pop!

Miraden was gone, as always, with little explanation. *Maybe it's better that way*, Daniel thought. *Explanation seems to limit the choices available.* Daniel stood taller as that knowledge overcame him.

"Better be on our way, lads! Ever been on Crystal Lake at night, Daniel?"

"No, not that I remember. Oh, yes – one time when Father

and I escaped Zantha at the Castle."

"When you arrived in that funny little boat?"

"That would be the time."

"Waning moon t'night. It will be a pretty one. Well, into the boat."

Daniel was understandably uneasy on the crossing even though it was a gorgeous night and the lake was especially sparkly. Not a hint of the trouble that was brewing in Caladon. They sailed up the Straits of Light and over between the Isle of Fear and the Point of Little Hope at the northern end of the Isle of Light where Zanadon and Mirador almost met. Then they were able to cross over straight to the Glen of Goodness. Elias and Matthew got out. Daniel remained frozen in the boat.

"Daniel, we're here."

He didn't move.

"Daniel?"

He was breathing strangely again. "I can't. The last time I was here … people died."

Miraden was standing in the dungeon, in the new Room of the Talisman of Caladon. The twelve Dwarves were there, solemn and serene, surrounding a stone box, triple locked and chained to the floor, containing the Talisman. Two score of the Palace Guard lined the walls. Without the full moon, Rosenblad would be of little help tonight. Guildenblad must take the lead. The two Taradalnock mercenaries would be hard pressed to defeat over fifty armed guards. Plus there were wardings that only Miraden and the Dwarves knew about. Seven protective wardings surrounded the Dwarves and the box. Each would have to be defeated before the Dwarves could even be touched. Miraden had done his work well.

But where was Miraden, now? He had just been here! It was only the Dwarves and the Guards and the box. Without them the room would be completely empty.

Red light flashed from the barred window high above. Two

Guards went down, bodies smoking. All the Guards moved directly under the window, where nothing could reach them from the opening. Red light streaked towards the Dwarves and bounced off their warding.

"Miraden!!!!" Guildenblad's hatred echoed off the walls.

Red light – ricochet ... Red light – ricochet ... Red light – ricochet – Guard down. Red light – ricochet – Guard down.

The Guards began to move continuously. Red light – ricochet – Red light – ricochet.

Another yell came from outside the window. Then there was a terrible banging on the door. It splintered and shattered into the room. Ten of the Taradalnock Brethren entered the room! Guildenblad smiled above. The ten mercenaries rushed at the thirty-six remaining soldiers. Swords flashed at each other, shields groaned and evil black steel knives penetrated Caladonan hearts. Caladonan blades severed Taradalnock heads from their black-clad bodies. Red lightning filled the room. Soon, only four Palace Guards were defending their safety under the window from the two remaining black-clad mercenaries. Death was more than palpable in the room; a physically demoralizing presence all its own.

The Dwarves had not moved. One mercenary leaped into the air, sword raised high in an arc and took the heads off two Guards. The other two Guards impaled the remaining mercenary. As that leaping mercenary landed on his feet, the door was swarming with more Palace Guards who ran at the swift moving mercenary. He died with ten blades thrust through his chest and abdomen while two more impaled him from behind. His eyes were wide and white as he hung there, suspended in midair by a dozen pieces of Caladonan steel. They lowered him to the floor. Once his feet touched, they pulled out the blades and his body oozed onto the stones, dead.

Red lighting flashed and took down five or six more Guards.

"The hall!" rang out from a Dwarf.

The Guards retreated to the hall, losing two more on their way out.

The red lightning began turning colors as it flashed at the warding guarding the Dwarves.

Blue – Gold – Green – Black – Orange – Purple – and a shimmer filled the room. The outermost of the seven wardings vanished in a flash of purple light. Then purple light was streaming from a statue in the corner as Miraden came to life and stunned Guildenblad through the window with his first blast of light. A wand dropped through the barred window and shattered on the cold, stone floor of the room fifteen spans below. Angry shouts began to fill the courtyard outside and above as the Guards searched for the Necromancer, Guildenblad.

But he had vanished. It was hoped that Miraden's blast of purple light had destroyed him. But it was proven, later, that the Necromancer had escaped, by the brown footprints left on the green grass by a retreating Dwarf who spread death and decay wherever he went. Those footprints headed away from the castle to the outer wall in the north and then just disappeared.

ML

CHAPTER TEN
THE CALL
(3rd Month)

WHEN HE HAD SEARCHED THE last spot where the Brother Blad had stood before his disappearance, Miraden had found something in the Courtyard outside the little barred window in Caladon; a bit of parchment with a curse on it. At least it seemed like a curse. He assumed that Guildenblad had dropped it.

To be aged and infirm -
Your body now shall squirm.
The blood of youth, the threads of truth,
Will leave you for a term.
Offensive to the senses,
If some come to your defenses
Then certain traits the spell has brought
Will fade away; become as naught.
Younger you will grow again
Remembering what was once forgot.
Still, knowledge can't be spoken then,
The truth and tongue is tied, as in a knot,
Until the death of me,
It unties and sets you free.

He had found it but he had no idea yet what it really meant or whom it concerned. He must get to Panador.

The Court of Panador was in session. People had packed the hall to listen to Miraden. They were anxious for a solution – something to return their Kingdom, and their lives, to some sense of normalcy. Miraden had explained about the brothers Blad from their turning to the theft of the Talismans of Aradon and Panador – and he added the recently attempted theft in Caladon. Panador was warned that the Kingdom itself could even end up like Balador or, Creators forbid, Zanadon. But then, once they heard about the terrors of the creatures of the night, they were not so bold as to be a part of the solution, although they still wanted one.

That seems to be pretty much as it is in our world. That is why the heroes of the War of The Realms are so honored by the people – in their praise of others they try to make up for what they have come to realize as their own shortcomings. They are happy to let others take the risks, even though they will all receive the benefits (or consequences) of any action. After all was said and done, only one stood forward. (Although another would have if she could have.) Boncaster, himself, volunteered.

"Who better to find a flower than a flower-grower?" was all he offered in defense of his wish to go.

There was the sound of applause and approval. (Of course, there was! It wasn't them volunteering. They might as well support the fool who did – it would save them the trouble.)

"Shall we outfit an expedition?" ventured the King.

"I shall go alone."

"I think *alone* would be best," Miraden added.

"What weapons can the Crown provide you?"

"A good stout quarter-staff and a bow with a quivver of arrows is all I need."

"Done."

Boncaster was so equipped, but there were two eyes watching him – and not from afar. Someone at the Court had developed an interest in Boncaster – the vagabond Master Gardener. Who was he really? Why did he show up when they most needed him? He seemed to be always there to do what no one else could do. The brain behind those two watchful eyes determined to be yet even more vigilant where Boncaster was concerned.

Boncaster asked, that before he left, if there could be a sparring partner available to meet him in the yard with quarter-staff in hand to make sure that his skills had not deteriorated.

There was laughter. Phineas, the Captain of the Guard, stepped forward. He would meet Boncaster in mock battle on the morrow.

Boncaster had figured that the Panadorians would feel better about the mission if they saw a demonstration of his skill – after all, to them he was only a gardener.

Guildenblad was more than exultant as he held the long-knife with the red handle in the air, magically, with the new wand that his Mentor had provided him. The names of Gregory and Daniel were prominent as the enchanted object spoke of its recent owners under the powerful spell of the Necromancer. But as to its origins, those names and places were not forthcoming from the knife. It kept some of its secrets despite the magical intervention of the former-Dwarf. He lowered the knife to the table in his cottage. He turned and waved his hands over the scrying bowl and called the name of Phet. A grizzled face appeared in the waters of the basin. Holding the dagger up so that his mentor at the other end could see it, he heard the words come through the scrying basin, "That was my brother's!"

Guildenblad noticeably startled and asked, "Miraden's?"

The voice clarified, "Anandoral's. Where did you get it?"

"From the ruins of Withera's castle."

"Destroyed?"

"Totally useless. I'm sure that the brat left it there after he finished tearing it apart!" was spat out by Guildenblad.

"The Prophecy?"

"Yes. My spells tell me that it has been in his family for a very long time – since the Great War at least."

"He was the one who destroyed the Castle?"

"I am sure of it."

"All the better for the revenge you will soon have upon him. Flay him. Strip him of his skin and his dignity. If he begs for mercy, give him none! Dismember him, disembowel him, let him die slowly and painfully. That boy shall never live to be a man. You will see to it?"

"I will."

The scrying basin went suddenly dark as Phet's image disappeared from its surface. The knife was held in Guildenblad's hand and he raised it to the sky. No magic appeared, as he thought it would. He lowered it and grumbled at it. He did not have the key or the authority to use it! But he did not know that. It would only come to power in the hands of "The Prophecy."

Boncaster was in the yard early the next morning. The staff was spinning and twirling in his hands. He stopped it, bounced it off the hard-packed earth of the parade ground, turned around three times and caught the staff in a position so that it was perfectly parallel to the ground. Not unlike a modern baton twirler would work with her baton, or a martial artist with his staff. Those two eyes were watching him again. A crowd was starting to gather. Not that they were bloodthirsty or anything – they wanted one of two things to happen: Boncaster to beat their glorious Captain or Boncaster's own defeat. Not that they wished to see the defeat of the one they were hailing as their champion. On the contrary, they wished him success, because the Captain had a little bit of bluster in his swagger – he was good by fact and reputation – but not as good as he himself thought he was.

The two combatants bowed and backed away from each other. The crowd murmured. All eyes watched – especially two! Miraden was smiling. He always seemed to know something that the people around him didn't know. Boncaster had staved off a first hit! The Captain didn't fare as well. Better hope that he ate a light breakfast. *Crack – crack – crack – ooof!* The Captain again, down two. Smiles crossed the faces of the onlookers.

"Two to naught, Boncaster."

Crack – crack – crack – swoosh – crack-crack – swoosh – thud – ooof!

"Three to naught, Boncaster."

The Captain gave a mighty swing and Boncaster jumped over the stave and landed with his staff in a vertical position to ward off another blow. He then angled the bottom end between the Captain's feet and pushed, and the Captain went down on his backside. Boncaster then stuck an end in the ground again and went over the Captain's head using his stave as you would use your arms and hands in a cartwheel. He landed right behind the Captain and had his stave pressing against the Captain's neck before the man could move off the ground.

"Yield?"

"Yield."

There was applause from the crowd. Boncaster helped the Captain up. There was not hatred in his eyes. Had he been a lesser man there could have been; there was only wonder and amazement for he had never been beaten.

Laughter, backslapping and more applause from the crowd for both Boncaster and Phineas.

"Guildenblad better be shaking in his boots," the Captain yelled, "Boncaster is coming!"

Three cheers went up. Some Panadorians were happier than they had been in a long time.

Miraden quieted the crowd. "My fine Boncaster – may I anoint your stave – though it needs it not – as a token of our trust and good wishes and as a blessing of protection?"

"You may."

Boncaster kneeled and Miraden withdrew his wand and potion and traced a line along the length of the staff and then a drop on the back of each of Boncaster's hands as they held the staff out to him. Boncaster stood and after final congratulations the crowd began to break up. Two eyes were still watching him from the shadows across the yard. Miraden held Boncaster back.

"I have recently found that Guildenblad has been hiding in the Anan Forest – for a long time; maybe centuries. He is well protected and thinks himself invincible. Lack of detection is a false confidence builder. His power is Dark and its results can sometimes defy death. He is a Necromancer and quite skilled. What you will deal with will not necessarily be "alive." It may be reanimated. I know there are, certainly, two types of wardings and two types of creatures. Every inch of the forest could be guarded now by Taradalnock."

Boncaster's eyes widened at the implications.

"I will 'pop' in to check on you from time to time. If I were you I would leave tomorrow. Rest well."

Miraden was gone. Except for the two eager eyes that had seen everything and the two ears that had heard every word, Boncaster was alone in the yard. And tomorrow, after a good night's rest, Boncaster would leave the castle and head west to Panadar Village; there to catch the Laketon Road to AnanWater and the forest beyond it.

It may have taken only two hours by coach but it was a full day's walk. As Boncaster set out the next morning, those two eyes that had been watching him, were watching again. A shadow, dressed in brown with a full, dark cape, followed the gardener westward.

ML

CHAPTER ELEVEN
STALKED
(3rd Month)

AFTER A PEACEFUL NIGHT AT the Glen and an uneventful morning ride to the Plains of Youth, Daniel stood silent and staring, in front of the remains of Zantha's Castle. His breathing had not been abnormal since last night. He seemed resigned to this confrontation. But when he looked around, all he could see was the blood of his friends – the youths of Panador. It wasn't really there; it was seen only through his mind's eye. The land was stained as if with a curse. But the real curse had been there long before his friends had died. He knew that. This was Zanadon.

One turret and two partial walls were all that remained above the foundation. His arms akimbo, feet spread squarely, fingers flexing, and breathing becoming more rapid – he waited.

"Daniel, best to move on, mebbe?"

Daniel paid no attention to Matthew. Elias, then, placed his hand on Daniel's shoulder and Daniel stepped forward away from it, his shoulders and chest heaving. Suddenly his arm raised, the hairs on his body and his head stood on end and the lightning bolt shot out of the palm of his hand, which was directed at the castle. One of the walls disintegrated in front of their eyes. Then another bolt and another and another and ... there was absolutely nothing left above the ground. Zantha's Castle hadn't been a stronghold for several years. Now, it was no longer even a ruin. It was like it had never existed. What was rock had become dust. What was still Dark in Daniel's heart and mind was now nothingness.

Matthew and Elias were very startled, if not more than a little frightened. This was something that they had never seen in Daniel. Not knowing just what to do, Matthew wrapped his arms firmly but kindly around Daniel. Elias hugged Daniel around the waist and the lightning stopped as his arms returned to his sides.

Daniel's shoulders continued to heave, but this time it was sobs that were wracking his body. His best friend and his best friend's father just held him until the anger was released; had purged itself, hopefully, from his soul. After a few minutes Daniel grew quiet again. Matthew started to release his hold on the boy but Daniel pulled his arms back around him. He stood there, tears streaming, but sobs quieting. He dazedly took some chocolate out of his belt. This seemed to signal that Daniel was ready. His friends released him. He, and they, turned around to face the east. Daniel pointed at the land from forest to lakeshore.

"The Plains of Youth – my friends died there."

"Mine too," injected Elias quietly. There had been two older boys from Harborton who had been massacred.

Daniel realized for the first time that others had been touched; it was not his burden to bear alone. Daniel nodded and looked at his best friend. Great sadness existed between them. But youth is resilient. It can weather the most difficult of storms.

"I'm ready now. Let's go."

The trio mounted their horses and started off to the north to head around the cleft in the mountains and follow the River Blad eastward, up to the DragonBeck: a small, fast-rushing stream with many cataracts and falls tumbling down the DragonMount. There was no road, just a footpath, so they would be leaving the horses at the base of the mountains, tethered and safe. As they entered the low valley that led from the Plains of Youth to the Valley of Dotham, Daniel spoke:

"I'm sorry I lost my temper. I didn't even know that was in me."

Elias, who had a natural talent for easing any difficult situation said, "Yeah? Well, remind me not ta make ye mad!"

It was a good laugh they all had. It broke a little of the tension but Daniel was still growing concerned. Was he ready for the power that was rising inside of him? He was having some serious doubts about his ability to control – anything.

Matthew could see it in his eyes. Daniel was scared.

Not of death, or injury or danger – but of what he might be capable of doing if he didn't stop to think about it. He worried about the responsibility of it all; its inability to be controlled.

It was a bright and beautiful day but somehow the trees, grass, rivers and mountains around them seemed to suck the light right out of the very air. Zanadon! The Dark Kingdom. It hadn't always been such. It had been a place of Light – once. Briefly. The horses managed to clop along as horses did, unaffected by the gloom. So it was the human riders who were solemn instead of joyful. Maybe it was more than the surroundings? This was a quest – searching for DragonSign – the preparation for the return of the most noble of beasts! There should be joy. But what existed was, at best, thoughtful contemplation.

The pass or valley was low, the trail was easy and level and Daniel hitched his heels and snapped his reins and his horse responded. Elias followed Daniel's example (as always) and the horses began to race each other. First Daniel's grey, then Elias' bay. One, then the other, would creep ahead. The boys were crouched low, hiding behind the powerful necks of each horse as their strides lengthened into a gallop and their hooves clawed for traction and speed against the earth. It almost seemed like the horses were enjoying it as much as the boys were. Judging by the smiles on their faces, the boys had finally broken the boredom factor – and the solemnity. Maybe they had even chased away the struggles that had beset Daniel.

Elias had the advantage with his lighter weight but Daniel had more skill in horsemanship, where Elias was most comfortable in watercraft. They shot out of the mouth of the canyon, Daniel's head almost resting on the horse's mane, and into the Valley of

Dotham where they hauled up on the reins slowly as, at last, they came to the River Blad after racing for what must have been about three leagues.

They dismounted and led their horses around to cool them down and then to the water to drink. The water here was not like the water in the Crystal Lake. Nor was it dark and muddy like the water of The River of Fear. Once the horses had had their fill, they began cropping the grass and other plants at the water's edge while the boys ran their hands down the smooth, moist necks of the beasts, trying to help them to cool down. They grabbed some dry grasses and rolled them against the horses hides. The horses nickered in response. They obviously enjoyed it. Matthew finally clopped up to their location and set his horse to drink.

The sun was high, the horses were feeding and it was a good time to break out the food for lunch.

Daniel wasn't sure yet, whether he preferred the solitary journeys he took to the DragonMounts of Aradon and Caladon – or this journey to the Green DragonMount with his friends – and on horseback! This one wasn't over. There could be all sorts of things ahead. (There would be all sorts of things ahead.) He said a quick and silent prayer that he would make the best choices possible.

Twenty leagues left to reach DragonBeck. They would be to the base of the mountains by this evening if they set a fair pace for the horses and rested and fed them twice along the way. As they packed up again and started east they saw a lone traveler walking towards them from the East. He wore a black hooded cape that flared out behind him in the breeze. He sauntered along at a speed that seemed unnaturally fast for a walker, and soon he was abreast of the trio.

"Ho there, stranger. It's a good day to travel."

The stranger stopped and stared at them. But all they could see was his mouth filled with uneven, yellowing teeth. The eyes were hidden beneath the cowl.

"I sense magic in you and Enchanters are not welcome in Zanadon! There is no peace for you here. Be warned," the stranger snarled as he pointed his long, slim, dirty finger at Daniel. "You are in great danger." The stranger took off running towards the southern mountains.

Daniel went to mount his horse and give chase but Matthew restrained him.

"Let 'im go. We've no truck wit' crazies."

"Did you hear his voice?"

"Yeah," Elias squeaked. He was obviously scared.

"He sounded like an animal, father Matthew."

"Aye, Daniel, 'e did at that. But 'e's gone now. No worries."

It had been said but that didn't make it come true. Matthew was still watching. Daniel mounted his horse and simply stared after the back of the departing stranger who seemed to be awfully far away so very quickly. *Did I see what I just thought I saw?* Daniel rubbed his eyes. "Can you see him?"

"No!" Elias was a little downcast, and still a bit frightened.

"I thought I saw him running on all fours. But that would be impossible. It must've been my imagination." Daniel reached into his belt and nibbled on another piece of chocolate.

"What's that?" asked Elias.

"Candy." Daniel said absently as he was still searching for sign of the departed stranger. "Want some?"

"Can I?" he pleaded with his father.

"Yes, son."

Daniel broke off a piece and handed it to Elias. Elias chewed it with relish!

"Put it on your tongue and let it melt."

Elias stopped chewing and placed it on his tongue and allowed it to melt as he sucked on it gently.

"Mmmm! Even better."

"That's what Miraden taught me. Oh, Elias!!! Ahh! Matthew – that's Miraden's special – I mean it's the stuff that – I gotta talk to Miraden."

He pulled out his orb and Elias' jaw dropped to the ground as Miraden appeared in it at the mere mention of his name. Daniel explained about the candy and Miraden said it would do Elias no harm, but not too give him too much. That he would make some more without the secret ingredient in it for Elias. Elias looked towards his father, hopefully, like a boy wanting a puppy. (Chocolate is almost better than a puppy.) Matthew nodded and Daniel confirmed it to Miraden. Then an unease overcame Daniel's voice and manner.

"Grandfather – we met a stranger on the road a few minutes ago. He was filthy, terrible brown teeth and we never even got a look at his eyes."

"Tell him about the voice!' Elias offered.

"What about his voice, Elias?" There was a nervous excitement in Miraden's own voice.

"Well, he kind of growled when he talked. And he – it was scary!"

"Thank you for telling me, Elias. It sounds like Nightbane is on the prowl. As the full moon is three days past, he can only turn to a wolf at night. Daniel, you know the warding for animals. Protect your camp. Be watchful."

"Yes, Grandfather."

The Orb went clear. Elias held out his hand and Daniel put the orb in it.

"Whoah! This is great!"

Elias handed it back after turning it over and over. Daniel put it in his rucksack and hitched his horse onto the road. The others followed at a good clip. The sun was at their backs. Daniel and Elias ended up singing silly songs to pass the time and Matthew laughed along with them.

> *The Ploughman and the Drover*
> *Both lived with cows, alack.*
> *The Ploughman ploughed them over*
> *And the Drover drove them back.*
> *Oh – hi-ding a derry, ding a derry o-i-oh!*
> *High ding a derry, sing a derry, Oh I know.*

After an hour of this Matthew begged the boys to stop. It was not the same song for the entire hour but many more songs like it; the kind of songs that children sing in our world when they are on long trips in the backs of cars. They did stop – but only because they both loved Matthew (and maybe a little bit because he could still give each of them a good hiding, since his hands were not on a steering wheel at eighty miles per hour.)

After the songs had left his mind, all Daniel could think about were the warnings of the stranger. They rang in his memory: *'There is no peace for you here. You are in great danger.'* Was this man a prophet? Because if it was Nightbane, why would he warn Daniel? He all of a sudden thought he'd rather be singing again.

"Ready, set, go!"

And Elias' voice brought Daniel out of his reverie. He saw Elias and Matthew tearing off on their horses toward the east. Daniel kicked his steed into motion and let him run. The horse, again, seemed to enjoy the exercise. As Daniel caught up to the two they were already watering their horses in the river a few leagues further along the road. As they had raced along the road though, they had lost sight of the river on their left for those few leagues but now the road and the river were side by side again.

Daniel put his finger to his lips and he and Elias stole away and as quick as a wink the two boys were up to their knees, splashing in the shallow, pleasant waters of the river. They splashed water out at Matthew and the horses. Matthew is the only one who moved out of range. The horses enjoyed the occasional shower of cool water. Matthew whistled and the boys got out. Daniel used his 'hot hands' to dry his legs and feet, but then hesitated to help or touch Elias when Elias looked over at him expectantly.

"Brace yourself."

Elias leaned into the wind from Daniel's hands. Soon, Elias' legs were dry, while his eyes were wide. The boys were on their horses and on the road again for the last few hours of their journey.

They looked off to the South as the sky was growing darker there. The sun was sinking behind the western mountains and twilight was lingering. The grasses of the valley off to the right were moving as if something was traveling through them parallel to their own course. They spurred their horses to greater speed (of course, they weren't wearing spurs, that is just an expression). The grass continued to wave and part as whatever it was passed through and kept up with the horses. They were nearing the place where DragonBeck came down from the mountains and joined with the River Blad. The rustle in the grasses suddenly changed direction – toward them – converging somewhere in the road ahead. The horses were urged forward and fairly flew into and through the waters of the River Blad. Then the grey and brown bodies of the wolves broke through the edge of the grassland and ran up to the bank of the river and howled. Daniel froze – his horse kept moving, but he froze. Deep water – Nightbane – they would be safe until the wolves could find a shallow way across or around. Daniel and party trudged up the trail along the beck and found a campsite on a small island in the middle of the stream. Double protection. They tied their horses at one end of the island and rolled out their bedrolls at the other with a fire in between. Daniel worked on setting up the warding.

He created a small bubble of energy around himself. He then started pushing the sides of the bubble out with his mind and the power in his hands until he had covered the entire little island, had surrounded it with the red bubble of the warding. He was exhausted.

The sky was black with occasional stars appearing and the fire was blazing. Six to eight pairs of eyes appeared out of the darkness. A howl issued, followed by the combined howl of the pack. Daniel walked to the bank closest to the wolves. One wolf charged at Daniel and encountered the energy warding. It hit so hard that its muzzle sizzled and it whimpered and limped back to its fellows. This was so familiar to Daniel. This time he knew who had created the warding. Daniel held out his hands and bolts of lightning again shot from his palms. All of the wolves but two yelped and collapsed. Once shining coats were now singed where death had claimed them.

"Let that be a warning to you, Nightbane."

One wolf looked at Daniel as if startled to hear it's name. It snarled, hatred in its eyes.

"I defeated you in battle two years ago. I have stopped you now. I will not allow you to follow me."

Daniel imagined ropes and chains binding the wolf. And ropes and chains wrapped tightly around the legs, paws and body of Nightbane, who yelped. His companion started gnawing at the ropes. Daniel sent another bolt of lightning and the companion snarled and stared at Daniel but did not go down. The charred flesh and burnt fur of the animal regenerated itself in front of Daniel's eyes. It looked towards Nightbane and then took off into the growing darkness.

"So, Nightbane, you have bitten yourself a companion."

"Don't worry," was snarled through Nightbane's muzzle, "I will not just bite you. I will not be satisfied until I tear you to pieces with my fangs and claws so that you cannot live to become one of us."

"Miraden and I can turn you, Nightbane. He has found a cure, but you must ask for it."

"Never."

"Then lay there. You will be a naked human, and defenseless by morning."

Nightbane reacted to that one. How did this human youngling know so much about him?

Daniel recognized the question in the eyes of the wolf. "I've heard all of the stories. It matters nothing to me either way. I was told not to kill you, but to offer salvation. But I could kill you now, could have killed you a few moments ago, as easily as I killed your pack." His voice was calm, almost serene – but its sound belied the true depths of Daniel's feeling. "Do you know why?" This was difficult for Daniel. "Because I can hate now; because you are the spawn of the ones who taught me to hate. But I obey Miraden, first. I am stronger in my obedience. I swallow my hate. Because of Miraden, I offer you your life and the chance to think about change. Which is more than you did on the Plains of Youth as you massacred children."

Nightbane was silent – impressed, but wary. Who was this

youth? His eyes searched Daniel's. He saw nothing but truth there. It had been a long time since he had been associated with anything or anyone truthful. He reflected back to his days as a human, before Reugella's curse came upon him. He dimly remembered truth – and how he had valued it then. He also saw an enemy in front of him, now. But it confused him because his enemy did not act like an enemy.

"I accept your chance. I will think."

Daniel motioned with his hands and the ropes and chains vanished.

"You are strong for such a young one! I would know your name?"

"I am Daniel Gregoryson."

"The Prophecy!"

"So I am told."

"We <u>have</u> met before." (On the Plains of Youth.) "We will meet again, Daniel Gregoryson."

"I hope you make the right choice, Nightbane. Or our meeting will not be pleasant – for either of us."

With a howl Nightbane departed alone into the darkness. The howls came regularly after that but each sounded further and further away. Daniel returned to the fire to stare at the remains of Nightbane's pack. Daniel collapsed and Elias caught him as he fell. Matthew rushed over and grabbed some chocolate and fed it to him. Daniel revived enough to let it melt on his tongue and swallow. He then let his head fall back into Elias' lap. Matthew brought blankets and covered the boys. He moved his own bedding to be closer to them. They all fell into a deep sleep protected by the energy around them.

Miraden was on the Laketon Road about two leagues from Panagon Hamlet looking west into the Forest of Anan. He had an idea and was there to test it out. He threw a bolt of purple light into the trees and the trees moved aside, actually bent and twisted to dodge the lightning. He then 'popped' to the border where

Forest met mountains on the west. He threw a stone at the trees and it bounced off a warding – some shield was up all along the edges of the forest. He 'popped' to a peak of the Great Southern Range at a point where he could see into the Forest of Anan. He sent off bolts and tossed rocks and saw them either absorbed or deflected by the trees of the forest. He then transfigured into his favorite animal – a little bluebird – and flew north. He soared over a clearing in the forest where he saw a small cottage and lots of activity. He saw a path that wound cleverly northward through the trees, almost like a maze, until it spilled out on the Laketon Road nearer to Ananwater. He flew back over the path, southward, and saw the trees and rocks shift into new positions as the path changed its course like water through sand. This was a clever enchantment and would be difficult to defeat.

Daniel awoke and grabbed some bread and cheese. With his sword in his hand he 'popped' outside the warding to see if he could sense Nightbane's whereabouts. All wolf tracks led to the beck, only one pair plus a pair of bare, human footprints led away. Daniel followed for a few spans and Nightbane rose up out of the grass in front of him. In his human form he was naked and he stared at Daniel out of disturbingly red eyes. But Daniel stared back through his piercing blues. Nightbane's body was hideous and scarred from all the transformations but he was still lean and very strong.

"Acquire Nightbane's cloak!"

A black cloak appeared in Daniel's hand. It stank, literally reeked of unwashed human. He handed it to Nightbane who took it, but snarled.

"Fine trick, Daniel Gregoryson. I have no magic. All I can do is kill. It is all I know. It is all that was left to me."

"I am sorry, Nightbane. There are better things than killing. Choices are better than killing."

Nightbane snarled again and disappeared heading south towards the River Blad. Daniel watched and saw that this time he ran only on two feet, but he was fast.

Daniel returned to his friends. "Nightbane will not bother us again, Matthew. I chased him away to the South."

"Ya did a very dangerous t'ing!"

"It seems that that is all there is for me to do lately!"

He looked at Matthew – directly in the eyes. Matthew looked away.

"Don't be mad at me Da, Daniel."

"I'm not."

Daniel gave Elias a friendly punch in the arm.

"Ow!"

"Sorry!" Daniel thought he had hurt his friend.

"Got ya!" and Elias giggled.

Daniel put Elias in a headlock and gave him what we would call a noogie. Elias screamed and laughed as he could not break away, so they went to the ground rolling. Daniel, as usual, ended up sitting on Elias' chest.

"Ooof. Tub o'lard!" was Elias' assessment of the situation.

"I'll show you lard."

Even though there was not an ounce of fat on Elias' lean body, Daniel poked Elias in the sides, belly, neck, and armpits, pointing it all out.

"Here's some lard. There's some lard ..."

Elias screamed with laughter, because he was horrendously ticklish, but Daniel soon stopped and Elias calmed himself. Then Elias gave Daniel a solid double punch on the inside of each thigh.

"Ow! Ye little beggar!"

Even Elias was a lot stronger than he used to be! Daniel picked up Elias and lifted him high into the air. He had never done that before. It was like Elias weighed nothing. He realized that he didn't know what he was going to do with his best friend now that he had him high over his head. He felt a little uneasy about it and set him down and offered his friend his hand. Elias took it and they stood, eye to eye, not at the same height yet, for Daniel was still taller, but there was present between them a great and playful bond of brotherhood.

"You two gonna start packin' up or start kissin'?" came from Matthew, with a large smile on his face.

"Sorry, Father."

"Sorry, Father Matthew."

The boys rolled up their kits, spluttering and hissing like a couple of snakes all the while. They packed their rucksacks, got their horses ready, mounted up and moved out without any other shenanigans. Daniel led them to the edge of the warding, touched it and it collapsed into his hand. Elias let out another exclamation of wonderment at Daniel's powers.

They turned north and headed for the base of the mountains that hid the Green DragonMount. A slight breeze cut across their path from the west and brought the pleasant early morning smell of heather and other wildflowers to their nostrils. Daniel and Elias started singing again. Matthew just shook his head, joined in and sang along. After all, he knew the songs.

"There once was a lass who filled every glass
With Aradonan brandy.
But the stuff was bad, made the customers mad,
Cause it tasted just like candy.
Then she pulled a flask, didn't even ask,
And she refilled all the glasses.
And the air grew rank, you could say it stank,
For that liquid quickly passes.
Oh, the Panadorian Wine is good.
Caladon makes ale that's dandy!
And the beer in Mirador is fine,
But the best of all,
Is what people call,
Aradonan Brandy!
Oh, oh, oh, Aradon-an Bran-dy!"

This last line was so fully and badly harmonized – they had more fun than finesse – that after the peals of the song faded from off the mountains, there was nothing but silence. It must have scared even the crickets and toads into a hush.

The boys sang that song (and the other songs they loved about bodily functions) at least ten times each. Matthew gradually stopped singing but tolerated it this time, because he remembered what it was like to be a boy! From what he understood from Miraden, Daniel would not get to be one much longer.

They finally arrived at the foot of the great mountains of northeastern Zanadon: The Barrier Peaks, which extended eastward into Balador, northward into Caladon, and southward into Panador and northern Mirador. They tethered their horses and then Daniel got an idea. He constructed, or rather magicked, a corral together where the horses could get grass and water from the beck and walk around instead of being tied to one spot. At Daniel's command trees, little more than saplings, came dancing out of the forest and he lopped them to the proper length and stripped the bark off the boles. The enchanted poles lifted themselves high up in the air and imbedded themselves into the ground. (Under Daniel's direction, of course.) More trees were brought, lopped and trimmed, then were held tight to the uprights as long dry grasses were twisted together and wrapped themselves around the joints to lash them tightly to each other.

Soon the horses were set and three travelers had their packs on their backs. They started up the footpath to the Green DragonMount. The beck gurgled as they traveled. But up ahead they heard the not too far off roar of rushing water. They came to a small pool where the water streamed over a ten span high cliff above them and cascaded down into the pool. It was a terrifically beautiful sight but the problem was that the path dead-ended at the rock face of the cliff in front of them. There appeared to be no footholds or handholds on the sheer-faced, cantilevered cliff with which to climb, either. Daniel threw several 'reveal' charms at the cliff face. There was no magic here. He created a protective bubble, about five spans in diameter and collapsed it to a dome over his and Elias' head. They walked under the falls, in their giant umbrella, which deflected the cascade of water away from them. Behind the falls was a cave-like entrance. Elias wriggled in and before long he appeared at the top of the cliff yelling and waving. Daniel motioned Matthew in and then followed after collapsing his dome. The way was narrow – very tight – but they made it to the top, up a series of ramps that were carved out of stone behind the falls.

From the top, the view to the South across the Valley of Dotham was almost too nice for it to be inside the borders of Zanadon. Maybe things were changing already? Daniel felt that he might be doing some good. From worse to better? The best would be a long time coming. You could just see the Crystal Lake passed the southern peaks of the Barrier Range – called The Peaks of Tranquility. They glistened through the haze of Zanadon's past curses.

The three pushed on and found that the pathway led onward and upward. The trees were mostly scrub oaks and sumacs and many of them were growing right out of the rocks of the cliffs around them. The beck jogged a little to the right and seemed to be coming at them over a series of short cataracts. There was a herd of deer at the top of the last cataract, just across the beck. Deer and Humans stared at each other in fascination for a few minutes until the Humans had to move on.

They came to a narrow pass where two large boulders, flattened on one side, had fallen in from the tops of the surrounding cliffs. The passage, forming the shape of a capital 'A', was tiny and Elias scrambled through it and turned around to grab Matthew's and Daniel's packs and drag them through. Matthew then wedged himself into the opening. Elias pulled from one side and Daniel pushed from the other and Matthew was through. Not that Matthew was fat – not at all – just bigger than the opening, which was proven by Daniel, as he was barely able to get through without help due to the widening of his shoulders and deepening of his chest. He could have shimmied through it easily back when his father was alive.

When they stood up out of the crevice they found that they were in a narrow mountain valley and they could see the DragonMount – unmistakably – across the valley and a little to the right, or east.

They followed the Beck along the little valley to the foot of the DragonMount – about fifteen minutes' walk. They stared up the steep sides of the cliff-based mountain. The cave was a good hundred spans up the side of that cliff. They could see several openings that appeared too small to admit humans – even one of Elias' size. It was also well beyond Daniel's 'popping' range. There was no ledge at all – and no path, no trail or climbing holds with which to get there.

Daniel pulled out his notebook from the rucksack on his back. He examined each page about the Green DragonMount. He kept coming up with nothing that would help him get up to the cave. He found that the layout of the cave was exactly like the other three he had already visited. Once he got there he would know where to go – but how to get up there!

"Where'd ya tike the notes from?"

"What?"

"Wot book?"

"Elias, you're a genius! Acquire "Zanadon's Green Dragons!"

It appeared in his hand. Elias fell back on his buttocks, stupefied and mouth agape. While Daniel thumbed through the book, sitting on a rock, Elias took a swim in the pool at the base of the cliff. He splashed and dove and walked the bottom, for you see, being the son of the Master Fisherman of Mirador, he himself was almost a fish! Daniel, the scholar, read on until Matthew interrupted him.

"Might be it's fed from a spring or somethin'," offered Matthew. For he could see nowhere that the water could be coming from except from down below. This spot seemed to be the origin of the DragonBeck itself.

Daniel found it in the book and his mouth was open to speak as Elias popped out of the water sputtering: "Daniel – come see – I found the entrance!"

"Good! So did I! Return Zanadon's Green Dragons." *I need to take better notes!* was mentally muttered to himself.

The book disappeared as Daniel shucked his clothes, threw Elias his breeches and tied his own breeches around his waist.

"What do we need these for?"

"You'll see!"

"Take a deep breath and follow me!"

Elias surface-dove and Daniel leaped in the water almost on top of him. Elias pointed down and to the cliff base in the clear, deep water and Daniel followed. Elias led Daniel into an underwater cave. The cave finally turned upwards. Daniel was afraid his lungs would burst. But soon enough the boys' heads were above the water of a grotto. Daniel was gasping for air. Elias was breathing easy. Hmm! Daniel's not better at everything. Elias noticed it, was pleased, but remained silent. A small hole in the cliff-face let a tiny shaft of light into the chamber above the water line, but it was enough for them to see the contents of the cave – a ledge, an archway, the roof and the water's surface. They pulled their naked bodies out of the water and onto the ledge.

"The book said it was cold in here. It was right!" Daniel shivered and cupped his hands around his mouth, "Matthew?!"

They heard a far-away-sounding "Yes?"

"We're all right and we're going up to the cave."

"Good – I'll await ye here."

"All right."

Daniel turned and caught Elias staring.

"You're arms and chest are huge. Make a muscle!"

Daniel hesitated but flexed the biceps of his arms. Elias' eyes sprang out of his head.

"Your arms is bigger than me leg!" Elias often lapsed into his regional dialect when he was excited. Most of the time he was able, through recent schooling with Miraden, to lessen the effects of his rural upbringing.

"I told you things were changing."

"Yeah, there's that too! Cor!" Elias shook his head as if to rid it of an unwanted image. Then there was Daniel, larger than life, right in front of him. The image kind of stuck. "I don't t'ink I'll ever get used ta ya bein' all white, neither. Ya don't even have a mole."

Daniel had indeed been marked white by the Light;

irretrievably claimed by the Creators. The only colors remaining on his body were the piercing blue of his eyes and the light pink tint to his lips and nipples.

Daniel, still not completely adjusted to his own changes, broke the moment of the Immortally uncomfortable reminders.

"Hot hands" – and they were dry. Daniel slipped into his breeches. Elias followed suit. "Come on, let's go!"

The boys started through the arched opening at the other side of the ledge onto which they had crawled. They stood up in the opening and the path rose on a slant and in a circular manner away from them.

"When do ya think I'll start?"

"Start what?"

"Changin.'"

"I think you have already!"

Elias looked at him incredulously.

Daniel defended his opinion. "Honest! Look how tall you are!"

Elias stood facing Daniel – their eyes were almost at the same level, maybe a couple of knuckles of difference.

"Cor!"

"Your Da's tall."

"But I'm still skinny!"

"I have two years on you, 'Lias! Everything takes time – or so Miraden says. It just doesn't take much time anymore where I'm concerned!"

Each time they came around to the cliff side of the winding tunnel in their walk upwards, a small shaft of light projected across their naked torsos. After who knows how many turns, but it was a total of twelve, the floor leveled out and they found themselves in a good sized room.

"It's a good thing it's still daylight."

"Daniel, what did the book say about this room?"

"Didn't mention it as far in as I got to read. Guess I should have read further."

The impatience of youth.

It was a strange room; not like one that was at any of the other DragonMounts. There was a long, central wooden table surrounded by a dozen chairs. But the chairs and table were all even a little too short for Elias' legs. There were sconces on the walls most likely meant to hold torches. But where were the torches? A painted crest hung on the wall behind the head chair of the table. It had a yellow, chevron-shaped field with a diagonal banner of red across it from upper left to lower right. Across the field and banner was a green tree or branch, seemingly on fire. It was quite stunning.

There was a large cabinet or armoire on one side with intricate carvings of Dwarves, Humans and Dragons on its doors. A hutch sat on the other side. Hung over the hutch were two gleaming swords with orange hilts crossed across an upright Dwarven battleaxe. There was also a chest or trunk in the corner by the arch through which they had entered. Another trunk was by the arch Daniel supposed they were to exit through. Daniel sat at the head of the table. Elias sat on his right, toward the outside wall and the hutch.

"Light!"

Nothing. Daniel got up and searched the armoire and the drawers of the hutch – they were empty. He walked to the trunk by the entrance – it had a torch – in fact several torches. He placed them in the sconces.

"Light!"

The torches were aflame. Daniel sat again in the chair. He looked over at Elias to say something, and he noticed that his friend's eyes had gone wide at something behind Daniel. Daniel turned in time for two large hands to reach for him and pick him up and place him on his feet on top of the table. The creature, or thing, seemed to stare at him; study him. The thing – which almost looked human but was dark green in color – had the curved boar-like tusks of a warthog growing out of the corners of its mouth, long dark hair, black eyes and a lean human like body. Even standing on the table, Daniel only came up to its chest. It poked Daniel in the stomach, legs, chest, it ruffled his white hair between its huge fingers, pulled at Daniel's breeches, ripping a hole in them at his hip, pulled out the waistband to peer inside and Daniel pulled the cloth back against his belly, ripping another hole in the waist there also. As Daniel's hands grabbed at the ripped places, to keep his breeches up, the thing felt his feet, legs, arms and hands.

"Daniel – what is it?!"

"I don't know!"

It didn't seem to mean any harm, it was exhibiting a great deal of curiosity, but Elias was still terrified.

Then Daniel became terrified as the thing in front of him changed from its monstrous, human-like form into an exact copy of Daniel. White hair, blue eyes, muscular chest, arms and legs – a perfect young warrior. Even Daniel was almost impressed. Then Daniel screamed and jumped back off the table. The creature screamed and jumped back also.

The room was suddenly colder. Daniel and Elias shivered over by the hutch, wishing that they had brought more than just their breeches. How did the Dwarves get in? They can't swim! Daniel eyed the swords. He took one down off the escutcheon and held it to his side. Elias tied the rips closed in Daniel's breeches so that he wouldn't lose them to gravity. The Mirror-Daniel approached the opposite corner. Daniel checked both corners and saw that one trunk was missing. Then he saw the other grow and change into a copy of the first creature as it had first appeared.

"Great – there's two of them. Elias grab the other sword!"

Elias took the blade off the wall. The creature approached Elias and prodded and poked him almost like his partner had Daniel. And suddenly Elias was staring into two green eyes just like his and a face that was a remarkable mirror image of his own surrounded by long, dark hair. His body was lean and strong. But on the Mirror-Elias there were some things missing: clothing and the things that clothing covered up. There was nothing there. Elias started to laugh. Daniel laughed too, as Elias pointed out the mistake.

"What do we do?" was spoken through suppressed giggles.

"I don't know. The book didn't say anything about this."

The Mirror-Daniel approached Elias and the Mirror-Elias approached Daniel. More prodding and poking. Each boy held on to his breeches with his free hand, sword ready in the other. The Mirrors changed and turned into the boy they were currently facing. Daniel and Elias backed up against the outer wall no longer laughing. The Mirror-Daniel that used to be the Mirror-Elias reached for the axe on the wall. It held it above its head. Daniel pushed Elias to make him go around the table – safer there – maybe. Daniel took his hand away from holding up his breeches and extended it outward, palm forward in the direction of the axe, hoping to make it heavy. The creature toppled backwards under the added magical weight and the strange balance of the new object. The axe sliced into the table and stuck there firmly. The creature looked at the axe, the table, at Daniel – and it growled in a very un-Daniel-like voice and rushed at the young warrior, leaving the axe in the table behind him.

Daniel held out his sword and saw his mirror-self merely impale itself onto the blade at the end of his arms. It's blue eyes grew wide as if this was an unexpected happening, and then it slumped forward on to the blade and Daniel's arm, knocking him back into the wall under its weight as it changed back into its towering, nearly human but still monstrous form. As Daniel was wriggling free, the Mirror-Elias approached his original. The younger boy's sword flashed – a slice ran across Mirror-Elias's chest and blood dripped – another slash and the blood gushed from the Mirror-Elias' thigh. A scream erupted from the Mirror-Elias and the boy rushed to his mirror image, driving the sword into what appeared to be his own body. Its green eyes bulged out of its Elias-like face, and its boyish body slumped to the floor. Then it changed back into the creature.

Elias backed up and Daniel caught him. Elias began to shed tears, not cry like a child, but weep, releasing the fears and tensions pent up inside. Daniel comforted him – for he himself had already been in that place where Elias now stood – many times since he and Elias first met had The Miracle of Mirador witnessed death at the end of his own arms. Many times he had won the battle and looked on the face of death in another being. Not something quickly recovered from. Daniel sat down and pulled Elias into his lap and reached his strong arms around his 'little brother' and let him cry. For until now, Elias had not been touched by death in any way. Even his grandparents were still alive.

Elias eventually came to the cessation of his emotions and stood up wiping the wetness from his face and neck; almost in an embarrassed way. Daniel put his arm over the shoulders of his best friend and led him over to the exit archway where they found a set of steps going up. It was a long straight run. Leaving the swords behind, they started up. Daniel stopped abruptly.

"Be right back."

He ran down to the room and grabbed two torches. Not only would they light the way but they would help to warm them up for it was growing colder the longer they stayed in the cave.

At the top of the steps was a long, sloping corridor that seemed to double back in the direction they had just come except that it went further up – higher into the mountain. They also saw a ramp that went down slightly. Hmmm? Which one to take?

"Did you, by any chance, read this far?"

"No, sorry."

A gust of wind came up behind them and blew out the torches. Daniel thought a few seconds.

"Light!"

The torches relit and Daniel chose the upwards corridor. At the top of the ramp they entered a small, domed chamber – much too small for a Dragon, so they couldn't be in the Mount yet. But the walls seemed to move, to be alive with motion. Daniel felt things dropping onto his bare chest and back. Elias felt it too. Everywhere they stepped now in their bare feet, there was a crunch and a squish. Six legs, eight legs, a hundred legs slithered across the boys' skin. They slapped at each other and ran across the cavern. They jumped through the door there, hearing a lot of sizzling as they did so. They went to slap at the remaining bugs, but they had disappeared from their bodies. They looked to the archway of the chamber where the few who tried to escape either popped or sizzled and disappeared at its entrance. The bugs were not allowed out of the room.

Still checking bodies and clothes for possible hitchhikers, the boys found themselves in a long hallway. Satisfied that there were no unwanted travelers, they crept along searching for a door. They reached the end of the corridor, not having found one. They frantically pressed their hands to the walls on a return trip looking for a way out. They knew what was behind them and they did not want to go back there again. But there was no escape – no other egress. It was a dead end. They looked at each other as a sick and disgusted feeling crept across their stomachs.

"Maybe you should've read farther?"

"Maybe I should have?"

"Bugs again?"

"I guess we chose the wrong path."

"Guess <u>you</u> did."

"Eat bugs!"

"Already had some, thanks!" Elias again, diffusing the situation.

The boys laughed and then looked back to the room full of the creepy-crawlies. They carefully made their way there. Daniel touched his torch to the floor and the bugs scattered away, except for those who ended up sizzling on the floor. He pushed his torch ahead of them and Elias placed his torch on the floor, keeping the bugs at bay behind them. They minced across the room, on their tip toes. (Looking kind of like the alligators in the movie 'Fantasia'.) Stepping on burnt bugs was worse than squishing them right off – in bare feet especially! But they made the other side of the room, ready to heave themselves out the door. Daniel turned around.

"Follow me!"

"I 'lready did and look wot it got ... Ahhhhh!"

Elias pointed to Daniel's belly where an arm-long centipede

type thing was crawling either into or out of Daniel's breeches. Daniel grabbed at it. Elias shoved him out of the room. The crawlie popped and sizzled leaving Daniel drenched in bug juice. Both boys checked themselves and found that their bodies were now – once again – insect free.

Then it hit Daniel. "A warding!" Elias just looked at him. "I should have used a red warding to get us through!" Hindsight is a great, but inconvenient teacher.

"Next time," Elias reassured his friend.

"Yeah," Daniel muttered.

They took the slightly down-sloping corridor. At the end of the long slope they found themselves at the base of another set of circular steps. They ran up the steps, torches blazing and bare feet slapping on the stone. It turned out to be a short run and Daniel found himself, suddenly, somewhere familiar. It was the central corridor of a DragonMount.

It's funny how Daniel's life keeps running across those circumstances where he had to make choices: Choices to continue reading, learning; choices as to which way to go when presented with numerous possibilities. Daniel stopped, to gather his thoughts. Elias waited – patiently. Everything in The Prophecy's life was reiterating to him how important the choices in his life were, and also, how with the right preparation – like reading everything in the books instead of just scanning them – he could help to avoid the poorer choices. He began to wonder if these quests were really about the DragonSign. Could they be about another way to educate 'The Prophecy?' Or could a Quest have multiple lessons to be learned and goals to achieve? He liked the second question better than the first, even though the answers to both of them would benefit him.

They hurried to where the cave entrance should be. It was almost completely walled up, leaving just a small opening. Daniel shouted down the 'all's well!' to Matthew below.

"All right?" came the reply.

"Yes! Do we have stories to tell you!" Daniel turned back to the cave. "Light!"

The torches in the corridor blazed to life. Daniel turned and stopped, "Noble Vendamere and Noble Eldradar, we seek for sign to bring you back to life. I am Daniel Gregoryson on a mission for Miraden Light."

With that Daniel took Elias to the hatchery. Elias saw the smashed up eggshells and Daniel handed him a sherd. Daniel also found a green scale in one of the broken eggshells. It was an adult sized scale so it had to have come from one of the parents. He tucked it and the eggshell down the leg of his tattered, now tied up and tight fitting breeches. They went back up and searched the twelve rooms. They found a fang and a claw and Elias put these down the front of his breeches for safekeeping. Daniel pointed and laughed, Elias looked down and blushed and moved the items to the tightness of the cloth at his hip. They ran to the stairs, took them two or three at a time and then came to a dead stop at the ramp to the bug room. With a sideways glance, they shuddered and continued down the slope, then the stairs, and into the chamber with their dead mirror-selves, where they slowed down, easing along the wall in avoidance, afraid that the creatures would come back to life – glad that they had turned green again instead of still looking like corpses of the two boys. Then down the circular ramp they ran, into the grotto. They stripped off their breeches and wrapped up the DragonSign in them securely. Holding their bundles, they dove into the crisp, cool water. Daniel was grateful to be able to wash off the dried bug guts. Elias moved through the water with a minimum of effort. While Daniel seemed to have no problems, Elias just made it look so easy.

As Daniel swam through the grotto, he noticed a set of stairs descending from the interior ledge to the cave bottom under the water. He passed through the entrance and noticed another set of steps from the bottom of the pool, up behind the rocks at the base of the cliff. Why had he not seen them before? Why had he not read about them? Daniel halted his swim for a moment. That's how the Dwarves got in! There must be an enchantment that rid the pool and grotto of its water. He didn't know the words. (He probably should've kept on reading!) So he'd better keep swimming because he surely couldn't breathe down here!

They were at the surface of the pond and Matthew was there to haul them out. He wrapped their shivering bodies in the bedroll blankets and warmed them up by the fire. Matthew had fixed dinner so there was something warm for both the inside and the outside of their bodies. They unwrapped the DragonSign. Elias handled and fondled the strange items. He had never imagined that with all the stories of Dragons, they were real. But here was the evidence – in his own two hands – gathered by those hands. Daniel watched his little brother. He hoped that the expressions on his own face at the sight of his first DragonSign were close to the wonder on Elias' face now. As Elias finished examining the green scale he put it, with the other sign, in Daniel's rucksack. Daniel took their breeches and did his 'hot hands' thing. Daniel thought *Weave it, mend it, no more tears or rips.* And the monsters' slashes re-knit themselves as Elias watched in further fascination. They put on their breeches after holding them to the warmth of the fire to make sure they were good and warm; kind of like when we run down to the clothes dryer and take out the clothes still warm and put them on after a cold day of sledding, snowball throwing, skating, or even after a day of swimming!

They ate. They were dry. They were warm. It was dark and they were tired. They curled up in their bedrolls and were asleep before they had the presence of mind to tell Matthew about the stories of their day.

Ah, well, Matthew thought, *I'll hear all about it in the mornin'.* Matthew cleaned up, tinkered around, then sacked out himself. Waiting around to be assured of the safety of your son and his best friend can be a very wearying experience.

The night was a restless one for both boys. Not that they didn't sleep. They did. But they dreamed. They shared a recollection of their trip through the Green DragonMount. Elias startled a couple of times. He cried. He heard himself yell out, not in his sleep but inside the dream. He saw his own dead body, pierced through with a giant sword, change into a monster. His father snored on but Daniel awoke and reached across Elias and cradled him close; just like he had his real little brother, Abraham, when he had had a night-fright. Daniel's dreams, too, had been disturbing. Elias snuggled into Daniel and they fell asleep again.

In the morning Matthew found the boys still snuggled close to each other, not having moved from their position after their dreams. He didn't wake them, but he did wondered what could have happened inside that cave. He was certainly grateful for the strong, upright youth that Daniel was becoming, because it was helping his own son to act in the same manner, with the same courage and strength. Matthew puttered with breakfast and through his noise the eyes of the boys opened. Elias turned his head and they both looked at each other. Daniel nodded toward Matthew, whose back was to them, puttering. Elias turned over to stare at Daniel. His green eyes bored into Daniel's blues.

"Thanks" came from Elias' mouth. Daniel just nodded.

Miraden was in the Mountains of the North speaking with Urso North, the leader of the Dwarven Clan of North. He was requesting their help in keeping the Taradalnock out of the Realms. Somehow these mercenaries were sneaking through the desert or over the pass near the Dwarves' home – or coming in somewhere else. The Clan had friends both Human and Dwarven throughout the eastern borders of Balador and Panador. They would all be watching! No one would get through if they had anything to say about it!

Miraden then 'popped' back to various positions around the Forest of Anan. There seemed to be no increase in the wardings or in the activity in the forest – yet.

The sunlight slowly crept into the narrow valley of the DragonBeck as Matthew, Elias and Daniel made their way down the canyon to their horses. On their trip down they told Matthew of the wonders and dangers of the cave, of the bugs and their 'deaths.'

"Your deaths?"

Daniel explained and Matthew's features grew dark and concerned. He hugged Elias to him a little more tightly. Daniel should call on Miraden. Daniel did so and Miraden expressed the same concerns.

"Two, you say? Only two?"

"Yes, Grandfather."

"Then there should only be six more. Somewhere."

"But what are they."

"Morphalls – changelings – Dark but stupid creatures. The only way they can learn is to change into things and experience by doing. It is good you killed them when you did, before they learned how to think like you. Give them enough time and you would have had real trouble. You would have been fighting yourself with your opponent knowing every move you made before you made it."

The orb went clear. Something must have drawn away Miraden's attention.

They were at the top of the falls. They entered the tunnel and Daniel had his warding ready when they stepped out under the cascade of the falls. They came out dry and moved down to the corral. The sight that met their eyes there, filled them with horror.

Miraden was called away from the orb by a sudden development in the forest. A shaft of, well, there is no other way to describe it, black light, not the halloweeney stuff, but true black light (as in absence of light, black) ascended in a pillar of Darkness from the clearing in the forest near the cottage of Guildenblad. Miraden grew alarmed. He 'popped' to the slopes of the mountain nearest the clearing. He tried to get some sense of the dark beam. This was not good. He transformed to his bluebird self and flew towards the clearing. As he looked down, the black light was streaming out of the bell of a cauldron.

Something had been brewing and had either gone very wrong (we hope, we hope, we hope!) or unfortunately right. (Please no, please no, please no!) A flash of red light missed him by a knuckle or two but, thinking quickly, he pretended to be hit and dropped to the tree tops where watching eyes could no longer see him. He waited. He transfigured to a squirrel and scampered down the limb to the bole of the tree. He noticed why he had been spotted: there appeared to be no other animals in or above the forest. Then a branch took a swipe at him.

At the corral, their horses – all three – were slashed, torn, bitten, bloody and dismembered. As they entered the fence, Nightbane appeared across the paddock from them – calm, serene – menacing in his silence.

"Let us see how great an Enchanter you are Daniel Gregoryson. I'll be watching."

"I will also be watching you, Nightbane."

Daniel took Elias and Matthew by the hands and thought, very fiercely concentrated on, the confluence of the DragonBeck and the River Blad. He breathed, squeezed their hands and they were there.

Nightbane was suddenly alone at the corral – surprised – maybe even disappointed. He now had a lot of thinking to do. This Daniel Gregoryson was even more prodigious than he had heard.

Daniel was amazed, himself. Elias was shocked. Matthew was speechless. Daniel had just transported them over ten leagues. Before, he couldn't even do fifty arms by himself!

"If I'd known I could do that I would have 'popped' us up into the cave. We wouldn't even have had to use the stairs."

"But then there would be all sorts of things that you wouldn't know about – you would have missed the opportunities to learn. Right, Daniel?" Miraden had also appeared; right behind them, at the moment of their appearance.

"Yes, Grandfather!" was said from a tight hug.

Miraden rested his hand on Daniel's head. He saw the mixture of emotions roiling behind the eyes of both Daniel and Elias. He reached out and cupped the back of Elias' head in his magical hand. It felt full of healing and comfort to the boy, who pressed back against the hand, almost nuzzling against it.

"One stop on the way and then I'll have you two home."

With a look at the grateful Matthew, he then 'popped' them all to the Crystal Dome, the home of the United Orb and Sceptre itself. The Matthewsons were spellbound by the power streaming from the Crystal Orb and Sceptre. They had never even been in the room before. They stood and gawked while Miraden and Daniel approached the source of power and wonder. Daniel was not fully certain as to what they were doing here. He looked back at Elias. Miraden held out his hands. Elias pointed behind Daniel and Daniel turned and put his hands in his grandfather's. Miraden squeezed and then closed his eyes. Daniel closed his and squeezed back. Elias and Matthew saw the power in the room begin to shift and change. It detoured from its straight up course through the apex of the dome, to wind and curl around and down, enveloping the bodies of the Enchanters. Elias took a step forward but Matthew restrained him.

Miraden and Daniel were lifted up, off of the floor. They turned slowly as the streams of white appeared to caress their bodies. Father and son watched silently as their friends seemed to be deep in some sort of trance. It was not long, several minutes maybe, before the power shifted again and Miraden and Daniel were gently deposited onto the floor of the room as the beam of light straightened out and sped towards the roof once more.

Elias could not begin to form his thoughts into words. "That was ... I ... what ..."

Matthew wrapped his arms about his son and pulled him to him. Miraden smiled and extended his hand to the boy. Elias took it and felt a keen warmth coming from it, infusing his own body. Daniel smiled quickly at the sight of his friend and grandfather. But his smile faded as Miraden looked at him.

"That has never happened before."

"What, Grandpa?"

"There was no answer. I could not see anything."

"All I saw was light," Daniel offered.

"That's all we saw, Uncle Miraden."

Matthew nodded.

"The Orb could not see into the Forest of Anan. There is greater power there than I had imagined. I will have to reevaluate our tactics. I cannot imagine where such power could come from ..."

"What power?"

"Dark power."

Matthew looked at Daniel, Daniel looked at Elias and Elias looked back at Daniel. Matthew spoke. "I know little of such t'ings, Miraden, but it seems to me that power of that magnitude is centered on more than a Necromancer."

Miraden nodded. "My thoughts precisely."

"So, what does that mean, Grandpa?"

"It means that we may have to look beyond the Forest of Anan. The missing Talismans may have given power to Guildenblad as well as weakened the borders of the Realms by their absence. Plus, their loss has diminished the power within the Realms."

"But we can still work magic."

"Our power comes directly from the Creators and is magnified by the Orb and Talismans. We still have our Talisman."

"So there are four kingdoms in danger?"

"Four for sure. Maybe all six. But I also think that in not being able to see what I wanted to see, I have received an answer of another sort." Miraden chuckled. He rubbed his hands together. "Guildenblad is not as clever as he thinks he is. I sense that his power comes from elsewhere. He is a conduit, not the sole originator of power. Once he is stopped, then we will have to deal with whoever else it is who is supplying that power and support."

"They are interfering in our choices, right Grandpa?"

Miraden nodded, then held his hands out to the three. They

159

joined hands and Miraden 'popped' them back to Harborton where they said goodbye to Matthew and Elias, who had plenty of stories to tell their family. Miraden and Daniel continued on to the Pinnacle with more DragonSign to cultivate. They also had Nightbane and Morphalls to worry about. Not to mention the Taradalnock Brethren, and Guildenblad – and whoever it was that was behind him!

ML

CHAPTER TWELVE
APPRENTICE∫HIP
(3rd Month)

AS DANIEL WAS FACING HIS fears again at the Plains of Youth; while Boncaster was walking into Panadar Village at the juncture of the High Road and Laketon Road; Guildenblad was busy in the Forest of Anan. The night potion he was brewing, which would turn every creature of the forest to his whim, was bubbling nicely. He had been rounding up all of the animals of the forest for months now and had cages full of them everywhere, protected by his invisibility wardings. There was not an animal to be seen anywhere except inside the cages within his glade. If the charms he had placed on the forest failed, if the wardings did not repel, if specially created magical creatures did not succeed, he knew his night creatures would triumph. This was a strange potion – it changed nothing on the outside of the creature – a squirrel still looked like a squirrel, even acted like a squirrel as long as there were no Human or Dwarven enemies around. But when an enemy was sensed, the bites and scratches from any of these cute and cuddly little animals was deadly! And the potion made them attack anything that entered the forest, especially if magic could be sensed in the being. Guildenblad almost committed the most unforgivable sin in his book – he almost smiled.

Panadar Village was an atypical village with a central residential green off of which people built row-houses. This green joined to the market square where the farmers and ranchers would sell their products in open air stalls surrounded by the merchants, inn and tavern of the Village. The beautiful little two-storey houses were made of brick and wood with stone chimneys and foundations. The green was large enough to accommodate about sixty houses, twenty on each of three sides of it, all with front doors facing the green. In the corners of the residential area were two rooming houses – one for the single men and the other for the single women, fifteen and over who had no other family to live with. As the green met the market square a cobbled type of courtyard took over and the stores and shops made another 'u-shape', except for the alleyway in the center of the short side, which led out to the High Road. As a result of this planning there was no traffic in the village proper. All roads were outside the enclosure. But the town was so popular that another little green-square arrangement was being constructed on the other side of the High Road. They may graduate from village to town soon. Then, from a townsman to a mayor. Farms and ranches were located outside the village limits so there would be room enough for people, crops and animals.

The brown-clad figure following Boncaster was seen working through the busy market crowd, trying to keep up with Boncaster as he entered the Graceful Grouse, the largest Inn and Tavern on the square, to take a room for the night. Boncaster entered the halved-door, we call them Dutch-doors, and the brown-clad figure waited and watched outside. When Boncaster came back out the brown-clad figure entered and took a room also.

Boncaster roamed the market buying his dinner. The Inn seemed a little too expensive with meals included, for his apparent station in life, and he had eclectic tastes in food anyway, so he had gotten only a sleeping room. He bought some small cheeses, a loaf of bread and a small flask of sweet wine from the open-air merchants. Then he procured a small cake, from the Baker's shop in the corner of the square. He then plunked himself down on the edge of the green and ate his supper. He was roundly smacked by a ball hit by the children who were playing a game similar to our lacrosse.

They apologized profusely and Boncaster tossed the ball back into play, not remembering the many games he had played as a youth, and the children screamed off chasing the ball and each other, and trying to be careful not to hit the nice man again.

The brown-clad figure had re-emerged from the Inn after feasting on stews, bread and wine. Boncaster was content with simpler fare. He didn't need to waste money. Boncaster finished his meal and returned his flask to the little wine seller who returned to him half a pence in exchange for the empty bottle. He proceeded to the Inn and paused in front of the brown-clad figure.

"Why are you following me? Who sent you?"

The brown-clad figure tried to walk away but Boncaster grabbed his arm.

"Let go unless you want to lose your hand!" the figure warned.

"Ah – a young pup just off his milk and trying to prove he's a man and doing a very poor job of it."

"So you say!"

"Yes, I do say!"

The brown-clad figure wrenched his arm away and fled to the green. Boncaster followed, smiling, and caught up to the figure as they charged through the middle of the children's game.

"Who sent you? Guildenblad? The King and Queen? Miraden?"

"No one sent me." There was a sigh from the person hidden inside the dark cowl. "I merely wanted to travel with you and didn't have the courage to ask you up front. There. Now, you know."

The figure just stood there, shoulders slumping.

"But you had the courage to come, to follow?" Had Boncaster gone too far?

"Yes – I did."

"Even though you're masquerading as a man – Princess Rose?"

"No – I – How did you guess?"

"Most would not, I suppose. You're pretty convincing – 'pretty' being the operative word. But I know you, your manners, your voice; your walk. It is still a little soft for a young man."

"I'll show you how soft ...!"

Rose raised her hand to slap him but he caught it, laughing. Not at her but at the situation. She smiled. He let go of her hand. Only a little. She still did not laugh. If there was one thing that Rose could claim to be successful at it was being stubborn.

"I must come with you now. I just must! The Blood Rose was partly my responsibility!"

"I do not mind your company."

"You don't?"

"No.

It's your tongue I mind!" and he laughed. "Two heads could be better than one. But four arms are not if two of them are useless. What can you do?"

"I am a fair marksman. I can handle a staff – not as well as you, but I hold my own. It also helped to have only a brother to fight with!"

"Fine. But you must stay a young man. Let's see – Sebastian – no – Cesario – no – Ganymede? Yes! A perfect name for a woman in disguise."

Rose shot him a doubtful look, "I preferred Sebastian."

"It doesn't suit you. You have mystery."

She smiled, 'Why do I have to be a boy at all?"

"They do it all the time in stories and plays. Women are always disguised as men."

"That is only because not enough men are man enough to be actors so they must cast a woman or a boy. And to make it easier for the woman to play a man they have the female character play a young man. It is for convenience only!"

"Yes, it does sound convenient."

"Oh, all right! Ganymede it is."

They shook on it.

"Besides, a man is less likely to be attacked by other types of lowlifes! Now, it's sleep we'll need to be at our best tomorrow. I'll see you after sunup."

"Yes. Goodnight, Boncaster. And thank you."

"Goodnight, my – Prince."

Boncaster strode into the inn smiling. Rose lingered a moment or two enjoying the coolness of the evening and watching the children play. She almost didn't mind being found out. A burden shared is a burden lightened. Then the parents called their children in for the night and the open air market dismantled itself for another day. She wandered across the cobbles towards the Inn. As she was about ten spans away, five men in black cloaks, on horseback, came to a crushing halt at the alleyway near the door of the Inn. A boy got up off the stool by the door and walked up to the men. They dismounted and each of them threw the boy a penny and the reins to their mount, and went inside the Graceful Grouse. The boy led their horses to the stables behind the Inn to be cooled, curried, fed and watered. Rose had seen it all and wondered who those men could be. She'd never seen their like before.

All too soon, there were crashes from inside of the Inn. The door opened and two men were ejected through the door so that they fell to the cobbles gagging and sputtering. Through the open door Rose heard:

"Now you have two rooms that you can rent to us, Innkeeper! Praise Dal!"

The door closed. Rose walked over to the men on the ground in front of her. When she got close enough she saw that their throats had been cut from ear to ear and they were not moving. There was nothing she could do to help them, after all. Those five men had killed them for a room to sleep in! This was definitely unheard of in the Realms of the Crystal Orb

Inside the inn, the noise was deafening, the laughter raucous and the food and drink over-plentiful. The Great room of the

Graceful Grouse had been taken over by the black-cloaked men whose cloaks were hanging on the wall. No others were present in the room as they were probably upstairs cowering in their rented quarters. The five men all wore the same habiliments and long hairstyles. Their eyes, brown; their skin, tanned and leathery. Most wore beards. Their tunics, breeches, boots and chemises – all were black. They wore long curved swords at their waists and two shortened curved daggers were tucked into their belts; ready to be grasped by either hand. Their weapons were made of black steel in black scabbards. The only color on their bodies was a little red symbol located on their headbands and on the hilts of their weapons.

That symbol was also tattooed on their skin underneath their left eye.

They were Taradalnock. Rose didn't know what it meant as she entered and crossed to the stairs. They quieted down in seconds and watched him/her cross the room. Some whistled and some guffawed. Boncaster appeared at the foot of the stairs and startled Rose. He motioned to her to say nothing. She passed him by and tripped up the stairs – literally. The men laughed and Rose ran up the steps where a door slammed. Boncaster took a seat at the table nearest to the stairway.

The men watched Boncaster. He was brought a mug of ale by the serving girl, which he drank as she scuttled quickly to the back room. They went back to talking, in lower voices, amongst themselves, with only occasional glances at Boncaster. Soon, they were back to their boisterous, room-clearing worst.

"From whereabouts do you gentlemen hail?"

Silence.

Five men stood with hands on swords and daggers.

"Since when is our business your business?"

"Just trying to start a polite conversation."

"We do not 'converse' with the infidels of Panador."

"Well, then you can talk to me because I am not from Panador."

Silence. Hatred in their eyes.

"Makes no difference to me. But you are the guests here. This is not your home, your native land ..."

"It will be soon."

His fellows shushed him – that was too much – yes, too much drink can set any tongue wagging.

"Pity to think that five men could hope to take a Kingdom."

"With fools like you to stop us? It will not take long."

Now Boncaster was getting to them. That was it! The men rose with daggers drawn. Boncaster sat still along the side of the table. The men approached him laughing.

"Poor fool!"

Five swords and five daggers in ten hands – the swords raised as if to slice a man into fifths. They were within striking distance now and Boncaster acted. His staff, from under the side of the table's edge, was in his hands and whirling and four swords were shattered with the first blow and sent to the floor in pieces. Two skulls were stove in with the second blow. Boncaster faced three men with three daggers and one sword. He liked these odds better.

"Wouldn't you prefer a little conversation to death, friends?"

The three backed up to the door, the top half of which suddenly burst open, knocking two of the three into Boncaster's reach. He brained one, who hit the floor with a dull thud. The other's back was broken by the power of Boncaster's back swing. The third rushed to the door with his sword flailing and ended up impaled on Rose's Panadorian blade. The man's eyes went wide and his last words formed as "Praise Dal!" bubbled blood across his lips.

Rose simply stepped out of the way, tilted her sword toward the ground and the man slipped out the door, off her blade and laid there leaking blood all over the once clean cobbles of the square.

"Who's Dal?"

"Probably their god. We'll have to ask Miraden. We should see him along the road later today. Better clean these up."

"Too bad we didn't get any information from them."

"They weren't in a talkative mood."

They dragged the bodies of the Black Warriors to the center of the Market Square and had the Innkeeper and the boy bring wood for a funeral pyre. This was the Panadorian custom and enemies should always be taken care of immediately. The two slit-throated travelers would be given their final rites at noon – later today, as befitted citizens of Panador.

"Well, Apprentice Gardener Ganymede, it is now time to try to get what sleep we can. We leave at six."

"Six hours, I'll see you then."

"And thank you."

"For what?"

"For having two arms that work."

They laughed as they shuffled up the stairs leaving the Innkeeper and the boy to tend to the burning bodies. The Great room remained empty for the night. No one dared come down. What could possibly top the defeat of five by two?

CHAPTER THIRTEEN
BAD DWARF
(3rd Month)

MIRADEN WAS PAGING THROUGH ANOTHER book, <u>Sad So Sad, When A Dwarf Goes Bad</u> by Aradella Light. (Miraden's first wife.) Her sense of humor was evident and he missed it terribly. As he read, the memories tumbled into him.

The Dark Creatures were created during the Age of Magic, and as she discovered them, she wrote down the spells and enchantments that had been used to create them or turn them. Then she created the other potions to counteract the turnings. So, spells and counter-spells were written down, carefully. And Miraden was not just reading, he was adding the latest creations of Tophet, from the scrolls he found. His own counter-spells and other methods to destroy the created creatures, were also added to the document. He had to keep the book up to date.

With the book about curing and/or killing turned creatures, not just Dwarves, Miraden was hopeful that he finally had a weapon to use against the present Darkness. But after reading the whole thing through several times, and adding the new information, he closed the book with a sense of disappointment and resignation.

Guildenblad and his brother probably would have to be killed. There was no way around it. He regretted it, but there was nothing more that could be done. But it was possible to turn

Nightbane – and maybe the other remaining Morphalls, also. He was glad that Daniel had done as instructed and planted the seed of change in Nightbane's mind. Maybe it would reach his unbeating heart?

The Dark creations had not been given the chance of a choice in the first place as to how their lives were to be conducted. They found that the act of their creation forced them to do the cruel things of the world to gain the selfish ends of their Dark Masters – their creators: the Dark Sorcerers and Sorceresses. The creatures were bound to them. And it was all they knew.

It was sad to Miraden, and Daniel, also, to think of killing something – someone, even Guildenblad – who had no part or choice in determining whom he was to be or what he would obey. Compulsion was the way of the Dark, not the Light. One choice brought freedom – the other, slavery.

Miraden was determined to give the Dark creatures their choice. They deserved that; at least he thought so.

He had been looking for a way to cure a Necromancer, a Vampire and a Werewolf – two Dwarves and a Human turned: Guildenblad, Rosenblad and Nightbane. He had found that the same potion worked on curing Vampires and Werewolves, whether created from Dwarf or Human. But the turning of a Necromancer – that potion was strange and complicated and it took decades to brew; just like it had taken a thousand years to create him. He would probably have to settle for destroying Guildenblad. In all actuality, Guildenblad was already dead. It was only Dark Magic that was keeping him 'alive.' So it was the magic that had to be destroyed for Guildenblad to finally be able to die.

Most of the citizens of the Realms believed in the Creators and in the powers endowed to the Race of Enchanters. They followed the precepts that had wisely been laid down for them. They did it because they wanted to – because their friends and neighbors did – because they chose to; because an example was set for them.

Miraden was aware that there were other citizens who didn't

necessarily support the Creators, but believed very strongly in choosing the way that would make all happy – not just one that would content themselves. After all they were each a part of a community.

Then Miraden reflected on those persons who chose not to believe in either of the better choices. Most of them ended up journeying beyond the borders of the Realms, never to be heard from again. They could get out through the wardings surrounding the Realms; but once out, they could not get back in! Or at least they weren't supposed to be able to.

A disturbing thought began to nibble at Miraden's consciousness: *How did those Taradalnock arrive?*

"This's gross, Uncle Miraden. 'ow many fish 'earts does 'is potion tike?" balked Elias.

"Three dozen for the scale, one dozen for the claw and one dozen for the fang."

The boys were making the preparative paste to cure the DragonSign before it would be needed later.

"I'm never eating fish again, Grandpa."

Miraden laughed.

"Then ya better not come over ta our 'ouse fer dinner!"

They all laughed, for, Elias and his father, were fishermen by trade. The boys returned to the mashing of the fish hearts into a paste. They added roach antennae and yak urine to the mix to preserve and prepare the Green DragonSign for resurrection. Each color of Dragon needed a different kind of paste.

"Who thinks this stuff up, Grandpa?"

"It's all in the books," was a dismissal by Miraden.

"Who wrote the books?" inquired an innocent Elias.

No comment from Miraden.

"Yak urine? Disgusting!"

Daniel and Elias shifted from foot to foot as they finished their work standing at the laboratory table while Miraden read at his desk. Miraden kept scrawling out list after list of ingredients for various turning potions with his quill.

At last the preparative potions were in the beakers and the DragonSign had been situated amid the paste. The boys capped the beakers and placed them on the shelves with the other DragonSign – White, Blue, Gold and now Green – They were on their way to resurrection. Soon, Dragons would live again!

The boys, task done, were looking for a snack. They found it.

"Which is which, Grandpa?"

"Which is which which?"

"The chocolate. There's two stacks."

"Daniel's chocolate is on the left and Elias' is on the right."

Each reached for a bar and marched out of the cave.

"Green DragonSign's done! We're goin' swimmin'."

"Thank you, boys!" Miraden was entirely and truly grateful. It was nice to have company again. And assistants!

They raced to the ledge at the mouth of the cave and looked out over the waters of the Crystal Lake with the Crystal City shimmering in the distance. Everywhere he chose to look, there was something spectacular and magical. Daniel was convinced that the true Miracle of Mirador was in its very creation. He held out his hand to Elias and Elias took it. He then thought, *I can see the nearest lake shore down below – right down there in the bay – I want to be there.*

Pop!

And they were there. It was another beautiful, warm spring day. The water was most refreshing. They splashed each other; they played dunkem', where Daniel lifted Elias out of the water and threw him, laughing and limbs flailing, back into the water a span away. Elias would try it with Daniel but usually managed only to get him just out of the water before having to drop him back in it – but it was fun. They raced – and Elias usually won those, as he was a near perfect swimmer. Daniel was strong but Elias was born to the water and his body seemed to slice through it. They climbed up on the high rocks overlooking the bay and they dove – tricks and flips and twists – Daniel was the better diver and really quite good. Elias didn't care about fancy, he just loved hitting the water, parting it with his hands, sliding through the cool wet and then breaking up through the surface again.

"Dinner time!"

The boys raced to the shore and Elias won. Daniel 'hot handed' the water off his own body. Then he pointed his hands at Elias and the burst of wind knocked Elias onto his butt. "Sorry." Daniel placed Elias against the rock.

"Brace yourself."

Elias held on and Daniel 'winded' him, which whipped the water off his skin, front and back. (He looked a lot like someone in a modern wind-tunnel.) They dressed and Daniel 'popped' them up to the cave.

"What's for dinner?"

"Fish!" came the reply.

Still hungry after dinner, as what little fish they could choke down didn't really fill them up, the boys each kiped a bar of chocolate and went out to Daniel's thinking rock and let the candy dissolve on their tongues as the sun melted into the western mountains on the horizon.

Miraden found them, later, staring at the lake. He almost hated to interrupt their peaceful reverie, but interrupt he must.

"Boys?" He was leaning on his staff. "I have another mission for you. There are just too many things happening and I need your help. I cannot be everywhere at once. This particular mission has no inherent danger. But what will happen after the mission – Elias – I need your promise now that you will come directly home when told to do so."

"O' course, Uncle Miraden."

Miraden told them of the Taradalnock Brethren, most of which Daniel already knew, but Elias was paying close attention, fascinated. They were to find the weakness in the warding wall of the Orb, where the mercenaries were sneaking through. He would be transforming them both to hawks, but once the boys had found the break, Elias was to return here to the cave and Daniel was to go on to the Red DragonMount for the DragonSign there.

"As a hawk?"

"Yes. I will give you the charm to affect your change once you fly there. I will change Elias once he returns here."

The boys agreed to do it. Miraden told them that they would leave tomorrow.

"Now, go and hop into bed."

"Oh, Grandpa – why so early?" Even if it was midnight it would have been early! Boys!

"Because I know it will take you hours to get to sleep!"

Daniel grabbed Elias' hand and he 'popped' them in to bed. Daniel thought it – one minute they were on the rock outside the cave and the next they were lying on the covers of Daniel's federdekked bed. Daniel looked over at Elias and smiled. Elias returned the smile with anticipation.

"Hawks!"

"Yeah! Flying!"

"Daniel?"

"Yeah?"

"Aw, nothin'. Never mind."

Daniel poked and goosed Elias who returned the poking and prodding with equal abandon. They were poking and laughing and giggling and goosing – a regular riot on the bed. After a while they laid back, hands behind their heads, elbows spread, looking at the intricacies of the rocks in the ceiling with thoughts about their fortunate circumstances. They had friendship, they had family, health, youth; all those things that boys can't usually seem to find the appreciative words for. Those were the things that washed over them with the warm contentment of silence. They drifted off to sleep and when Miraden came in to check on them he was surprised to find them really asleep. He pulled the covers over them and whispered,

"Light out."

The room was in darkness and the Enchanter went to his chair on the ledge to think and plan and hope that all would work out in the end. He had a certain knowledge about the Creators that no one else on Colabos possessed. But there were times that his knowledge was tested, his faith was tried and his hope was pushed to a breaking point. The end, he had found, was always a desired result. It was getting to that end that was troubling – even problematic.

The next morning Elias woke early, looked over at Daniel still sleeping, and got out of bed to take care of his morning duties. When he got back Daniel was stirring and Elias had a smirk on his face. Elias, repeatedly looking toward Daniel then retreating and looking down at his own hands, finally worked up the nerve to ask the question that had plagued him most of the night.

"Who's Tilly?"

Daniel's face went as white as his hair. Well, it was already white – but it went whiter. (If that was possible.) He had not told anyone about Tilly! Only Miraden knew.

"She yer girlfrien'?"

"How do you know about Tilly?"

"'ow could I not know about 'er? You were sayin' 'er name 'alf the night."

Daniel turned even a brighter shade of white. "She's a girl I met when Miraden took me over to Laketon Hamlet for the Spring Festival," was mumbled through his extra whiteness.

"She yer girlfrien'?"

"I like her."

"Did you kiss 'er?"

"No. But I think about it – a lot!

Both boys smiled at the implications of that statement.

"Then she kissed me."

"Whoah! Wot's it like?"

"Tingley."

"Tingley?"

"All over!"

"All over?!"

Silence, a smile, then a nod from Daniel.

"Whoah!" then Elias got quiet. 'Do ya like 'er mor'n me?"

"I'll like you forever – no problem there. But I don't even really know her yet. Who knows? She and I could end up hating each other. Like her more'n you? Naw. Differently from you? Yeah. 'Sides, I can't marry you – but I could marry her. You'll always be there, Elias!"

"Not always." Elias was all too aware of his own mortality – and Daniel's Immortality.

Now Daniel became silent. He realized what had made Elias sad and he loved him all the more for it. He voiced a secret wish.

"I wish you <u>could</u> always be there."

"Yeah. Me too."

Miraden had been watching and listening. "Here's breakfast!"

"Wot is it?"

"Chocolate, bread and tea."

He held up his hand and onto it came a little salver with two sets of each of the items mentioned and he placed it before them on the bed.

"Which is which?"

"Daniel left, Elias right, as usual, Elias is always right!"

"Hey, Grandpa, no fair!"

Daniel pouted while Elias snickered. Daniel gave him an elbow.

"Are you sure you've got the right chocolate, Grandpa?"

"Absolutely positive."

After they dressed, the boys launched into their tasty breakfast, one they were sure their mothers would never have approved of, and soon it had been polished off.

"Time for a mission! First we'll pop over to wait for Boncaster. He'll help with the procuring of the ingredients for the potions. Ready?"

They nodded, all joined hands and Miraden 'popped' them to the Laketon Road, just a little south of Panadar Village, near AnanWater, to await the arrival of Boncaster.

ℳ

CHAPTER FOURTEEN
RED QUEST BY REQUEST
(3rd Month)

BONCASTER AND GANYMEDE, EACH ASTRIDE two coal black chargers, came down the Laketon Road from Panadar Village. The people of Panadar had given them the horses, grateful for the service they had rendered in defending the village from the Taradalnock. The two talked about Panador and this mission; spoke of life past, present, and hope for the future; how they appreciated the horses; how Ganymede (Rose) appreciated Boncaster's help with the gardens. In the road ahead were a man and two boys. Boncaster reined in as they came abreast of the little group.

"Boncaster! And who's this?"

"Ganymede." Rose said nervously.

Daniel was not to be fooled. "Oh, no – you are not Ganymede! He is a friend of mine."

Rose gave a look to Boncaster like, *'You betrayed me?'*

Daniel continued, "You are that rotten and spoiled Princess Rose of Panador!"

Rose's jaw dropped. "How did you know, Daniel?"

He almost said that he never forgot a pair of lips – especially when they were his first – but he settled for: "I never forget the tormentors of my childhood."

Who are you kidding, Daniel – like that tickling incident was more than days ago? It was a good cover anyway.

"Tormentors?"

"My ribs and armpits still hurt!"

"So do mine!" quipped Elias.

Daniel gave him a playful punch.

Boncaster and Rose dismounted and they left the road with Miraden's party.

"It's good to see you again, at least, Daniel."

"It's good to see you too, cousin." Daniel's smile was, perhaps, a little too broad, thinking of that kiss and the possibilities that it raised.

They sat by the shores of the northern tip of AnanWater. It was a small but breathtaking lake, rimmed by trees and mountains and reflecting the clear blue of the Panadorian sky. Miraden told them of Guildenblad and the wardings and other possible dangers of the forest – creatures he could not yet describe, but would be able to soon. He talked of the mercenaries, the men in black capes, and Boncaster and Rose shared a quick glance between them.

"You know of them?" asked Miraden.

"We had to kill five in Panadar Village last night."

"Whoah!" came from the boys.

"We are riding two of their horses – a gift from the villagers. Who are they?"

Miraden told them what he knew, who they were associated with, and to plan on their presence around the Anan Forest.

Boncaster assured Miraden. "We can kill Taradalnock. But how do we kill Guildenblad?"

Miraden thought. *There is more to this 'gardener' than I see in front of me.* "First we make a potion – and he must drink it somehow – it will turn him mortal for just a very few minutes. Then his heart must be pierced and he must be burned and then decapitated. It is the only way to destroy the spell cast in a Necromancer, for you see he is already dead. It must happen fast while his tissues are still living again."

"Where do we get this potion?"

"We must gather it, and Daniel must brew it."

"Me, but I can't do ..."

"You can make potions. The potion maker must be the one to get him to drink or it will not work. It is all very complicated – all interconnected."

"Magic always is, Grandpa."

"First a copper pot from Panadar – only the right type of copper is forged there. Pour in four flagons of water from Mirror Lake."

"Tilly!" Elias giggled.

"Shut up!" Daniel said, giving him a poke with his elbow.

"Add to that one crushed bloom of the purple flower found on the shore of AnanWater. In that mixture, pour the powdered scale of a Red Dragon. Then add one drop of the potion of the Orb. Daniel and I each have two vials of it with us at all times."

"And that's it?"

"That's it. Rose, you will get the pot. I will go for the water from the lake. Boncaster gets the flower and Daniel will get the scale for us after he and Elias scout out the Eastern Chasm for Taradalnock. We will meet back here tomorrow morning. After I return with my water I go to scout the forest again. Boncaster and Rose – Ganymede – off you go."

They mounted up and went off to their intended destinations.

"Boys? Ready to be hawks?"

"Yes, sir!"

"You will fly to the eastern border by the Great Eastern Desert and follow the Eastern Chasm southward. Find the break in the warding. Then, Daniel, you will fly to the Red DragonMount and say 'boy again' and you will change back to you. Elias, you will fly straight west to the Pinnacle. I will be there tonight to change you back. You have clothes there, I presume?"

"No, sir."

"I'll pop yours home. Daniel, once you retransform, you will need to use an acquire charm to get your clothing to you from here."

"Umm – are we flying naked?"

"Birds do not wear clothes – cannot wear them. Remove them behind that rock."

The boys stripped down and stood there. Miraden, wand in hand, muttered an incantation. Daniel's skin felt tingley. Elias had a sudden itch in the middle of his back. Tiny down started to sprout all over their bodies – little fluffy feathers extended from the tiny hairs in their pores.

"It tickles!"

Elias leaned in to Daniel – "Bird puberty!"

Daniel laughed.

Then the down changed to feathers of flight, bodies became more oval, human legs and feet were replaced by bird legs and talons, heartbeats speeded up, their arms and hands disappeared and wings folded out and flapped to maintain their places on the rock. Their faces grew round and the curved beak of the hawk replaced their mouths and noses. Their shared, exultant laughter ended in a caw. Then their eyes changed and they could see in ways that they never had imagined before. Daniel became a snowy white hawk and Elias turned a lovely, speckled brown. They could not speak to each other but found, quickly, that they could transmit ideas through their thoughts. Daniel hopped up to the top of the rock and Elias joined him. They fluttered their wings and looked at Miraden.

"Avoid humans if you can. Now, off you go!"

They could understand Human speech! The boyhawks leaped into the air and flapped their wings like they had never lived to do anything else. A screech came out of each beak. What they had meant to say was *'Goodbye, Miraden.'* Daniel was sure that he had understood anyway. So was Elias, even though only the screech came out. They circled and flew off to the Northeast already able to see all the way to the Eastern Barrier Ridge, twenty leagues away.

Miraden 'popped' off to the Hamlet of Laketon. He stopped

at the Lakeside Lion. Miraden noted that Tilly's eyes lit up when she saw him; then dropped a little when she noticed Daniel's absence.

"Is Daniel not wi' ye?"

"Not this trip, my dear. He is on a mission in the east."

"When will I be seein' 'im?"

"Soon – the mission will be over soon." Miraden was trying not to chuckle over Tilly's infatuation with his grandson.

"Would you be likin' somethin' to drink?"

"Yes, a nice lemonade, please."

"Comin' right up."

Lemons were one of the things grown in the orchards of Laketon Hamlet. Along with limes, oranges and grapefruits, they made up most of the economy of the area. Tilly brought Miraden his lemonade. He sipped quite contentedly. Tilly sat. No one else was there this early in the day.

"Miraden, sir – would Daniel be likin' me?" burst from a very anxious girl.

"I think that would be a safe assumption."

"Really?"

"Why are you surprised? Dear child ..."

"I'm sorry – it's just that – I be likin' 'im alot. Why hasn't he be comin' by?"

"I am sorry, Tilly. But I have kept him and his friend, Elias, very busy. We have had no time to stop by. But you can be sure that we will be at the Midsummer Festival."

"That long?"

"Sooner, if we can."

"All right – I'll be waitin'."

"Tilly, you can help Daniel and I, if you will?"

"Of course."

"I need four common empty flagons with carrying straps. I will be able to return them soon. Maybe even Daniel could return them."

"There be some in the back. Not be a minute."

Tilly disappeared for a few moments and then reappeared

with four flagons on cords around her neck. Miraden placed two copper coins on the table next to his empty glass.

"Will these do?"

"Perfect. Walk with me?"

"Where be we goin'?"

"The lake. I need to fill these."

"We have the water in the pumps right here."

"I need lake water."

They walked a few dozen spans across the road to the lake where they filled two flagons each, stoppered them and hung them about Miraden's neck.

"I'll leave you now, and thank you for your help."

"You're welcome – be seein' you soon?"

"As soon as is possible."

Miraden 'popped' out leaving Tilly alone and surprised at the suddenness of his departure – and thinking of a handsome, white-haired, pleasant mannered boy named Daniel Gregoryson.

Daniel and Elias skirted the population center of Panador City by flying to the North and west on their way to the Eastern Chasm. The chasm was a natural protection against the expanse of the Eastern Desert, that surrounded the Realms except across the seacoasts on the West. Another chasm was located on the North and an escarpment protected the southern lands. The Creators had placed it all there to assist in the wardings of the Orb. For twenty-seven hundred years, until the loss of two talismans and the theft of two others, they had helped keep the Realms safe.

The boyhawks were over the Forest of Ral and sighted the Dwarves' cabin. The Dwarves must be at their mine because there was no other sign of them close about. They closed in on the Eastern Barrier Ridge.

"Screech!"

An updraft lifted them and took them both a hundred arms higher in a matter of seconds. They looked over at each other. If they could they would have been smiling.

"This is so incredible!" Daniel thought to Elias.

"This's m'favorite mission so far."

There was the Great Eastern River shining far below them, rushing through the canyons of the Anandoral Mountains into Balador. They flew northeast now, until the mountains ended and the desert began. There it was – The Eastern Chasm – two hundred spans across in most places and three hundred arms deep in some! This Enchanter-made canyon cut a deep and wide gorge to help mark the eastern border.

Daniel and Elias turned south and arched over the chasm. They flew along the Baladorian border for a while and saw no signs: footprints, hoof prints, fires, camps, all the usual and expected tracks were missing in the sandy bottom of the gorge.

Soon, they were flying along the Panadorian border and the sandy bottom of the chasm was changing to bare rock with only occasional soil covering. Here the Great Eastern River did the strangest thing: it ran along the top of the side of the plateau where there was only a five span high upthrust of rock that created a channel to keep it from spilling over the edge and into the chasm. The Springs of Peace were ahead and to the South, just two leagues off to the right. The springs were the source of three of the major rivers of the Realms: The River of Peace that flowed westward to the Crystal Lake in Mirador; the Great Eastern River which flowed north to Lake Estrella in Balador; and an as yet unnamed river flowing into the Unknown East, now being labeled 'the Taradalnock Lands.' It was really called the River Nock by those of that land but none inside the Realms knew of its name – yet. But it was the most spectacular of the three. It flowed to the edge of the Panadorian escarpment where it tumbled over a cliff and into the chasm with a waterfall that was two-hundred arms high and half a league wide. At the bottom of the falls was a small lake. Then the river continued eastward through the shear-cliffed canyon that led into the Taradalnock Lands and was lost from the sight of those in the Realms.

Before crossing from the North side of the lake, Daniel thought to Elias, *"See it! There it is! Their way in!"*

On the south side of the lake boats were pulled up on the shore among the rocks to partially conceal them. These were larger boats, they could possibly hold more than just Humans. *"The river must be navigable to this point all the way from their settlement far to the East,"* was Daniel's supposition.

Elias nodded, mentally.

They had to have brought the horses on the boats because the river canyon to the east appeared to have no shoreline, just a deep cut in the earth. The boyhawks took off to the East for a few leagues and proved their theory true. No riverbanks, no beaches, no sandy spits – no footholds of any kind – just sheer cliffs all the way to the desert.

Daniel and Elias doubled back and Daniel thought, *"Elias, do you understand how they are getting in up to this point?"*

"I think so – yes."

"If the wardings were up along the chasm they'd never get through. We must find the break in the warding."

They flew south along the canyon. The hamlet of Eastridge came into view a few leagues to the West and they looked below them where, in the chasm, they saw a canyon floor of dirt. In that dirt, hundreds of hoof prints. The chasm turned southwest and the hoof prints continued. They flew for twenty leagues, or more, following the prints until they disappeared. They just stopped. Daniel and Elias doubled back again.

The boys flew higher and westward, into Panador. At the very narrowest part of the Eastern Barrier Ridge, which were the mountains of the escarpment, they picked up the prints on their western slopes, appearing out of nowhere, inside Panador. They banked and went lower.

"Elias, fly around here in a tight circle and screech every little while. I'll go back to the East and go lower. When you screech twice I'll answer and we'll meet up again here. If I screech twice you come to me."

Daniel headed east again. He flew into the gorge and out over the place where the hoof prints stopped. Whing! Whing! Whing!

Three arrows flew past him. He veered higher and peered into the gorge. He could see nothing. He flew back over the mountains and returned to the spot from above and behind. He came in low and that's how he saw it – a paddock that held horses, sheltered behind and below the rocks at the base of the cliff. And archers placed high in the rocks looking eastward across the chasm. Daniel hugged the cliff face and edged lower. Whing! It almost clipped his wing tip! There it was – a cave entrance, hidden from prying eyes by a beetling overhang.

He flew up and over and screeched. Elias answered.

"I found a cave entrance on the West slope, Daniel!"

"Good work! I think I found the other end of it at the bottom of the gorge. It must have been magically dug. I'll join you and we'll follow their trail out to the West."

Once Daniel had flown back to Elias' position, the boyhawks, again inside Panador, picked up the trail of horses moving out through the fields, crossing the Hamlet Road and the Anandoral River, then across the farmland to the Laketon Road and into the Anan Forest. No one was on the trail today. It should be good enough for Miraden.

"Elias, we've got them. Go tell Miraden. I'll see you tomorrow."

"Be careful, Daniel." Elias admonished.

"Aren't I always?"

"Be careful, Daniel!" is what Elias said, but he meant 'Are you ever?'

"Thanks – I will."

Boncaster was trotting along on his sturdy Taradalnock mount. The desert peoples were certainly able to breed great horses. Not only beautiful animals but strong and hardy. He was traveling down the border of Mirador/Panador between the MidRange Mountains and AnanWater. He was looking for a flower – a purple flower. There was plenty of heather but that was too simple. He rode over closer to the shore of the lake. There was a narrow plain here full of heather and gorse and other meadow-like flowers, but no large purple blooms. Miraden had said the <u>shore</u> of AnanWater. Well, he would simply have to ride the entire shore. It would be about twenty leagues – he could do that in a few hours.

The sun was directly overhead by the time the western shore had been covered. Boncaster headed for the broad southern tip. Nope, no flowers there either. Then he curved around to the North. After he had ridden the entire eastern shore he saw an area of the lake covered in purple water lilies right along the shore. They were located at the mouth of the Anandoral River, where it emptied into the lake. He got off his horse and pulled six large and soggy blooms out of the water with their plants attached – beautiful, bell-shaped, striated flowers of purple with white. He tied them to his saddle and finished skirting the shore back to the meeting place; which is where he had started his journey. As he dismounted he was sure hoping he had picked the right blooms.

Rose was back at the Graceful Grouse. The boy from the Inn was holding the reins to her horse in one hand and two bright pennies in the other. Rose was asking about copper pots. The Market Square was setting up and she was directed to a certain stall. She walked up to the merchant.

"I need a copper pot that will hold four flagons."

"Is that a standard or an imperial flagon?"

"I'm not sure – which is larger?"

She must have only dealt with the imperial.

"The imperial."

"I'll take that one."

"Don't have any. Try two rows over."

She walked over two rows and found a lady who was unpacking all sorts of copper items.

"Excuse me, I need a copper pot that holds four imperial flagons."

"The flagons themselves or the contents of them?"

Was everyone trying to be funny? "The contents."

She rummaged and clanked and tossed aside empty crates.

"Ah! Here it is. It's me last pot of that size."

Rose could see others. The lady stepped into the view so that Rose could no longer see any of the others.

"I'll have to have that lazy dog-of-a-husband make more this size. That'll be fifteen talens."

"Ten talens."

"Fourteen."

"Eleven."

"Thirteen."

"Twelve."

"Done."

Rose thanked the lady. She didn't know why, the pot still cost too much and she had lied about it being the last one. Oh, well. She returned to the boy holding the reins to her horse and gave him another penny and his eyes lit up and he went inside the Inn. She took the reins and tied her prize to her saddle, mounted and trotted out through the alleyway.

Boncaster had placed his flowers back in the water, at the meeting place, just in case they needed to be fresh. He was sitting on a rock, whistling an aire and digging in the dirt with the toe of his boot. Miraden 'popped' in and handed him four flagons of water (not imperial in size, but that's all right) and a small vial of his potion of the Orb.

"Daniel knows what to do. I must go!"

He 'popped' out.

Boncaster placed the four flagons at the base of the rock and discovered the boys' clothes.

"Ah – must be swimming somewhere."

Miraden 'popped' back in and gathered up Elias' clothes and 'popped' out again.

Talkative, isn't he? Boncaster thought.

He took his boots off and rolled his breeches up and put his feet in the water. It was refreshing and cool. He sat on a rock by the shore, feet in the water, throwing stones, skipping stones, trying to hit anything he could see – *just like I used to do when I was Daniel's age* – he thought. Funny, that he should remember that and nothing else about his boyhood. His past was an empty page; except for that strange little memory. He turned around at the sound of distant hooves and saw a black horse with rider approaching from the North. Something was glinting off the saddle in the sunlight. It turned out to be Rose, of course, – uh, Ganymede – Rose! She dismounted and brought the pot to the rock and left her horse to graze with its brother.

Ganymede/Rose looked over at Boncaster with a sly smile. "How old did you say you were?"

"I didn't."

"Hmmm. That looks like something Daniel would do."

"Some boys never grow up – they just grow older. And some girls think they grow up too fast."

Ignoring the comment, Rose pushed on. "Do <u>we</u> put the ingredients together?"

"No, Daniel must do that."

So, she took off her boots and waded into the water. She threw and skipped stones. She and Boncaster had a little contest, which she let him win. They broke out some bread and cheese and ate.

A dust cloud appeared to the east of them heading in their direction across the plateau. They got the copper pot and the stoppered flagons and sunk them into the lake to hide them. They took their weapons and entrenched them into the grass and dirt by the rocks. They put their boots back on and secreted a dagger in each boot top. Then they sat down again and pretended to eat. Boncaster noticed that Daniel's clothes were gone. He must have called for them.

Daniel was cresting on the updrafts and downdrafts and having a wonderful time. He hoped Elias was getting home all right.

"I'm fine!" was the thought that Daniel heard.

"Elias?"

"Yes."

"Where are you?"

"Past Panagon. I'll fly south of the forest to the Pinnacle. See you tonight."

Daniel adjusted his course a little to head southwest. He could see the DragonMount in the distance, tall and stately. He soared around three or four peaks following on the air currents of the valleys. The Red DragonMount loomed in front of him. He suddenly realized, *no climbing – I can land in the cave entrance!* He fixed his angle of descent to match his trajectory with the cave's opening. He found was too low. He pulled up at the last minute and conked right into the roof of the cave. He dropped to the floor and landed on his feet (talons). He held out his hand (wing) and thought, *Acquire clothing!* A dress covered him. He flapped frantically to get it off. He then hoped no one was wearing it when he acquired it! He thought, *boy again!* He started to change immediately.

First, his beak disappeared and his Human head was on his bird body. His wings changed back into his muscular arms, his legs and feet grew back, his body regained its Human proportions. The feathers fell off and his skin returned to its immortalled whiteness. Then his white hair was back in place. He stood, "Acquire my breeches!"

Pop!

"Acquire my boots and chemise!"

Pop! Pop!

"Acquire my sword!"

Pop!

Then he had another thought – a deep request – "Acquire my dagger!" Nothing. *Well, it was worth a try!* He slipped into his breeches, put on his boots, struggled into his chemise – it seemed a little small – and buckled on his sword.

He twitched. He itched. He felt something crawling under his clothes. He danced around. He slipped off his clothes again, faster than ever before, and found ants swarming through his breeches (and other places) – and a few worms and other insects hanging on to the inside of his chemise.

He held each garment in his left hand and opened the palm of his right and a gust of wind cleaned off the ants from his breeches and the worms from his chemise. He double-checked them, brushed his body off by doing his windy-hand-thing and slipped back into his clothes. He stepped into the cave a span and did his windy-hand-thing again at the cave floor and blew all the little critters over the edge.

"Light."

The torches flared to life and a moan came at him as if from the deepest recesses of the cave.

Daniel startled, recovered and walked stealthily into the cave with his sword drawn. He went straight back and to the right, heading for the hatchery. He eased himself along slowly, down the ramps, still wondering about that moan.

"Rindamere and Andradar, honored Red Dragons of Panador, I am here on an errand of Light from Miraden. What I take from here will help you return to life."

He edged around the final curve and there were two skeletons lying on the floor, facing each other. But the more disturbing sight was the one of two smaller skeletons that were lying between the two larger ones. Daniel stopped.

"Murderers!" was spat out under his breath. Daniel was referring, of course, to whichever Human or Sorceror could have done something like this. Then he took a good look. He kneeled down and reverently touched the tiny Dragon skull from one of the offspring's skeletons. His heart ached over the senseless destruction of the creatures. As his eyes slowly adjusted to the light he saw red.

There were red scales everywhere! How could he make sure he picked up scales belonging to each Dragon? *Go to the outer edges* came to his mind. He gathered two scales from the far left and two from the far right. He picked up a large sherd of eggshell. He looked at them in his hands. He took off his chemise and ripped it in half. He wrapped up the shell and two scales from the left in one part of the shirt. He used the sleeve to tie it to his belt. He did the same with the other two scales and the other half of the chemise. Then he looked carefully to confirm which skeleton was male and which female. The males were larger and had a longer jawline. He had been correct – male on the right and female on the left – by instinct or by luck he had guessed it right.

"Thank you, Rindamere and Andradar."

He walked to the front of the cave.

"Lights out!"

The torches went out and the breath of wind blew passed him again. He crouched on the edge at the opening and thought *southern tip of AnanWater behind the rock.*

He went nowhere. Suddenly, he felt a pressure around him. Darkness crowded in. He backed up to the wall of the cave and the pressure only increased. He couldn't get away from it. He couldn't breathe. His chest was tight. He was physically pressed up against the wall by an unseen force. He felt flat.

He saw the bundles of DragonSign that were tied to his waist burst into flames. They flared up and disappeared. His breeches disappeared with them. But before his skin was seared by the heat and flame, he had managed to free one arm from its invisible restraint and call for water.

His palm gushed forth and all the flame was extinguished. His skin had been reddened, like a sunburn, but he was not seriously hurt. The pressure that had pushed him against the wall of the cave suddenly vanished. He fell, naked, to the floor of the cave. He quickly summoned a new pair of breeches from his own cave. This time he was surprised as they arrived – they 'popped' directly into place on his body.

He was still on his hands and knees, panting at the effort it had taken to extinguish the fire and claim his clothes. He was exhausted. He pushed himself back to sit on his haunches. He sat for a few minutes, trying to gain his strength. Then, with the imaginary heel of his hand, he mentally thunked himself on the forehead. Chocolate!

He summoned a bar and devoured it. Within minutes he felt renewed. He stood. He had no DragonSign. He had to do it all over! He took a step or two into the cave and stopped. It would all just happen again, wouldn't it? Whatever that Darkness was that had overcome him before would certainly attempt to do the same again. A smile crossed Daniel's face.

He summoned two sacks; sacks he could cinch closed quickly. He thought, *eggshell – two scales on the left – two scales on the right*. They were in his hands as a breath of air exited the cave. He stuffed them rapidly into the sacks and pulled the cinch closed while thinking: *southern tip of AnanWater behind the rock.*

He disappeared with a 'pop' as a cloud of Darkness tried to enshroud him. As he vanished and reappeared at the rock near AnanWater's southern shore, he heard the echo of an angry scream as if from far away. Then the echo left him alone surrounded by sky, water and grasses.

The dust cloud from the East appeared closer, larger and as it got within eyesight, Rose and Boncaster saw eight coal black horses with eight Black Riders.

"We're travelers, Rose! We found the horses. We're heading to Laketon. I'll do the talking, you're just a boy, remember?"

Rose nodded. "I hope Daniel doesn't come back too soon."

Boncaster looked around hoping the same thing. They waited and the horses and their riders pulled up to the rock.

"Those are our horses!"

"Could be – we found them wandering along the road. We have our food – take them. We were originally walking to Laketon anyway."

One of the Black Riders whistled, in a very peculiar way, and both horses trotted over to him.

"Where did you find them?"

"Up the road near the village."

"When?"

"This morning."

"There should be three more."

"We only found two."

The dark eyes narrowed and the man dismounted. He swaggered toward Boncaster, who was so unimpressed, he almost smiled.

"Yes – so I see – there would be no honor in killing you. But there might be some fun in flaying you open and leaving you for the buzzards."

Rose's eyes reacted as the Riders laughed in agreement.

"How old are you, boy?"

A look at Boncaster, "Nearly sixteen."

"Tall but too thin. Are you sure you have what it takes to be a man?"

"I think you'll find, sir, that the boy has everything you have."

Rose almost lost her composure – she nearly cracked up at the double meaning. There was another chuckle from the Black Rider's fellows. The leader drew his sword. He slipped it along Rose's cheek.

"Not even a stubble yet."

More laughter.

"Is this the bravery of the Taradalnock? Abusing a child?"

The sword pushed through the back of Rose's hood and sliced upward and the cowling fell away. It's a good thing that Rose had cut her hair last night to a boyish length.

"A very pretty boy."

"Give me a sword and you will not look half so pretty, sir!" Rose was fuming.

The Rider turned to his fellows and held out his hand. A curved sabre was placed in it and he handed it, hilt forward, to Rose.

"Name, Boy?"

"Ganymede."

"Well, Ganymede – no blood – just a friendly contest. Three hits with the flat is the winner."

Rose took the hilt and examined the sword. She raised the

blade to her nose. The Rider did the same. They backed off from
each other. Boncaster did not like this, but there was little he
could do about it. The other Riders had come forward in front of
the rock. The Rider and Rose circled each other. Boncaster stood
by the shore. The Rider slashed and Rose parried. He struck
down and from the left and Rose parried again and slapped the
Rider's shoulder with the flat of her blade.

"One!" Boncaster cried out, surprised.

Pop!

Daniel made it – all in one piece. He stood up slowly, out of
his crouching position, from behind the rock. Only Boncaster saw
him, and motioned him back down. He untied his bundles from
his waist and peered around the edge of the rock at the scene
before him.

Slash-clang – slash-clang, slash-clang, whoosh! Clang-clang-clang-slap!

"Two!"

The Rider lost his temper and came after Rose with blood in
his eyes. Daniel thought *black sword in the lake* and flicked his wrist.
The sword flew out of the Rider's hand and landed in the lake.
Daniel then pushed his palms at the seven others and knocked
them to the ground with a burst of wind. Either the impact of
the wind, or the landing itself must have been forceful, because
they acted as if their breath had been knocked out of them.

"What sorcery is this?"

"Mine!" and Daniel jumped to the top of the rock, shirtless
and powerful, white hair blowing in the wind. He pointed his
fingers at the Rider.

"Daniel, don't!" came from Rose.

Daniel ignored Rose and pushed the man into the water with
another gust of wind. The others were getting up. He knocked
them down again – all but one. Daniel's hands flew right, left, up
and down and the single Rider's cape, headband, tunic, boots and
weapons disappeared – they just vanished. Daniel lifted him out
over the lake, about ten spans away, in just his breeches. He
repeated this same action with the remaining six. The Black
Leader made his way to shore with a fierce grimace on his face

and Daniel was not kind. He removed all clothing and weapons from the man's body and threw him back into the lake naked.

"Sorry, Rose." Daniel whispered as she averted her eyes. "I could have killed you, Taradalnock!"

The man's eyes grew wide with a mixture of hate and fear.

"I will not be so kind next time. Stay where you are, all of you, or I <u>will</u> kill you. After we leave, you will go back to where you came from and not enter the Realms of the Crystal Orb again."

Boncaster was grabbing the potion ingredients from the lake while Rose uncovered their buried weapons. He knew when to make an exit. With one eye watching the Taradalnock, Daniel grabbed his bundles and refastened them to his waist.

Rose then stood at the edge of the water. The Riders moved towards her. Daniel stood fast at Rose's side and the Riders backed down.

"By the way, Taradalnock, I am Princess Rose of Panador. It was a girl who beat you, Rider. Unfortunately, from what I have seen, I am more of a man than you'll ever be!"

The Rider made a menacing move toward her and then realized that he was still naked and what she had meant – connecting the smile on her face with her previous comment. He and his fellows made a move together and Daniel raised his hands and set them all into a waterspout, removing their breeches in the process. They whirled around and around screaming and cursing against the day they would meet again.

Daniel, Rose and Boncaster, with their potion ingredients, mounted three of the black horses and gathered the reins to the others between them. Rose turned to the men who were falling out of the dying cyclone and back into the lake.

"I can't say I'd like to see more of you – I've already seen all of you and it was certainly not a pleasure."

The trio laughed and rode away southward, from eight, fearsome, mercenary warriors – helpless and naked in a lake. It just did not get any better than this!

ᕟ

CHAPTER FIFTEEN
POTIONS AND PASSIONS
(3rd Month)

DANIEL WAS PUTTING HIS ORB of Communication back in his pocket. He had shown the sacks to Miraden through the orb. Miraden had called through to him. They had vanished from Daniel's waist. This time there was no flame. (For which Daniel was very grateful.) Miraden confirmed to his grandson that the articles had arrived safely at the White DragonMount.

Daniel felt reluctant to tell it, but he knew that Miraden should hear the story of what happened to him at the Red DragonMount – all of it. So, he told him. Miraden was enraged – not at Daniel – but at what had happened and demanded that Daniel return to the White DragonMount immediately.

Daniel refused. "You have the DragonSign, Grandfather. The Darkness hasn't pursued me. It has to be bound to that cave. I'll be all right."

Miraden didn't argue. He knew he could never change the youth's mind. If he forced the lad to come home it would only end badly. He wondered if he really wanted to change Daniel's mind. Then something that Daniel said hit him. *Bound to the cave.* He realized that his rage was indeed not at Daniel, but at the Dark. He began to wonder if the Red Dragons of Panador had been approached by the Dark; had they been turned before their deaths? Could this have been the reason that so many Humans were enlisted in the annihilation of the species? Had the Red Dragons enflamed the sentiment against DragonKind with Dark actions of their own? Were those thoughts unworthy of the noble Rindamere and Andradar? It was a lot to think about in a second or two. Miraden just gazed through the orb at his grandson.

Daniel may have been overly optimistic, but he really wanted to stay with Boncaster – and Rose – on the Quest. He pleaded with Miraden, who finally relented. The old man's thoughts were filled with one thing at the moment: *What was the extent of the power in this child?* He had escaped this dangerous situation with his magic and his cunning.

Miraden sighed and then reported to Daniel that Elias was safe and had done exceptionally well. Daniel was grateful that the Darkness hadn't gone after his friend; that it had attacked him, instead. He was older and stronger – somewhat practiced in the arts of Enchantment. Elias was a mere mortal. Daniel took no pleasure in that thought. Miraden smiled a worried smile as he closed their communication, uncertain of what would be thrown at them next.

Daniel told Boncaster – and Rose – the news as they headed to Panagon Hamlet.

"Daniel, the last time I saw you I thought you were just a skinny little kid."

"I probably was."

"Where did all this muscle come from?"

There was a gleam in Rose's eye. Daniel almost enjoyed it. He still liked Rose. She saw the surprise and a little recognition of her interest reflected back to her in his piercing blue eyes. Although not a man yet he certainly looked like one to Rose – and to many others. He probably had appeared especially fearsome to eight naked Taradalnock in the lake. The whiteness of his appearance was unquestionably fearful and strange – yet, startlingly attractive to the females who were given the chance to see his physical power and glory.

Daniel swallowed, trying to maintain his composure. "I've trained a lot with the Master at Arms in Mirador. And Miraden says that everything will be happening to me faster than it does in others until I am fully grown – and then – I just won't age – at all. I'll probably look twenty-something years old forever. Look at Lily!"

"Are you all right with that?" His explanation had surprised her.

"I suppose so. But it really doesn't matter if I am or not. There's nothing I can do about it."

"Daniel, this may sound like a strange question but, where is your wand?"

"I don't have one. I never have." He remembered his long-knife – he missed his long-knife – but it wasn't really a wand.

"It looks like you don't need one."

"Yeah. It does, doesn't it," puzzled Daniel. He would make it a point to talk to Miraden about that!

Rose leaned over to Boncaster and whispered, "If he only weren't my cousin-in-law and five years younger. Ooh!"

"Yes, but remember – from what I understand about it – in ten more years he'll still be fourteen and you will be nearing thirty. And in twenty years he still won't look like he's out of his teens and you will be …"

"All right! All right!"

As they rode, Daniel often caught Rose looking at him. Although he was comfortable and pleased with his body, and he was flattered by the attention Rose was offering him, he thought that he would like to offer her that same attention; Rose was certainly more than pleasing to look at; even dressed as Ganymede! But still, it felt awkward. He didn't know why. Besides, he figured that if he couldn't have Bianca – on whom he had had that serious crush at first, but she was now his sister – then why not Rose? She may be Bianca's cousin but that is so much different than being someone's half-sister! Is there such a thing as half-cousins? Even though her hair was cut short, she was so pretty. Daniel noticed pretty girls. After all, he was thirteen! But then there was Tilly!

Daniel suddenly felt really uncomfortable and wished he had

a chemise. He should have kept one of the Taradalnock's.

Kept? Hey, why not? he thought. *Acquire Taradalnock tunic.* It appeared in his hand and he put it on.

Rose looked over and a shocked expression appeared on her face. Daniel looked even more striking in black. That was, of course, due to his white skin and hair being set off against the darkness of the clothes.

"Sorry, if I made you uncomfortable, Daniel. It's just that you're like a little brother to me and … well, never mind."

"I know, Rose. I know." Daniel slumped into his saddle. *A brother? A little brother!*

The reality of the situation hit him square in the chest. His feelings for and attraction to Rose were immediately quelled by her statement of 'like a little brother.' It was enough to douse any fires he may have had smoldering around inside his rapidly changing and confused mind and body.

He smiled a game smile. He wondered, briefly, like a flash in his head, if he would ever be able to live a normal life. Would there ever be someone to satisfy his need for affection; his longings? He smiled that brave smile again, not sure that that would ever happen. Even Tilly was only a mortal.

Rose noticed the tentativeness of the smile. She hoped she hadn't hurt one of the most special people in her life. She did indeed love Daniel, but not in any way that was romantic. She realized that her attention to him over the last few weeks may have inculcated in him the same type of silly crush that she had had for him earlier; and that he had had for Bianca. She was a little melancholy at the thought that Daniel would be out of her reach forever. Not because he was her half-cousin, not that he was five years younger than her; those are silly reasons. What does age matter to an Immortal? (Look at Miraden and Lily's mother, Kylara.) It was because of the fact that his Immortalled status put him beyond almost anyone in the Realms, including herself. She felt a little sadder for this uncommonly fine boy, youth, young man – friend. Would he come to know the joys and fullness that life offered? She hoped so. She truly did.

Then she saw the black tunic again. She tried to forget how striking Daniel looked in it. It stirred those feelings in her, again.

"Where did you send those, anyway?"

"Home to the cave – mementos." And he laughed.

"Can I have one sometime?"

"Me too?" added Boncaster.

"Of course! I have eight sets, breeches and tunics. Enough for everyone!"

They laughed at the recollection of the 'dangerous and fearful' Taradalnock they had left behind in AnanWater. Rose's and Daniel's victory kept them talking and laughing, reliving each moment, each detail, until they reached their destination. Daniel was glad, now, to have been distracted from the thoughts that kept puzzling him so: Rose, Tilly – someone else?

They rode into Panagon Hamlet, stabled the horses and took two of the four rooms at the one and only inn – The Boastful Boar. They stashed their kits in their rooms along with the potion ingredients and went down to a supper of potato and cheese soup, venison, vegetables, potatoes, cakes and wine. The small town inns always had the best food. Small town inns – Daniel started thinking of Tilly again.

He was confused. He liked her but he did not want to like her. He was still a child, not a man yet. (In mind, maybe, but not in body.) Not yet ready. Or was he? He could take a man's part! Or could he? She was as young as he was. They were children! Others had been married at thirteen! Did she even like him? He thought not. Impossible. Just someone to meet and have fun with at a party. But then there was that kiss ; and the uncomfortable tingling in his body, and that look in her eyes, and her smile, and her voice – and the way her red hair blew in the wind when she danced. And then there was her dancing ...

"Potion time?" Rose whispered in Daniel's ear, jolting him out of his more than pleasant daydream.

The three returned to Daniel's and Boncaster's room. They lined up the ingredients. Daniel set out the pot, the flagons, the flower, the scale and the potion. Daniel was very meticulous and the other two indulged him since it was he to had to make and use the potion. They would just assist if he would need them.

Everything was in order. Daniel was nervous. He had made potions for Miraden before but now his friends were watching. He picked up the flagons one by one and carefully poured each one into the copper pot on the chest, waiting until the last drop fell before taking the flagon away and lifting the next one to pour. He crushed the flower petals from one bloom of the purple water lily and added the pasty mess to the water of the lake in the pot and stirred until it became suspended in the water as Miraden had taught him to do. Wouldn't your chemistry teacher be proud if you were Daniel? (For chemistry is merely potion-making for mortals!) While he was working on the flower, he had Rose and Boncaster crush the Dragon scale into a powder. When they finished, they passed it to him and he added it to the suspension and stirred thoroughly. The mixture sat there with kind of a mini-whirlpool-thing going on in the center of the pot. Magic was beginning in the cauldron. He then slowly unstoppered the vial of the Potion of the Orb; as he had come to call it. He held the vial in one hand and the stopper in the other, ready to stem any excess flow, and tipped the vial ever so slightly. One drop fell into the slowing whirlpool. He stoppered it and quickly set the vial aside. The mixture bubbled. Smoke arose from it. It was tinged slightly green, then it turned brown and a red puff of smoke came out of the pot. After the red, the liquid turned a bright purple and a puff of white smoke wafted out of the pot and into the air around their heads. Daniel took the orb out of his pocket.

"Miraden."

"Yes, Daniel," came the reply.

"Potion's done."

"What color is it?"

"Purple."

"And the last puff of smoke?"

"White."

"Perfect. Very good."

Daniel, Boncaster and Rose, together, took a deep breath of

relief as Boncaster patted Daniel's back and Rose squeezed his forearm.

"How's Elias?"

"No feathers. And yourself?"

"Back to normal. Although once in a while I long for the taste of a mouse or a squirrel."

There was laughter from Rose and Boncaster.

"Normal after effect. My bird form eats bugs and worms, so you know what I long for sometimes!"

They all laughed again. Miraden's laughter ceased as he peered intently into his orb at Daniel. Daniel saw the confusion, the question on his face.

"Why are you wearing a Taradalnock Tunic?"

"Because we had a run in with them and I had to teach them a lesson."

Miraden reacted.

"No one got hurt, except maybe their pride when I had to separate them from their clothes in front of Rose. By the way, those clothes should be on my bed."

Footsteps were heard, Miraden turned around as the laughter of Elias came from the bedroom through the orb to Daniel and the others.

"Miraden?" Rose had borrowed the orb.

"Well, Princess Rose – or is it Prince?"

"Princess. Did you know – I mean is it normal for – I mean – how is it possible for Daniel to do his magic without a wand?"

"It is normal and all a part of the Prophecy."

Daniel took the orb back – a little angry.

"No wand? But you said ... said I would have one soon! What else haven't you told me?"

"Everything will be revealed as soon as we take care of Guildenblad. I promise. You would know it all of me already if it were not for the things that keep getting in the way."

A reluctant "All right, Grandpa," came from the young Enchanter.

"Good night, Daniel. Oh – Tilly says hello."

202

Before the orb went clear Elias' raucous giggle was heard in the background. Boncaster and Rose looked expectantly open-eyed at Daniel but he ignored them, and placed the orb back in his pocket again. He busied himself with putting the potion into the flagons, casting nervous 'I-don't-want-to-say-anything' glances over his shoulder at Rose and Boncaster. The other two gradually realized that he was not going to tell them anything so they helped him with the storage of the potion.

"With four bottles we each will have one, with one extra maybe on one of the horses? That way some potion will be on hand, unless all of us are stopped and searched.

"Good thinking, Daniel," had a bit of an edge to it.

"Thanks," as Daniel pretended innocence, still trying to deflect their attention from asking about Tilly. But he knew it wouldn't work for long.

Sleep! That's what they needed. It had been a long eventful day and there would be a longer more eventful day tomorrow. Rose went, reluctantly, back to her room. Daniel sloughed his tunic and boots and slipped into bed. Boncaster just fell on top of his and they both were soon fast asleep.

"Who is Tilly?"

"What?" Daniel's mouth opened wide in astonishment.

"Who is Tilly?"

"Why? Didn't you hear all you wanted about her last night?"

"Just her name."

"Oh. In the orb?"

"Yes. And ..."

"All night?"

"You mentioned her once or thrice in your sleep."

"She is a girl I like, well, more than like!" A grin spread across his face. Boncaster smiled, too. "But I am too young."

Boncaster pursed his lips and then drew them into a tight line. "Remember, Daniel, your entire body, your being, even your mind has changed. You may have lived for a total of only thirteen years

203

but you have matured closer to eighteen, even nineteen and you must remember also that everything you have done has made you more mature in many other ways; more than anyone else your own age ever has been before.

"Is liking Tilly normal?"

"Absolutely.

"I'm not strange?"

"I didn't say that!" There was a friendly push and a shove between the two. "But with your being Immortalled, you will probably be married within the next two years anyway!"

"Married?!" Daniel looked at him, fully astonished.

"I am serious. Most boys marry between sixteen and eighteen. You're not there in actual years but in bearing and maturity you are way passed that age. And I have heard that some marry as young as thirteen."

Daniel's thoughts turned to Tilly, the dance, the talking – her eyes.

"I think I'd like that. But I'm not 'most boys.' I'm '*The Prophecy*.'"

"I think that it is a good thing that you are not 'most boys.'"

Daniel looked at him and Boncaster smiled again.

"Trust your feelings and talk to Miraden."

"I will – thanks."

Daniel offered his hand and Boncaster shook it heartily. The older man was terribly impressed with the resolve, strength and ability of this mere boy-suddenly-almost-man. There was a knock on the door. It was Rose calling them down for breakfast.

They trooped down the steps and Daniel hung back. He was uneasy all of a sudden. Rose hit the bottom step ahead of them and was taken to the right. Boncaster had no time to react and was taken to the left. Daniel 'popped' to the outside and looked in the window. There were the eight Taradalnock, albeit in some funny clothes, holding Rose's and Boncaster's swords, each to their own necks and looking like they were missing something. Daniel thought harder than he ever had before. The swords disappeared. He then burst through the door and fired bolt after bolt of lightning at the men formerly in black. Each one went down with a fist sized hole all the way through his body. There was no blood because of the cauterizing effect of the bolt. Boncaster had broken his man's neck and Rose had kneed her man in the groin and then had stove in his head with a stool. The Great Room of the inn was littered with dead Taradalnock.

They grabbed the bodies and dragged them out back of the inn and burned them. Enemies get taken care of first!

Daniel had warned them!

Why didn't they listen?

He refused to feel guilty. He paced and fretted and cursed at the stupidity of the Riders – at their arrogance! His pacing stopped abruptly. Was it really their arrogance he was angry at? That thought had not occurred to Daniel, until this very second. It made him feel even more guilty than before.

Rose stood in front of Daniel, sensing his tension. He angrily walked around her. She stepped into his path again and wrapped her arms around him. He stopped – every muscle was tensed – he was a solid mass – his body was alive with fearsome anger – holy power – but she felt him soften the longer she held him and he gradually put his head on her shoulder and sobbed.

He did not like the choices he was forced to make sometimes. He forgot that he should be grateful for the opportunity to make them. But they were too much for a thirteen year old! Rose continued to hold him in her sisterly embrace. Boncaster placed his hand on Daniel's shoulder. The sobs subsided as the fire inside Daniel grew as dim as the one that had consumed the bodies of the slain Taradalnock. A reluctant smile came to his lips. He hoped no one was watching – after all it was Ganymede who appeared to be hugging him!

Daniel stood still, dazed, tension gone. It was almost like he was defeated, this time. He took the orb out of his pocket.

"Miraden – I'm coming home!"

And Daniel disappeared from in front of Rose and Boncaster. They stood, shocked, alarmed and uneasy. *Had Miraden expected too much too soon from this fine boy?* The thought brought

Rose to look deep into Boncaster's eyes. He had been thinking the very same thing. He returned the gaze and merely shrugged his shoulders.

ᘒ

CHAPTER SIXTEEN
COMPLICATIONS
(3rd Month)

"I CAN'T DO IT, GRANDPA! I just can't. I can't go on killing people. I'm still a child; despite what I look like! I <u>want</u> to be a child. I don't want to be – responsible! I don't want to be an adult. I don't want to fight. I don't want … I don't want to hate anymore." He was out of breath. His energy had dissipated. But it would return momentarily. Miraden was silent because he knew that there would be more.

"I want to swim, ride horses, run across the fields. I want to sleep in the woods and not be worried about werewolves, witches, vampires, necromancers – Taradalnock Mercenaries. I want to fish with Elias – I want to – to hunt with my father!"

Daniel had been pacing in front of Miraden and now he threw himself onto his bed, punching the pillow repeatedly. Elias looked on, not knowing what to do; except be glad at the fact that Daniel wanted to fish with him – and swim! He looked over at Miraden who came to him and put his arm around the bewildered boy's shoulders. Miraden ushered Elias out to the front of the cave, leaving Daniel alone for a moment.

They seated themselves – the eleven-year-old Elias settling his now taller, still slender frame into Miraden's lap like a little child. He seemed to instinctively sense something wrong. He also sensed that he had no idea what it was, nor how he could help his best friend.

"Uncle Miraden ... How ..."

"Be patient and love him like you always have."

Elias leaned against Miraden's chest and Miraden held the boy close. Elias shuddered as he breathed in, terribly upset.

"What's wrong with Daniel?"

"Not a thing. We all go through it. Especially Immortals."

"Will I?"

Miraden nodded.

Elias pouted. "I'd rather not grow up then."

Miraden did not reply but let Elias sit on his lap and think. Elias thought of all the things he and Daniel had done together; the fun, the missions for Miraden, the adventures – all the chocolate they had eaten! He realized that he loved Daniel like a brother – the big brother he had always wanted! It was not really a new thought, but over time it had been fully recognized and even realized. It was a confirmation.

It had also been a lot of responsibility to be Elias Matthewson – the oldest in his family. Daniel had helped to ease that burden for him by just being there. He was like Daniel in that way – Daniel was the oldest in his family – until his entire family had been killed. Daniel was still the older – the first to do everything – the first to have the great responsibilities heaped on him; the first to try the abilities of the parents of the family. Elias was doing it. Daniel had done it before. But, he was being asked to do it again with Elias. Elias took another shuddering breath.

"I have not told you, nor have I told Daniel, something that you both should know."

"What should I know?" Daniel appeared, unnoticed, after having listened for a while, snuffling and drying his eyes a little.

"That you, Daniel – and Lily and I – are not the only Immortals in the Realms."

"Who?" was spoken by Daniel and Elias, simultaneously; attention riveted on Miraden's potential answer.

"There have never been two different piles of chocolate. It has all been one kind."

"Are you saying that Elias is my Immortal brother?"

"I am."

A smile crossed Daniel's face and Elias hopped off of Miraden's lap and threw himself into Daniel's arms.

"I've got a real big brother!"

"And I've got a litt ..." (*Nope – Elias' head was already up passed Daniel's chin.*) – "... a younger brother."

Daniel thought something else that calmed him some: he would never be alone. There would always be someone there to share the load and help him to bear up under the burdens placed on him. Now, Elias grew thoughtful.

"But what about my family?"

"You will be with them for all of their lives. I have come to discover that you, like Daniel, once grown, will never age even slightly, like Lily and I do. It is a new Immortality that has entered the Realms. There is so much for you and Daniel to do. And you must have the time to do it. You will do that together as brothers. The Prophecy is being fulfilled." Miraden recited it.

"Many others will also rise to aid him in his eternal quest."

"It was written before Daniel's birth; before your birth, Elias. And you were a part of it – even then."

There was a silent contemplation from the 'brothers' for a moment. Then Daniel voiced his concern – no, his hope!

"What about being husbands? Will there be wives for us? When we are ready?"

"Yes, there will be."

"Immortal wives or someone like – sorry, Grandfather – like Kylara?"

"Immortal."

"Do I dare hope?"

"You may dare hope." The Enchanter smiled.

"Hope what?" Elias was confused.

"Miraden – I don't know what to say!"

"How about – 'let's go to Laketon?'"

Daniel had never, in all of his thirteen years, smiled a smile as large as the one that enlivened his features at this moment. He positively glowed. (Well, more than he already did, anyway.)

Elias finally found his way into the current train of thought – "Ohhhh! Uh-oh!"

"What, Elias?"

"Um – me too?"

"Yes, you too."

"Will I turn all white?"

"No. That only happened to Daniel and Lily through the United Orb and Sceptre and because of the Prophecy."

"Oh. Who am I going to marry?"

Daniel looked at him and raised his eyebrows in that way that always arouses fear and trembling. Elias' face went white.

"Grandpa, I thought you said that Elias wouldn't turn white!"

"Well, not permanently, at least."

"Daniel – Tilly?" Elias was putting the pieces together.

"And Elias – Nancy!" Daniel cided and laughed as Elias backed away.

"I can't do that, Uncle Miraden. I'm not old enough!"

"It won't be necessary for a while yet. There is plenty of time."

"Nancy!" Daniel giggled.

Elias stomped his foot and glared at Daniel. Just like a brother, kind and loving one minute, teasing and ready to tear someone's head off the next.

"Nancy!"

"Daniel, that's enough." The ever calm Miraden cautioned.

Elias stuck out his tongue and Miraden hexed him so that he couldn't get it back in.

"Shall we go see the girls now?"

Elias shook his head violently and whimpered pitifully. Daniel snickered.

"Daniel!"

"Sorry, Grandpa. Come on, Elias. It is not bad. I never thought it would happen at all. Just like you. But lately, I can imagine a life with Tilly … forever. I can't imagine a life without her. Really, Grandpa?"

"Yes, Daniel."

Miraden unhexed Elias' tongue and the boy slipped it back into his mouth.

"Better to not let things get out of place in the future, right, Elias?"

"Yes, Uncle Miraden." He was properly cowed.

Miraden got the boys to apologize to each other and impressed upon them the importance of their relationship – their brotherhood. Then he focused on the relationships that they would develop with the girls. Could they be fond of them? Would the girls return those feelings to the boys? Miraden hoped so.

"Are we ready?"

(Are we ever really ready? Especially for whatever romantic entanglements come our way!)

"Yes," came simultaneously from two contrite throats.

Well, there's an answer!

Pop!

They were standing at the gate of the side yard of the Lakeside Lion Inn, in Laketon Hamlet. Miraden left the boys for a moment and Tilly emerged from the door through which Miraden had entered the Inn. Tilly and Daniel rushed together in a brief embrace and then they held hands and moved off to a table.

Elias looked around to be sure no one could hear. "Mushy stuff!"

Daniel heard him and laughed. Elias <u>was</u> just like him. As Daniel and Tilly engaged each other in conversation, Elias started to stare. After all he was supposed to do everything Daniel did. Elias' eyes grew big. Daniel was talking to a girl like she was his best friend or something. Elias was sure he couldn't do that.

"Ahem, Elias. It's not polite to stare."

Elias turned in the direction of the sound of Miraden's voice but his eyes did not make it all the way to the Enchanter. They stopped on someone who looked an awful lot like Tilly. Red hair – green eyes – and freckles.

"Elias, this is Nancy. Nancy – Elias."

Or <u>could</u> Elias do what he had seen Daniel do? Possibilities spread out in front of Elias like the vista of Mirador did from the cave at the DragonMount.

She held her freckled hand out and Elias shook it. He liked the feel of its softness, and the girl had a grip. But he just didn't really care about anything other than the fact that he could not seem to tear his eyes away from those green eyes in front of him. It was like staring into his own soul – but he didn't realize that then; at least he wasn't conscious of it, couldn't express it in words. Miraden retired into the inn to talk to the girls' parents.

Nancy tugged the stricken Elias over to a table, a little away from Daniel and Tilly, and sat him down. She sat on the bench of a neighboring table and looked at him. He startled as she waved her hand in front of his face. He looked down at her hand in his. He gently took his hand back. She folded her hands in her lap and smiled at him. His throat went absolutely dry. He tried to swallow – and figured that his throat must be directly connected to his armpits, because all he could do was sweat.

"Hello?"

"Hello," was said a little too quickly.

"I don't bite."

"I – didn't think you did," he managed to squeak.

Nancy looked over at their older siblings. *They seem to be doing fine.* She looked back at Elias and he was looking over at Daniel and Tilly.

"They seem to be doing fine," she half mumbled to herself.

"Yeah – how does he do it?"

"He's older."

"I'm eleven – and a month."

How quick we are to claim every second of our age when we are young and how loathe we are to admit any part of it at all as we grow older.

Nancy laughed. Elias gave her a quizzical look. "I feel the same way about Tilly. I never get to be first at anything. She's already done it."

"But you're the first to like me – besides me mum and sisters."

"Yeah, I am. And I do." Also said a little too quickly, but not insincerely.

Is there anything to the notion of love at first sight? Well, maybe there is when there is magic at work. Not the type of magic that forces love or lust or even attraction; just the kind of magic that allows opportunities to choose and connects people more quickly than the mortal kind.

Elias blushed.

As the ice had been broken, so to speak, the fishing started. A question from Nancy would be answered by Elias and so on, back and forth, until they had found out that they liked lakes, swimming, fishing, citrus fruit – their older siblings, but they didn't want to admit it to them. They found that they had a lot in common. Nancy was eleven. Elias was eleven. Nancy's birthday was six days away from Elias' – just like Daniel and Tilly. She sounded to Elias, the longer that they talked, like she could be a really good friend. Elias loved having friends but up to now, he realized, none of them had ever been a girl. But she sure was better looking than Daniel – there were those eyes!

Nancy ran into the house suddenly and Elias wondered what he had said, or not said, but she returned quickly with a checkerboard and checkers.

"I've never played checkers. I fish wit' me Da. We're always out in the boat."

"I'll teach ya. It's real easy."

Elias sat there, hanging on every word out of Nancy's mouth. Nancy was stricken by Elias' handsome, and innocent face. His simple, eager fascination endeared him to her. And he was quite tall.

Miraden had planned long and well. Although he hadn't counted on implementing his plans for a while yet, circumstances sometimes dictate a change in the timing of any plans. Choices, to be made, right? Sometimes people just have to be more important than saving the world.

Miraden came out of the inn eyeing the two couples who were in rapt attention with each other in the side yard. He loved it when plans turned out to be totally beneficial. He worried a lot that things he would plan somehow wouldn't turn out.

"Time to go, boys."

"Do we hafta?"

"Yes, I'm afraid so."

Elias stood and offered Nancy his hand again. The chocolate had already begun its work on Elias. He would not be aware of it for some time, but he was, already had been, rapidly changing.

"I 'ad – it's been – I'm glad ..."

"Me too, Elias. Come again?"

Elias looked over at Miraden, who nodded.

"Yeah! Um – thanks!"

Elias continued to hold Nancy's hand. Daniel held Tilly's hand to his cheek and then kissed it tenderly. She leaned up and kissed his cheek. "I'll um, see you – soon!"

Elias dropped Nancy's hand reluctantly and went over to Miraden, leaving the smiling Nancy alone.

"I should 'ope so!" Tilly giggled. "I love you, Daniel Gregoryson."

"I, um, I love you, too, Tilly FitzMichael." Daniel hadn't realized it, yet; hadn't put it into words. Until now.

"Mushy stuff!" Maybe Elias wasn't changing too fast!

Miraden, Daniel and the girls laughed and that laughter rang in Elias' ears as the trio 'popped' home to the cave.

"You've not enchanted anything? Me or Tilly or Elias or Nancy?"

"I guarantee you that everything that is happening between you, everything you are feeling for each other is perfectly natural – even though it is magical in its own right. I have created no charms, or potions to alter or enhance your feelings." Miraden left the bedchamber.

As the boys settled down, or at least tried to stem the excitement of life's changes and surprises – of hope's fulfillment – they got into another punching, poking, goosing match.

"Admit it, Elias – it was exciting and tingly – right?"

"All right, yeah, It was excitin' – but it don't mean I'm gonna get all mushy like you! Kissin' 'er 'and! Makin' those cow eyes!"

Daniel 'noogied' Elias and Elias smacked him back, playfully of course. And then Daniel attacked, tickling and poking. Elias had never been able to withstand the 'Daniel attack.'

"Uncle! Uncle! I said, Uncle!"

"Yes, Elias?" and Uncle Miraden popped his head into the chamber. Daniel settled down.

"I was pretty stupid earlier, huh, Grandpa?"

"Not in the least, Daniel. What you felt was perfectly normal. And you must always tell me how you feel – sooner than later, preferably – both of you. Don't bottle it up inside. No one has ever gone through exactly what you two will be going through. I need to know."

Daniel snickered. "More books you need to write, Grandpa?"

Miraden looked long and hard down his nose at his grandson, whose snicker turned to a beaming smile.

"Thank you, Grandpa. I think I can say that I love Tilly."

"I think you already did that, son."

"Oh, yeah."

Elias giggled. "I don't know 'bout love, Uncle Miraden, but Nancy an' me get 'long better'n me and me sisters do!"

"All the best relationships start out as friendships."

"Kylara?" Daniel offered.

Miraden nodded. "And Aradella."

"You chose well, Grandpa! I could never have found Tilly on my own."

"Yeah, thanks – Uncle Miraden."

"You're welcome. Now, sleep – and no more poking." Miraden waved his wand and Daniel's arms were trapped at his side. Elias noticed this as Daniel struggled to free his hands. Elias smiled a wicked smile and panic spread across Daniel's face as Elias started to poke the now defenseless Daniel.

"Sure is great to have a big brother."

"Hey, Grandpa – not fair! Elias stop it! Grandpa?!"

Miraden waved his wand again and Elias' arms were trapped at his sides.

"Uncle!"

There was no reply and no release of their arms.

The Boastful Boar had been quiet since the removal of the Taradalnock threat. Rose and Boncaster spent a peaceful and restful night in their rooms. After breakfast they waited and waited and waited for Daniel. They decided to walk the lanes of the hamlet which consisted of the Inn, Stables and Blacksmith (kind of like a modern travel-plaza), a market square filled with vendors hawking their wares, and ten to twenty homes and cottages and a few other shops along the main street. Children ran through the square totally unaware of the Dark presence growing in the forest just a few leagues away. They had also slept through that Dark presence in their village last night, and so had their parents. No one had been aware of the danger, except those at the Inn, and they were sworn to secrecy. Maybe at this time, a public knowledge of that kind of danger so close to home would be detrimental to that very public, for they would want something done about it – or they would do something about it themselves. And that would lead to more casualties. There had already been too many casualties: the entire Dwarven Guard of Panador, nearly forty soldiers of Caladon, the Taradalnock – ten in Caladon and now thirteen in Panador. Just how many more Black Riders were there? The footprints in the chasm had indicated many more than a hundred.

It was only twenty leagues to the Eastern Chasm. An easy ride. Rose and Boncaster left a note in his room for the absent Daniel, if and when he returned. They stashed the potion, mounted their Taradalnock horses and left the Hamlet for the rest of the day.

There was no trouble in finding the tracks of the Taradalnock who thought that no one knew they were even inside Panador, so confident were they that they did not take the time to cover up the signs of their passage. The swath cut by the hoarde of black horses led all the way to the Eastern Barrier Ridge where a large cave opening yawned before them. They rode up on the slopes above the cave and secreted themselves among the rocks and scrub trees to watch and wait. They broke out bread, cheese and dried meat, and ate and talked.

Boncaster was worried about Daniel. Rose assured him that Miraden would sort it all out. Daniel would be fine. Rose was concerned about the recovery of The Rose. Her kingdom was so vulnerable without it. That brought her to think about the missing Gentle Jewels of Aradon. What it must be doing to the citizens of that Realm.

They must close up this entrance. If Daniel was correct and magic had opened it up, then magic would be required to close it up. Miraden or Daniel would have to do it. They were swamped, at the moment. Rose sat up straight and listened – the echo of horses' hooves – someone was coming quickly through the cave.

They hunkered down behind a boulder – their black horses concealed and tied securely. The clops of the hooves became lighter, less resounding, and the first of the group appeared at the western entrance to the tunnel. Twenty-four Riders on horses emerged at a canter, gleaming in the noonday sun, their black metal sword hilts flashing at their waists.

Rose and Boncaster waited until the Riders were well down the trail before they came down with their horses in tow. They moved into the cave, keeping to the sides and the shadows. Daniel had said that the tunnel was about a league in length. They mounted and rode the edges of the tunnel, slowly, listening for the approach of more Riders. After the light from the East end of the tunnel came into their view, they rode as far as they dared and then dismounted and walked to the opening.

They peered around the edges of the opening and saw the archers, six of them, three on each side – two up high and one down low. Rose unslung her bow and aimed at the lower one on the right, closer, easier. Carefully, she let fly and he slumped over without a sound. She turned to the other single on her left, nocked her arrow and released. He shifted at the last moment and took it through the neck with a scream. A quick second arrow through his chest silenced him. The other four looked around for the sound, even to the skies because echoes were tricky in this chasm. Finding no source, they went back to scouting the horizon. Rose turned to Boncaster. He was gone. She saw him behind the two sentries up on the right. So she covered the two on the left. She did not see Boncaster drop in behind his two, staff twirling, heads being stove in by the might of the blow. All she saw was one archer, on her side, stand and release — she released and he fell forward over the cliff. His partner stood and faced Rose as Rose sent another arrow straight into his eye — he took the fall forward, screaming, until he hit the bottom of the chasm with a sickening, bone-crunching thud. There was no one left to hear it except Rose and Boncaster.

She also hadn't seen the arrow that hit Boncaster. When she looked over to where he had gone, she could not see him standing. She rushed to the place where she had seen him last and found him lying back against the rock, an arrow through his shoulder, muttering and cursing to himself over his rash stupidity.

She knelt by him and he asked her to hold the point behind him steady, while he broke off the arrow's shaft in front. She did so. He snapped the arrow and she pulled the remainder of the shaft through his tissues. She ripped the cloth from the edge of her tunic and packed the wound on both sides. She then helped Boncaster to his feet, into the cave and onto his horse. They must get back to the Inn. They dug in their heels and their horses took off at a gallop.

It was less than twenty leagues back to Panagon and they galloped and rested and galloped again and within an hour they had pulled into the yard behind the inn. Rose helped Boncaster up to his room. Daniel was there. He assisted Rose in laying Boncaster out on the bed. Rose was going to go for a doctor but Daniel asked her to wait.

They cut Boncaster's shirt away. Daniel put his hands together. He rubbed them. He placed them over the festering wound just under the knob of the shoulder. Daniel felt the heat go through him and Boncaster moaned. Daniel thought his way all the way through the wound; he saw the muscles, tendons, ligaments, flesh and capillaries reunite. It all played across a mirror-like surface in his mind. He pulled his hands away. The wound was gone and the skin was pink and clear.

That's funny, Daniel thought. *It doesn't look like the rest of his skin.*

He leaned Boncaster forward and applied a small amount of healing to the wound in his back. Soon, new skin appeared, again differing from the old, but Boncaster was breathing easily. They covered him up and he fell asleep. Rose took Daniel downstairs. They sat at a table and she looked at him – and looked.

"What?" he finally asked her.

"I've never known anyone like you, Daniel. Where did you learn to do that?"

"It was the first thing I could ever do by magic. I didn't learn it. It was just there – like an unasked for gift. I healed your brother, my father ... and others." He waited for his emotions to catch up with his mind.

"So that's what Valerius means when he says he owes you?"

Daniel nodded. "But I wasn't able to bring my father back from death."

Rose didn't take her eyes off of the youth.

"I don't suppose you know how incredibly unique you are?"

"I'm different, that's all." Daniel got up and walked outside.

Rose debated going after him but stayed seated.

Daniel strolled through the Farmer's Market and bought a peach and bit into its sweet, juicy pulp. He let the juice run down his chin. He decided that, through something as simple as a peach, he was grateful to be alive. It didn't even take his thinking rock to do that, this time. He walked back to the inn and Rose was there, waiting for him. He sat down and Rose put her hands over his – a great comfort filled Daniel. Rose's power wasn't magical or Immortal. It was heartfelt and Human. She loved this little man and would do anything to help him.

"Daniel, Boncaster and I killed the sentries today at the

tunnel in the chasm. We also saw twenty-four Riders heading for the forest. We need to destroy that tunnel!"

"Let's go!"

"It would take too long!"

"No, it won't. Take my hand?"

She did and Daniel thought of the western entrance to the cave which he had seen as a hawk from the air.

Pop!

He and Rose were standing on the road in front of the western part of the tunnel. Rose wobbled at the suddenness of it all. Daniel walked as close as he dared to the tunnel and Rose stood behind him. He planted his feet and squared his shoulders. He raised his hands and sent bolt after bolt of lightning into the recesses of the tunnel, trying to collapse it from the inside. The mountain shuddered and dust and rock came rolling out of the cave's mouth. He sent more bolts of lightning and the mouth of the tunnel collapsed in front of him. He took Rose's hand, not seeing the expression of consternation on her face, and

Pop!

They were in the chasm facing east, looking out over the Unknown Lands.

"It's so beautiful, Daniel. I never even knew it was here."

"Neither did I 'til a few days ago."

After a while, Daniel turned around and saw Rose's arrows in two Taradalnock bodies.

"Nice shooting."

Daniel sent more bolts into the cave. The rumbling started again and the tunnel filled up with debris. He stood back with Rose and collapsed the cliff face. Then he just stood there. Sunlight was leaving the chasm.

"Should I put up a warding?"

"Then they would know someone had been here and done this. If you leave it like this they may think that it was just a collapse. We'd better burn the bodies though."

Daniel and Rose piled all six of the bodies behind one of the rock outcroppings. He stood there and imagined flame – and the bodies burst into flame. It was quite unsettling – both for Rose and for Daniel. They could not, did not speak. When the bodies were consumed, Daniel erased all traces of ash and fire. He took Rose's hand again.

Pop!

They were back at the Inn in Panagon, Rose wobbly and dizzy. They checked on Boncaster who was sitting up in bed.

"The tunnel?"

Daniel and Rose shared a look.

"There was a cave-in."

"The archers?"

"Cremated."

Boncaster sighed. He would have liked to have been a part of it all. "The forest tomorrow?"

"Miraden wants me to scout it tonight. See what happens in the dark."

"Can you use some company?"

"I sure could."

Boncaster wondered how he ever could have accomplished this alone. Or was he always meant to have help? Or maybe, just to be the help?

There was little light – just a waning, three-quarter moon. The trees were moving and there was no breeze. Not only leaves and branches writhed, trunks swayed and their very roots, unnaturally above the ground, having unearthed themselves, so to speak, were wriggling, grasping and finding nothing to grab a hold of, as they spiraled into the air and fell back to the earth empty, angry. The trio stood at the western edge of the forest by the MidRange Mountains and watched in horror as the Forest of Anan seethed, teeming in anticipatory hunger for it's enemy, hungry to feed. For that is what the trees did with a captured enemy. Guildenblad's invention.

Daniel picked up a rock and threw it at the forest. He had expected that it would just bounce off the warding, but, instead, the warding absorbed the rock and then spit it back out at the trio who ducked to avoid a direct hit. Then four Black Riders appeared and searched for the location the rock had come from. Daniel, Rose and Boncaster walked in an invisible warding so that their explorations could be done undetected. They also wore some of the Taradalnock black that Daniel had summoned from his cave. So, in the darkness, they were twice invisible. The trio headed north around the end of the forest and every hundred arms or so they tossed in a rock, which was returned. Each time four more Taradalnock Riders appeared at the edge of the moving trees searching for the rock thrower, but were never able to find him. After several hours and many leagues of exploration, one Rider came out of the forest and through the warding itself, swinging his curved sabre, slashing at the air. Daniel and the others laid down and hugged the ground, flat and motionless, hoping the sword would not reach them. The hooves of the Rider's horse came within knuckles of the trio's invisible fingers. They felt the air move above them from the slashing of the sword. The horse nickered – it sensed something. But the Rider did not, and turned the horse around, heading back to his fellows. As he reached the edge of the forest and its warding, he raised his left hand and said,

"Praise Dal."

He and his horse entered and were absorbed back through the warding, like it wasn't even there. He rejoined his three fellows who had not ventured beyond the safety of the forest. The trio agreed on further silence and moved off to the east, away from the forest, before they spoke in hushed tones.

"A password gets us through the warding. We have their horses and their clothing. We might have an easier time of it than we thought," was Boncaster's assessment of the situation.

"What about the slashing trees?" was Rose's worry.

"They don't touch the Taradalnock," Daniel stated, simply.

"But we're not Taradalnock." Rose countered.

Boncaster smiled. "We'll have to wait and see if the trees think we are."

Pop!

The three were now at the entrance to the forest on the Northeast corner near AnanWater, at the path that Miraden had said led to the clearing where Guildenblad was hiding. The trees were moving here, too. While the entrance stayed the same, the path within the forest seemed to shift every few minutes. The trees appeared to get up and walk on their roots and replant themselves as the soil opened up and accepted them, thereby blocking the former path and creating a new one.

Have you ever looked into a can of worms? I mean a can <u>full</u> of worms? Or maybe into a container full of maggots? A solid moving mass of individuals – that's what the forest was like. As Daniel watched the trees of the forest in their Dark enchantment, it gave him that same feeling of dread as the one that creeps up the back of your neck.

"So the trees themselves move and the path continually changes?"

"Appears so, Daniel."

"Maybe we had just better find a way in somewhere else and forget about this path."

"Maybe."

"We need to know what the creatures are. Guildenblad has been able to guard so many of his secrets much better than his master, Tophet, ever did. I need to know. I can't go in blind."

"We won't have to. We can look like Taradalnock. They seem to be protected from the warding and most likely from the creatures, too, whatever they are."

"Daniel, the Taradalnock marking – we need them under our – which eye?"

"Left."

Daniel traced out the delicate marking on Rose's, Boncaster's and his own cheeks and an ornate, red 'T' decorated the left cheek of the three pretending Taradalnock.

"We must return to Panagon to retrieve our horses."

Pop!

Once back in the hamlet, Daniel shook off the warding.

"Sleep. We'll start for the forest tomorrow by horseback. I have an idea."

"Praise Dal!" Daniel had raised his left hand and now rode his horse through the warding. Rose and Boncaster did the same and all three were inside the moving forest. Daniel, especially, had had to paint his face and hands to match the desert tan of the Taradalnock. Rose and Boncaster had natural color from working in the garden and did not need as much colorization. But Daniel, once Immortalled, could not seem to tan naturally no matter how hard he tried. He couldn't yet transfigure himself so he had to settle for make-up.

As they moved their horses forward, animals of the forest gathered around them – silent – watching – tense.

"Praise Dal?"

The forest animals settled back on their haunches and seemed to relax. They kept their sharply pointed teeth inside their mouths. The trio moved forward. The animals moved aside and let them pass. Four Taradalnock approached.

"Praise Dal!"

"Praise Dal."

"We've just come through the tunnel."

"Where are the others?"

"They were killed in a cave-in – we barely escaped. Twenty-one gone."

The eyes of the four Riders grew wide.

"Is there a way back?"

"There is always a way back, Praise Dal. Just no more way in."

"Come with us, we must inform the Dark One."

The horses moved off. The trio regarded each other with wary eyes. They were going to Guildenblad! But Boncaster and Rose had gotten the gist of Daniel's plan now. It was a clever idea – if they could maintain the ruse.

The forest around them was strangely quiet after last night. In the distance the trees were moving but as the party passed, the trees grew silent. Daniel turned to look around behind him. The trees had started their motion again, with the lack of any Taradalnock presence.

"What's wrong?" demanded the leader of the Riders.

"It's hard to get used to trees, let alone trees that move."

"Yes – it is a strong magic but once Guildenblad has his full powers, our master and mistress will be able to regain theirs, Praise Dal."

"Praise Dal."

Daniel's thoughts went wild. *A master and mistress without magical powers in the Taradalnock Lands? Miraden will be delighted. It must be Tophet and Withera!*

The closer they got to the glen, the darker the forest became except, again, right in their immediate travel path. It was like another warding protected each group of Taradalnock as they traveled – marking them, keeping them safe from something – but what?

They heard a 'thump-thump-thump-thump' coming from what sounded like far away, when all of a sudden their horses reared up and the canopy of the trees in front and above their heads parted as if two giant hands had grabbed them and pulled them aside to peer at something down below. There was nothing there, yet the treetops were parted – stationary – unnaturally ominous. Daniel continued to look up as he passed beneath the place where the trees were parted.

"First time in the forest?"

"Yes. Praise Dal. There are some – some strange things here."

"It is a Yetrall. There are six of them that guard the forest. They are copies of the original Yetrall that live far to the North. They will not come down here so Guildenblad had Morphalls imitate them so they could protect the forest."

"Are they always invisible?"

"Guildenblad has made them so. Were you not trained for this mission?"

"We are part of a group of last-minute conscripts. No time for training. They just sent us off to the forest." Boncaster interrupted.

"Praise Dal."

"Yes, Praise Dal." The leader drew his sword. The other three Riders drew theirs as well, slowly and menacingly.

Daniel acted quickly. He freed his hands and pointed all of his fingers out in a splayed position and shot lightning through the four Black Riders. They fell off their horses, holes blasted through their chests. Daniel then threw his hands up and created a red warding around himself and extended it first around Rose and then Boncaster. A tree root rose up before the warding closed around their feet and it took Rose's horse out from under her; dragging it off whinnying and neighing in terror. She quickly climbed on behind Daniel while her horse was taken up and thrown into a nearby tree where blood rained to the ground, as the horse was ingested. Daniel placed another layer of protection around them, this time a purple warding; but only above them. The red warding would be sufficient as it contacted the ground. The trees came alive and assailed the new, purple bubble that surrounded the red, which by this time was a complete sphere covering top, sides, bottom, front and back of the group. The animals arrived and threw themselves at the warded Humans continuously bouncing off the purple warding while the red warding helped to defend from the attacks of the tree roots. The wardings took a heavy blow – then another.

"Can you move with this warding, Daniel?"

He nodded and Rose, holding the reins around Daniel, and Boncaster kicked their horses into gear. (Of course they didn't really have gears – that's just an expression.) As the two horses raced eastward there came a 'thump-thump-thump-thump' following them, animals continued to throw themselves at the warding. The trees continued to assail them from all sides. A root would raise up in front of them to try to trip them and the red warding would pulse and shear it off as it passed over it. The tree would scream – a most human-like, yet unhuman wail. Blackness was all around them as was the noise of the trees and creatures.

Daniel held up his orb – "Light!" and a beacon shined,

cutting through the darkness ahead, illuminating their way.

Crash.

Another huge blow came down on the warding from above. Daniel was sweating, trying to keep all three enchantments going at the same time. Rose and Boncaster urged their horses to greater speed. The blows rained down on the wardings. The trees continued to move into the path of the fleeing Humans and the warding continued to splinter and raze them in its passage.

Thump - thump - crash! The purple warding shattered.

Daniel slumped a little. Rose squeezed her arms around his middle to hold him onto the horse. He then redoubled his efforts and strengthened the red warding around them. The horses were flying across the root-filled ground. The trees cracked, the flying animals sizzled to a crisp now that the purple warding was gone; and the Yetrall, with a fearsome yell, tried to shatter the red bubble that hurt him each time he hit it.

(NOTE: If it had had just half a brain it would have stopped hitting something that hurt it every time it hit it. Any child knows that once you touch a hot stove, and get burned, you never do it again!)

A line of dead and dying animals littered the ground on the back-trail of the fleeing Humans. Off to the left, Taradalnock Archers had been put in place and a storm of arrows now disintegrated as they bounced off the warding. Daniel was tired but there was light ahead. Rose looked at Boncaster and they signaled each other. They reached the edge of the forest and took their horses into a mighty leap. Finally, they were outside the warding.

They turned and saw the Yetrall emerge from the shadows of moving boles. No longer protected by the spells contained in the forest, it was revealed to be at least four spans high with white and tan fur and tiny red eyes. It had a Dwarven type of face rimmed by a brown beard and monstrous, uneven teeth. It wasn't like the green Morphalls at all. Daniel dropped his warding and aimed all his lightning power at the monster. A hole the size of an oak tree's trunk ripped through the body of the Yetrall from both of the hands of the young Enchanter. It slowed, tottered, looked at its belly and crashed to the ground, with its insides now spilling outside.

Rose flew into action and dropped off her horse as it was running and nocked three arrows in quick succession. At a full run she downed three of the Taradalnock archers. Boncaster had dropped off at the edge of the forest and was behind the remaining six-archers. Three more were taken down by Rose's arrows. Boncaster broke three enemy bows and three heads with several swings of his quarter-staff. He then rushed to Rose as fifty mounted Taradalnock emerged from the forest and raced toward the three Humans. Boncaster and Rose each grabbed one of Daniel's hands, as much to hold him up as to have the necessary physical contact with him.

"Daniel, now would be a good time!"

"I don't know how far we will go!"

"Try for the Hamlet!"

Daniel thought – the three disappeared as a great roar came out of fifty Taradalnock throats, closing in on only two riderless horses.

The trio could see the hamlet at least. They were close.

"Daniel, the potion!"

"Acquire the potion from the horses!"

And the two flagons of the potion that they had taken with them were in his hands. Daniel collapsed.

When Daniel awoke the next morning, he couldn't determine where he was. It was all familiar but ... Miraden and Elias entered with bars of chocolate. Daniel sat up and devoured them. He needed the energy. Rose and Boncaster entered the room. Daniel was home! Then his brain finally kicked in.

"Grandpa – in the forest ..."

"Rose and Boncaster have told me everything. At least we know where the other six, now five, Morphalls are."

"Morphalls?"

"Yes, the Yetrall copies were ... are Morphalls. It was very foolish, what you did ... brave, but foolish."

"Yes, but Grandfather, look what we learned!" Daniel always used 'grandfather' when he was trying to convince him of something.

"But think, Daniel, what I ... what we could have lost."

"But I'm immortal!"

"Daniel, you won't die, but you can be killed. It would take immense power or force to do so, but it is possible."

Daniel stopped short, then continued anyway. "Oh, I see. One of those things you were going to tell me!" But he had been told, by Lily, shortly after his Immortalization; he had just forgotten about it.

"Daniel!" and Rose shook her head as she held his hand.

"Sorry." Silence. "When do we go after Guildenblad?"

"In a few days the time will be right. We will have a big surprise waiting for the Taradalnock. Your venture into the forest may have been foolhardy but it was a very smart thing to destroy their tunnel. In the meantime, all five of us will go to Balador to get the DragonSign there. Four to protect and one to retrieve. Prince Valerius will tend to the surprise."

"You mean that only I can get the DragonSign?"

"Yes, you must fulfill The Prophecy."

"Will I ever know The Prophecy in full before I fulfill it?"

"No, you will understand ..."

"Later, I know."

Miraden spoke very particularly in remonstrance of Daniel's interruption, "When - it - is - fulfilled - you - will - have - a - full - understanding."

Daniel was properly cowed.

Miraden smiled. Lesson learned. "Sleep. Dream of Tilly."

"Grandpa!" Daniel was aghast!

Elias fell off the edge of the bed, he was laughing so hard. "Tilly, Tilly, Tilly," came out of Elias but he continued to giggle.

The grownups chuckled and left the room.

"Nancy, Nancy, Nancy!" came tauntingly from Daniel's lips

before the three escaped beyond the range of hearing necessary to embarrass Elias. He shut up and got into bed. He gave Daniel a test punch after a while, as if to ask 'still friends?' Daniel returned it, in the way Elias had hoped, a friendly one, if a little more forceful than necessary.

"I'm glad you're all right, Daniel."

"Thanks."

Elias couldn't resist it. "I bet Tilly's glad too!!" He busted up again.

Daniel pounced and Elias felt as if he was being murdered as the goosing, poking and tickling drove Elias to distraction. Both of the boys were howling with laughter.

"Sleep," a disembodied voice echoed around the chamber. The boys were quiet. They looked at their arms, which could still move. Then the light went out.

ML

CHAPTER SEVENTEEN
ORANGE AID
(4th Month)

CASTLE BALADOR WAS A DISASTER! No one had lived there for over eight hundred years. The turrets were toppling. The moat was dry and overgrown. If you didn't know better you'd think that Sleeping Beauty lived, or slept, in the uppermost remaining tower just waiting for some Prince to hack his way through the briars and brambles to rescue her. But there was no Sleeping Beauty here. The drawbridge outside the King's Gate on the west no longer drew. In fact it was missing entirely. Vines covered the walls and the ground. Even Dragon-built, Castle Balador couldn't outlast the Great War's Dark Magic; due to the untimely loss of its Talisman, The Flaming Sword.

The town below and to the North, formerly a city, had fared little better. Once home to thousands of people who had thronged its streets, Balador City was now nearly a ghost town. Maybe three hundred people lived there and they resided in the quarter farthest away from the castle. They kept close to their north gate, as if the ruined castle portended bad omens for them. It was a walled city and had been quite spectacular throughout its history. The walls ran uphill to the South from the inhabited quarter to touch the curved northern outer walls of the Castle battlements. A large open bailey of at least two hundred spans contained a circular castle keep which sat on a natural mound.

This added to its protection, except when the war was against Sorcerors and Sorceresses, who had almost torn it completely apart.

Daniel, Miraden, Elias, Boncaster and Rose stood in the center of the circular Great Hall. A four storey vault, it had once been a magnificent court proudly displaying the orange crest of Balador: a single, vertical shining sword, balanced on its hilt, encircled by golden flames. The sword was laid against a rectangular royal purple field. Around that field was a border of lavender crowns, finials pointed to the center of the field. The whole field overlaid a shield of orange.

The parapets and towers of the white castle would normally have flown alternating orange and purple banners for important visitors. Not only were the banners missing, all but one of its eleven towers was gone. So, our five visitors received no welcome whatsoever.

"Why are we here?"

"Where is here?"

"This is Castle Balador. I have never been to the Orange DragonMount, so I could not take us directly there. The Orange Dragons were reclusive; maybe part of the reason that Balador fell so quickly in The War. This is the closest I could get us. Daniel must take us the rest of the way. The mount is ten leagues south of the castle along the western edge of the Anandoral Mountains."

"Are we to walk, Miraden?"

"Yes, Daniel.

"It shouldn't take long. We'll be there by noon."

They walked out the Barbican of the keep and down the mound via a roadway whose edges were also crumbling away. They followed the roadway to the west gate, or King's Gate and met their first obstacle – no drawbridge. The moat was wide and empty. Miraden 'popped' over with Elias. Daniel brought along Rose and Boncaster.

The clouds were boiling in the Southwest and it looked like the rain over Zanadon might reach them. Maybe they wouldn't be going far enough south to be affected by that rain. Besides, a simple purple warding could keep them dry, if they needed it.

With the adults present, Daniel felt strangely free of responsibility and felt that he could be a child again with Elias; like Miraden had encouraged. So, they chased each other and raced each other. Daniel piggybacked Elias for a while and then Daniel had ... a strange idea. He wanted to see if he could make it work. They ran ahead of the grown-ups and Daniel had Elias lay on the ground flat on his back. Daniel concentrated hard and opened up his palms to face the sky with his fingers pointing at Elias. He then raised his palms to the sky about the distance of the length of his forearm. Elias floated off the ground, startled and fell back to the earth.

He was smiling from ear to ear before he was even up off of the ground.

"Whoah! Do it again, Daniel!" He laid back down.

Daniel concentrated, this time a little harder, and Elias did also. Elias lifted off the ground and floated in midair at the level of Daniel's waist. Daniel used one hand to keep him in the air and the other to move him along the road. The little group of adults applauded as they came up and joined the boys. So, Elias floated along for several leagues. It became very easy for Daniel to keep him floating along and moving forward.

"Can I try?" Rose asked Elias.

"It's all right wi' me!"

Daniel lowered Elias and Rose laid down. Daniel levitated her easily and she stayed put in midair as Daniel moved off the road at an angle heading towards the looming DragonMount. Elias ran back and forth under Rose as they traveled along. It almost looked like a magic act with Elias as the assistant proving that there were no wires or supports to hold Rose up, but this wasn't an act! Daniel was an Enchanter, and although young, he was a very powerful one. How powerful was yet to be fully understood.

Daniel pointed out the Orange DragonMount almost right in front of them. He lowered Rose to the ground and she stood up. Daniel ate some chocolate and felt renewed. Miraden's chocolate seemed to be able to fix anything. He hated to imagine having to drink that green stuff! Nasty!

You could not only see the top of the mount from where they were, but the cave entrance was clearly visible along with a strange spiral of smoke coming from the back side of the mountain.

"I can see the cave. Can we 'pop'?"

"You try it first, make the decision, and then report back to us."

Daniel thought.

Pop!

Pop!

Daniel was back.

"I got there and back in one piece."

"Take Elias and Rose. Boncaster and I will follow."

Pop!

All three were gone.

Miraden turned to Boncaster. "I have seen trouble here, my friend. This will not be as easy as Daniel thinks it will be. There is very little known about the Orange DragonMount. Please be watchful and ready and tell only Rose to be so as well.

"Why not tell Daniel?"

"I have. But sometimes his enthusiasm carries him away."

Boncaster nodded.

"Ready?"

Boncaster nodded again.

Pop!

There they were at the entrance to the cave and Daniel had already lit the torches.

"Gondomere and Istradar – I am Daniel Gregoryson, here on an errand with Miraden to ..."

The cave shook.

"... to collect DragonSign so that you may return to life."

The cave shook again and knocked all but Miraden over.

"Daniel, keep Elias close to you. Rose and Boncaster at my side, please."

Boncaster whispered in Rose's ear as Daniel placed his arm over his little brother's shoulders while Elias quite naturally placed his arm about Daniel's waist. Daniel led them along the central corridor and into the last room on the right where the entrance to the hatchery would be.

Another tremor shook the mountain. The group waited until nothing crushed them and started down the circular ramp that led to the hatchery. Then the mountain cracked. Literally. The floor in front of them opened up and rocks fell away beneath their feet. Elias grabbed onto Daniel tightly and the group backed up a few steps. The floor shook and the crack in front of them got wider and deeper and steam started escaping. It was hot and difficult to see, but there seemed to be this orange glow reflecting off the bottom of the steam cloud. The chasm in front of them had grown to about a span wide.

"I have heard of a mountain of fire in the eastern lands. This mountain might very well be connected to that mountain somehow."

"What is it, Grandpa?"

"The Orange DragonMount is an unerupted volcano – until today. I have been sensing the eruption for a year or so. I thought we had more time. It will require all of us in order to get what we want and escape with our lives."

"I can 'pop' to the hatchery and 'pop' back."

"Go!"

Daniel 'popped' and the floor opened further. The orange glow was brighter – closer. The mountain shook violently and the magma rose to a level that was just knuckles below the floor level. Another tremor and a scream from Daniel.

"Daniel?" shouted Rose.

"Daniel! Daniel!?" Elias was terrified and then he just vanished. He was not there!

"Elias!" Rose screamed again.

"I'm all right! I'm with Daniel. I 'popped'!"

The adults let out a sigh. Elias 'popped' to Daniel – right to him. Odd.

"Daniel's leg is caught under a rock!"

Miraden took Rose and Boncaster's hands and 'popped' to the other side of the crack in the floor of the cave. They walked carefully downward and found, through the dim haze of the volcanic glow, Daniel levitating the rock off of his own leg and Elias tugging him out from under it. Once he was clear, Daniel released the rock and it thudded to the floor while the echo rang through the chamber.

"It fell from the ceiling and hit the floor. Then it rolled onto me – or over me."

There was no real damage other than the normal scrapes and a pretty good bruise that would develop tomorrow, especially on Daniel's white skin.

"I'm all right."

"A good thing."

They looked around and Daniel's heart sank along with Miraden's. The hatchery was empty. Clear. Clean. Vacant. There was nothing in the room but the rock on the floor. Miraden held his wand aloft.

"Light!"

And the cave was fully illuminated. It was barren. No shelves – no brass, no ledges – no nothing. Just five humans recently arrived and a rock. Daniel looked up to the place from where the rock had fallen. There was a hole in the roof of the chamber.

"Miraden, look!" Daniel pointed up. "Boncaster, lift me up!"

Daniel climbed to Boncaster's shoulders and got his hands around the edge of the hole and pulled himself up. Yes, he could have 'popped' up but he was in explorer mode now and sometimes that didn't include magic.

"Grandpa, I need your wand. Acquire Miraden's wand." During the transfer the light went out. "Light!" and the wand in Daniel's hand glowed again. That was one thing he couldn't do without a wand! Unless he had stones or torches.

"Elias 'pop' up here! 'Pop' to me! Grandpa, bring the others!"

Pop!

Pop!

Elias and the others stood in the room above the hatchery – eyes growing accustomed to the eerie light. This was a very unusual DragonMount – fourteen rooms! The mountain shook and the hole in the floor lost another rock. But this cave was bigger than the hatchery below and it was full – not of DragonSign but of treasure or what appeared to be treasure, or maybe artifacts, but at least things; Human things.

After examining the artifacts, Miraden determined that everything here was from the court of Balador. It all had the markings of the Kingdom. He even recognized some of the items specifically.

"The Dragons must have brought it here during the wars for safe keeping. Gondomere and Istradar were wise Dragons."

The room shook again. As they looked around they thought that there would be no way to save it. They all had a single thought and it was not an encouraging one. Miraden came up with the plan.

"I think we can do something. If we put wardings around several items at a time we can 'pop' with them to the Castle, then come back for more. Arrange things into piles and hurry.

The five worked feverishly and got everything separated into smaller groups of, well, stuff. Miraden and Daniel each stood by a grouping and created a warding around it and themselves, thought *'throne room of Balador!'* and 'popped' out. The mountain shook. They were back within a minute for another two groupings. The mountain shook again – violently.

Pop! Pop!

Elias pointed to the hole in the floor. The glow below was brighter.

"What's that?"

Boncaster looked down, "The hatchery floor is being covered with lava."

Pop! Pop!

There were four stacks left.

"Elias and Rose – each of you get with a stack. Boncaster, we'll be right back."

Pop! Pop!

Elias was still there but Rose was gone with Miraden. Daniel just couldn't do it every time. He was tiring. Elias rushed to the hole. He pointed, speechless and terrified. The lava was rising in the chamber below.

Pop! Pop!

"Elias!" Daniel hugged his brother. "I thought I'd lost you!"

"No, ya just left me!"

"Elias – stand by a stack," Miraden commanded.

Pop! Pop!

Boncaster was alone. The only light now was the ever-brightening orange glow from the hole in the floor. The room was otherwise empty. Boncaster paced the edges looking for higher ground – just in case. He could see the lava nearing the ceiling of the hatchery below.

Pop!

Miraden took Boncaster's hand as the lava spilled over the edge of the hole in the floor and raced toward their feet.

Pop!

They were back at the Great Hall of Balador – and 'stuff' was everywhere.

"Grandpa, what about DragonSign? We have to go back!"

"Yes, you and I, Daniel. Elias, you help Rose and Boncaster move these things to the safe room, the Lesser Hall over there." And he pointed to the Southwest.

"I can set up a warding to protect it when I return. Daniel? Cave opening. Ready?"

Daniel nodded.

Pop!

The three remaining in the Great Hall looked around and let out their breath at the same time. They laughed.

"Shall we sort this out? Furniture on one wall, trinkets on another and miscellaneous 'stuff' on another."

"Sure. Why not."

They looked at the stacks and sighed, again. Then looked at Elias. Elias only shook his head as he thought, *What a time to not have an Enchanter around.*

Miraden and Daniel stood at the entrance to the cave. The lava appeared, surging out of the last room on the right. Daniel rushed to the middle room on the left – where he had found male DragonSign in most of the other DragonMounts.

"Acquire Gondomere!"

Nothing. So he said it again and again and nothing appeared.

"What if they didn't live here, Grandpa? What if they made a new DragonMount and just hid the castle stuff here before they were destroyed?"

Miraden nodded.

"Acquire <u>Orange Dragons and Their DragonMount</u>." The book was in Daniel's hand.

They opened the book and flipped through from front to back. The pages in the last half of the book were blank. Miraden waved his wand and the book opened right to the last page with writing on it.

"Mmm-hmm. Yes. Ho!" Miraden was reading from the book.

"What is it, Grandpa?"

"Castle treasure ... hidden cave ... mountain unstable ... moving hatchery ... under the waters of ..." and the record stopped.

"Under what waters, Grandpa?"

"I'm not sure. Great Eastern River, Wolf Pond."

"Wolf Pond?"

"Yes. Hasn't anyone ever told you the legend of William of Waterside?"

"Um – yes, Grandpa – I've heard it."

"And?"

"Is it true?"

"Well ..."

"It scared the stuffin' right outta me!"

"I'm afraid it is true."

"Grandpa!"

"Sorry – it is."

This was disconcerting to Daniel as he had met Nightbane several times and Miraden knew about it. His nightmares had lasted for months after the first telling of the story.

"What other water is there, Grandpa?"

"Lake Estrella."

"And?"

"There is only one person who may know something about where the Dragons were."

"Who?"

"Anna – The Lady Of The Lake. Take my hand."

Pop!

They were on the shores of what Daniel supposed to be Lake Estrella, near a little grove of trees with a lone cottage occupying a prominent place by the lakeside. Daniel was bewildered that there was a person called ...

"Miraden, who is the Lady of the Lake?"

"Estrador's illegitimate daughter. Estrador was my niece."

"I've never heard of her before."

"I have not seen Anna in over a thousand years."

"What happened?"

Miraden continued as if Daniel had not spoken. "She's an Immortal who has always kept a low profile, not ever knowing who her father was."

"Is she still alive?"

"She should be."

Daniel sensed something in Miraden's demeanor. There was another Enchanter, well, Enchantress, and he had not been told about her? What was Miraden hiding?

"Are we welcome here?"

Miraden paused and looked deeply into Daniel's blues. "Very good question."

Miraden walked over to the cottage and rapped lightly on the door. Miraden's and Daniel's eyes looked everywhere but to the lake. Out of the lake, like a trained diver in one of our old movie musicals of the thirties and forties, Anna rose up, dry as a bone and as beautiful as any woman ever born. She floated across the lake and up to the visitors at her cottage door. Daniel screamed and stepped back as Anna glided by. Miraden simply turned.

"Anna!"

"Uncle."

Miraden was hopeful. Anna was a little cold – a chill not resulting from the waters of the lake. But then her eyes shifted and alighted on Daniel, whose startling and angelic appearance could melt any woman's heart; especially one who was over two thousand years old and only appeared to be, say, twenty.

"Who is this?"

"My grandson, Daniel Gregoryson."

"The Prophecy!"

"The very one."

"Pleased to meet you, Lady Anna." Daniel bowed and Anna was taken aback, amused at the polish of the young man.

"Such a gentleman as this belongs to such an old goat?"

"I <u>have</u> been remiss, niece."

"Well, in that case, I accept your apology."

"You have it."

"What brings you to my lake?"

Miraden explained all that had happened with Daniel interjecting a word here and there.

"So, the book mentioned my lake?"

"No, it said, 'under the waters of …' This is the only place in Balador with waters large enough for anything to be under. Gondomere and Istradar are long gone but I would like to bring them back. We already have the DragonSign of all the other Dragons. You don't want Balador to be the lone Kingdom without a Dragon, do you Anna?"

"Of course not, but a promise is …"

"Sacred, yes – but Dragons were sacred and never should have been killed in the first place. It will be different – this time."

"Come with me." She eased her arm around Daniel. He wasn't wholly comfortable with it. Miraden followed as Daniel mouthed the words "help me" back over his shoulder. After all,

Daniel looked at least eighteen to Anna, maybe even a little older. Anna looked only twenty or thereabouts. It could happen – in Anna's mind at least. Besides, they were both Immortals. What did physical age matter?

All three strolled westward along the lake for a half-a-league or so until they came to a large rock outcropping which rose up suddenly from the level ground and jutted out into the lake.

"The entrance is there. Give me a kiss, Daniel, so I will have the strength to open it."

Daniel leaned over and gave her a sweet kiss on the cheek. She patted his face and pulled his lips to hers. Daniel rose up on his toes but she had him in her grip. After a few breaths and a heartbeat or two she released him. He was stock-still.

"Did that do something for you?"

"I'm only thirteen!" was exhaled in a very uncharacteristic and breathless soprano – so unlike Daniel's robust baritone. Now, he was very uncomfortable – it had done something all right. Anna was not in the least abashed and gave out a little giggle. "Lady Anna – you are very pretty – very pretty – but I am promised to another – and I love her very much."

"At thirteen?" she mocked him.

"Yes, Ma'am – uh, Lady Anna."

Anna giggled again and stroked Daniel's cheek. Then she folded her hands in front of her, took her right hand out in a circle to the left, then up and over her head and down to her right side repeating over and over, "Gondomere and Istradar."

The rocks that were strewn along the shore, and inland a ways, began to hop up on top of each other, like they were playing piggy-back, or leap-frog, magically creating a pyramid of stones and revealing a tunnel into the ground which headed out under the lake.

A Dragon-sized tunnel! Daniel hoped.

"Rose, come look at this, please?"

They had just about finished sorting through the artifacts of

Balador. Elias had been opening everything he could. Boxes, chests, caskets, jars, drawers, cabinets. He had found a medium-sized chest and discovered something wondrous inside, but he wasn't sure what it was.

"It looks like an egg to me, Elias."

"But it's gold, Rose."

Boncaster passed by, his arms full of books – he stopped, staring.

"Looks like a Dragon's egg."

"I know, but gold?"

"What's it doing here?"

"What was it all doing at the DragonMount?"

"Could it have been there not to save it all but just to conceal the egg?"

"Miraden needs to see this, right Rose?"

"Yes, Elias. I think so."

Elias closed the lid to the chest and without speaking his intention he disappeared.

Pop!

"Elias!"

"He's gone to Daniel. That is a very extraordinary talent."

"You sure?"

"Yes. There is a bond there that can never be broken. When he transports – every time he transports – he goes right to Daniel's side.

"Well, then let's see what else we can find around here."

Elias appeared next to Daniel with the chest in his hands. It is strange how he could go wherever Daniel was. Normally, he couldn't even 'pop' across a path if Daniel was not on the other side.

Daniel, Anna and Miraden almost got wet at Elias' appearance. They slipped on the rocks on the shore and only Miraden's quick spell kept them dry.

Without a hello or any preamble, Elias opened the chest and

Lady Anna gasped.

"The Golden Egg of Istradar! Where did you find it, Young Man?" She caressed his cheek.

Miraden interjected, "He's eleven, Anna."

"Hmmm, looks older," and her hand fell to her side.

Elias hitched his shoulders back, standing up as tall as he could – almost liking the attention – then, launched into an explanation of the treasure and the sorting that was happening back at Castle Balador.

"You were right, Elias, in coming here."

"Lady Anna?" Miraden was curious.

"As far as I can reason from what Gondomere and Istradar told me – this is the key to opening the one room in the DragonLair under the lake, where I have not yet been able to go. I thought it had been destroyed."

"Let's go!" urged Daniel.

"Bring the chest, Elias."

Elias grinned and followed Lady Anna, Daniel and Miraden into the subterranean world of the Orange DragonLair. It was dark, which Lady Anna soon fixed by calling for 'Light.' The torches blazed. It was mostly dry, which surprised Daniel, after all they were beneath the water of the lake. However, it did have the smell of stale air – air that had not been used in a long time – unlike the open caves he had visited.

"I know this, Grandpa! It is the exact layout of the DragonMounts. Six rooms along each side of the main corridor. One room underneath accessed through the last room on the right?"

"Correct, Daniel – hmmm, handsome and smart."

"And young, niece."

Daniel rushed to the last room on the right.

"You can't get through without Elias," was Anna's helpful statement.

"Hurry up, Elias!" Daniel called, as impatient as ever. Maybe he wasn't growing up too fast.

Elias hurried and Miraden and Anna hastened along as well.

Daniel stared at the place where the opening should be. It was a solid wall, as the one in Miraden's laboratory had been. Elias arrived and opened the chest.

"Whoah! Where does it go, Lady Anna?"

She waved her hand over the place where the door should be and a pedestal arose out of the floor. It brought up with it centuries of dirt. As it rose, the caked dirt flaked and dropped off revealing a shining glass pillar in the shape of an hourglass. An eerie orange translucent opaqueness filled the room with a warm glow as it rose, throbbing and pulsing. Elias walked toward the pedestal with the egg. He set the chest down on the floor and took the egg out of its velvet-lined box. The egg started to hum — a low, constant pitch — Miraden recognized it as the thrum of an angry Dragon and he almost stopped Elias, motioning him to turn the egg over so that the large end was on the bottom.

Elias didn't know why, he just did it.

The hum changed to a buzz — higher, happier almost. Miraden nodded and relaxed a little. Elias held it in front of him and approached the pedestal and looked over his shoulder. Lady Anna motioned him onward and nodded, smiling sweetly; clutching Daniel's hand, a pained expression on the youth's face.

Elias lifted the egg and placed the rounded bottom of it in the carved out hollow of the top of the pedestal. The glow from the pillar increased and the light was soon flashing on and off. It rose up about another arm's length from the floor. The egg opened like a flower does to the sun. It opened! There were no marks, no cracks, evident hinges, lines — no anything, a solid surface — and it opened. Elias was astonished.

The others were taken aback. As the egg unfolded, the fruit at the center, a golden key, was revealed. A beam of light directed itself at a small spot on the wall, where a very obvious keyhole appeared as the dirt fell away. Miraden nodded and Elias hesitated. Daniel motioned him to go on! Elias lifted the key out of the center of the egg and the wall started to shake. Elias crept slowly over to the wall and pressed the key into the lock. The hole collapsed around the key. Elias then jumped back to save his hand from being taken off and Daniel caught him and steadied him. Daniel motioned to his brother to turn the key. Elias reached out tentatively, placing his fingers around the key's handle, and twisted his wrist in a clockwise fashion.

Again, where there were no lines, cracks, hinges – just the keyhole – the rocks covering the door twisted and folded in and away from those standing awestruck in the center of the room. An archway opened up. When the movement appeared to have stopped, Daniel ushered Elias through and followed. He knew what they would find at first and wound their way down the slanting, winding corridor. This was familiar territory to Daniel but that changed as soon as they rounded the last curve of the corridor. Daniel hadn't seen it before he got there, but it was dark in the hatchery.

"Light!"

Six torches blazed and lit up what was in the room.

Daniel and Elias screamed at the face of a Dragon as it appeared, staring out through the darkness, motionless, from a clear chest in the center of the room. Daniel thought that it was kind of like Bianca's bier. The face seemed to be looking right at them, even with its eyes closed. It was floating in some kind of liquid behind the glass – or whatever the clear barrier was. It was a bright orange Dragon in orange liquid. The glass box sat on a raised rostrum. Daniel and Elias walked around peering into the chest. We would probably call it a tank or aquarium.

They got around to the other side as Miraden and Anna entered the chamber. The boys pressed their faces up to the glass. It was warm. They turned each cheek toward that warmth, soaking it in. The Dragon's eyes opened. Red stared out at the boys through orange. They jumped back. Miraden and Anna came forward in front of the Dragon.

"An offspring – only days old."

"Gondomere and Istradar's child?"

"Yes, Elias. He won't be an adult for nearly two hundred Human years. Dragons, unlike immortal boys, grow very slowly, no matter what potions they ingest." She had finally noticed that

Elias did not look eleven. Not any longer.

"How do we get him out, Lady Anna?" asked Daniel.

Elias gave Daniel such a look – like – duh! "Use the key?"

"But the door took it!" Then Daniel thought a moment. "Golden Key come to me!"

It wasn't as immediate as Daniel had grown used to, but the key was soon floating in the air in front of the youth."

"Go on, Elias – take it."

"Where do I put it?"

Daniel searched quickly and pointed to a key shaped hole on the rostrum just under the front of the glass bier. Elias placed the tip of the golden key at the opening and slowly slid it in. It didn't bite at him this time, so he then turned it to the right – it wouldn't move. He turned it to the left. He felt ancient tumblers click and revolve as he twisted his hand to the left until it could go no further. A bright, warm, orange glow appeared in the liquid around the little Dragon. Bubbles floated upwards through the viscous fluid. Daniel and Elias pressed their hands on the glass and squashed their faces close. The glass was now hot and the liquid was really starting to boil.

The little Dragon moved a foreleg, a hind leg. It's tail started swaying and then the liquid started draining out of the glass case. The Dragonet was moving and placed its nose against the glass on the opposite face from the boys' noses. It blinked and the top hinged open on one side and folded down against the outside of the case.

Once the liquid was gone, the case started sliding down and into the rostrum until its edges had disappeared below the surface that the little Dragonet was now standing on. The Dragonet nuzzled Elias, then Daniel. It wasn't cold and slimy; it was warm and soft. The boys reached up and stroked the Dragonet's long neck and it nuzzled deeper into the boys' necks. Anna stepped in and caressed the Dragonet's head. It blew a warm breath at her and reached out to nuzzle her as well.

"Is it a boy or a girl?"

Miraden lifted the spiked tail – "Boy!"

"Istramere!" Daniel and Elias shouted together. "A fine name for a fine Dragonet!"

ᛰ

CHAPTER EIGHTEEN
TRANSFORMATIONS
(4th Month)

ELIAS AND DANIEL WERE RELUCTANT to leave the Orange DragonLair under Lake Estrella. Not that Lady Anna couldn't care for Istramere. She could. They just wanted so much to be a big part of the little Dragon's life. Boys and their pets!

Could you just imagine your mother's face when you brought a Dragon home and asked, "Can we keep him? He won't eat much!"

"He won't eat anything because he's not staying!" would have been my mother's answer.

No, the boys knew that the DragonLair was the best place for the Dragonet. The Lady of the Lake would be a great substitute mother until Gondomere and Istradar could be brought back to life. The boys had found all the DragonSign they would ever need in the hatchery. They had Gondomere's teeth and Istradar's claws and an eggshell. All twelve original Dragons would live again! But Daniel was a little bit worried about the Red Dragons. He hoped that his and Miraden's fears about them were groundless.

Miraden 'popped' them all back to the little village of Panadar; back to the Graceful Grouse for a good night's sleep. Elias had never slept at an inn before. Campouts with his Da, and staying over at Miraden's cave with Daniel, yes, but sleeping at an Inn where people served you, and waited on you – it was exciting for the eleven year old.

The food was good, not as good as the food at the Boastful Boar in Panagon, but perfectly acceptable. They were full and ready for bed. It had been more than a long day. Miraden had 'popped' out for a minute to place the warding of protection on the treasure room at Castle Balador. It was a small chamber and he was back before the little group had even made it up to their rooms. Daniel and Elias had a room together. Elias could hardly contain himself. Rose had her own room, of course, while Miraden and Boncaster shared a room, at Miraden's expense. Miraden magically hung his hammock and would sleep above his bed while Boncaster simply fell on to his – out like a light!

Rose stared out her window for hours. It seemed as if the Blood Rose of Panador was farther away than ever before. She sometimes thought that it might be unrecoverable. But Boncaster seemed very capable. She enjoyed his company. Miraden and the boys, they were family; and they had always managed to accomplish what they set out to do in the past – so ...

Her fears were based on the stories of the past. Even her own past. She was only sixteen when the War Of The Realms had claimed so many of her countrymen, including boys younger than she was. It had affected her to her core. That war was terrible and the Dark forces didn't even have a Talisman, then. Now they had two – that Miraden knew of. One was her very powerful Blood Rose. The other was supposedly the Gentle Jewels of Aradon. How could she ever retrieve her Talisman? She had been it's principal caretaker and she had failed in her duty. (She seemed to be forgetting about twelve Dwarves who had been unable to stop its theft.)

She had to redeem her honor along with the honor of her Kingdom. Sleep could not claim her now. A vigil is what was required of her. She removed her tunic and sat cross-legged on her bed in her chemise and breeches. She folded her hands in her lap and tried to connect with the Creators. At least to let them know that she was theirs to command. But they already knew that. Maybe Rose just needed to know that they knew that; that she knew that they knew that.

Daniel and Elias played a game. They couldn't decide which bed should be who's. Daniel would sit on a bed and Elias would join him on that one. Daniel would 'pop' to the other bed and Elias would follow. They would test, lie down and then sit up again and 'pop'. Daniel – Elias – Daniel – Elias – Daniel – Elias – Elias!

Daniel had not 'popped' this last time and Elias had. They were now on different beds. Elias sat there clueless for the moment while Daniel was smiling. Could it be that Elias had just been borrowing Daniel's strength until he had enough of his own to 'pop' by himself? As children, we all – most often – hang on to the coattails of others, especially parents or older siblings, until we have either enough skill, strength or confidence to set out on our own; to do things for ourselves. It happens at every stage of our childhood. It sometimes even happens in adulthood, where it is not always healthy.

"Elias, what are you doing over there?" Daniel chided.

"I like this bed better." Elias didn't realize what he'd done.

"So, how did you get there?" Daniel played.

"I 'popped'."

"Yeah!?"

Daniel 'popped' over to congratulate Elias. At the same time Elias 'popped' over to hug Daniel and they seemed to barely miss each other in midair but still ended up on separate beds again. Daniel got up off of his bed and held out his hand. Elias stood and took it, smiling broadly, finally getting a hold of the fact that he had 'popped' on his own.

Then Daniel put Elias in a 'headlock' and 'noogied' him back onto the bed that Elias ended up choosing. As usual, Elias burst into fits of laughter. Inevitably, there was a knock on the wall from the direction of Miraden's room. The boys quieted – slowly

– with stifled giggles and hissing and sputtering. The room sounded like a snake pit for the next few minutes. Gradually the room quieted. The boys lost consciousness as Miraden worked a little magic from the next room. Too bad he didn't know about Rose's disquiet.

Boncaster was snoring and Miraden put a silencing charm over Boncaster's bed. Ahhhhh! Blessed silence! Miraden then drifted off in his hammock.

Rose was still watching out the window, which happened to be on the Market Square side of the building and faced south. She saw light reflected off the bottoms of the distant clouds from the direction of the Forest of Anan. Lights meant that Guildenblad was not asleep either! Red light, orange light, purple, blue, yellow – black. Tomorrow was the day. Rose knew the risks. She wondered if Guildenblad, with all of his magic, was even aware that they were coming or, especially, aware of how much they knew. How much did they know? Was it enough? Did those lights over the forest indicate that he was trying to brew additional, last minute surprises for Miraden's little force of Light?

Fifty men in Panadorian red and gold camped out at the western edge of the Eastern Barrier Ridge. They were near the former entrance of the collapsed tunnel. All had been quiet there for days and seemed like it would remain so. Guildenblad could not afford the energy it would require to re-carve that tunnel – at least not at the moment; that's what Miraden was counting on. Valerius and the Panadorians knew that. But it did not hurt to be careful. So Valerius had agreed with Miraden and stationed the small detachment of troops to guard their rear.

There was a darkened ring around the Anan Forest – if you

were looking at it from above, like a bird would. A circular haze, a mist, covered the five hundred Panadorian soldiers as they lay unseen in the tall grasses encircling the trees. Miraden had placed an invisibility warding on them days ago as he had silently and without revelation to anyone, moved them into place. Guildenblad was completely unaware of the enemy without.

The cry of a newborn rang through the halls of Castle Panador. A boy! Just as Miraden had predicted! But Miraden was not there. This was the first royal birth that Miraden had missed in ages. This time, his great-grandson! Not that he would have been much help with anything; but his presence was always reassuring. Bianca, his granddaughter, missed him, but had a fairly normal time with the birth; nothing magical was needed. Miraden was more than occupied by events elsewhere in Panador and Balador. The Child of Promise entered this world with little more than the fanfare of trumpets announcing that he had arrived. The city tingled at the news. Many of the citizens remembered the new Prophecy. Miraden had spoken to them – for them! For the Realms, too? They still wondered who this Child of Promise was to be. How great was the Promise?

The sun was up and Miraden was gone. The four remaining travelers were breakfasting on eggs, bacon, potatoes, milk and porridge. Elias was in heaven again. Boncaster had been loathe to waste the money but he certainly enjoyed the feast that was set in front of him; at Miraden's expense. Before they had finished, Miraden had walked through the door and joined them. After stuffing themselves, Miraden tipped heavily and they all returned to the stables for Boncaster and Rose to get new horses. The three Enchanters would be 'popping' to the forest.

They reviewed the plan of attack. They had been going over and over it all through breakfast.

Pop!

Miraden, Daniel and Elias were already at the southernmost end of the Forest of Anan while two familiar Riders in black approached the northern path to the forest. A third Black Rider appeared, alone and apparently waiting. Rose and Boncaster decided to approach the lone Rider.

"Praise Dal!"

"Praise Miraden!"

Rose's jaw dropped as she recognized the voice.

"Aunt Lily?"

"Yes, Rose."

"What are you ..."

"I am here to shield you as you travel through the forest."

"I thought Miraden would be doing it."

"Miraden is needed elsewhere."

"It's going to be a rough ride."

"I know."

They stood just outside the forest warding. Lily had her wand out. The horses were chomping at their bits, ready for what, they did not know; but they sensed the excitement. Boncaster started forward. The ladies followed closely.

"Praise Dal!"

The warding was penetrated. They had not changed the password. Evidently yesterday's little foray had gone unnoticed. Lily called out, "Sphere!" and her wand circumscribed an arc from six o'clock to six o'clock. A red protection surrounded them. "Animal Warding!" and the purple globe encircled them inside the red one. The trees and animals, sensing the use of magic within the forest, descended on the Red/Purple warding. The Taradalnock were, however, conspicuously absent. How long it would take for word to reach the clearing, they did not know, but the Darkness was one thing that found them quickly enough. It was a thickness, a blackness, an absence of light that surrounded the bubble of their protection. It felt like you could reach out and cut it with a knife; and it seemed to be only in their immediate area, shutting out a glimpse of what was beyond.

"Light!"

And the wand in Lily's hand pulsed its light through the wardings, which dispelled the Darkness in the forest through its beacon. They rode on, slowly and surely, then they heard the shriek of a bird.

Elias was standing behind a large rock in the meadow – his clothes piled neatly on top of it. Miraden's wand waved and Elias grew feathers, wings, talons and a beak – much faster than last time – as he changed into a brown hawk. He hopped up on the rock and flew away to the North. He swooped down to the ground and picked up a rock in each talon. He flew over the forest and dropped first one and then the other. They bounced off the warding and Elias shrieked twice and flew onward. He sighted trees moving below him, other trees being pushed apart – the Yetrall – all clustered around the clearing near the cottage of the Dwarf. Elias continued his trip north. He saw black shapes, groups, moving through the northern half of the forest, out to its edges. He then picked up a bright Red/Purple warding just inside the forest on the very Northern end and he shrieked once.

Miraden and Daniel were ready. Two shrieks, the signal that the rocks had not penetrated. Then a single shriek: their party had entered the northern part of the forest. Lightning erupted from their hands and hit the forest's edge. It was absorbed. The trees swayed. But it had drawn the attention of the Necromancer, as the penetration of the North end had not. Miraden and Daniel walked apart from each other, Miraden heading west and Daniel going east. More lightning. Daniel and Miraden turned around and headed back towards each other but stopped. Miraden fired lightning. Daniel shot flame, which followed the path of the lightning and set a part of the forest ablaze as it crept through the warding on the lightning's path. The warding was as they had thought. It could only repel one thing at a time!

They then turned and walked around the western edge by the mountains and continued to set the forest on fire. Before long the flames covered many leagues and the screams of the dying tree-creatures were loud enough to drive you close to madness. Then the first Taradalnock appeared. Two groups of twelve were galloping towards Miraden's and Daniel's position. The forest was continuing to blaze as the trees screamed in agony while turning to ashes. It hurt Miraden and Daniel also, this destruction of trees. But the trees were, really, no longer trees. They were turned, flesh-eating creatures of Darkness.

Elias had returned to his rock and thought 'boy again!' and had rapidly become his human self once more. He got dressed and 'popped' to Daniel's side – not that he needed to, or that it was all he could think of to do – that is where the plan called for him to be.

The Taradalnock were still approaching Daniel and Miraden's position. Miraden simply destroyed them and twenty-four riderless horses ran across the meadows to the west. The Enchanters turned back to the forest and sent more lightning and flame as the tree-creatures continued to scream and burn.

Guildenblad looked into the see-all eye of the waters of his scrying cauldron. He was losing trees and Riders, yes, but the little force was falling into his trap. Miraden and Daniel would be crushed. Boncaster and Rose would die a painful death. And Lily – Queen Lily – and the other little brat would not see tomorrow's sunrise. The outer warding would hold long enough. The warding on his clearing would not be penetrated. The Morphalls were merely a diversion, simply expendable, like the thousands of changed forest animals, and everything else in Guildenblad's life so far; just a means to an end. What end? To deceive and usurp. *Stupid Taradalnock!* he thought.

Boncaster, Rose and Lily were being assailed by tree limbs and roots, and animals were still playing 'kamikaze' at the warding around them. The bodies of possibly thousands of animals littered their path already. The creatures were drawn to the purple energy and thus, to their own deaths, as the red energy was in their way. Their ferocity catapulted them at the warding which reflected them away, the animals having crushed themselves in the process against the walls of the warding, which pulsated as they sizzled on the red.

The trio was halfway through the forest and began to hear the stomps and thumps of the still faraway Yetrall. Then all of a sudden, the ground moved underneath them and trees parted and a long ribbon of earth passed under their feet, like a long, wide, flat jump-rope. The path from the South end had shifted. It was an eerie feeling to see the ground bending and rippling toward you and then have it pass harmlessly under the warding.

Guildenblad was growing frantic now. How was Miraden doing it? The forest was aflame, the animals were dying and Taradalnock were down. He saw it all through the power that the stolen Talismans had given him. The Rose and the Jewels had been a great combination. They had rendered Miraden's orb sightless. (But not Miraden himself.) They had given Guildenblad that which he had thought would be an advantage. Guildenblad sent the word and the Taradalnock moved out in force – left the warding of the forest – and advanced on Miraden's position.

A wall of Black, over a league wide, appeared to be centered on the position of the Enchanters as it drove at them out of the forest. The wall advanced quickly. Miraden and Daniel kept the forest blazing as long as they could. Elias sent a few small bolts of light at the advancing Taradalnock. Here and there Riders fell. Elias thought he should be elated that his powers were working. But he couldn't help thinking about magic that helped people rather than hurt them. He continued, for that is what he had to do to save himself and his friends.

The hoarde of some three hundred Black Riders came to a full gallop with the Enchanters still in the center of their collective target. Swords were raised in their hands and knives held between their teeth. Miraden stood his ground and the boys stood with him. The Enchanters kept hurling their magic at the forest, a good quarter of which was aflame now. The swords were beginning to swing, the flame and the lightning were still flashing, the Taradalnock were still charging and falling and imagining dead Enchanters who, then, unexpectedly, vanished!

Miraden and the boys were just gone!

As they vanished, Guildenblad, through his scrying cauldron, witnessed five hundred Panadorian Warriors on horseback and on foot appear out of the shimmer of Miraden's invisibility warding. Arrows were loosed, cavalry charged and the threat of the Black Riders was met.

The Taradalnock charged on. Arrows decimated their front ranks. Soon, curved black swords clashed with shining straight swords. Black tunics fell to the ground. Red tunics were tinted a deeper red. So many of both colors were covering the heather, staining the purple flowers crimson.

Miraden had homed in on Lily's position and had 'popped' to her location with the boys. For father and daughter had a connection, also, like Elias and Daniel had. Lily and company had cleared away a large number of trees with their warding as it moved through the forest. The Yetrall attacked. Miraden 'popped' Elias inside Lily's warding. The thumps and stomps were all around them. Daniel kept 'popping' from place to place around the Yetrall and they were becoming terribly confused and more and more irate. Miraden and Daniel began again flashing their lightning. Trees screamed into flames and a Yetrall crashed, visibly to the ground, his body changing to the green-Human-like form of its Morphall original. The one that had so terrified Daniel and Elias in Zanadon. It laid still. Four to go! Flash – flash – flash! Trees screamed again and another Yetrall crashed to the forest floor. Three! Animals were converging on the magic-made clearing that was growing larger by the second. Lily moved to the center and dropped her wardings. Boncaster's and Rose's bows

258

went into action as animals fell now to both bow and magic as lightning flashed from Lily's and Elias' hands. Miraden and Daniel worked back to back clearing trees and felling another Yetrall. Two were left unseen, as three green bodies now blocked parts of the clearing.

There were no more stomps to be heard. The whereabouts of the remaining Yetrall were unknown. They didn't seem to be here. Yet. The air was filled with the stench of dead and dying animals and expelled magic. Smoke from the burning trees was also brought to them on the acrid breeze. No more sign of the Taradalnock. The battle in their tiny warding-made clearing grew quiet. Red/Purple wardings went back up around Lily-Boncaster-Rose and Miraden-Daniel-Elias. They went southward, to the cottage of the Dwarf.

What was once the Taradalnock 'threat' now covered the heather-dotted meadows, intermingling with many a red tunic. But no Black Riders remained seated on their horses or stood amidst the bloodbath. Guildenblad was tearing his hair as he witnessed the complete annihilation of the first wave of his defenses. Not one of them would be able to fight their way through to his glen. Not one! He was right.

The two interchanging Red/Purple wardings of The Forces of Light were cutting their way toward the cottage through the twisting, squirming and burning trees. Branches were crashing down and roots were flailing up and around, trying to penetrate into the impervious barriers, only to be recoiled as the trees flailed in agony over their own severed limbs and burning branches.

Miraden called to Lily: "Merge the wardings!"

The two bubbles touched and arced at the contact. As the edges overlapped, the electricity tingled. Elias' hair stood on end!

"Boncaster, Rose – come with me! Elias and Daniel go with

Lily."

They exchanged places. Miraden moved off to the right and Lily off to the left. They were very near the edge of Guildenblad's glen. While the Darkness around them had not necessarily impeded their progress, it was powerful enough so that they could not tell their exact position. A thunderous crash came down on the top of both wardings. Lily and Miraden felt the impact and they wavered and reeled for a moment. Then another crash hit and Lily's bubble cracked and shattered. Lily shielded Elias immediately but as she extended the protection toward Daniel they both saw him lifted into the air as if by some giant, unseen hand.

"Noooooooo!" issued from five throats at once and a thump-thump-thump-thump was heard receding into the distance toward the South.

Elias ripped off his clothing and yelled to Miraden, "Change me, Uncle!"

Miraden spoke the charm. Elias' body changed as he ran and soon his wings took over where his legs had begun and he flew off, lifting high on the warm currents wafting through the forest. All he had to do was look down to see where the trees were parting to find the direction in which Daniel was moving.

Daniel had never seen a forest from the height of its branches before – at least not moving through it like he was. He suspected that a Yetrall had him but he couldn't be sure. His arms were pinned to his sides, so there was no chance for him to throw a spell. He just grew angry and pushed the anger out through his body; expelling the heat into the monster's invisible hand. What must have been the other hand swatted him and he lost consciousness.

The Yetrall continued on. Miraden and party hurried after the monster as they could see Daniel appearing to float, hanging limp and unconscious in the air, arms dangling. Elias buzzed the air around where he thought the Yetrall's head was. A hand came swatting at him and he flew off a little way.

The Yetrall came to the edge of the glen of Guildenblad and magically passed through the warding. Miraden threw up a quick invisibility spell. They crept to the edge of the clearing where they saw Taradalnock all around on the outside of the warding of the clearing. There must be at least a hundred guarding the entire perimeter of the glen. They heard the thumps of the Yetrall as it advanced and stopped in front of Guildenblad. Another set of thumps was heard after the first stopped, but nothing more was seen.

Daniel's body was lowered out of the air and to the ground at Guildenblad's feet and a triumphant sound of laughter erupted from the Dwarf's throat. Guildenblad pointed his wand at Daniel and Miraden's party saw that Daniel was lifted back into the air and dunked into the nearby well, head first. Yes, the Dwarf had another wand. Miraden could only think, *Where did it come from?* The answer was unavoidably obvious: Tophet and Withera probably knew.

As soon as the Necromancer sensed movement in Daniel he lifted him out of the well-water and set him down. The shriek of a hawk was heard above. Guildenblad pulled two flagons on a string away from Daniel's waist, stripped him of his utility belt and chemise and, with enchanted ropes especially created and conjured for the purpose of holding an Enchanter, tied him by his arms and legs spread-eagled between two trees so that he was held, suspended in midair – shoulders, arms, chest and back straining – but face and eyes still proud and defiant in front of Guildenblad. He violently shook his mane of long, white, wet hair!

The Dwarf pointed his wand at Daniel and an arc of black lightning reached out and seared a line of flesh across Daniel's newly bulging chest. The youth did not even flinch, although his teeth were gritted tightly.

"So, you're the upstart brat who defeated me in Zanadon? Not much to you now!"

Another arc of black seared Daniel's legs through his

breeches as the cloth was scorched into the burned flesh. Some of the cloth, below the seared mark fell away to the ground, having been separated from the rest of the breeches.

"I want your secret."

Daniel merely looked at him, hatred rising, or at least appearing to rise. A bird cried out and a hawk floated to the treetops just outside the warding of the glen. Guildenblad sent a ray of light at Daniel. Daniel's long white locks fell to the ground leaving a dark, almost burned out stubble on his head.

"Taradalnock?" was spat out by Guildenblad.

A Rider approached.

"Flay him little by little!"

A grunt of approval and exultant, anticipatory satisfaction escaped the Rider's throat as he pulled out one of his curved, black knives — sharper than a razor! He approached Daniel and touched the point of his knife to the top of Daniel's breastbone.

"Here, Taradalnock — use this knife."

Guildenblad retrieved a long-knife with a red handle from his robes. Daniel saw it but couldn't react. He could not let the Necromancer know that he recognized this enchanted object. It was his knife; his father's knife! Where had Guildenblad found it? The black-bladed knife of the Taradalnock withdrew and the long-knife's tip was placed against his breastbone, instead.

"The secret!"

Daniel spit at the Rider.

The Rider pressed ever so slightly. (The Taradalnock were masters at flaying their captives until all the flesh was missing from the body and the person was still alive, begging for death. That was the legend, anyway.) Nothing happened. The knife had not penetrated Daniel's skin. The Taradalnock pressed harder, going for bone. The knife would not penetrate. The Rider slashed at a nearby tree branch and it fell to the ground, severed from its parent. Daniel saw the knife drop to the ground from the Rider's hand.

"Useless."

The black steel blade replaced it. Daniel felt the pressure. He fought what he felt. A layer or two of Daniel's skin opened as the mercenary drew his knife towards Daniel's navel cutting across the burned flesh on his chest. He stopped at the bottom of the breastbone, leaving a thin line of red in the knife's wake. He then placed the knife tip at Daniel's rounded, muscular shoulder.

"The secret."

Silence from Daniel.

The knife was drawn similarly down Daniel's shoulder and across his biceps. Blood flowed this time, as it was a deeper cut. Red drops were purged from Daniel's skin through the slit. Still Daniel gave no evidence of his pain and no satisfaction to his torturers.

"Tell me, Realmer Brat!

Daniel's eyes widened as the Taradalnock placed his knife tip at Daniel's groin. Daniel used his arms and pulled up a little, biceps knotting. The knife-point followed him. *That was stupid*, he thought. *Now I have to hold myself up here.* He looked momentarily toward the flagons on the ground. Guildenblad caught his eye movements.

"Do not geld him yet! What is in the flagons, boy!"

More silence.

Sharp pressure against his groin. Arms straining to escape the knife-point and pull even higher. Then the ropes on his legs pulled tight and he could escape no further. Blood dripped from the point of the knife. Was it fresh or was it still there from the cut on his shoulder? As the pain increased in his groin he knew that it was fresh blood dripping.

"Potion!" finally escaped Daniel's lips. He could endure no more.

"What potion?"

"The potion that builds my powers!" Daniel cried out.

"The one that also gives you immortality?"

Daniel hesitated. The knife-point, flicked, cutting a slit through the crotch of his breeches, moving in, touching flesh and more fresh blood was dripping.

"Yes!" Daniel cringed.

"Hold off!"

The point made a downward departure from its tender target and Daniel's arms released a little; but the blood continued to drip, collecting in a small pool on the dead grass below him. The knife-point now pressed against Daniel's inner thigh. First there was a sharpness felt on one leg, then on the other, as the tip circumscribed Daniel's leg. More of Daniel's breeches fell away. More blood began to trickle and seep from the red lines around Daniel's thighs.

"Enough!" screamed the Dwarf.

The Rider reluctantly backed off about a span's distance.

Meanwhile, the Dwarf moved to the flagons and picked them up. He draped the strings of both flagons across his own neck, opened one flagon and sniffed its contents. He held it out to Daniel.

"Drink!"

Daniel opened his mouth and the Dwarf poured some of the liquid into Daniel. Daniel swallowed and returned to stone-faced silence.

"Taradalnock – drink!"

The Black Rider who had begun to flay Daniel backed away in confusion and fear and Guildenblad sent a bolt of lighting at him that fried him clear through his body which then fell, incinerated to the ground. Guildenblad signaled another mercenary to drink. He crept forward and drank; not wanting to end up like his companion. He looked up and down his body. He felt his throat. He pressed against his stomach. Nothing happened. Guildenblad snatched the flagon and upended it into his own mouth, opened the other and drained it of its contents as well.

Guildenblad stood waiting, anticipation written in the grey lines of his Dark skin. Guildenblad screamed as he looked down and saw that his skin was changing to a more Human-like, more alive and pinkish color. The Dwarf's scream mingled simultaneously with the screams of a hundred Taradalnock on the outside of the glen's warding as hundreds of Panadorian arrows pierced black tunics and Riders fell off of their horses, almost as a single body!

Daniel jerked his legs and arms towards his center and snapped the enchanted fetters as if they were paper. Immortal enchantments had vanished from the ropes as the Immortality and power of the Dwarf began to leave his hideous re-mortalling body. From his place between the trees, Daniel gained the ground running, and then shot lightning at Guildenblad to stun him. He then lifted the Dwarf up into the air as his body was re-mortalling. The warding around the clearing disappeared, no longer sustainable by a mortal Dwarf. Miraden and Lily raced to Daniel as they heard the thumps of two Yetrall advancing on him. The Hawk screeched again. Miraden placed a warding around himself, Lily, Daniel and the Dwarf. Arrows flew through the air and both Yetrall screamed in agony as their now-visible bodies were pierced by a hundred shafts. They fell. The ground shook. Green, half-Human shapes emerged out of the dust and detritus of the forest floor; they remained silent and stilled on the ground, oozing their dark blood into the leaf-packed earth of the forest.

Boncaster, with his staff, and Rose, with her bow, went into action at the same time that Daniel gained his freedom from between the trees. They took out the six or seven remaining Taradalnock who had been inside the warding of the clearing. Miraden and Lily released their warding again and Boncaster placed an arrow through the Dwarf's heart, then another and another. Daniel was still magically supporting the Dwarf's limp and sagging body in the air. Miraden and Lily launched flame at him and Guildenblad's now mortal body started to burn. Daniel lowered the blackened Dwarf to the ground where Rose cut off his head. His dead-but-reanimated remains quickly disintegrated in the fire. Daniel, Miraden and Lily released their streams of magic.

Too much energy had been required and Daniel collapsed.

A hawk landed on the ground by Daniel's head. Elias thought 'boy again!' and he turned to a boy, fast and furiously, in front of the others who marveled at the speed of the transformation. As he was a naked boy, Rose was there to cover him with her cloak. But as he knelt by Daniel he threw the cloak aside; it just got in the way, as he pressed his hands desperately to Daniel's chest. The burns, scars and slashes on his brother's body began to disappear. Lily and Miraden joined Elias and they had Daniel's wounds sealed and his flesh back to its extra-whiteness in a matter of minutes. Only then did Elias acquire his clothes and slip on his breeches and, at a smile and a nod from Miraden, knew that Daniel was going to be all right.

Miraden pulled chocolate out of Daniel's cast off belt and gave it to Elias who pushed it into Daniel's mouth, first, and then took a bite himself. Four hundred Panadorian Warriors knelt around the body of the boy who had once again saved them. There was only one thing missing from this circle of gratefuls: Boncaster!

Just beyond the circle of warriors who were clustered around Daniel and Elias, Miraden noticed Boncaster was down and struggling to do something; get up? Close a wound on his face? When did it happen? Who had done it?

"Boncaster!" was screamed through Rose's lips.

Rose went to him and helped him to his feet as he tried to wave her off. There was something wrong with the man's face! He was pulling the skin off his face in large strips – almost like a rotting corpse. Maybe even more like an actor who would be removing the prosthetics and latex appliqués after a performance as the Hunchback of Notre Dame. It hadn't been just a performance for Boncaster. It had been a curse that had finally found its cure: The Death of the Dwarf who had cast the spell. Boncaster's 'command performance' was over.

With no ability to speak the truth about himself, or what had happened to him in his past through and because of the curse of a Necromancer, Boncaster had been unwillingly and unwittingly in disguise all along. Guildenblad had enchanted him to live in a shame he could not reveal; and without solace for his failure, as he was encased in the made-up body of another man, another face – a new, cursed life had taken over.

Twenty-year-old Prince Emeron of Aradon had taken his turn as guard of the Gentle Jewels in the Room of the Talisman in the Purple Palace of Aradon. Guildenblad, under a warding of invisibility, had snuck into the room and struck the young Prince unconscious and had stolen the Jewels. He then magically cursed the young man for his failure, and left him to live with the guilt of the loss of his kingdom's Talisman.

"So, you are not Boncaster?"

"Yes – but no, Princess Rose. I am Emeron, Prince of Aradon."

He was still pulling bits and pieces of skin off his face. A young and handsome Prince had emerged out of the middle-aged enchantment that had been Boncaster.

Daniel realized something for the second time in his life: appearances not only can be deceiving – they *are* deceiving. Who could have guessed, could have known, could have even suspected that the answer to the missing Jewels of Aradon had been with them all along. "Grandpa, what about that parchment?"

Miraden held the piece of parchment, suspended in the air in front of Daniel. Everyone, including Boncaster, read it.

To be aged and infirm –
Your body now shall squirm.
The blood of youth, the threads of truth,
Will leave you for a term.
Offensive to the senses,
If some come to your defenses
Then certain traits the spell has brought
Will fade away; become as naught.
Younger you will grow again
Remembering what was once forgot.
Still, knowledge can't be spoken then,
The truth is tied, as in a knot,

Until the death of me,
It unties and sets you free.

Rose couldn't help it, she was gawking. It was the same physical Boncaster – tall, strong, silent, compassionate, talented – just a new face! Young again; even more handsome than Daniel, but older than she. She remembered Emeron – suddenly saw him as he was six years ago – one of those silly little boys she had so easily dismissed. Rose had only one more thought: he was no longer silly, nor was he little.

Elias helped a renewed but nearly naked Daniel to his feet and covered him with Rose's cloak as Miraden emerged from the Dwarf's cottage with an open casket containing a Blood Rose in one hand, and the bag of Jewels in the other. Daniel saw a flash of steel as he lifted his gaze towards Miraden, who was smiling. Daniel reached down and retrieved his long-knife, tucking it carefully in the less than secure waistband of his tattered breeches. Miraden placed the casket in Rose's hands. The bag of Jewels he gave to Prince Emeron with a hug of 'welcome back.'

Daniel was hugging Lily. Elias hugged Daniel. Rose gave her young hero-cousin a kiss on the cheek. Elias put his cheek up, available, and the Princess kissed him as well. So did Daniel – playfully – and Elias wiped it off and smacked Daniel, not quite so playfully, across the chest. Emeron took Daniel's hand in friendship and Miraden stood behind Daniel, as ever he was wont to do, hands on the boy's shoulders, squeezing them and smiling proudly.

ML

CHAPTER NINETEEN
REVELATIONS
(4th Month)

DANIEL AND ELIAS, UNCOMFORTABLE IN their stiff dress tunics, fidgeted nervously as the procession headed up the hall of the Throne Room of Panador. Daniel's long white hair returned and hung to his shoulders, magically restored by Miraden. Valerius and Bianca were seated on the thrones. Miraden and Lily stood by Bianca's side, Comera and Alidah were near Valerius. Rose and Emeron were advancing up the aisle. The boys were restless next to Miraden, but he looked at them and they stopped all extraneous movement.

As Emeron and Rose reached the dais there was in the air an overwhelming feeling of curiosity; everyone was wondering who this man was. Where was their Champion? The tale of Boncaster and his whereabouts, was solicited out of the handsome Prince to quell the questions as to where their prized gardener had gone.

"And that is why Boncaster can no longer stand before you, Your Majesties."

Emeron and Rose had just finished returning the Blood Rose in its casket to Valerius. Valerius turned and handed the Talisman over to the Dwarves of the Clan of Ral who would be moving from their beloved Forest of Ral and its diamond mine to guard the Talisman of Panador in place of their brethren, The Clan of Hand – destroyed in their totality by Guildenblad and Rosenblad.

Queen Bianca came to the front of the dais and signaled for her newborn son to be brought to her.

"In honor of the Royal Birth, the return of our Talisman, and the services performed for this Kingdom by Prince Emeron (and others, of course) we propose that the name of our newborn son and heir be – Boncaster. Miraden has already pronounced him as a Child of Promise, and we add our seal upon his head."

Miraden then took the child and he and Valerius held him up to the assemblage, placing their hands on his little head as if in a blessing. They then gave the child back to Queen Bianca to great applause and cheers.

Prince Emeron stepped forward.

"I am honored, as is the Kingdom of Aradon, to be recognized by the throne of Panador, especially for what I did not do alone." He looked around at his companions. They all nodded. "So, I hesitate to ask another favor. I ask King Comera and Queen Alidah for the hand of their daughter, Princess Rose – to be my wife and the future Queen of Aradon."

King Comera stood. "Prince Emeron, we would be delighted for this marriage to occur, but only as long as it is also the wish of our daughter."

The entire room turned, as one, and looked at Rose.

"It is," Rose said meekly.

Her father looked at his daughter out of the corner of his eye, unaccustomed to the demure demeanor in his youngest child. "Then you have our blessing!"

The audience applauded. Rose and Emeron were in each other's arms.

Elias, squirming and fidgeting, looked at Daniel. As the applause died down he shouted over the sudden and unanticipated quiet: "Mushy stuff!"

Daniel, as well as the rest of the room heard. Daniel nodded in agreement as the rest of the room laughed. Then the Child of Promise unintentionally added his strong voice in positive affirmation of the union of Aradon and Panador.

ℳ

CHAPTER TWENTY
NO MORE MUSHY STUFF
(4th Month)

MIRADEN AND DANIEL HAD TALKED so long, Daniel asking every question that had entered his brain and heart. Miraden answered them all, even the ones Daniel didn't ask, not sidestepping a single issue. It took twelve trips around Halla Tarn before Daniel was finally satisfied and silent. Overwhelmed. He knew everything that could or would happen as far as Miraden could tell him. Everything he could be called upon to do. Everything he was or would be capable of doing.

Elias and his father, Matthew had fished all morning, side by side – father and son. Elias often looked over to wherever Daniel and Miraden were walking, then back at his father, grateful that he had not been taken away from him like Daniel's had. He always wondered how Daniel had held up under the strain of it all – he, himself, certainly couldn't have held up without his father! How had Daniel managed and kept it all together?

Miraden 'popped' back over to the cabin side of the tarn. Elias saw Daniel over on the far shore, throwing rocks. He didn't look angry. That was a good sign. Daniel saw Elias looking at him and motioned him over. Elias 'popped' to Daniel's side. Something he felt that he would always be able to do.

Daniel pointed off to his right. "Water's warmer over here. Sun's been on it all day. Shall we?"

Elias took this as *'I'm not ready to talk about anything yet,'* and said, "Sure!"

Miraden and Matthew sat, deep in conversation, on the porch of the cabin looking out over Halla Tarn. Elias and Daniel were in the water, across the way, swimming, splashing and playing dunkem'; just being boys – forgetting their cares – not acknowledging the approaching responsibilities that only Daniel was cognizant of at the moment; losing their worries in a very pleasant aquatic activity; as Miraden had advised Daniel to do as often as possible.

There were no Warlocks, Wizards, Witches, Necromancers, Vampires or Werewolves in the little valley that surrounded Halla Tarn. Not today. Just one Enchanter and two apprentices. This was a special place. It is where Miraden had spent months with his second wife, Kylara. Where Queen Lily was conceived. Where memories of a good life, well-lived, now washed over the oldest man in the Realms.

Miraden looked up at the sun, winked at Matthew and 'popped'. A few minutes later he 'popped' back and soon the playful screams and splashes of the boys grew silent, replaced by looks of horror! Tilly and Nancy, along with their father, Michael, stood at the near shore of the Tarn.

Daniel and Elias suddenly sunk up to their necks in the nearly transparent, thigh-deep water. Their faces turned red (as red as the rest of their bodies). The girls, who were so suddenly standing there, were giggling at the boy's discomfort. Michael smiled and took his girls to the cabin. The boys waited until all the signs were that the girls were safely inside. Then they summoned their clothes from the far side of the tarn. They dressed in the water, just in case. When they got out they used the 'hot hands' drying technique that Daniel had developed, that Elias could now perform for himself. Elias' powers had manifested quickly. (It was all the fault of that second type of chocolate that never really existed!) Their clothes and bodies were soon dry. They 'popped' to the cabin to find everyone there seated around the dinner table.

There was silence as the boys entered, as if the boys had been the subject of conversation prior to their appearance. Daniel moved to the empty chair between Tilly and Michael. Elias stood behind the empty place between Michael and Nancy.

Daniel took Tilly's hand, kissed it and sat down. Elias watched closely and copied Daniel's actions. Nancy giggled, good-naturedly, but was still flattered as the boy she had grown to really like sat down next to her. She even blushed a little.

Good thing, Elias thought. *Serves her right! Seeing me in my ...*

Both girls gave their hero, Enchanter, boy, a quick peck on the cheek, interrupting Elias' thought. Elias, who was next to his father and now feeling all warm inside, leaned over to Matthew and whispered: "I never thought I'd like the mushy stuff!"

Daniel whispered loudly, as he leaned across in front of Michael, "I told you so!"

That chocolate is pretty magical and wonderful, huh? Works fast!

A mock-hurt, mock-smile crossed Elias' features. He hadn't intended anyone to hear him except his father. Roars of laughter rose and fell as they dug into the feast that Miraden had prepared, while Tilly found Daniel's hand and clasped it tightly in hers, proud of the accomplishments of her good friend. And Nancy? She smiled a smile that melted whatever resistance might have been left in Elias' suddenly adolescent heart.

All's well that ends well. (But that is just an expression.)

ML
(The End)

THE BLOOD ROſE OF PANADOR

Glossary of Characters

Year: End Month of 2701 to 4th Month of 2702

KING VALERIUS RED OF PANADOR – formerly Prince Valerius. b. 2682

QUEEN BIANCA OF PANADOR – formerly Princess Bianca of Mirador. b.2684

PRINCESS ROSE RED OF PANADOR – the King's sister. b.2684

KING FATHER COMERA OF PANADOR – former King and Father to Valerius and Rose. b.2663

QUEEN MOTHER ALIDAH OF PANADOR – former Queen and Mother to Valerius and Rose. b.2665

MIRADEN – ancient Enchanter of the Realms, Immortal.

DANIEL GREGORYSON WHITE – The Miracle of Mirador, a young Enchanter. Immortal. b.2689

BONCASTER – a traveler, He first appears as an older man. b.2682

GUILDENBLAD – a Dwarf Necromancer, apprentice to Tophet. created by Withera: 1812

ROSENBLAD – a Dwarf turned Vampire, brother to Guilden. created by Withera: 1290

ELIAS MATTHEWSON – son of the Master Fisherman of Mirador, Daniel's best friend. b.2691

MATTHEW MATTHEWSON – Elias' father, Master Fisherman of Mirador. b. 2676

SARAI MATTHEWSON – Elias' mother. b.2677

RUTH(2692), HESTER(2694), JEREMIAH(2695), & JONAH(2700) MATTHEWSON – Elias' siblings

MATHILDA (TILLY) FITZMICHAEL – daughter of the Innkeeper of Laketon. b.2689

NANCY FITZMICHAEL – second daughter of the Innkeeper of Laketon. b.2691

ANNA – The Lady Of The Lake. b.476

NYARA – a Nymph of the Blue River.

DRYAD of the Forest of Caladon.

GNOMES of Caladon.

NIGHTBANE – ancient Werewolf, created by Reugella in 1050

TARADALNOCK BRETHREN – outlanders from the Unknown East, formerly a people of the Realms, their ancestors left over a thousand years ago. They hire out as mercenaries when they can get into the Realms.

THE DWARVES OF THE NORTH – the miners of Balador.

JEREMIAH – Master at Arms of Mirador.

PHINEAS – Captain of the Guards of Panador.

MICHAEL FITZPATRICK – the Innkeeper of Laketon – Tilly's and Nancy's father. b.2673

DON'T MISS THE NEXT TWO NOVELS IN THE SERIES:
**DANIEL LIGHT AND THE
CHILDREN OF THE ORB**

BOOK THREE: PART 1

THE PROPHECY
AND THE
CIRCLE OF LIGHT

What if the enemy without turned out to be even more dangerous than the enemy within?

The true nature and source of the Darkness that threatens all is revealed in its many-faceted horror to Daniel as he endeavors to build his Circle Of Light; his army of Young Enchanters. As they search out the long forgotten and almost discarded places of their continent, they find hatreds, uncertainties and distrust about the Realms and those who lead them. In addition to fending off attacks by separated but still united factions of the Darkness, Daniel has to mount a Good Will Campaign that has never been attempted before in The Realms of the Crystal Orb. Miraden then comes forward again with a new prophecy. One of a helper for Daniel: The Child of Promise.

AND

DANIEL LIGHT AND THE CHILDREN OF THE ORB

BOOK THREE: PART 2
THE PROPHECY
AND THE
CHILD OF PROMIƒE

What would you be willing to do to serve those you love?

To come at a time of greatest need, this Child Of Promise, is born and begins to grow. A favored child in every way, as most promised children are, he is nurtured by loving royal parents, grandparents and a peculiarly powerful uncle, Daniel Gregoryson -- the Miracle of Mirador. The Child of Promise and The Prophecy (Daniel) continue to learn and grow and fulfill their individual prophecies in ways that are surprisingly linked together. The Darkness is alive. It seems impossible to just snuff it out. Now a new threat to the Realms of the Crystal Orb arises; a threat also to the Prophecy, and to the Child of Promise. What sacrifice will be required at their hands to usher in yet another victory? Is victory even possible?

C. Michael Perry, Author, Composer and Lyricist, is a graduate of Brigham Young University. He is the composer of more than thirty musicals including <u>Cinderrabbit</u> for PBS, which won an Emmy Award and a "Best Of The West" Public Television award. He spent nearly a decade in television assisting in over 300 weekly episodes and commercials for ABC and PBS, Hasbro Toys and Toyota. He has performed in front of over 2000 live audiences from Utah to Italy in various plays and musicals. He has received acting awards for his many leading and supporting roles, won awards for lighting and scenic designs, more than forty shows have seen his directorial hand, and he has choreographed over fifty productions in is career, including <u>Big River</u> at the Sundance Summer Resort summer of 2010. Also a playwright and lyricist, he has written more than twenty plays and award winning musicals that have been published and produced across the nation and around the world. He is the founder and former President of Encore Performance Publishing, a publisher of plays and musicals for amateur, educational and professional markets, now owned by Eldridge Plays and Musicals of Tallahassee, Florida. He has also been a freelance writer for Scottsdale MultiMedia, of Scottsdale Arizona.

His previous volume of fiction, the first book in this series, THE MIRACLE OF MIRADOR, is also published and available. He is working on several other stories, in addition to the sequels to this series, and hopes to soon have the first novel of his WEMBLEY TEWKES ON THE EDGES OF TIMES series, IMPERFECTIONS ON THE EDGS, available by the end of 2014.

He resides in Utah with his wife of 30 years and his son, Jon-Christopher. His daughters, Jessica, Janalynn, and Joelle are out on their own; married and such.

www.ingramcontent.com/pod-product-compliance
Lightning Source LLC
Chambersburg PA
CBHW021511240626
47154CB00002B/580